LOST VEGAS SERIES, VOLUME ONE

AVELINE, TIANA

LIZZY FORD

CAPTURED PRESS

AVELINE

ONE

THE CORPSE on the makeshift dais at the center of the two-room cabin was still warm when the dreaded knock resounded off the walls.

Not yet, Aveline thought. *I'm not ready.*

She gripped her father's lifeless hand. His scarred features were serene, as if he had found the peace in the afterlife he never experienced in the ruthless criminal underworld of Lost Vegas. She studied his aquiline nose, silvery hair and pale features. Death did little to lessen his commanding presence, and for a moment, she was unable to accept the demise her own eyes had witnessed.

They had both believed he would die in a fight or in the prisons of the Shield, the police overseeing the inner and outer cities making up Lost Vegas. His illness caught them both by surprise, and his unexpected death left her feeling as if her entire world had been swept away by nothing greater than a sneeze. It did not seem possible for a child to die from a minor illness, let alone someone as strong as her father.

Would he wake up, once this stage of his illness was over?

She felt for his pulse, already knowing it would not be present but desperately wishing she had been wrong the previous dozen times she checked it.

The knock came again, this time harder, and dashed her hope. Many people were waiting for her father to pass. One of them must have paid a clairvoyant to know the exact time, for Aveline had not left her father's side in a week or spoken of his condition to anyone. The men at the door had come as much for her as for her father's body.

At seventeen, a half-breed with no family would not last long in the city that readily devoured the lost, friendless, or weak. Her father was gone, and her survival depended upon her accepting this and moving on, before she followed in his footsteps. She could almost hear her father lecturing her to be practical, logical, to think of her own life now that his was over.

But I don't want to leave him.

Aveline reached for the knife at her waist and glanced over her shoulder to ensure the door remained locked. Either she stayed and faced those sent to enslave her, or she fled and left her father's body exposed to those same people. Fresh organs sold for the same price as a newly orphaned teen in the city. They'd strip his clothing and hack apart his body and then destroy her home in the search for valuables.

The thought of anyone dishonoring him stoked her anger, and she yearned to disregard her father's insistence she always control the hereditary curse she bore, the part of her touched by the devil. In a moment such as this, she wanted to let the devil's wrath free upon anyone who drew near her father's body.

"Avi! Come on!" The urgent hiss came from the direction of the crawlspace leading under the back wall of the cabin and into an alley. The black-haired head of her closest friend, Rockford – known as Rocky – poked out of the crawlspace, and his dark eyes settled on her.

Her fury fizzled, and the devil's hunger for blood loosened its grip on her. Aveline's mouth went dry. Her heart pounded loudly enough to fill her ears. Part of her understood Rocky's urgency, but moving did not seem possible when she realized she would never return here, never see her father again. This was their last time together, and the infuriating knocking was ruining it. The door bucked beneath the fists of the fate awaiting her, if she did not flee.

"Avi!" Rocky insisted.

Wiping warm tears from her cheeks, Aveline sucked in one last breath laced with her father's familiar scent then leapt to her feet. She hurried to the lopsided dresser where they stored their weapons and yanked open the bottom drawer. Her father had drilled into her the importance of never allowing their only possession of value to fall into the hands of anyone outside their family. More than once, he had shown her the envelope in the drawer and reminded her how dangerous his position was, and how likely it was that she would one day need to protect his treasure.

Those coming to dismember her father would take his body, but not his only treasure. The small gesture was all she could think to do to honor him before he was lost to her forever.

Shoving the envelope into her pocket, she dropped to her knees in front of the crawlspace and shimmied beneath it just as the front door splintered under the blow of an axe.

Waiting for her, Rocky reached in and hauled her out of the hole into an alley reeking of rotting refuse and human waste.

"There are ten of them, including the Shield and Miguel's men," he whispered to her. "They were arguing over who decides what goes to who. Hopefully it will be enough to distract them, so we can run."

Aveline barely heard his words. Rocky's eyes darted up and down the alley, aware whereas she was numb. The sting of winter nibbled on her ears, fingers and nose, and she shivered reflexively. Her breath floated over their heads in tiny puffs towards the night sky, away from the alley, from the damned city. Was her father up there somewhere, looking down upon her?

What remained of the thick wall that used to surround the city formed one side of her father's cabin, which was the last dwelling in a line of shacks and cabins. With the crumbling wall to one side, the intruders on another, and the cabin on a third, there was only one direction for them to run: across a wide road and into the city's criminal underbelly.

Her focus, however, was not on escaping but on the sky. The stars and moon were hidden behind the puffy gray clouds which covered the skies for the greater part of three months every winter. Was her father able to see her through the clouds? Was he finally free of the devil's curse? Of the hunger for blood and death?

The sound of people ransacking her home made her wince. If she let herself envision them ripping his body apart, she would lead the second greatest massacre the city had ever known.

Rocky was at the corner of the cabin, peering around to the front. Those who came for her father's body and possessions held torches that sent shadows dancing across the dark features of her best friend. "Six inside, four outside. Now's our chance," he whispered.

"I don't want to leave him," she said. Tears further blurred her surroundings.

Rocky approached her and gripped her arms. "You remember what you told me when my Papaw died?" he asked.

Aveline swallowed hard and nodded. "Crying is a weakness."

"That, too," Rocky said with a tight smile. "You told me your mother's people believe the dead return to where we all came from, and they're happy spirits again. This," he motioned to their surroundings, "is probably hell."

"I don't think I said that," she said, a small smile tugging up one corner of her mouth despite her tumultuous emotions.

"You said the first part. I'm declaring this hell," he answered. "Your father is happy and he wants you *not* to be caught by those bastards. You deserve a chance to start a new life. It won't happen if we stay here."

Less than two years older than she was, Aveline often wondered how Rocky had become so wise. She suspected it had something to do with the scars running down the side of his body, from the tip of his scalp to his toes, stemming from his run in with the Shield last year.

"Maybe we should let them catch us, so I'll match," Rocky added and motioned to the side of his face without scarring.

"Burn you, Rock," Aveline replied, though she appreciated his attempt to lighten her mood. She shook off his hand and then rolled her shoulders back. "I'm ready."

Energized by the cold, she became more cognizant of their danger as her emotion was pushed back in favor of surviving the next hour. Rocky was right. She could mourn her father later. For now, she needed to hide. It was not possible to guess how many of her father's enemies would seek her out. As the former head of the Assassin Guild, he had collected enemies for twenty years and was wanted by the Shield and city leadership for thousands of deaths. Trained by him secretly, possessing the feared curse, she would be hunted by hundreds, if not thousands.

She hoped some of the Guild members would remain loyal to her father long enough to help her apply to the Guild's council for permission to complete the final trial required for her to become a full-fledged assassin. Her plan had been to one day lead the Guild as her father had. As an assassin-in-training whose sponsor was now dead, she would have to appeal to the new leadership for consideration, alongside hundreds of other applicants eager to join the elite, discreet organization.

This morning, she had confidence in her father's recovery and her fate. Standing outside her home, without her father to guide her, she no longer knew where she belonged.

"Almost time," Rocky said. He lowered the assassin mask over his head.

At least I have one friend, she thought.

Despite his warm eyes and ready humor, Rocky was second in lethality only to Aveline's father and one of his favorite students. Her friend carried a bone machete and wore his full Guild blacks, the coal-hued uniform of the assassin. She envied him for his position as a newly sworn in member of the exclusive Guild. She had become an outsider the second her father died.

Rocky peeked around the corner of the cabin once more then motioned for her to follow.

Aveline shifted to the balls of her feet, ready to sprint when he did. She watched him calculate the movement of others she was unable to see from her position. With a quick nod, he focused on their destination – crossing the wide road on the other side of the men – and then ran.

She sprinted after him. Small and agile, Aveline caught up to him quickly. No sooner had they reached the point where they were fully exposed to their pursuers than a shout came from the direction of the cabin.

Aveline risked a look over her shoulder and almost tripped. The door to her home was open. Her father's body had been dragged off the dais she built and was in the process of being dismembered.

She stopped, unable to take her eyes off his form.

"Avi!" Rocky shouted from across the street. "Happy spirits, remember?"

It was her mother's belief, not her father's, though her father had been diligent about teaching her about the woman who died in child-birth. Would it matter if he had not believed in spirits? Would he still become one, if he were touched by the devil, as she was?

As if to reassure her, the clouds above thinned until the moon spilled silvery light around her feet. She glanced up.

"Happy spirits," Aveline repeated, wanting to believe the rare sighting of the moon in winter to be a sign from either her father or mother.

With dread heavy in her stomach, Aveline turned and ran, joining Rocky on the other side of the street. The heavy footsteps of pursuers sent both of them bolting for the relative protection of the shadows.

They plunged into the dark alleys making up the inner city of Lost Vegas and filled with criminals, the poor, orphaned, and anyone else who did not fit neatly into the strict social castes of those privileged few who dwelt in the outer city.

"We'll lose them in the markets!" Rocky told her.

She nodded. It normally did not take more than five minutes to shake any kind of pursuer, and evading the Shield members was a skill every child on the street had learned by the time he or she turned five.

Aveline and Rocky leapt over obstacles, slid around corners, ducked through closed merchant shops, and doubled back periodically to confuse their pursuers with the innate familiarity of their surroundings only those raised in the streets possessed. Past a statue of the Lost Vegas Founder and the Wynn monument, into the narrow maze making up the oldest of the city's markets, through the brothel and neighboring slave districts, and around the heavily guarded central water and food storage buildings. Navigating the familiar footpaths and landmarks was second nature to them both.

By the occasional change in Rocky's speed and the increasingly erratic route, he sensed what she did. Someone had managed to track them long past the markets. Her heightened instincts picked up the periodic brush of cloth, the scrape of soft soles against stone and the pungent scent of the polish used solely on metal and iron weapons, which were reserved for the upper castes, their elite protectors, and decorated members of the Shield. Even if assassins did not prefer bone and stone weapons, the Guild built around discretion and secrecy would have avoided the attention possessing steel weapons drew.

The longer Aveline and Rocky ran, the clearer it became their pursuer was having no trouble tracking them.

At long last, Rocky paused inside an abandoned dwelling in the middle of the temple ward to catch his breath.

Aveline stopped beside him. They listened, panting in the darkness. The sense of being followed did not abate and yet, no one charged through the door to confront them, either.

"This isn't right," Rocky said quietly. "No one from the outer city could've followed us. We learned these routes from your father himself."

She silently agreed. Her father had been the city's most wanted for twenty years. No one had been able to find him, once he entered the maze of streets, alleys, and paths making up the inner city. At one point, the Shield had ordered a manhunt with no less than five hundred foot soldiers and still her father escaped and returned home by dinner.

How were they being tracked? More importantly, which one of them was being followed? Rocky, because of his forbidden profession as an assassin, or Aveline, the daughter of a wanted criminal? And why did either of them rate this persistent level of attention?

"There's more than one," Rocky said and held his breath.

She did the same, listening.

Voices came from two directions. Unable to make out their words, Aveline could estimate how far they were. The two search parties were no more than a hundred feet away – and closing in on the abandoned building where she stood.

"Maybe they have the help of Ghouls," Rocky said.

"Maybe they *are* Ghouls," she growled in frustration.

"My mother used to say you could hear them scream from ten miles away and devour a horse in -"

"I'm not in the mood for stupid fables meant to frighten children," Aveline interrupted. It was the worst night of her life, and she was being given no chance to mourn before her world fell spectacularly apart. She never asked the Great Spirit or people around her or the city for much of anything, but she needed a small break this night. "We need to split up."

Rocky hesitated before agreeing. "Meet at Guild Main at dawn?"

"Yes. If something happens ..."

"... we always come back for one another," he finished their friendship motto. Raised on the streets, their survival had been a matter of working together from the time they met, when she was five and he seven.

"Stay alert. I'll see you at dawn," Aveline said and stepped outside the building. Listening once more, she decided to go left, towards the center of the city.

Aveline deftly wove through forgotten and abandoned routes, across streets and crossing the different wards dividing the sprawling inner city. Passing through the slave ward once more, she paused at one point and let her senses fill with the late night sights and sounds.

From one of the buildings near her, a man had been seized by a round of coughing. Music on ill-tuned instruments floated from another direction, while the movement of the vermin living within the city came from several directions. A rat was dragging what appeared to be a human hand towards the sewers, and larger scavengers were tossing inedibles from heaps of refuse in their search for food.

And then the faint scent of metal polish reached her.

She took off once more, vowing this would not be the night she joined her family as a spirit.

Whipping around a corner, Aveline was halfway down the street before she realized it had been recently rerouted. Streets often were dammed and changed in attempts by the Shield and city leadership to curb crime in the worst parts of the inner city. She had been at her father's side the past week instead of exploring the streets as she normally did.

The sounds of pursuit grew louder. She hesitated too long, her mind racing to find an alternate route. As she tried to decide what to do, a low whistle reached her from above.

Aveline looked up. A figure in dark clothing was framed against the night sky, crouched on the edge of a roof of the building flanking the alley. The figure stood, revealing the tall, lean form belonging to a man. He tossed a rope down towards her and motioned for her to take it. The figure was too wiry to be Rocky, but it was difficult for her to determine anything else about her rescuer.

Aveline snatched the rope and began to haul herself up the side of the building, pushing and bracing herself with her legs.

"Hey!"

She glanced down and saw two dozen men had jammed up the entrance of the alley. Her thoughts went again briefly to why she and Rocky rated a search party before she concentrated on climbing. When she reached the top, she slung one leg over the edge of the roof and hefted herself over. Her heart flew, and she yanked the rope up before any of the men below could grab it.

Aveline leaned over, trying to identify something about her pursuers that might tell her who they were or why they were so doggedly chasing her this night. Rocky had seen the Shield members as well as the men working for the largest debt collector in the inner city, Miguel. She fully expected both to show up the night her father died. Miguel would sell off her father's possessions – which included her – to the highest bidder to settle the debts of the Guild, and the Shield had an interest in confirming the assassin leader was dead. Why the latter insisted on chasing her, though, was not something she understood at all. What was one orphaned street dog to the Shield?

These two parties were joined by men in maroon she did not recognize. There were four of them. She ducked back from the edge of the roof when the men on the ground spotted her peering down at them. It was better to find safety first then spend time debating who was chasing her.

"You're welcome," a low, unfamiliar male voice said from nearby.

She had nearly forgotten the man who threw her the rope. Aveline whirled to face the shadows cast by the neighboring building. The man was there, hiding from the night. She breathed in deeply, using all her senses to pick up any clues as to who he was.

No smells, no sounds, no impressions. He was being very, very careful.

"Do you work for my father?" she asked.

"Sort of."

She frowned and ran through the voices of every assassin or client who had ever crossed the threshold into her father's cabin.

"You are for hire, are you not?" the man asked. His accent was polished, the rhythm of his speech slow and enunciated.

He was from the outer city. What was he doing here?

Wary, she shifted one hand to the knife at her thigh. "Why do you care?" she replied.

"Because, if you are, I would like to hire you."

"Hire."

"You are a seventh generation assassin, are you not?"

If he were one of her father's men, he would know she was not allowed to call herself thus yet, because she had not completed her final trial.

"I assume you need a benefactor of some sort. Or were you running through the inner city for exercise?" he asked.

"Thanks for the help, but I'm not interested," she said.

"You have not yet heard what the job is or what it pays. I have never met an assassin who did not wish to know how much I was willing to donate for my wishes to be carried out."

"There are dozens of assassins. Hire one of them," she said shortly. "I'm not currently looking for employment." Aveline started away, towards a ladder leading up to the roof of an adjacent building. Roof walking was dangerous. She had done it before but generally preferred not to risk falling through anyone's ceiling. With her current route blocked, she had little choice.

"You bear the devil's blood, do you not?"

She stopped in place at the polite question. It was not chance that placed this man in her path. *Devil* was her father's nickname, earned from his actions during the single deadliest massacre ever to occur in the inner city of Lost Vegas. Those who coined the nickname did so out of a sense of admiration, claiming her father had to have the blood of the devil flowing through his veins in order to kill a thousand people in three days time.

They did not know how accurate they were, and very few outside the two of them knew the truth about the curse she bore. Her father's family really was touched by the devil. To relinquish one's control over the blood curse was to become possessed by the spirit of the devil himself, and by a rage that burned so hot, it turned everyone in its path to ash. After he witnessed for himself how lethal his curse was, her father had raised her to control it at all times and forbidden her from ever unleashing it.

"Only you can complete this task," her rescuer said.

"Who are you?" she asked, facing him once more.

He remained in the shadows.

"Why are you hiding?"

"The girl possessed by the devil wants to know why I do not wish her to see my face?" he retorted. "My name has no meaning here, but my money does. I know enough about the Guild to understand those who bring in benefactors often advance more quickly than those who do not."

It was true the Guild relied upon funds from outsiders to maintain its locations and care for the families of those assassins caught or killed during their missions. Assassins earned their place in the Guild by the merit of their ability to fight and kill. In payment for blindly obeying orders, they received a stipend, along with free living quarters for the rest of their lives. Those who purchased assassinations paid the Guild rather than the individual assassin. The Guild was a large family; money went where it was needed, and it was understood among the Guild members that no one would be rewarded more than his brother or sister, no matter what the circumstance.

Except when someone brought in the kind of grateful benefactor who could fund stipends for a year or build a dozen new living quarters. The assassin favored by a wealthy benefactor received none of the money but moved up the ranks faster.

She would need a benefactor, if not before she appealed to the Guild's board to take her trial, then soon after to gain status.

More importantly, she would need a benefactor to settle her father's debts. There had been a dry spell in assassinations the past three years caused by the emergence of a second group selling similar services to the wealthy. Her father had taken out large loans from

Miguel to fund the Guild, loans she was now either responsible for repaying or dying for.

The timing of this stranger's appearance, however, coupled with the death of her father, left her suspicious. He had not been waiting for anyone to come through the alley. He had been waiting for *her*.

To accept a mission when she was not a full assassin would not only earn her a reprimand but hinder her ability to find a sponsor and take the final trial. How could she justify potentially spending days, weeks, months on assignment, and disobeying the Guild's council, when she needed to focus on drawing the attention of a Guild sponsor?

Her future was shaky enough without the added challenge.

"Find someone else. The Devil's blood died with my father," she said and spun away. Reaching out to grip the wooden ladder, she was trying to figure out how this man, and the others, had found her this night when the stranger spoke.

"We will discuss this again."

Something stung her neck, and she slapped it, expecting to feel a mosquito squish beneath her palm. Instead, her fingers met the long, slender arrow of a blow weapon. Before she could react, the world slid out of focus, and her body grew too heavy for her to stand. She sank to the ground, helpless to move or speak.

"I apologize for this," came the low male voice. "You have forced my hand."

Alarm spun through her mind as darkness swallowed her.

TWO

A WOMAN'S shout awoke her.

Aveline's eyes snapped open, and she stared at a wooden ceiling. A cacophony of activity pummeled her groggy senses. The events of her night were clear; the world around her less so. The splashing of water, strange moans, and at least two women barking orders were joined by the sound of knocking at a door and someone else stomping across the floor.

Where was she?

She started to stand up only to realize her body was unresponsive. She tried again. Nothing happened.

Aveline attempted to lift her hand next, then her foot, then her head. Not even her lips would form a word or part for a sigh.

She was paralyzed, with the exception of her eyes.

Panic surged through her. She strained against her wooden body, unable to make sense of what was going on around her. Gradually, she realized she was not staring at the ceiling but at a wall, and her back was to the activity. She smelled nothing, and her skin was numb to the roughness of the wood beneath her.

"Bring the mixed one next!" one of the women shouted.

Seconds later, hands gripped her ankles and yanked her onto her back while another woman bent over her and lifted her upper body beneath the shoulders. They jostled her; she felt none of it. Her head fell helplessly back against someone's torso, and she was relieved to see she was not missing any limbs or wounded.

But she was completely naked.

The person supporting her torso dropped her. She heard her head smack hard against the ground without feeling anything. The woman cast a quick, worried look towards someone before hastily lifting her again.

Aveline struggled to contain her panic. She was a prisoner of her body and could not scream for help or fight off these people as much as she wanted to. She was all but flung onto a table on her side long enough to see a row of four other young women lying helplessly on tables. The girl beside her was little more than thirteen, and a woman was at the bottom of the table. The girl's legs were apart, the woman sticking something into the sacred pocket between them that only women possessed.

"Virgin. Clean her up and put her in the pile," the woman ordered two others standing by. She rose and moved towards Aveline.

Brothels. She was in the processing line to be assigned to a brothel. Aveline knew the brothel ward as well as any other ward in the inner city. She had seen the creepy displays of beautiful girls and boys at the front of each prostitution house meant to entice clients into the brothels. They appeared more like living dolls, and she had wondered in passing how these kids managed to stay so still. There had always been a chance she would have been sold to a brothel to work as a whore in order to repay her father's debts, but she had taken comfort in the smug knowledge she could kill anyone who tried to touch her.

Realization sent a streak of fear through her. She could not defend herself, or escape, if she could not move.

She was shoved onto her back and stared at the ceiling before wildly trying to look around at what she could with the only part of her that worked. Whatever was done to her, Aveline felt and saw none of it until the woman in charge rose and towered over her.

"Virgin. But mixed," she said, peering down critically at Aveline. "How'd the other mixed girl do?"

"Forty ounces," someone else answered.

"Decent," the woman said. "Clean her up. Put her in the pile."

What the hell was going on? Aveline screamed the question at the people who could not hear her. She was hefted and half dragged across the floor, through a doorway into a bathing room consisting of six wooden tubs filled with murky water.

She was shoved into one.

Water closed over her head, and she started to panic as water entered her lungs. Unable to breathe or move, Aveline strained against the prison of her body once again. This time, she lifted a finger. But one finger was not going to save her.

A blurry form reached into the tub and hauled her up. Her upper body was pushed over the edge, and the sound of her bather slapping her back was followed by the involuntary expulsion of water. Able to breathe again, Aveline sucked in as much air as she could.

Her bather went to work scrubbing her with movement born of routine. Had she been able to, she would have grimaced at the amount of force the older woman put into scouring every inch of her skin. Aveline's skin blazed red from the harsh scrubbing. Instead of spiraling into panic, she closed her eyes to block the surreal world and focused instead on moving her body.

Two fingers lifted when she ordered them to.

Burn me, burn me, burn me! she chanted mentally, frustrated by the weak progress.

"Lori!" a man bellowed.

Aveline's eyes cracked open to see a large man missing most his teeth standing in the doorway.

"Yes!" Lori, the woman in charge of the other room, entered.

"Which are these?" he gestured to the floor.

"Rejects. Send them to the butcher!"

He grunted and bent. When he straightened, he had both fists wrapped in the hair of two girls around the ages of ten.

Aveline stared at them, horrified to witness the circling of their eyes as they struggled to take in what was happening to them. Her bather dragged her out of the bath, severing her view of the girls being dragged away to be slaughtered. Aveline was dropped onto a pile on top of several other women stacked like logs and dripping from baths.

Faced with another truth, Aveline was not certain what to think.

Food in Lost Vegas was heavily rationed, with the outer city receiving the fresh meat and the inner city left to fight over rotten scraps. It was an unwritten rule that no one in the inner city ever asked where fresh meat came from, whenever it was available. She had always hoped only the worst criminals were put down to feed the rest of the inner city.

Residents of the inner city would starve without a steady supply of fresh meat, but those girls were too young for such a fate. Aveline had met too many dishonest grown men and women for *children* to be sacrificed to feed the rest of the criminals in the inner city.

Caught in her own perilous position, all of her training and skills were not going to help the girls when she could not move.

Frustration mixed with anger and fear, and Aveline continued to fight her body.

Four fingers.

The activity around her remained at the same level as more immobilized young women and men were bathed and then stacked by the wall. Every once in a while, she heard one of those around her moan or utter some other kind of panicked squeak, but no one could speak.

The longer she struggled to move, the more disappointed she became with her slow progress. When she had managed to lift all five fingers on one hand, another body was stacked on top of hers, pinning her hand between them.

While discouraged, Aveline was not ready to accept her involuntary fate as a whore. How much time passed, she had no way of knowing. She used the mental discipline her father had instilled into her to prevent her panic from consuming her and instead, channeled all her focus on moving the fingers on her free hand.

She watched the shadows on the wall, unable to track the movement of the bathing room any other way. Only when the mound of shadows began to decrease did she start to become unsettled once more. The boys and girls stacked around her were being removed, one by one. The sounds of bathing soon quieted as well, signaling a change in her environment.

Enough time had passed for her to coax all five fingers on her free hand back to life and even to straighten her palm. Her wrist was still frozen by the incapacitating drug they had given her, and she concentrated on moving it next. Aveline doubted she would have a chance to do anything without at least one arm and her legs in working order. Her toes and feet had yet to respond to her mental orders. With one arm free, she would feel slightly less vulnerable. If anyone armed came within reach, she could snatch their weapon and ...

This part of her plan, she had not yet figured out. One arm free could stab as many people as she could see, assuming they remained directly in her line of vision. The thought of spilling blood stirred her Devil's curse but provided her no real means of escape. The devil was not interested in anything but blood. Once she attacked, she would be easy to subdue, and the element of surprise would be completely gone. They might even inject more of the numbing drug into her.

Wrestling with what to do, Aveline fought back the urge to act without reason, to kill – or try to – without caring how she was going to escape. Fleeing this place was more important than revenge. When her body was itself again, she would find this place and mete out the kind of revenge that made the devil in her gleeful.

Determined, she urged her body to free more of itself as her eyes stayed trained on the diminishing shadows on the wall. The body atop hers was lifted, the one beside her, and finally, it was her turn to be picked up and slung over someone's shoulder. She hung helplessly and watched the flooring. Her captor left the room and walked down a narrow hallway flanked by several open doors before he descended a set of stairs at a jog and left the building. He walked down a short alleyway and to what she judged to be the rear entrance of the neighboring building by the muddied stairs and flooring.

The scent of cooking meat reached her nose, and a thrill went through her. She could smell again, and her wrist was cooperating.

When her captor all but dropped her onto the floor of another room, she was almost grateful she was unable to feel anything. She would be in pain from the rough treatment otherwise. Her gaze fixed to the ceiling, she tested her wrist to ensure it had not been trapped beneath her body before looking around.

To her delight, her neck moved several inches. It was small progress, but she was able to see more.

Several other boys and girls were propped up on benches, slumping and held upright by large pieces of wood. Two middle aged woman and a man were going down the line, very carefully applying makeup to the lifeless bodies of the new whores. The process took a solid ten minutes per child, and then another toothless, large man armed with a bone machete and a small knife hefted the human dolls and took them to the neighboring room.

Aveline's fingers twitched instinctively with the need to hold a weapon. She glimpsed vast piles of clothing in the second room. The armed man moved back and forth between the rooms, carrying one at a time.

Her neck did not cooperate enough to let her see directly into the adjacent room, so she shifted her attention to the ceiling and returned to manipulating her free hands. The first hand whose fingers moved before being pinned between her body and that of someone else had regained feeling up to her elbow, her other hand just past the wrist.

Her legs remained useless. Fortunately, there were ten people ahead of her waiting to have their makeup done, and the process was slow.

By the time only four bodies remained between her and the next station, her arms were both free to the shoulder. The brothel workers did not seem concerned with looking after those who were paralyzed.

Aveline tested her arms. She tried to lift her small frame off the floor. The awkward angle prevented her from succeeding. She waited, thinking furiously of any way to leverage her weight and what strength and mobility she possessed. Finally, she reached out and gripped the arm of the person next to her with her right hand and pulled herself towards him. With her left arm, she shoved away from the floor.

With little grace and no control over the rest of her body, she managed to maneuver onto her side. She rested for a moment, cursing herself for putting her back to the people she needed to keep an eye on. She gripped the arm of the boy once more, this time with both her hands, and pulled.

She landed on her belly, half on top of him, with her nose planted in his cheek. His eyes were wide and terrified as he tried to look at her through his peripheral. As much as she pitied those around her, her first priority was to escape.

Aveline tugged the arm pinned beneath her body free, braced both, then pushed her torso off the ground to test her strength. Her arms were feeling almost back to normal, and the sensation was spreading slowly through her shoulders and down her back.

But not her legs. She blew out a breath in frustration and lowered her body to the ground once more. Resting, she was debating whether rolling out of the room was a valid option when someone snatched her off the ground. It took every ounce of control not to fight back, and she went limp as the thug in charge of moving bodies dropped her onto the bench between another teen girl and a log.

Aveline pretended she was numb and tried once more to work on her stubborn legs. Too soon, her face was covered in makeup and the man transferring her to the next station on her journey to becoming a whore.

The clothing room contained only four would-be whores at a time and a team of three dressing each. She was placed on the ground. The three workers clothed her in a blue dress with lace edging and then braided her hair and tied it into a topknot. Aveline forced herself to ignore the person applying lotion to her hands and painting her nails.

Another man picked her up when she was deemed finished and carried her more carefully out of the dressing room and down a hallway.

"Mixed girl goes there," someone else directed. "Someone already paid for her."

Another dose of anger, mixed with apprehension, tore through Aveline. She resisted the urge to fight the man carrying her. She needed more time for her legs to work.

The man deposited her into a cramped room and on a bed that smelled of sweat and then bent over her to smooth out her dress and arrange her body. A small window overhead brightened up the space, and she calculated it was almost dawn.

Aveline waited for the man to position her head and reached out, snatching the small knife from his waist and quickly tucking it in the space between her arm and body.

When he was satisfied, he left and closed the door.

She refrained from unleashing a cry of pure frustration, afraid of alerting her captors before she was able to run. Muttering curses under her breath, swearing vengeance against the brothel and anyone associated with it, she was quickly distracted from her anger by the pressing need to escape. Her arms and shoulders worked well, and she had regained feeling halfway down her back. She rotated her head another two inches but still couldn't lift it. She pushed her body up, lowered it down, and stretched out to either side.

Her lower abdomen, legs and hips remained useless. She would not get far dragging herself away, and her heavy head and numbed neck made it next to impossible to keep an eye on her surroundings. She would be dead in seconds in an outright fight.

Her hope for the time needed to regain control of her body soon vanished.

The door opened. "Your first time with a mixed?" one of the brothel workers asked someone in a voice far too cheerful for their surroundings.

Aveline gripped the knife. She did not hear the response through the clamoring of her thoughts, except to notice the low male voice. The first rays of dawn formed a line along the top of the ceiling, and the sounds of the city awakening drifted through the window.

The night had started as the worst she could recall, with the death of her beloved father. By now, Rocky knew she was not coming, but could he possibly find her here? Even if he did, he would never reach her before the man in the hallway. It was one thing to go down fighting and quite another to be put down when vulnerable.

Tears stung her eyes. She hated crying and in the span of a single night, she had cried twice, once for her father and once for herself. What would her father think of her if he knew she had not lasted a day after his death? That all his training had been wasted? That she was weak?

Aveline swallowed the sob stuck in her throat and ran half a dozen scenarios through her mind, seeking one that allowed her to live through this unscathed.

The results of her mental exercise left her with one terrible option – and the determination she would rather face the punishment for her actions in the afterlife than remain here as a whore.

Aveline steadied her breathing and closed her eyes. She thought of her father, who was hopefully waiting for her among the other spirits, and then of Rocky, who would mourn her death. He would seek revenge on her behalf, once he discovered what had happened here. She would do the same for him, and knowing vengeance would be obtained stilled some of her fear.

Farewell, Rocky, she told her best friend silently. *I have no choice.* Death was not feared by assassins. At least, it was not *supposed* to be feared by them. She could not help thinking there was too much she had not accomplished with her life to die now. But she was too proud for the alternative: losing all control over her body and life.

Had her father experienced the turmoil of his stomach and his pulse quicken with fear when he realized he was going to die? Had he wished for one more day or one more chance at life?

Her heart felt like it was being squeezed in a clamp when she thought of her father. Aveline gritted her teeth. She waited until the door closed, clenching the knife. When the man who came to violate her took a step towards the bed, she acted.

Aveline plunged the knife towards the major artery in her neck.

The man snatched her wrist, and her eyes snapped open. He disarmed her and stepped back quickly, as if sensing the blow she was in the process of flinging towards him. Her sloppy attempt at a punch did nothing but twist her body and nearly knock her off the bed.

Aveline righted herself with some difficulty then pushed her torso up and glared at the stranger.

He wore a mask. "I thought I would give you another chance to accept my offer."

She blinked, registering his familiar voice. "You sent me here!" she snarled.

"I did not," he countered. "I simply enabled your capture by the pursuer I believed would do the least amount of harm. I thought this could be a lesson."

"A *what?*"

"You should accept an offer from a man like me when it comes. I am not accustomed to being turned away."

This man's ego had sent her to a brothel and driven her close to suicide? She narrowed her eyes in disgust and propped herself up against the wall.

"The assassins have an extensive set of rules," he continued. "I believe one of them involves a life debt. If I save you, you owe me."

"It doesn't count if you're the one who puts someone in danger!"

"I can leave you here to take your chances with the next man or woman who comes through the door. I was not the only person interested in the exotic beauty your owners claimed you to be. Or you can agree to work for me, and I'll ensure your safety."

Aveline bit back the acidic retort at the tip of her tongue. She was not in a position to offend him. Perhaps, after her night, entertaining her strange new stalker was not the worst idea she had ever had. "You put a lot of effort into convincing me to work for you!" she snarled.

"That should show you how important this is to me, should it not?"

The fixated man had to be insane. But she was smart enough to understand his lesson and leery of what happened if she turned him away again. "Who do you want me to kill?" she asked reluctantly.

"No one," he answered.

Her brow furrowed. "Then why do you need an assassin?"

"Let me clarify. I want you to protect someone from anyone else who tries to kill her. In the potential circumstance where someone tries, you can kill whoever it is."

"I'm not a guardian. I'm an assassin. Well, almost. I'll be an assassin soon," she said.

"You have something the other guardians and assassins I spoke to do not: the blood of the devil in your veins."

She crossed her arms, uncomfortable discussing the curse no one else was supposed to know about. He was not an assassin or from the inner city. Who had revealed the closely held secret?

"I believe this will make you more effective in protecting your charge."

"I will never allow the Devil's blood to control me," she said firmly.

"I accept this condition."

Aveline's mouth dropped open and then closed. The man was not making sense.

"All will be clear soon," he promised, reading her confusion. "You will be rewarded above and beyond what you can imagine."

"I don't care about money. I care about becoming an assassin. Unless you can sponsor me, which you *can't*, because you're not one of us, there's nothing you can do for me."

"You seem to underestimate the importance of money, assassin. I can *buy* you a sponsor. If you want the new chief of the assassins as your sponsor, I will arrange it."

Aveline laughed. "The Guild leader cannot be bought! It'd take more money than half the inner city sees in a year to tempt him!" she exclaimed.

"I can pay it."

"Just for me to stand at someone's doorway and *not* unleash the one trait behind the reason you're hiring me?"

"Yes."

It was the craziest proposition she had ever heard. Whether he could pay that much money, or if he were concealing an additional agenda, she did not care. At the moment, she had one convincing reason to accept, no matter how bizarre the proposed employment sounded.

"You will get me out of here?" she asked cautiously. Although willing, she had not felt ready to die, even for the just cause of preventing anyone from dishonoring her body.

"Immediately. Give me your word you will do as I've asked, without question, and I will see you free," the masked stranger vowed.

Aveline said nothing, pensive. Her father warned her against trusting someone who appeared to be offering her exactly what she asked for.

"As a sign of good faith." The stranger pulled something from his pocket and held it out to her.

Aveline accepted it, and her breath caught. The envelope containing her father's treasure she had sworn to protect. She had never seen its contents and fingered the lumpy envelope, relieved to have it returned.

The stranger was offering her a form of freedom and help becoming a real assassin. In the face of the alternative, no objection held merit. "Very well. I'll do it, whatever *it* is. If this is a trick, I will find you and burn you alive."

"Excellent!" The man seemed far too excited. "Remain here. I will send someone for you." Without another word, he opened the door and left.

Aveline stared after him, unable to understand what exactly her new employer wanted.

If he were lying about being wealthy, she would soon know. The expectation for a whore was to make money, and no brothel owner would let her go cheap, especially when the money she made was supposed to be split between the owner and debt collectors. This madman would have to pay off two people in order to free her.

The longer she waited, the less convinced she became about the masked stranger's ability to follow through. Aveline returned to testing her body. She was mobile from the waist up and leaned down to rub her legs, uncertain what else to do to encourage them to wake up from the drug.

Eager to be away from the brothel, she waited and prayed to the spirits of those who had come before her. The sun was fully in the sky and lining the wall in front of her when the door opened again. With one leg awake and the other useless, she was at least able to stand.

Turning warily from her position leaning against a wall, she eyed the two men in Shield clothing in the doorway. Her nose wrinkled at the scent of metal polish, and she sought to place the significance of the green sashes they wore across their normal scarlet uniforms.

"We have been ordered to escort you to your new position," one said and looked her up and down critically.

The same enunciation and cultured lilt shaped his tone, and she realized what the sash signified. These men were part of the personal guard for the elite living in the outer city.

Her benefactor, whomever he was, was as wealthy as he claimed. She had never ventured once into the outer city; she would not know the city's leader from a privileged servant or citizen, so why had he hidden his face?

The two soldiers stepped aside.

Aveline limped forward, dragging her sleeping leg with a curse.

She trailed one of the soldiers while the second followed her. As she walked through the brothel, she made an effort to memorize the features of every worker who crossed her path. When this mission was over, she was returning and driving a bone knife through the right eye of everyone enslaving the boys and girls. When she was done with the workers, she would track down those making meat out of children, slaughter them all, and feed the inner city.

She breathed a sigh of relief when she stepped into the cold winter day. The gray sky had never been so welcome to her.

The soldier led her to an enclosed carriage led by four bay horses and opened the door for her.

Aveline climbed in, ready to fight anyone who tried to attack her as she did. The inside of the carriage was built more for practicality than luxury with bench seats and blinds across the windows.

She sat down, uncertain what to expect. She pitched back as the carriage jolted forward and caught herself on the seat. Straightening, she sat back against the wall, tense and leery of the stranger who bought her freedom in exchange for her not being what she was. Beyond puzzled, and concerned she would be at the mercy of his true intentions, she pulled the envelope containing her father's treasure out of the pocket of her gown.

Her father never offered to show her its contents, and she had never requested to do so. In hindsight, she wished she had asked him if she were permitted to see it, or if she were supposed to protect it without ever knowing what the envelope contained.

She had lost it once and had it returned by a man she dared not trust. His offering was not lost on her, though, either. The stranger did not have to return anything to her after what he had to have paid to free her.

As curious as she was about what the envelope contained, she feared dishonoring her father. Aveline returned the treasure to her pocket and started to sink into the memory of hearing her father's last breath and feeling the warmth of his skin fade away. Her night had kept her from such a thought. But alone, uncertain and reeling from her experience at the brothel, her emotions were far more raw than she wanted, and her father was forefront on her mind, along with uncertainty about what she had involved herself in a mere ten hours after his death.

The jarring ride in the carriage left her wishing she could walk. She massaged the thigh of her numbed leg. A tap came from one of the doors. Certain she had misheard, she ignored the sound.

It came again, and she leaned forward to lift the blind.

Someone was on the runner outside the door. He wore a familiar uniform.

Thrilled by the idea Rocky had found her, she unlocked the door and opened it.

The assassin in all black leapt into the carriage and closed the door. He sat down across from her and peeled off the skintight mask.

"Karl!" she exclaimed, startled to see her father's most trusted advisor.

"Avi," he replied curtly. With dark hair and green eyes, the middle aged man was leaner and faster than most new members to the Guild. His ruthlessness had earned him a position at her father's side and his trust as well. "The news of your father's death has left me speechless." He bowed his head in honor of her father.

Aveline smiled, touched by the thoughtfulness of the assassin she considered to be an uncle. He had been around her entire life, faithful to her father until the very end, and often took the time to train her.

"Thank you, Karl," she said. "You can't know how shocked I was."

"We recovered his body," Karl told her. "We will see it buried, outside the city, where no scavengers can find it."

Her eyes misted over, and she ducked her head to prevent him from witnessing her tears.

"I came to discuss a different matter," he said.

Aveline waited.

"The man who hired you. What has he revealed?"

She looked up, surprised. "How do you know about him?"

"Before he came to you, he came to me. I was suspicious, and for good reason. Soon after the man in black approached me, a second man did, this one without a mask. He wanted to sponsor a murder, to which I was more than willing. But he would only deal with the blood of the devil."

Her face grew warm. Karl had known the family secret longer than she had. However, the second mention of her curse within a twelve hour period, when she had not spoken about it in years, left her uncomfortable.

"He wouldn't say much at all," she said, perplexed. "I'm supposed to protect someone. That's all he would reveal."

Karl nodded. "You agreed?"

"He saved me from the brothel," she hemmed, not wanting to upset someone she admired by admitting she had accepted employment before she was a real assassin.

"I understand, Aveline. I am not upset," Karl said.

She released the breath she did not know she was holding.

"I am here to convey a message, from both the Guild and the benefactor I spoke of earlier," he continued. "You have no sponsor for your final trial?"

She shook her head.

"I will sponsor you, if you kill the person you were hired to protect."

Aveline blinked, her initial excitement fading. "But I gave him my word. Wouldn't I be breaking the Guild laws?"

"You aren't a member of the Guild yet, Avi," he reminded her gently. "The oaths you take before you enter are of no consequence, once you pledge your loyalty to the Guild."

It was not exactly what her father had told her. He insisted all oaths had to be fulfilled, for integrity was a key requirement of an assassin's personality.

When she hesitated, Karl spoke again.

"I may be able to negotiate Rocky's release as well."

"Rocky?"

"He was captured by the Shield last night when they were trying to find you. He was very brave. He refused to tell anyone where you were," Karl explained. "My benefactor will pay for his release, once the kill he commissioned has been committed."

Not Rocky. Her heart began to pound hard in her chest. Her closest friend did not deserve to be tortured because the men last night found him instead of her. Guilt fluttered through her at the thought of Rocky in pain. She had helped nurse him back to health after his first encounter with the Shield that left him scarred. She had already lost her father; she could not handle a second loss so soon.

"I don't want to see Rocky hurt any more than you do. He's suffered enough, and it's not fair to him that he was captured because you chose to run instead of fight, as your father would've wanted," Karl said. "My sponsor will ensure he remains untouched, as long as you agree. Once the job is done, he will pay for Rocky's freedom."

"Yes," she whispered. "I'll do anything for Rocky."

"The two of you are similar to your father and me," Karl said approvingly with a faint smile. "You will make an excellent Guild leader some day, and Rocky your right hand."

Aveline could not smile in return. Knowing Rocky was in danger, and she had put him there, left her feeling sick to her stomach. Betraying a man who would not show his face was surely forgivable by her father, if it meant saving Rocky.

Integrity. The voice of her father was in her mind, and she recalled his lecture on honoring every oath. The man she had promised to serve had saved her life, another consideration the Guild took very seriously.

She had never heard her father require an assassin to break an oath, and her father would kill any assassin who failed to honor a life debt. But Karl would never ask her to do something her father would disapprove of, would he? At least, before this moment, she had not considered he might.

What was so important about her target? And why would only the Devil's blood be able to either protect, or kill, this person?

What were Karl and the masked stranger keeping from her?

Did any of it matter, if Rocky's life was on the line? Aveline studied Karl, troubled by the request and just as concerned about Rocky. The night that started as the worst in her life had turned into a morning more bizarre than any she could remember with two men asking her to perform actions that ran counter to her training.

"My sponsor will contact me when he wants the murder to take place. I believe it may not happen until spring," Karl said, oblivious to her inner turmoil. "This will give you time to earn the trust of those you need to in order to isolate your target."

She nodded.

"Your father would be pleased to know you will soon become an assassin. It was his deepest desire for you to follow in his footsteps."

Some of her doubt melted. "It's all I've ever wanted," she admitted.

"I believe, once a new leader is chosen for the Guild, I might be able to convince him or her that this task should be considered your final trial."

"You would do that?" she asked, startled by the offer.

"My ... *our* benefactor will be swept away with gratitude. His money will support the Guild for years. In honor of your father, it only seems right that such a task is rewarded in a way benefitting you as well," Karl said.

Aveline smiled. "I'd be forever grateful, Karl, if you can speak to the new Guild leader about this. And ... please take care of Rocky."

"My pleasure." Karl bowed his head again. "Consider this a sign of good faith." He pulled the strap of the satchel he wore over his head and handed it to her. "Standard assassin's tool kit, awarded upon acceptance into the guild."

Aveline accepted it. "Thank you, Karl," she whispered, starting to tear up once more, this time out of gratitude edged by exhaustion. Her father had made her a kit when she was younger and taught her how to use the herbs, poisons, weapons and other tools of the trade within.

"I must leave before they notice I'm here. I'll contact you through the standard Guild methods in two to three weeks. Rest assured I'll speak to our benefactor immediately about Rocky," Karl said.

She nodded eagerly.

Karl pulled his mask on and opened the door, exiting the carriage the same way he had entered.

Aveline closed the door behind him and sat back down, her mind whirling with everything that had happened. Her father's death, her narrow escape from the brothel, Rocky's capture ... and the promise of becoming a full assassin. The events of the past twelve hours were some of the worst, and potentially best, of her life.

All she had to do to turn her life around, to make her father proud and take her place in the Guild, was break an oath to a stranger.

As the long ride out of the inner city continued, she sank into thought once more. Karl had been as vague as the masked stranger. What kind of person had one wealthy man willing to spend untold amounts of money to protect him and another to see him dead?

I'll do anything for Rocky. She was somewhat relieved to know her agreement would protect him while he was imprisoned. It did not quite seem like enough, but she trusted Karl to protect her friend when she could not.

Aveline focused on her numbed leg, on making her father proud, on how incredible she would feel when she became an assassin, on saving Rocky's life ... on anything except the whisper in her mind warning her that something was wrong, if Karl was asking her to break two sacred Guild rules.

THREE

"YOUR FATHER SHOULD HAVE burnt you at the stake alongside your mother."

"Yes, Matilda," Tiana replied stoically. With her eyes on the floor, she dared not wince as the woman behind her wrenched a brush through her tangled hair. Fingers laden with expensive rings containing brilliant gemstones flashed by her face as Matilda leaned forward to grasp another handful of wavy hair.

"I was not born to be a slave to a freak! My father is the ..."

Tiana zoned out, accustomed to the lecture that came whenever her stepmother had to help her prepare for a ceremony. The events requiring her attendance were few and far between, numbering four annually. Somehow, each one this year only seemed to make Matilda angrier, and Tiana began to think her father was souring on his wife of seven years. Matilda was too determined to remain in the family for Tiana to understand what might have happened. In front of her father, Matilda was sweet, doting, and perfect.

In private, her stepmother's frustration had recently exploded into an increase in violence and ranting. Matilda's usual resentment had taken on an unusual vehemence. Tiana's father never saw what happened in private, and she never spoke a word of it to anyone except her brother.

Tiana traced her fingertips along the scars crisscrossing the soft skin of her inner forearm. Her latest cut still stung, though not as much as her eye, which was rendered black during another of Matilda's temper tantrums. She was accustomed to physical pain, too, to the blows and cuts and bruises.

Matilda flung the brush onto the vanity and stomped towards the wardrobe, a flurry of anger and tinkling sounds emanating from the bells on her slippers and layers of pearls sewn into her gown. The heavy gold necklaces around her neck glimmered with jewels, and even more gems had been braided into her hair.

Tiana released her breath and peeked towards her stepmother, a beautiful woman with pale skin and blue eyes. At twenty five, she was closer to Tiana's age of seventeen than to the husband twenty years her senior.

Matilda's fingers trembled as she yanked a gown from the wardrobe. She studied the different lengths of silk before selecting a veil featuring fantastical animals Tiana had embroidered into the silk. Her nose was red, a sign she had been using the medication she stashed in Tiana's room so no one else would find it.

Warmth bloomed within Tiana. As miserable as Matilda made her, she could find only pity for the woman who had dealt with her and her father for so many years. To be a member of this family was to wield great power – and to be confined by it as well. That Matilda had learned a slave's duty of dressing her was more than Tiana's previous two stepmothers had done for her.

"Do not look at me with those ghoulish eyes!" Matilda snapped. "One could never guess your mother's family bred with those creatures. Your father burnt every last Webster in the city after he saw your crippled little body, and rightly so. "

Everyone but my brother and me, Tiana corrected her silently and returned her eyes to the floor.

"You should be ashamed to bear the mark of a Hanover!" Matilda continued.

Tiana reached back instinctively to feel the raised tattoo on her shoulder. Every Hanover born was etched with the symbol of a diving eagle, the family crest.

Matilda gasped. "Cease this display. Now!" she snapped.

Her stepmother was pointing at the pillows floating three feet in the air above Tiana's bed. It took effort to undo what she had not felt herself do. Tiana willed the pillows to return to the bed. They obeyed and dropped in place, where they belonged.

Matilda cursed at her then snatched slippers from the wardrobe and slammed it closed. "Be quick. Your father does not forgive tardiness. I will deal with this incident later!"

Tiana stood and closed her eyes to shield Matilda from the most repulsive of her deformities. She tugged off her sleeping gown and then lifted her arms. Matilda pulled the ceremonial gown over her head with gentleness she never showed Tiana, careful not to wrinkle any of the layers of silk, lest she earn the displeasure of Tiana's father. The green sash and metal insignia, marking Tiana's position as a colonel in the Shield – an honor bestowed upon the children of the city's hereditary leader – went on next. The last piece of her ensemble was the most important one: the translucent layer of silk preventing the public from seeing her deformity.

Matilda's long nails grazed Tiana's skin as she maneuvered, tucked and pinned the veil in place, skillfully covering Tiana's face and neck while leaving her hair exposed. The wrapping of the veil was a privileged art only select members of the city were permitted to learn, and it was one of Matilda's duties to approve which women from wealthy families were allowed to display the veil. The trend was started by none other than Matilda as a simple solution to the dilemma Tiana's father faced on Tiana's thirteenth birthday. He was required by the laws of the elite to present his debutante daughter. Doing so would have revealed her deformity and seen her burned at the stake, alongside everyone else who knew of the deformed girl.

Initially an act meant to conceal Tiana, the wearing of the veil had become an instant symbol of power among the women of the city, and teenage girls everywhere began copying the fashionable trend.

Once she had finished positioning the thin layer of silk, Matilda clipped strings of gems and gold to Tiana's hair around the edges of the veil and stepped back to examine her critically from head to toe.

"You look like a Hanover," Matilda pronounced.

The way she said it left Tiana convinced that Matilda was worried about her position in the family. Free to look around without anyone seeing her deformed eyes, Tiana looked Matilda's clothing over.

"May I straighten your gown?" she asked quietly.

"Drink your tea first."

Tiana did not grimace the way she wanted to. Every day, Matilda brought her an herbal tea meant to bolster her health. Tiana drank the warm tea down fast, hating the pungent flavor and the strange smell.

"Good. Now, with haste." Matilda went still, waiting.

Tiana smoothed out a layer of silk bunched up near Matilda's right hip and then very carefully realigned the strings of gemstone beads that had shifted out of position in her stepmother's hair.

Lowering her hands, she moved away before Matilda could shove her. Despite the rough treatment this morning, she felt a spark of excitement at the prospect of seeing the world outside the room where she was confined.

A rap at the door was followed by her brother's entrance sans permission. Dressed in the official scarlet Shield uniform, he also wore the same green sash and honorary medals and ranks as Tiana. His hair was damp from bathing, and the green-gray eyes he had inherited from their father flickered over both of them with similar coolness. The wealthy families had always cooed over how much Arthur Hanover resembled his father, from the strawberry blond hair to his near identical build to the natural leadership ability.

The only significant difference between father and son was one that made Tiana adore her brother. Whenever he saw her, he smiled, and the skin around his eyes softened with genuine warmth. No one else was ever happy to see her.

Lightheaded from being on her feet too long, Tiana forbade her shaky knees from buckling beneath her. She leaned against the wall to support her weak body.

"Arthur. You must wait after you knock. What if we had been in a state of disarray?" Matilda's reprimand was spoken with maternal affection and a smile. Her ability to switch from resentful loathing to dulcet sweetness in a fraction of a second never failed to impress Tiana.

"Father awaits us," Arthur replied without acknowledging his stepmother.

"Of course." Matilda's tone cooled.

Tiana did not need to glimpse her stepmother's face to understand the tension between stepmother and stepson remained. She was unable to pinpoint the day it began, but it had become much more apparent the past six months until the two barely spoke when in each other's presence.

Arthur stepped aside for Matilda to exit. She did so gracefully, a cloud of silk, tinkling and jasmine perfume. She began belting orders to the slaves awaiting her in the foyer, calling for her cloak and reprimanding one of them for the bunched skirt Tiana had straightened.

Arthur strode to Tiana's wardrobe and removed her heavy cloak, consisting of a silk shell lined by the warm fur of animals he had trapped for her fifteenth birthday. He placed the cloak over her shoulders, and Tiana reached up to button it around her neck.

"How are you feeling?" he asked.

"Like my body will collapse, if I let it," she replied candidly.

He held out his arm, and she eagerly slid her hand around it, relieved to have his support.

"One day, Tiana, I will take you to a proper physician," he vowed.

"Matilda would never allow anyone else to see me. I am well

enough, Arthur." Tiana spoke the words with what strength she could muster, already aware her brother would not be fooled.

"Our stepmother is fickle, but she can fold a veil like no other," he said dryly. Once Matilda was out of sight, his smile became wide.

"You should be nicer to her," Tiana said. "You have seen what happens to our father's wives."

"You should be less forgiving of her. She deserves our father's wrath for how she treats you."

"Father would not fault her for trying to fix what I am."

"But I do."

"At least she tries to heal me with her teas," Tiana murmured.

"Tea will not cure any malady, ever."

Tiana pursed her lips. She did not fully disagree with Arthur, but neither was she one to condemn a woman in a position like Matilda's. Their stepmother had seen the two women who preceded her burnt at the stake. She understood the danger inherent in her position, as Tiana did hers.

"I do not care to argue with my beloved sister over someone who means so little to me," Arthur added.

She hugged his arm and leaned her head against his shoulder briefly as they walked to the door. "I wish you would come see me more often," she whispered, thoughts on how displeased Matilda was going to be after Arthur's cold shoulder. When he was present, Matilda dared not touch her.

"I will, Tiana, after the Winter Hunt."

But that's three weeks, maybe longer. She almost sighed and shifted from her own inevitable peril to her brother's. "What will you do if you see the Ghouls?" she asked.

They exited her room and fell into line behind their stepmother, who was flanked by half a dozen slaves. The party began walking through the family's gilded, private quarters to the elevator at the center of the apartment.

"What I always do. Tell them to leave me alone," Arthur

quipped. "I do not fear creatures that may not exist, Tiana. The natives pose the greatest threat."

"We are at peace with them, are we not?"

"Meat is scarce in winter, and any truce we form with them during a time of plenty is gone when we are both trying to feed our people," he explained. "Those to the north, where the buffalo herds are, have never agreed to our treaties anyway."

"I would love to meet the natives in the villages near the city and see buffalos!"

"You are safe here."

"Am I?" She allowed the soft question to escape.

His jaw tightened to the point the muscles snapped in his cheek. "I know," he said. "I found someone to guard you while I am away for these two weeks."

"Matilda will not approve."

"Matilda will not know."

"You can take me with you," she said wistfully. "I want to witness snow fall upon the prairies and walk across the frozen lakes!"

"Someday."

It was all he ever said when she expressed an interest in leaving the city. Tiana's cheeks warmed at the reminder even her dear brother believed her deformities casted an egregious shame upon the family, one that had to be kept hidden from everyone forever. She would never leave her room, aside from obligatory events, let alone venture from the city to the world beyond.

"I heard the slaves talking about the Free Lands to the north," she continued and then held her breath, waiting to hear what her brother said on the matter. Slaves often spoke of nonsense, according to Matilda. Tiana, confined her entire life, had no real experience or basis to help her determine what was true and what was not.

"Tiana, if I knew somewhere you could go, where you would be safe, do you not think I would do everything in my power to send you there?" Arthur replied.

"You would," she said. She hid her disappointment, aware of how much her brother cared yet suspecting he either did not know about the Free Lands or did not wish to encourage her in her desire to eventually leave the city.

They fell into comfortable silence as they joined their stepmother's party. Trailed by her train of slaves, Matilda went first down the elevator from the top of the pyramid to the indoor village contained within its base, where their father and other members of the privileged awaited them. The massive structure, guarded by a sphinx and obelisk, had survived the destruction of the Old World, the period five hundred years before when Lost Vegas had existed as a city of luxury before it became a refuge for the few that survived the demise of the Old World. The wealthiest survivors had gathered here, and since then, only the most powerful families in the city were permitted to live in the great pyramid.

From the apartment at the tip of the pyramid, the word, *Luxor,* could be seen written across the floor far below. Tiana had often gazed at it and wondered what it meant, why someone had named the exotic building this.

She and Arthur followed in the second lift, lowered from the height of two hundred feet by electricity – existing only in the elite outer city – and by a team of mules at the bottom when the electricity was not working, which was half the time.

She kept hold of her brother's arm as they left the elevator and were immediately surrounded by throngs of the wealthiest members of the city. People always stopped to stare at her, curious about the elusive daughter of their leader. None of them had ever seen her face, and the slaves often spoke about how various men and women would try to bribe those working for the family for information about the mysterious Hanover daughter.

For her part, Tiana did not mind the excessive attention, as long as she was safe behind her veil and at her brother's side. She had eyes only for what lay beyond the confines of her home.

She and Arthur moved into place behind their father and stepmother, who led the small parade from the pyramid, outside into the outer city and onward to the top of the commemorative wall, where they would watch the Shield depart for the wilderness.

The procession out of the pyramid housing the elite families of Lost Vegas was solemn, a reflection of the importance of the Winter Hunt. It was the first day of the annual hunt, which began every year on winter solstice. Led by her brother, half the Shield members left Lost Vegas in search of the meat the city needed to make it through the rest of the winter. Her father spent the week before the Hunt honoring the gods of every major religion in the city and visiting various clergy members, scientists and clairvoyants to determine the type of weather to expect and in which direction the great herds of buffalo and deer would be found.

The men and women he consulted, as well as his advisors from the lower castes, joined the procession in positions of honor.

Tiana stepped with her brother outside for the first time in several months and drew a deep breath of frigid air.

The street before the procession was lined by Shield members in scarlet. Citizens from all castes were packed behind the lines of soldiers as far as Tiana could see, straining for one glimpse of the elusive, powerful Hanover family. Many people appeared worried, and she resisted the urge to tell them her father had never been wrong about where to find food in his thirty years of leadership. His uncanny knack for analyzing the information provided from the clergy, scientists and clairvoyants, and identifying where his men would find food, was one reason why he was regarded as the greatest leader of Lost Vegas in five hundred years. The other reason: his dedication to ridding the city of criminals and those suffering from hereditary deformities. His solution was simple. He burned anyone who exhibited any sign of disfigurement or who tried to protect such people.

Tiana looked from the expectant, concerned crowds to her father then to Arthur, who had led the Winter Hunt for the past five years in his father's place. She often wondered if Arthur would make the same kind of leader as their father, if his kindness and compassion would disappear once he assumed their father's mantle. It did not seem possible her father was born the way he was, and she had long since drawn the conclusion that her deformities had caused him so much grief, he simply stopped feeling and grew impartial to the entire world.

Would something equally terrible happen to Arthur one day and expel his warmth and smile?

The thought of her brother suffering as much as she imagined her father had left her chest tight with anxiety.

Soon, however, the dark thoughts vanished, and Tiana began to strain to see the world outside the open gates. Beyond the city's defensive measures, the world consisted of snow on snow, with white prairies meeting gray skies in the distance. The brown path leading away from the gates of the city contrasted with the frosted surroundings. Beyond the prairie, in the distance, she spotted the forest. Somewhere beyond it, too far to see, were mountains tall enough to pierce the sky.

Winter air penetrated her veil and chilled her face. She shivered, delighted by the sensation of being outside.

Arthur loosened her grip from his arm. "Can you walk without me, sister?"

She tested her body. She felt frailer than usual but also buoyed by the prospect of glimpsing the outside world. She would not embarrass her father by falling or collapsing.

"I am well, Arthur," she replied.

"I will see you soon," he said for her ears only before he strode from the procession to the small group of men and horses waiting by the gate.

Tiana clenched her hands together, wanting to beg him not to leave her, to take her with him. In the end, she remained silent and continued along the designated parade route a short distance to what remained of the great wall that used to circle the city. As part of the trade agreements and peace truces with the local natives, the wall had been torn down a generation before hers, except for this commemorative stretch, where her father gave speeches several times a year to the city.

The path running along the inside of the massive stone and brick structure was wide enough for two people to walk shoulder to shoulder and smooth from wear.

She trailed her father and stepmother and then took her place at her father's side looking out over the world outside the city.

It was the one time every year when she saw this world, and she stared, mesmerized by how large it appeared to be. The forest stretched in every direction. Her brother had told her stories of the kinds of animals dwelling in the woods, of lakes twice the size of the city, of wastelands where nothing grew in the far south, and to the west, of the ocean he claimed was bluer than the sky and extended across half the planet.

She had never set foot in any of it. If her family had it their way, she never would. At seventeen, she was not permitted to leave her rooms, unless it was for one of these special occasions.

Matilda snatched her arm hard enough to bruise, and Tiana blinked, snapping back from her imagination to her immediate surroundings. Her father had moved to the edge of the wall to offer his blessings to his son and the dozens of men in scarlet and his command to fill the empty wagons with meat.

Her stepmother motioned discreetly but frantically towards the ground at Tiana's feet. Tiana glanced down and saw the snow hugging her feet beginning to float upward, toward the sky.

Ordering the snowflakes to lie flat again, she shifted her dress in an effort to hide the unusual movement. Matilda released her, and Tiana forced her attention from the vast world she longed to explore to her current situation. When she let her mind wander, or when she was upset, strange powers emerged. As much as she wanted to drink in the sights before her, she dared not lose focus in front of so many people, especially not when Matilda was watching.

Tiana listened dutifully to her father give the traditional Winter Hunt speech, eyes on her brother. The Hunt was dangerous, and usually, only half the men who left the walls ever returned. Arthur claimed the Ghouls did not exist, but she had heard the slaves speak of seeing the creatures inhabiting the plains, awakened from hibernation when the Old World was destroyed five centuries before. Many cities exiled their deformed members rather than burning them, which meant the forests were filled with grotesquely disfigured men and women who behaved with the wildness of animals. Finally, the hostile natives who had reclaimed their lands when the Old World fell knew no boundaries and freely roamed all the lands outside the cities. They claimed ownership over everything and killed any city dweller they crossed.

As scared as she was for her brother's life, Tiana was unable to convince herself that life here was much better than what lay beyond the city's edge. She would rather be free and face all the dangers of the world combined. Or better yet – flee towards the Free Lands, where everyone was said to live in harmony, no matter what caste or deformity had defined them in their previous lives.

Her father's deep voice quieted. The soldiers below, led by Arthur, wheeled their horses and started down the path leading towards the forest.

Tiana wrung her hands once more, worried about her brother. Her gaze slid to the man riding at her brother's right, his closest friend, a man from a family lower in the social strata scale but still respectable. He had been trained as a guardian and raised with Arthur, who was his ward.

As with her twenty year old brother, the young man, Warner, had filled out almost completely, turning from a boy to a man within the span of a year. She watched him often through the peepholes and secret hiding spots in the family's apartments when he visited Arthur. Warner had a large, strong build and was handsome enough that the slaves giggled when they spoke of him. When Warner was with her brother, she did not fear Arthur's return. Her brother always boasted of how his friend was the best fighter in the Shield and the first to defend him, if he were in trouble.

Those on top of the walls watched in silence for a full ten minutes in the cold before her father shifted away. Everyone else followed his lead. With regret, Tiana turned her back to the outside world and obediently trailed her stepmother towards the outer city and into the pyramid where she lived.

As was customary, a feast followed the commencement of the Winter Hunt, though Tiana was never permitted to enjoy any of it. The other wealthy women removed their veils to eat, but she was forbidden from doing so and sat stiffly and unmoving at her father's left until he dismissed her. Her stomach growled, and she ignored it, fascinated by the people around her she rarely saw.

The leader of the Shield appeared to have aged twenty years in the past nine months, when she had seen him last. Matilda told her he had been very ill, and it showed on his gaunt features.

Matilda's father, Christian Cruise, the wealthiest man in the city, was old and stooped and fed by two slaves. His wife, however, was little older than Matilda, and the two women shot each other frequent looks of resentment that left Tiana amused.

The rest of the men and women privileged enough to sit with the Hanover's and the wealthiest man in the city were themselves from the original families to settle the city and were too busy trying to impress one another to be interesting to Tiana.

The adults talked around her and seemed not to notice her at all, to which she was accustomed. She paid no one any attention, until she heard her name on the lips of one of the men. Startled, she focused on him.

"I am afraid our sweet Tiana is of too sickly a nature to consider marrying," Matilda was responding smoothly.

"It is a shame, is it not? We have long wished to cement the relationship our families enjoy," the man replied, glancing from Matilda to Tiana's father.

"As my wife said, Tiana is too frail," her father replied with firmness no one would question.

The man bowed his head.

Tiana studied him. Did he mean for her to marry *him*? He was old and fat, and his teeth were crooked. When he looked to the man on his other side, she began to think he wanted her to marry his son, who was nowhere near as handsome or strong as Warner. If she were forced to wed any man, she hoped it would be the friend of her brother. Thinking of Warner twisted her stomach into knots and sent her blood racing.

No one said anything else about her the rest of the dinner. Tiana retired to her room before anyone else, accompanied by three slaves who left her alone at the entrance of the family's apartment.

She went to her room and lifted off the veil, able to see clearly once more. She took off the coat and hugged it in place of her brother then smoothed the fur lining and replaced it in the wardrobe. She removed the ceremonial sash and gown and placed them in the wardrobe in exactly the way Matilda had shown her. Changing into one of her sleeping gowns, which she wore most of the day, every day, Tiana approached the door and touched the smooth wood with her fingertips. She felt energized after the half hour she spent outdoors and ached to leave her room to experience more.

Without Matilda's overbearing presence, and with the slaves occupied by the feast, the apartment was quiet. She often stood before the door leading from her room to the rest of the family's quarters and debated what it would be like to be able to open the door at will and go wherever she wanted. She was forbidden from such action now by both her father and her stepmother. While she understood their reasoning, she still let herself imagine how incredible it would be to walk out, greet the slaves and go to a feast where she could actually eat the amazing food featured on the banquet tables.

Tiana smiled and began to hum then twirl around her room, imagining herself at a ball, dancing with Warner. In her imagination, her deformities did not exist, everyone in her family loved her, and she was happy.

A pillow grazed her arm, floating from the bed to dance with her. She snatched it out of the air with a giggle and hugged it. How her deformities allowed her to use her mind to move objects, to occasionally glimpse a person's thoughts, and to sense some events before they happened, she did not know. The strange magic was difficult to control and impossible to predict, except that it would always act up when she least wanted it to.

Tiana danced with the pillow and barely kept from tripping over her brush as it floated towards her, too. In fact, every piece of furniture and every item she possessed hovered in the air.

Matilda's sharp voice came from the hallway.

"Down!" Tiana ordered the inanimate objects urgently, panicking at the idea of Matilda witnessing her sorcery. Everything dropped back to its place, and she snatched the brush from the floor. She had barely managed to return it to the vanity and tossed the pillow back on the bed before her door opened.

"You nearly exposed yourself!" Matilda snapped and slammed the door. She marched to the drawer in Tiana's vanity where the white, powdery medicines were kept. Opening it, she stared. "Have you touched them?" she demanded and whirled.

"No," Tiana replied, eyes on the floor. "The vanity floated a little."

"Again?" Matilda snatched a bag from the drawer.

"I apologize, Matilda."

"You have no idea what it is like to live with you, to fear you will cause us all to be burnt, because you refuse to control this sinful sorcery!" Matilda shouted. "Do you want me to be burned alive? To hear me scream alongside the rest of the deformed freaks your father burns every Sunday?"

Tiana shook her head.

"Three incidents today, Tiana!" Matilda withdrew a small knife from her silk purse. "It seems this is the only cure to keep your ghoulish sorcery from happening. I did not insist yesterday, because I did not wish you to be distraught for today's event. It was my misguided judgment, and for this, you nearly exposed us all. I should have known better than to trust you."

Tiana accepted the knife and sat on the bed.

"Three. Do it now." Matilda planted her hands on her hips and waited.

Tiana drew a deep breath and pressed the edge of the knife against her forearm. There was no longer a spot devoid of scars on either forearm, so she randomly chose a few inches of skin to punish. The sharp sting was accompanied by a line of red blood.

"Deeper," Matilda ordered.

Gritting her teeth, Tiana pressed harder on the second cut.

"Do you want to remain disfigured? How do you expect to bleed out the sorcery if you do not cut deep enough?" Matilda leaned forward and snatched Tiana's wrist with one hand and the knife with the other. She slashed Tiana's arm, harder and deeper than usual.

Tiana gasped, and tears sprang into her eyes.

"I will cure you, Tiana, to stay in favor with your father, even if I must first bleed every last ounce of blood from your body. The clairvoyant who told me when I was six that I would marry your father swore this would work, but you are too weak to do it. Have you no love for your family? Do you want us to be burnt at the stake?"

"No, Matilda," Tiana whispered, distraught by the idea. She alternately admired and hated her strange ability. At the moment, she felt the full shame of being deformed and possessed by sorcery that alarmed even her brother.

"Then behave like the daughter of your father!" Matilda shoved the knife and powdery medication into her purse. She left, slamming and locking the door behind her.

Woozy from pain and the strain of venturing outside her room, Tiana stood. She went to the private bathroom off her bedroom and squeezed blood out of her wounds into the sink, as Matilda had shown her many times. The more blood she lost, the less magic was inside her. Or so the clairvoyant who had guided Matilda's life claimed. Tiana squeezed until no more blood bubbled then washed her forearm before binding the wound with trembling fingers.

Miserable, Tiana returned to her bed and curled up in a ball.

The outside world could never be as cruel as this one. At least, away from the city, she would be free to run from someone like Matilda instead of cowering, and no one would accuse her of sorcery when she lost control over her power to lift inanimate objects. Outside the city, she would not be confined for all but four days a year, and she could visit her brother whenever she wished.

Most of all, she would not feel the way she did now: ashamed of existing and burdening everyone around her.

But it was not the pain of her wounds or self-pity sending hot tears down Tiana's cheeks. It was the unspoken words in Matilda's mind that Tiana had read as Matilda cut her.

I hate this cripple.

Tiana wished she did not possess the ability to read minds at all, however erratic and inconsistent the skill was. She did not want to know how much Matilda despised her. She wanted to be able to believe that maybe, what Matilda did was to try to help her was out of some shred of human decency, however small that piece of Matilda was. Why should it matter that Matilda truly hated her and acted, not out of sympathy, but out of self-preservation?

Because I want her to love me.

The foolish, heartfelt desire embarrassed Tiana as much as her disfigured body.

Tiana cried harder than usual. Born into privilege, enslaved by her deformity, she wished her father had let her die beside her mother, seventeen years ago.

FOUR

A LARGE CELEBRATION was in full swing in the massive pyramid at the south side of the city, attended by swarms of men and women wearing jewels and silks. Aveline stepped out of the tunnel leading into the most privileged place in Lost Vegas. She had seen the pyramid from afar without fully comprehending how large it truly was. Her mouth fell open, and she stared upwards, towards the top of the structure, which came to a point some two hundred feet above.

Hundreds of lights lined the walls of each floor. Not torches – but lights that ran off of electricity. She had heard rumors of the outer city possessing the once rampant magic of electricity. The lighting was as bright as fire but colder, cleaner.

Behind railings on each level, where clumps of wealthy people gathered to look down upon the events of the evening, she was able to glimpse doors leading to living spaces.

"Each floor houses one to three families," her guide told her and pointed towards the individual levels stair-stepping up the interior of the pyramid. The closer to the top, the smaller the levels became. "There are thirty floors and two hundred families living here, with the Hanover's, who have been in charge for four hundred and fifty years, at the very top."

Three slaves jostled past her, laden with plates of seasoned meat whose rich scent made her mouth water. They hurried up the stairs leading to the second floor and the village at the center of the pyramid. Music filled the main floor, which still bore the word *CASINO* in large letters. The crowds were too thick for her to see what lay beyond the walkways leading into the first floor space.

Dazzled by the display of wealth, Aveline did not know what part of the new world before her was the most stunning: electricity, glittering gems, brocaded silks and fitted suits, cloaks lined with valuable furs, towering statues edging the stairs, or the full scale buildings in the village at the center of the pyramid. Wealth unlike anything those in the inner city would ever know was worn as casually as she donned shoes. One silk scarf or turquoise button would provide her food and shelter for a month. The four women in veils before her wore enough jewelry to feed the inner city for a year, if not two.

Her guide, George, sighed. "I told you. You need to try to fit in, if you can. Do not gawk."

"Shallllll I tallllk like thissssss?" she retorted, exaggerating his accent.

The slave who met her after her carriage ride to the outer city was old enough for his hair to be white and spoke with the same cultured lisp as the other outer city dwellers. He had not seemed particularly pleased to see her and even now, his gaze was skeptical. Rather than taking her to her new ward at once, he had sent her in for a medical exam, where they injected her with medicine to counter the numbing agent. She had then been scrubbed down and given clothing traditional to the slaves: gray, cotton shirts and pants, sturdy black boots and a dark gray cloak.

The clothing was more comfortable than she expected.

"What is this?" she asked. She plucked the sash he wore across his chest.

He pushed her hand away. "I told my master you would never pass as one of us," George complained.

"I'm not here to pass as one of you," she replied. "I'm here to do what I do best."

"You do not touch another slave's family mark," he said firmly. "This denotes who owns me. Every slave is identified this way."

She glanced down. "Why don't –"

"It's in your left pocket," he snapped.

Aveline had yet to explore this pocket, though she placed the envelope with her father's treasure in her right pocket. She pulled a green sash and a leather necklace from the left pocket. She set about examining the necklace to determine how much she could sell it for. The leather rope was simple, the wooden locket round and clunky and decidedly worthless.

No longer interested, she pulled on both sash and necklace.

"Not like that." George sighed again. He moved forward and expertly arranged the sash so it was not twisted or wrinkled. "You *must* try to fit in!"

"Why don't you have a locket?" she asked, ignoring him.

"Because your locket is meant to look like it belongs to someone from the street caste. It contains a special concoction."

"Really?" Her curiosity renewed, she picked it up. "Is it poison?"

"I do not know what it is. My master insisted you wear it. He gave specific directions for you never to open it."

Aveline smiled, and the older slave pursed his lips.

"On the streets, you can do what you want. Here, every one of these people would kill to be on the floor above them, and all of them want to be there." He pointed to the very tip of the pyramid. "You cannot behave with brashness or thoughtlessness or disobedience and survive here for long. Some of these families have been plotting their ascension for generations and manipulating everyone who crosses their path."

"I'm pretty sure I'll be fine," she said and shook her head. "These people wouldn't last a day on the streets. What do they have to worry about? Being served one pad of butter instead of two?"

"Not all danger is physical," he said with impatience. "You were warned."

Aveline snorted, amused he thought to warn *her* about danger. What in this obscenely wealthy enclave was a threat to the daughter of the assassin guild's leader, the bearer of the Devil's blood? She began learning to use her first machete when she was three. These privileged, overdressed, weakling snobs had never seen a knife let alone knew how to use one. Not one person in the pyramid, except for the occasional Shield soldier, remotely posed any danger.

"What am I doing here?" she asked.

"What my master hired you to do." Resigned, George led her down a quiet hallway populated solely by slaves that led around the base of the pyramid. He stopped at the first corner, and they stood waiting.

Aveline watched the scurrying slaves, each of whom wore a different color sash from the rest.

"If you find yourself in trouble, which I am certain you will, come to me," George said when they were alone. "But otherwise, you will have to earn your place among the slaves."

"What?" she asked, shifting her attention back to him. "Slaves are slaves, aren't they?"

"There's a hierarchy. You must adapt to our way of life quickly." He looked around then pulled out an elegantly wrapped bundle from the depths of his cloak. "My master bade me give you this along with a warning. You must only act in defense, and only use what force is necessary."

"I can do that." Aveline accepted the long bundle wrapped in soft, high quality leather. It was heavy and tied closed by a matching piece of leather. Sensing he did not want anyone else seeing it, she tucked it into her waistband.

"The slave quarters are below the main floor. The stairs are in each corner." George indicated the stairwell beside the doors in front of which they stood. "The kitchens and offices belonging to other members of the staff are also in the basement. This is the slaves' lift. Do not use the other lifts or entrances not marked for slaves."

As the said the words, the door before opened to reveal a small compartment lit by a light bulb.

Aveline frowned, not understanding the importance of the space. George stepped into it, and she followed. Before she could ask what they were doing, the box lurched and then began to climb swiftly.

Her breath caught and her stomach dropped as she realized they were being carried upwards, towards the top of the pyramid. Her attention went from admiring the fist-sized bulb that managed to light up every corner of the lift to the scene below them. She leaned against the front of the wooden box and stared down at the village at the center of the structure. It was filled with people, and the murmur of their talking echoed off the walls of the pyramid.

When the lift stopped, the people below were the size of insects.

"This way." George said from behind her.

She turned and trailed him past four Shield members and into a hallway whose floors and walls were made of polished marble. The ceilings soared, and stately paintings in heavy frames lined the walls, some taller than her. Glittering crystal chandeliers blazing with brilliant, white light hung from the ceilings.

The hallway opened up into an elegant, circular shaped gathering area with antique furniture, sculptures, more paintings and even larger chandeliers. George led her around the area to another hallway and then onward to a dining chamber featuring a table at least forty feet long. Aveline's eyes fell to the silver cutlery and delicate, porcelain place settings, and she automatically calculated how much she could sell just one for, if she managed to steal it without being caught.

Every room he led her into was more opulent than the last, until she was certain she was walking into a dream. They passed only one other slave wearing a green sash and none of the apartment's residents.

After seeing more spectacular chambers, their path dead ended in a cul de sac flanked by four gilded doors. George paused before the one on their right and turned to face her.

"You must not, under any circumstances, allow anyone to know why you are here, or that someone hired you for a position other than as a slave." His features were unusually grim. "Especially not her." He lifted his chin towards the door before him. "She will monitor your activities closely, and you must convince her you are nothing other than a dumb, mute slave. Can you do that?"

"Yes," Aveline said readily. Role playing was yet another skill children living in the streets mastered at a young age in order to manipulate passersby into giving them money. "Did you say mute?"

"Mute."

She sighed and nodded.

"Finally, do not lift your eyes from the floor."

George opened the door and entered an antechamber with a gilded fireplace, more chandeliers and statues. He went to the door on the right and tapped on it.

It was opened seconds later by a female slave, who bowed her head and stepped aside. The parlor beyond the door was large. Aveline was starting to become numb to the displays of grandeur and wealth, but this room lit a spark of anger inside her. Cups and goblets were inlaid with gems. Silk drapes were edged with pearls, items made of and gold and silver were everywhere.

She had always known the outer city citizens lived better than those of the inner city, but the divide between those who could barely find food and this sparkling, golden, bright world left her vowing she would steal as much as she could carry when she left. What could anyone living in such a place ever fear from anyone? Why had she been hired, when one gold plate would pay for an army of guardians?

"Forgive my intrusion." George bowed his head to someone.

Aveline focused on a raven-haired woman of exceptional beauty, dressed in silks and gems, who sat sipping tea and nibbling a pastry from a table laden with more food than Aveline had eaten in the past year. Different varieties of meats, savory pies, bowls of vegetables, pastries, breads and rolls, and other food covered every inch of a table. It was enough for several families, but Aveline guessed it had been brought for one person alone.

"What is it, George?" the woman asked crisply.

"My master purchased a slave for his sister."

The woman tensed, set her saucer down with great control and then rose, facing them.

Beautiful – and cold. Something about the woman made the hair on the back of Aveline's neck stand up. This wealthy woman could not possibly pose any sort of danger, and yet, Aveline's instincts – molded by the need for self-preservation on the streets – were never wrong.

"This?" the brunette asked, lifting an eyebrow in delicate offence. "This is who my stepson chose to bring into my home? A mixed slave?"

Mute, Aveline reminded herself. It took effort to keep her eyes on the floor when she wanted to slap the woman.

"Absolutely not. I will not have one of her kind in my household!"

Aveline sneaked a glance at George, who appeared unruffled.

"He did not believe you would approve of him spending more than an ounce, and he insisted upon buying a mute, dumb slave," George replied calmly. "He believed this would please you."

Aveline held her breath, uncertain what the woman would say.

George's mistress glided towards them and circled Aveline. Without warning, she reached out and pinched the soft skin of Aveline's inner arm – hard.

Aveline remained silent despite the pain.

"Hmm," the brunette murmured. "So she is mute. But Tiana has enough slaves."

"My master assured me this mixed girl is meant to become her *personal* slave," George persisted in a low, respectful voice.

"Interesting timing, when he is not around for several weeks," she stated. The woman shifted her cold, intent gaze to George, and she scrutinized his features long enough for the tension to become uncomfortable. To his credit, George did not so much as blink beneath her glare.

Aveline waited, uncertain what exactly was causing the dissent between the two. That this Tiana did not need another slave? The new slave being mixed?

The identity and importance of this family was beyond Aveline's experience to judge. She had been too enamored by the sensation of flying from the bottom of the pyramid towards the top to notice on what floor they stopped, except that it had to be near the top, which meant these people were among the most powerful and richest in the city.

She was learning hints about the masked man who tracked her. But a man who lived in this golden world was not likely to ever visit the inner city. Had he sent someone to do his bidding?

Did it matter? A wealthy brother had hired her to guard his wealthy sister. Aveline was starting to unravel the mystery behind her assignment – and becoming more baffled in the process.

"My master believed this slave would ease your burden," George added when the woman did not speak. "No woman of your position should be forced to sully her hands as you are."

"Burden," she repeated and whirled, gliding back to the table. "May no one else ever know such a life as mine!"

"My master understands this and wishes to help make your life more comfortable."

"I had thought my stepson wished me to suffer!" she snapped.

"He does not," George said firmly. "Consider this a gift to you as well."

George is a damned good liar, Aveline thought, entertained by how he was manipulating the fickle-tempered beauty.

"Then I accept. For now." The dark-haired woman lifted a plate and placed a heel of bread, three strawberries and a half-eaten piece of meat upon it. She leaned over to pour a cup of tea next, dropped a sugar cube into it, then reached into a pocket hidden in her sleeve for a small vial. She delicately dispelled two drops from the vial before replacing it. "Slave, serve your mistress her dinner!"

George nudged Aveline forward.

Is Tiana a dog? She thought, looking over the paltry dinner. She approached and accepted the plate and saucer held out towards her while the woman glared at George.

"It will be your life in the fire, if this does not go well, or if I find upon his return he did not arrange this," she warned him.

He bowed his head at her then signaled Aveline towards the door.

Aveline obeyed, not at all eager to remain in the presence of the wealthy woman. She exited and waited in the round cul de sac for George. He appeared after a minute and closed the door to the woman's chambers behind him.

"You will need to tread very carefully," he warned Aveline again. "Tiana has never had a personal slave, and her stepmother will object to her husband if my master fails to reassign you. At the very least, you should have three weeks, until my master returns."

Puzzled by the dynamics of the assignment, Aveline waited for George to explain.

"Do not ask too many questions and do not cross paths with Matilda, if you can help it," he said. "Her drugs have made her pleasant today."

"That was *pleasant?*" Aveline asked, eyebrows shooting up.

George said nothing. He knew far more than he let on, Aveline assessed. Surprised he had stood up to the stepmother named Matilda, she chalked it up to an impressive sense of loyalty to his master. She had never heard how slaves lived. By the nature by which they were bought and sold, she assumed loyalty would be diffi- cult to assure.

"This is Tiana's room. It's kept locked from the outside at all time," he said and approached the door right of center. "My master ordered for you to be provided a key. It will allow you to exit Tiana's chambers. You cannot give it to Tiana or to anyone else. She must not leave her room. Ever. You must not speak about her to anyone, ever."

Aveline's instincts were on edge. George's expression, always grim, had turned severe.

"What's wrong with her?" she asked when he finished the lecture. "Why is she locked up?" Her concern was not for some wealthy girl living in opulence but her own safety.

"It is not my duty to know," George replied and looked away.

But he did know. Aveline would wager every one of the gold candlesticks in Matilda's fancy parlor on it.

"Take Tiana her dinner. Remember, if we are caught, we both burn." By his tone, he had little hope of Aveline succeeding.

"You're as *pleasant* as Matilda," Aveline said. "Don't worry so much, George."

"I am old. At least, I will burn quickly." He handed her a large key.

She smiled, entertained by the dour slave. George left her standing before Tiana's door and Aveline focused on her mission.

The only obstacle between her and the ability to claim her place among her father's assassins lay beyond the elegant mahogany slab of wood with its gilded fixtures. Hired first to protect Tiana, then to murder her, Aveline doubted anything could surprise her more than the turn her life had taken since her father's death. Whatever reason Tiana was locked away was inconsequential when Aveline was determined to win Karl's support and save Rocky.

She could make it until spring in this ridiculous world of the wealthy. If Tiana resembled her unpleasant stepmother at all, she would be easy to kill.

This is how I will honor my father. She drew a steady breath.

When she was an official assassin, Aveline would be able to look up at the sky and know her father and mother were proud of her. She hated crying, hated how weak it made her feel, but when she thought of her father, she was unable to stop the tears from forming. He had been her mentor as well as her father, and she found herself wishing she could seek his advice one last time about her current circumstances. His sudden absence rattled her to her core.

She took a moment to regain control over her emotions then shifted the saucer to brace it against her body so she could pull the key to Tiana's room from her pocket. Her nose wrinkled at the pungent tea. Recognizing a very faint odor among the heavier smells of herbs, she leaned forward and sniffed.

An assassin learned early on how to identify poisons by scent and taste. Aveline lifted the cup to her mouth and took a tiny sip. Intermixed with the strong herbs was a familiar flavor: arsenic, a favorite among assassins.

That bitch, she thought, amazed by how brazen Matilda had been. None of the slaves had blinked when she dropped the poison into Tiana's drink. Were they ignorant as to what it was? Or too afraid to speak up?

If her only challenge to keeping Tiana alive was a woman too stupid to hide what she did, Aveline's duty to protect the Hanover girl was going to be easier than she thought.

Reaching forward to unlock the door, Aveline felt confident about her future for the first time since her father fell ill, although cautious about what danger lurked in the room before her. She envisioned a chamber similar to Matilda's or one of the sitting rooms she had passed through while following George here. Balancing herself on the balls of her feet, in case this Tiana was somehow dangerous, Aveline opened the door slowly.

FIVE

AVELINE BLINKED in the dim lighting of the room. The window across from the door had been boarded up, though light peeked in around the edges of the slab of wood covering it. The small bedroom was lit only by two candles and a dangling light bulb. For a moment, she stood in the doorway, puzzled. It was as if she had been magically transported from the outer city to the inner city. The room was barren of every sign of wealth and consisted of wooden floors and walls, weathered furniture and few personal belongings, none of which appeared to be of value, except for a glass perfume bottle on the vanity. Even it was only of moderate value.

She spotted the pile of books then, antique tomes from the Old World stacked on one side of the vanity. Each of the books was worth a small fortune in the criminal underworld. A bathroom with indoor plumbing – the only other luxury the room contained – was off to the right and a closet to the left. The room was clean and plain and smelled of the roses placed in a simple vase on the nightstand beside a skinny, wooden bed with rags for coverings. Neither pictures nor mirrors hung on the walls, and no sculptures stood in the corners.

This is worse than my room, Aveline thought, recalling her cluttered bedroom in her father's cabin.

The girl on the bed seemed to be frozen in place. Her eyes were downcast, her long blond locks loose around her. She was barefoot and clothed in a cotton gown, the kind Aveline wore to sleep when she as a child.

But this was not a child. Aveline estimated the girl to be around her age, slender to the point of gaunt – and breathtakingly beautiful with pale, flawless skin and small features. Aveline caught herself staring too long. She had never been drawn to women over men, but Tiana was the prettiest woman she had ever seen, prettier even than Matilda. She almost understood the appeal of a beautiful woman to a man.

Aveline closed the door. She started to ask where Tiana wanted her dinner then stopped, recalling she was supposed to be mute. Crossing to the small table near the boarded up window, she placed the meager meal on it. The food and room fit together – but nothing else about this place did. Why did Matilda's stepdaughter live in poverty, under lock and key? The girl contained absolutely none of the muscular toning Aveline did after years of calisthenics and weapons training. She was naturally slender without being athletic, leading Aveline to believe Tiana posed no physical danger to anyone.

Unless ... was she insane?

It was the only other conclusion Aveline could draw, and it left her leery. Some of the poorest people on the streets displayed an unpredictable, dangerous sort of madness characterized by fits of rage and violence. Her father had been kinder to them than most, teaching Aveline that they would starve without charity, since they were unable to work for a living.

If madness were the case, Aveline almost understood why Tiana was imprisoned in this room with none of the finery she might throw or break or damage in an uncontrollable state.

Aveline waited to be acknowledged in some regard, especially after she dumped out the tea and rinsed the cup out, or for Tiana to eat her dinner.

Tiana did not move or lift her eyes from the floor. Her shoulders were hunched, and she was tense.

After an awkward silence that stretched for over ten minutes, Aveline retreated to the door and debated leaving. She had formed no real expectation of the person she was supposed to guard, and she was still startled by what she found. If Tiana's family barely fed her and kept her locked up, what harm would anyone possibly want to cause her?

Why did Tiana's brother insist only Aveline could protect her? And why had Karl's benefactor likewise claimed only Aveline could kill her?

Aveline's instincts were whispering, but she could not quite understand what they wanted her to know. Unlike Matilda, she sensed no danger from Tiana, but there was a charge in the air that left her edgy. Combined with the Spartan quarters, she had the sudden urge to talk to George and ask several more questions about her new charge.

She made the decision to find him, and the slave quarters, then return before dusk. Most assassinations occurred between twilight and dawn. If Tiana's brother were concerned about someone attacking her, those were the hours Aveline needed to be wary.

She reached for the door to open it. Before she could unlock it, however, it was shoved open.

Aveline stumbled back.

"Dumb as promised," a female voice said coolly. Aveline caught her balance against the wall. "Your brother wasted a whole ounce on this slave."

Aveline lowered her eyes when she saw the familiar blue of Matilda's dress and ground her teeth to keep from reacting.

Matilda closed the door behind her and breezed obliviously into the room towards Tiana.

"This slave is yours, at least, until your brother returns and reassigns her," she announced. "I will no longer be forced to wait upon you, hand and foot. If I hear you displayed any incidents for her to see, I will have you whipped, Tiana."

"Yes, Matilda," came the soft, quiet response.

"And you, slave!" Matilda rounded on Aveline. "My step-daughter is of a delicate nature. Her blood has been poisoned by witchcraft and sorcery. She is forbidden by her father from leaving this room, unless her presence is mandated by him and him alone. If she displays any strangeness, you *will* inform me, or you will be the one whipped."

Aveline had a few choice words for Matilda but kept quiet. The bizarre explanation for Tiana's seclusion made little sense to her, unless *strangeness* was how the wealthy described madness.

"Nod if you understand, slave," Matilda ordered.

Aveline obeyed.

The woman in blue crossed to the vanity and yanked open a drawer. She pulled out a clear, glass vial containing what Aveline presumed was the kind of illicit drugs that often drove people into madness on the streets. By its color, pure white, it was of better quality than anything found in the inner city.

Matilda pushed the drugs into her purse and left the room. The sound of the lock sliding into place was followed by more awkward silence.

Tiana remained frozen in place.

Uncertain what to expect, Aveline studied her, this time noticing the bandages around one of the girl's arms. Extensive scarring marred Tiana's other forearm, and she bore bruises on the rest of her exposed arms and across one cheek.

An uneasy feeling slid through Aveline, one akin to pity. She shook it off, not about to empathize with the girl she was supposed to kill in a few months. But she did decide to remain here rather than leaving to find George. Whether the danger to Tiana was Matilda, or someone else, she was unable to shake the instinct urging her not to leave the vulnerable, mad girl alone until she had figured out a little bit more about her.

Her mind made up, Aveline crossed the room to the vanity, which contained one of the two chairs in the bedroom. The second was at the table. She withdrew the leather bundle George had provided and sat down to unroll it.

Knives of rare metal, spikes of silver, throwing stars of bronze, and other essentials for an assassin were contained in the bundle. Aveline unrolled the entire thing before lowering her hands and admiring the valuable items before her. It was almost a shame to sully them with blood!

Tiana's brother understood the kind of weaponry assassins preferred. These were high quality, well made, balanced, sharp and polished. They were perfect in every way. When this was over, she could sell them or keep them, depending on how attached she became to the beautiful weaponry.

"Can you use them?" Tiana's voice was so soft, Aveline barely heard it.

"Yes," she replied absently.

"I knew you were not mute."

Burn me. Aveline tensed and then twisted to see the girl on the bed nearby. Tiana's gaze remained on the ground, but there was a small smile on her features. Up close, her skin was so pale, it appeared translucent.

"I will not tell," she added. "I know my brother arranged for you to be here. It is our secret. Matilda would have you burnt, if she found out."

"I'm not afraid of her," Aveline said resolutely.

"I am."

The words gave her pause, and Aveline tried to understand the wriggling instinct.

Tiana shifted from the bed and went to the table, where she picked up a red berry from her dinner plate. "I love strawberries," she said. "Did you know they grow on plants?"

"Um, yes. Where else would they grow?" Aveline asked.

"On trees."

Aveline shook her head and rolled the weapons back up into a bundle. Madness had to be the case with Tiana.

"Have you ever seen one?" Tiana asked.

"Seen what?"

"A tree."

"Of course I've seen a tree," Aveline replied. "Who hasn't?"

Tiana's wistful sigh was her answer.

Aveline frowned. "How long have you been in here?"

"Since my father burnt my mother at the stake after I was born," Tiana replied.

The response flowed so easily, without emotion of any kind, that Aveline was momentarily taken aback by the brutal honesty. Was this the event that drove Tiana insane?

Tiana sat and began to nibble on the bread. She placed the strawberries in a line on one side of her plate.

"Why do they keep you locked up in here?" Aveline asked.

The blond girl's hands went to her lap, and she twisted them. Her head lowered until her chin touched her chest, and she slumped, a beautiful, wilted flower.

Aveline did not care for how seeing Tiana this deflated made her feel. "You don't have to say," she said.

After a minute, Tiana straightened and began eating.

It was too quiet in the small space. Aveline rose and paced. Whenever she gave herself enough time to think, her mind slid back to her father. Being active helped distract her. The room was not large enough for her to do any weapons or combat training.

"I think strawberry is my favorite color," Tiana said.

"I don't think strawberry *is* a color," Aveline snapped, frustrated she could not release her emotions.

Tiana went still again.

Reading the other girl's body language, as she had learned on the streets, Aveline sighed. "It can be if you want it to be."

"If you do not wish to be here, you need not stay," Tiana said softly, sadly. "I cannot leave, and you can return when you desire to. We can talk more when you come back."

"To be clear: we aren't supposed to be friends, Tiana," Aveline said. "I don't care what your favorite color is, and I'm not here to entertain you. Do you understand?"

Tiana had wilted again. "Yes." Her defeated tone was the same she used with Matilda.

Aveline felt lower than her street caste breeding. She gathered up her cloak and bundle of weapons, uncertain how to react. Her original plan nudged its way into her thoughts again.

"I'll return before dark," she said shortly and then left without waiting to hear Tiana's response.

The odd energy in the air around Tiana faded as Aveline walked through the apartment. This time, she did not glance once at the wealth she passed but strode as fast as possible without running to the slaves' lift. Another slave was waiting for the door to open, and Aveline kept her distance, troubled by her interactions with the other girl and the instincts she could not decipher.

Her initial impression, that Tiana was likely insane, left her dissatisfied. The girl, while different, had not seemed so mad once she spoke. If anything, she seemed lonely locked away in her room. Their interaction only perplexed Aveline more as to why anyone would want to harm the isolated, neglected Tiana.

As an assassin, it did not matter why anyone wanted her dead, if he was able to pay for the murder. Death was a business transaction, and the relationship between sponsor and target was not her concern. Aveline had this facet of killing drilled into her. So why did her instincts urge her to examine more closely the two conflicting jobs she was hired for? Why did Matilda's treatment of Tiana irritate her? For all she knew, Matilda was the benefactor Karl had discussed. Aveline had spent all of two minutes in Matilda's presence and would not doubt the woman's ability to murder her own stepdaughter.

Disturbed as much by her own thoughts as her circumstances, Aveline stepped into the elevator box when it opened and rode the lift down to the base of the pyramid. She paused to orient herself before descending the stairwell into the basement.

The halls were narrower here and whitewashed, lit by electricity but showing the wear of generations of slaves walking these paths on their way to serve their masters. She began walking without knowing exactly where she was supposed to go and soon discovered the connecting corridors and random intersections to be a confusing maze. She crossed the paths of several other slaves but feared asking for directions when she was supposed to be mute. Tiana was probably not going to tell her evil stepmother about Aveline, but she dared not risk trusting other strangers with the secret.

At long last, after half an hour of searching, she reached a long hallway lined by dozens of doorways, each of which was marked by a different color sash. She slowed and peered into the first few doors. Large bays containing wooden bunk beds stacked four high and armoires appeared well kept, if worn. Several people were sleeping in the bunks, and she quickly assessed the dorms on the right hand side were for men, those on the left for women.

Doorways designated by green sashes were at the far end of the hallway and numbered twice as many as any of the other sashes. She entered one of the three on the women's side at random.

"That's her." The quiet voice came from a corner near the door.

Aveline glanced towards the five women seated at a round table, eating. All of them glared at her with varying degrees of unfriendliness. Unconcerned, Aveline ventured farther into the dorms and sought some sign the bunks were assigned or claimed before she selected one.

"You don't belong here, new girl," one of the women called gruffly.

Aveline returned to the front of the bay. She pointed to the dorm on the right and then the one on the left then shrugged, hoping to convey she did not know which was hers.

"I don't mean you don't belong in *these* barracks," the woman said. "I mean, you don't belong here at all." She stood. Aveline was startled by her size. At close to six feet tall, with short hair and an athletic build, the woman before her resembled a soldier in the Shield.

"You stole Jacque's position. She was supposed to be promoted to a Hanover's personal slave," another piped up.

"My family has been serving the Hanover's for nine generations. *Nine*. And they give the position to a mixed girl off the streets?" Jacque, the towering woman, shook her head.

Don't push me, Aveline warned silently. While nothing suited her mood or spiked her Devil's need for blood more than a confrontation, she recalled how many times George had tried to tell her not to make waves. For his sake, she decided to ignore Jacque. Aveline paced towards the door. She could return later, after talking to George, or take up residence in one of the other dorms.

Jacque moved quickly to block her path.

Aveline assessed her with expert eyes. She had nothing to fear from anyone here. If they had been servants their whole lives, they had no experience surviving on the streets or fighting.

But she did.

"I don't like you, new girl." Jacque said and shoved her. "You ought to know your place here. You should be on the bottom floor, serving the Willows and not all the way at the top where I belong. I deserve this!"

Aveline's anger sparked. If only George hadn't claimed she was mute! Once again, she tried to avoid the confrontation she knew was coming by skirting Jacque to reach the door.

The woman moved into her way again.

Aveline sighed. A fight on her first day was not the best way to start off, but neither was she going to take a beating or abuse. She rolled the bundle of weapons into her cloak and set them on the ground nearby then returned to the position in front of Jacque, prepared to set the boundaries the tall woman desperately needed to learn.

Ready for a fight, Aveline was willing to let Jacque throw the first and only punch when her instincts blared a warning. Before she could whirl to face the danger, one of the other women had thrown a blanket over her head and torso and then grabbed her, trapping her arms against her body.

Blinded, Aveline grunted when Jacque punched her in the abdomen and then the chest.

The other women began to cheer and encourage the jealous slave, their voices swelling as more slaves joined their ranks to watch.

A familiar sense of calm fell over Aveline as her training and instincts synced with one another and began to guide her. She lashed out with her legs and felt them strike flesh. She threw her weight around to try to dislodge the woman holding her. More blows fell all over her torso, and she bore them without making any sound that might give away her secret.

Aveline managed to throw off the balance of the woman holding her by swinging her legs and knocking them both to the ground. She thrashed loose from the blanket amid vicious kicks. With her vision unhindered, she snatched the next kick aimed at her head and twisted the woman's foot, yanking her leg all the way around and sending her tumbling to the ground.

Launching to her feet, Aveline fearlessly entered the fray with fists and kicks swinging. The crowd around them was somewhere around a dozen, and six additional slaves were trying to hit her.

Six untrained combatants were a nuisance but nothing Aveline was unable to handle. She slammed the head of one into the wooden post on a bunk bed, smashed her heel into another's throat, and unleashed an avalanche of rapid punches into two more. Her father had required her to be trained in street fighting as well as the more traditional, dignified martial arts, and she held nothing back as she fought off the slaves who meant to bury her so one of them could take her place. Her Devil's blood cheered her on, urged her to every last one of her opponents.

"Stop this! Immediately!" The sharp command came just as Aveline dropped the last of her attackers.

The women fell silent and created an opening for George to walk through. He was accompanied by two Shield soldiers.

Aveline lifted her chin in mild defiance, not about to apologize when she had been the one attacked. Straightening, she dabbed at her bloody nose and mentally assessed her body as George stared at the damage she had done. By her count, two slaves at least were dead, another two unable to walk anytime soon and the final two unconscious. Jacque, who had started the fight, was one of those she knocked out.

"Check them and tell me who still lives," he instructed the Shield soldiers. His gaze settled on Aveline. "You. Come with me." He pointed at her.

She went, eyeing the crowd she walked through. No one lunged or lashed out at her, and she snatched her bundle from the ground near the door. Aveline did not start to relax until she was in the hallway. George continued walking quickly, down the opposite direction she had come, and turned a corner before confronting her.

"That cannot happen again," he said.

"I didn't start it."

"Did I ask?" he snapped. "You are here for one reason only! If you are expelled or worse, burnt, by the end of the first day, who will protect my master's sister?"

Aveline resisted the reaction of rolling her eyes. She dabbed at her bloodied nose. Bruises were forming on her torso and legs, and her nose was starting to hurt. The fight, however poorly timed, had the result of freeing some of the tension she had been carrying since she woke up in a brothel.

"Do you understand we cannot risk bringing anyone else in here? That you are the only hope?" he continued.

"I know how to do what I was hired to do. I don't need you

lecturing me," she retorted. "That bitch came at me. What was I supposed to do? Let her beat me?"

"Yes. Because then, she would have left you alone, and no one else would be talking about how the new slave to Tiana fought off six slaves! I thought your ilk were supposed to be discreet! Is that not one of your primary directives? Do you have no concern for what is at stake?"

Rocky's life.

George had a point, she ceded silently. Her indignation melted when she thought of her friend. His life depended upon her blending in. Assassins were never supposed to be seen and if they were, to leave no impression on the minds of others. Killing two slaves was not going to help her ability to move unnoticed among the slaves or earn her the trust of those she might need to help her at one point. By reacting instead of thinking, she had unwittingly endangered Rocky's life.

"By your silence, you know you were in the wrong." George was calming down. "For now, you will sleep on Tiana's floor, until I can find a way to smooth over the murder of the family's slaves and ensure you are not likewise murdered in your sleep."

As much as she hated being lectured by someone whose hands had never known a callous, Aveline nodded. "I apologize," she forced herself to say. "It was not my intention to cause a mess."

"I appreciate your humility," he said. "Do not do anything like this again!"

She said nothing.

"Come. We will fetch your bed linens." George turned away and began walking.

"Hey, George. Why is Tiana locked away?" Aveline asked, at his heels.

"It is not for me to say."

"Try not to be too helpful!"

"You are fortunate I am willing to hide the bodies and not force you to face Matilda for your crimes." He gave her a pointed look. "If preventing you from being burnt is not helpful, I am uncertain what is."

"Point taken," she grumbled. "I am trying to understand what I'm doing here."

"It was my master's belief the threat to her life comes from inside the family," George replied quietly.

"They already treat her worse than a slave."

He glanced at her. "I have heard this rumor many times before. No slave has ever seen Tiana or accessed her quarters. Matilda takes her food and prepares her for events where her presence is required."

"She lives worse than I did in the streets, and Matilda starves her."

George frowned. "Then you will obtain her food directly from the kitchens from now on. My master is permitted to see her monthly. He has no way of knowing how his sister is treated daily."

"He thinks Matilda will try to kill her?"

"He believes the threat comes from within the family, which extends to the cousins and extended family on the floor below the Hanover's," George replied carefully. "To speculate who is behind it without proof is irresponsible."

"What I can't figure out is why?" she asked again, perplexed by what value there was in spending the money Karl's benefactor had pledged in order to kill a girl who never left her room.

"It is not for me to speculate." George said and entered a massive laundry and linen room filled with pools of steaming water and red-faced slaves scrubbing clothing and bedding.

Aveline's nose wrinkled at the pungent scents of cleaners. The open bay was more humid than the hallway. Within seconds of entering, her clothing was sticking to her skin. George went to a shelf extending all the way to the thirty foot ceiling stacked with folded linens. He plucked a blanket from one shelf, sheets from another and a pillow from the third and piled them into her arms.

His gaze lingered on her before he strode down another aisle and pulled a cotton bag from a shelf then filled it with soft bandages and clean rags. He piled the bag on top of her other linens, blocking much of her vision, and motioned for her to follow him.

Aveline trailed him through the underground maze. Accustomed to learning and adapting to the ever-changing streets, she instinctively chose random landmarks and recorded them so she could find her way back. They passed several bays filled with metal, pottery, and cotton spinning artisans hard at work before reaching the kitchens located next to the stairs for easy access.

George stopped walking when he reached the stairs. "Return to Tiana," he ordered. "No more trouble."

Aveline snorted and started up the stairs, balancing the heavy armful of linens.

Ten minutes later, she passed the guards outside the Hanover's apartment and teetered through the opulent rooms and hallways to Tiana's door. Aveline dropped the bedding on the ground and straightened, checking her nose once more. The bleeding had stopped, but she was going to have a black eye in the morning.

Unlocking Tiana's door, she nudged it open with her hip while bending down to retrieve the linens. She entered and pushed the door closed and crossed to the table to deposit the armful.

Tiana had eaten everything except for one strawberry, which sat in the middle of her plate.

Aveline glanced from it to the bed, where the girl was curled up in a fetal position, her back to the center of the room. The defensive position drew Aveline's thoughts once more to the bizarre statement Tiana had made about her father.

Aveline's father, an assassin leader, had mourned the loss of his wife so much, he lost all control of himself and went on a rampage, the Devil's Blood Massacre, to try to soothe his pain. Their time on the streets had been rough, but he had always doted over Aveline, always spoken warmly of her mother and ensured none of Aveline's native past and history was lost.

Unable to imagine a scenario where her father hurt her mother, Aveline grappled with the idea of being abandoned by the only family she had. Was this why Tiana crumpled every time someone spoke harshly to her? Refused to look at anyone and curled up on her bed as if waiting for someone to hit her?

"You didn't finish your strawberries," Aveline said awkwardly.

"I saved it for you," came the soft response. "As an apology for angering you. I should not have spoken out of turn."

The words punctured the veneer of control Aveline had over her emotions. She imagined Tiana expressing the same exact sentiment to Matilda, after her unstable stepmother had hit or screamed at her. After George's explanation about no one being allowed to see Tiana except Matilda, Aveline did not doubt at all that Tiana's bruises and fear came from Matilda's wrath.

Not only that, but Matilda had given Tiana the most bruised of the bowl of strawberries sitting on her table. Tiana was already waifish and had admitted to loving strawberries. That she saved one, when she had to have been hungry, bothered Aveline.

Rarely did Aveline feel unable to adapt to her circumstances. This situation, which called for a level of empathy she was unaccustomed to receiving or sharing, stumped her. *Kindness* was not among her tools for surviving the streets, and she did not quite grasp how to express it to someone who appeared to need it.

Aveline returned her gaze to the berry then to the linens. Tiana's bedding consisted of rags sewn together, and she possessed three flat pillows.

"I brought you new bedding," Aveline said. "I need to strip your bed."

There was a pause and then Tiana shifted. She sat up and twisted, away from Aveline, and left her bed. Her eyes remained trained on the floor. The lighting of the room was too weak for Aveline to see their color.

She pulled the rags off Tiana's bed. The slaves had better bedding than the Hanover daughter, and Aveline puzzled over this as she moved. At first, she had thought Tiana's childlike fascination with strawberries indicative of madness. As she made the bed, a second possibility emerged.

Tiana never looked up. Was she blind? Or was it a combination of factors the wealthy Hanover's were ashamed of? A little madness and complete blindness certain to make Tiana clumsy in public?

Aveline reached for the pillow at the end of the bed and paused.

Was it just her, or was it floating?

She blinked, and the pillow was where it belonged on the bed. Chalking the incident up to her swelling eye, which was blurry, she grabbed and tossed the pillow at the head of the bed before stooping down to gather up the old bedding.

Without an explanation to Tiana, she left and traversed through the apartment quickly one more time, down the lift and to the basement. Using the landmarks she had memorized, she found her way back to the washroom and deposited the dirty linens into a random bin without caring what it contained. She followed George's initial footsteps through the aisles, invisible among the other bustling slaves, and collected her own bedding.

On her way back, she paused in the wide doorway of the kitchens. Massive stone ovens lined one wall while the far wall contained an entrance to a pantry whose entrance featured bundles of herbs hanging from the top of the doorway. Rows of counters stretched between the two walls along with a line of ten spits.

Aveline juggled her bedding and made a mental note of where slaves wearing different sashes were lining up to pick up trays of food. In the morning, she would join them and ensure Tiana was fed a full meal instead of scraps.

She returned to the top floor and to Tiana's room. The blonde girl was lying down again, hugging the fluffy pillow.

Aveline made her bed in the middle of the floor, where she would be alerted if anyone entered. She stretched out on the floor with a grimace, her body beginning to stiffen after her fight. The sunset edged the boarded up window, and she watched the orange-pink colors splattered across the ceiling.

Tiana's breathing was deep and regular. She was asleep at an early hour, though Aveline was accustomed to staying up much later. Bored, she stood and went to the books on Tiana's vanity. She picked up one. It was much heavier than it appeared to be, and she opened the cover. Reading was not an essential trait for an assassin, and she had never learned. The squiggles inside had no meaning to her, though she stopped to study the drawings and pictures when she reached them.

Her interest waned, and she replaced the book. Tiana's belongings consisted of the tomes, the empty perfume bottle, a brush and a few pins for her hair, an armoire filled with fancy clothing and shoes, a trunk of nothing but brightly colored threads and other sewing supplies, and a closet containing a dozen more of the plain sleeping gowns. Aveline assumed the drawer full of vials was not Tiana's but Matilda's. She examined one of them before replacing it.

Was this how Tiana had spent every day since she was born? Trapped in the most restrictive place Aveline was able to imagine?

As soon as the sun set, the poor lighting in the room became even more evident. It was downright gloomy. Aveline lay down and forced herself to stay still when she wanted to do anything else. She placed two knives under her pillow and another under Tiana's bed. The room was utterly silent, as if the walls had been soundproofed. Nothing was unusual or out of place, except for the strange charge that seemed to exist solely in Tiana's room.

Aveline's mind went again to her father and then to Rocky, and she stared at the ceiling, doubting she was going to sleep at all this night. Too much was depending on her success. Of everything to be concerned about, why was she hoping the kitchens had a bowl of strawberries for her to grab for Tiana in the morning?

SIX

ARTHUR AND HIS CLOSEST FRIEND, Warner, sat on one side of a bonfire at the edge of their encampment, their native tracker opposite them. Dressed similarly in layers of cotton, leather and fur, the native was distinguished from the Shield members by the three feathers in his long hair and the lack of sash anywhere on his body. Arthur wore his around his bicep and Warner around his waist.

Arthur gazed into the dancing flames, pensive. The night was cold enough that he wore a fur-lined hat with flaps to protect his ears in addition to thick clothing, winter boots and a scarf made by his sister he kept wrapped tightly around his neck.

"You have determined our path tomorrow?" Leaping Deer, the native tracker, one of the few surviving members of the Comanche Nation, asked quietly.

Arthur glanced up at him then around to ensure they were not being observed by the other Shield soldiers. Withdrawing a steel knife from the satchel at his side, he placed it on the ground before him, rested his hand on it, and closed his eyes.

Show me where we will find game, he willed the weapon.

It began to move beneath his fingers, and he lifted his hand and opened his eyes.

The tip of the blade pointed northwest.

"Then northwest we will go," Leaping Deer said with a half-smile.

Arthur replaced the weapon. His unusual gift, while saving the city many winters from starvation, was likewise forbidden. If anyone discovered exactly how his family was so successful finding food, he would be burnt at the stake, alongside his father and sister. His step-mother, he guessed, would probably lie her way out of everything. She had a survivor's instinct he would have admired, if not for the accompanying ambition he suspected would drive her to turn on her husband at a moment's notice.

Leery of one of the Shield soldiers noticing his magic, Arthur twisted all the way around to survey his surroundings.

"No one saw," Warner assured him.

"I would claim it to be native magic if they did," Leaping Deer added. A friend of the family for two decades, the native living in a village near the city was permitted to use magic whereas those inside the city were not.

"Thank you." Arthur smiled at his companions.

"You are normally more eager for the annual hunt. Your father would not allow his heir apparent to leave the city, if we did not need your special magic to find game," Leaping Deer observed.

"I am thrilled to be out of the city but also worried," Arthur assured him. "My father and his advisors have been at odds, and I suspect a shift in the alliances of the families around us, which makes this year's hunt ill timed."

"How is this different than any other year?" Warner retorted with a small laugh. "They are at odds when food is scarce and lovers when we return victorious laden with meat enough for three winters."

"True," Arthur said. He hesitated to speak of something far more private, even though he trusted these two men with his life. After a moment of internal debate, he charged ahead. "I have been plagued by a dream for the past month. It makes me believe it is not a dream but a ... vision. I have them from time to time." He glanced at both men, waiting for one of them to judge him and relaxing when neither did. If anything, Warner was studying him in concern while Leaping Deer appeared curious. They were more comfortable with him discussing his strange abilities than he was.

"Please tell me you do not see your death," Warner whispered.

"No," Arthur said quickly and reached over to squeeze the hand of his longtime guardian and lover. "Nothing of the sort. This dream is so bizarre, I have feared revealing it even to you. There is little sense to it, and I have tried to decipher it through reading and seeking general counsel from the clairvoyants Father permits entrance into the city. But the meaning of this dream eludes me, and I cannot speak to anyone else about the specifics."

Warner waited, his blue eyes glued to Arthur's face.

"Perhaps, Leaping Deer, you can help me interpret it," Arthur said.

"Me?" The native lifted his eyes from the fire. "I am not the one possessing magic."

"You make my *deformity* sound pleasant."

"You deny the gift your gods have given you. In the Free Lands, you would be beyond the wrath of your father," Leaping Deer reminded him.

Free Lands. The mention of the legendary place earlier by his sister made Arthur pause. How she overheard the slaves talking, he did not know, but she often picked up on information he wished she had not. The existence of the Free Lands was one of those trinkets of knowledge he did not wish her to possess. At least, not yet, not until he had verified they existed. She was too frail to be led on and then disappointed if he discovered they were not real. He would rather wait until he knew with certainty.

"I hear talk of the Free Lands but have never met anyone who has visited them," Arthur said.

"If they are as wonderful as we hear, who would leave?" Warner asked.

"True," Arthur agreed. "But then how would we know they existed in the first place?"

Warner turned his attention to Leaping Deer. "Have the people of your village visited the Free Lands?"

"No," was the response. "The tribal elders have spoken of the Free Lands to the north for many years, but no one has ever ventured that far to see if they exist. It is believed that there are far worse dangers than the forests, plains and Ghouls that lie between us and the Free Lands. Perhaps we have never heard of anyone returning from them, because no one who sought them reached them in the first place."

I need them to be real, Arthur thought. Leaping Deer's fears had been repeated to Arthur by everyone he asked about the Free Lands, including the clairvoyants he was only allowed to speak to in passing. Under the watchful gaze of his father, Arthur had little opportunity to pursue the questions burning hottest inside him and instead was forced to play his part and seize any chance presented to him to further his quest for knowledge.

But the older Tiana became, the less time he had. Their father had rebuffed both the council and the pressure other wealthy families put on him to marry her off and cement an alliance between powerful families, as was traditional. When she turned eighteen, people would begin to suspect she was disfigured, if their father did not announce her engagement to one of the many available heirs from other families wishing to climb the social strata.

"Your dream," Leaping Deer prodded him.

Arthur blinked out of his thoughts. "Nightmares are more accurate," he said. "Do not laugh at me, either of you!" He gave them looks of playful warning, self-conscious of sharing the odd dream. "No matter what dream I am having, a native man will appear and begin chasing me. He's not from the Apache or Navajo or any of the nations with whom your tribe, or our city, is at peace," he said to

Leaping Deer. "This native is different, and if you ask me why, I am uncertain what to say. I *know* it, just as I know which direction we must go to hunt game."

"Not all of the first peoples were destroyed with the Old World. It is said there are a few very old tribes from the Northeast, where it is winter for nine months a year," Leaping Deer said. "It is possible you have made contact with one of their holy men in your dreams."

"I hope not," Arthur said with a snort. "This man is not like us. He takes on the form of a bear sometimes and a wolf at other times and still other times, a horrible creature I have never seen before and cannot even begin to describe." He paused, recalling the dream, before continuing. "But he finds me no matter what dream I am having or where I am in my dream. When he appears, everything changes, and I return to the same place every time."

"Where?" Warner asked.

"I don't know for sure," Arthur admitted. "In every dream, I am running from him across the plains, but I cannot identify which grass-lands these are. A place I have visited? A place far away?" He shook his head. "I am always in a prairie."

"What else do you see?" Leaping Deer asked.

"Spring is in the air, a little cool, yet warm enough not to need furs or a cloak. The grass is high, the wind strong, and the full moon is above, bright enough to make the grass glow silver. I run, and he chases me, sometimes in one of his animal forms, sometimes in his man form. In his man form, I can see he is crippled. One of his legs is only half a leg, and he wears a contraption that allows him to move like a normal man. This ... contraption," he made motions in the air, uncertain how to explain the awkward sight from his dream, "is covered at all times in black leather. Whether he's an animal or a human, one of his legs is always black, which is how I always know he is the one pursuing me no matter what form he takes."

Arthur paused. His audience was completely enraptured. Warner appeared concerned, but it was Leaping Deer's narrowed gaze that alerted him something about the dream was of particular interest to the tracker.

"I started calling him Black Leg," Arthur admitted, a little sheepishly. "This magic that lets him change into animals, and lets him track me, no matter where I am in my dreams, and which pulls me back onto the prairie in Spring, is contained in his leg."

"His leg is magic?" Warner echoed, brow furrowed.

"Yes. I know it sounds comical or bizarre," Arthur said. "But his magic is stored or ... maybe just exists in his leg. I cannot rationally explain it."

"And Black Leg appears in every dream?"

"Every one for the past month."

"Does he ever catch you?"

"Never. He never comes closer than that tree." Arthur pointed to a tree ten feet away. "But he never stops trying, either."

Leaping Deer was frowning fiercely.

"What is it?" Warner asked the tracker. "Does this mean something to your people?"

"According to the spirits of my ancestors ..." Leaping Deer began and then winked.

Warner's face flared red, and Arthur chuckled.

"We are not all mystics and shaman," the native said. "But, Arthur, there are two elements of your dream I recognize. The first scares me less than the second. You frighten your children with tales of the Ghouls, and we tell our children stories about skinwalkers, men who can turn into bears or wolves or similar."

"But Ghouls *are* real," Warner insisted and then sighed at the tracker's patient smile. "Ah. So are skinwalkers."

"When the Old World ended, a lot of strange things happened. Skinwalkers became as real as the Ghouls."

"If skinwalkers are anything like Ghouls, how can anything else frighten you more?" Arthur exclaimed. "I have seen the forms a skinwalker takes. I would rather meet a Ghoul!"

"What frightens me more: this man who chases you in your dreams really exists," Leaping Deer said. "He is a boogeyman among my people. They fear speaking of him, lest they become his next victim."

Arthur's stomach twisted. He had sensed the dream was not entirely fiction but hoped he was wrong.

"He is from the far northeast, or the south or perhaps even the west. No one knows, except he is the last of his kind, a legendary bounty hunter who invited the dark spirits into himself so he could seek vengeance on those who murdered his family," Leaping Deer said. "In the meantime, until he can find them, he is hired by wealthy natives to hunt down and kill the descendants of the Old World and the invaders who stole our lands from us long ago. He has killed other natives, too, and worked for men of all nations and colors. He serves any master willing to pay his price, and he never accepts money as payment."

"What else is there?" Warner exclaimed.

"No one knows except those who pay him. They are sworn to secrecy." Leaping Deer shrugged. "It is also believed, and widely ridiculed, that the dark spirits he invited into his life live in his leg. If you have seen this, Arthur, without knowing the legend, maybe it is far truer than anyone thought."

Silence fell, and Arthur's heart began to skip beats. The part of his dream he did not reveal was that he was not himself when he was running. He had long, blond, wavy hair and wore a sleeping gown. Tiana had been the one fleeing the bounty hunter, not him.

"He is said to be ruthless, violent and invincible, and his magic leg protects him from harm. He has never failed to find his target," Leaping Deer continued.

"What would he want with Arthur?" Warner spoke in a hushed tone. "The natives do not trust us, but if they wished to kill someone, why Arthur and not his father?"

A better question: why Tiana? Arthur mulled.

"Shall I ask my ancestors?" Leaping Deer asked dryly.

Warner shook his head. "We have no enemies outside the city that we know of. Do we?"

"It might be possible the natives have hired him, perhaps thinking if they can topple the Hanover's, the city will crumble. Our truces of the past generation have pleased no one, inside the city or out," Arthur said. "Or, maybe our enemies within the city hired him to unseat my family. The fact someone wants me dead does not surprise me. My family has built up a long list of people who would like to see us gone over the past two hundred years. But the man chasing me in my dreams ..." he drifted off, more disturbed after Leaping Deer's explanation than he had been waking from each dream. "... every night, Warner. He is there every night."

It was one of the reasons behind Arthur's search for a guardian for his sister. When she turned eighteen, Tiana's continued existence would become a larger challenge. Matilda and members of other ambitious families had always hated Arthur's sister, but it was his father he feared the most. Tiana could not be married off when she turned eighteen for fear of someone discovering her deformities, and this caused his father a political problem. Arthur did not have enough faith in his father to hope for another creative solution to the issue of Tiana. A quiet assassination made the most sense.

However, a native with one black leg would not go unnoticed in a city that did not welcome natives in the first place, which meant Tiana faced potential threats from at least two directions.

With the Winter Hunt looming, two months before Tiana's birthday, Arthur grew concerned about leaving his sister vulnerable in her own home. Amongst the nightmares of being chased by Black Leg, Arthur had also dreamt nightly of a young woman of mixed heritage standing beside his sister in front of the window in Tiana's room, overlooking the city. The girl had not been among any of the slaves, and Arthur's search hastily expanded from the outer city residents to those of the inner city. When his spies uncovered the identity of the girl, he was confronted with another problem. How could he place Tiana's life in the hands of the Devil? By the rules of the Guild, an assassin-in-training would not be permitted to protect Tiana without the leader's permission.

Even if it had been possible to arrange for Aveline to become Tiana's protector, how did Arthur welcome the daughter of a mass murderer – both of whom were rumored to have the blood of the devil in their blood – into his home? His and Tiana's own faulty breeding was the reason Tiana could not leave her room.

Or was it the blood of the devil that would protect Tiana? In his discreet pursuit for more information, carried out by faithful slaves, Arthur had found no other explanation as to why Aveline was special, aside from her demon blood. At the last minute, a clairvoyant had slipped him a tip about the pending death of her father, the day before the hunt, and advised him as to how and where he could contact her. Aveline had possessed no other choice but to accept the only position that would guarantee her life.

One of Arthur's visions had been accurate, and it scared him to consider the other might be as well.

"I will die to protect you," Warner vowed, assuming Arthur's troubled silence was for his own life.

Arthur's gaze flickered to his friend. "I would not let you. Besides, I am not concerned for myself but for my sister. If anything happened to me, she would be alone."

"I will take care of her as well," Warner said without hesitation.

"I know, and I am grateful to have you in my life and by my side," Arthur said with a quick smile. "Do you know the name of this bounty hunter?" he asked Leaping Deer.

"No one does. He is called many names. Black Leg is one. Black Wolf. Black Bear," Leaping Deer shrugged. "The names are never the same but the magic leg is."

"Then he will be easy to identify, if I pay for a bounty of my own," Arthur responded confidently. "I will have him killed before he reaches the city."

"If you can find him. He is known for his stealth."

My sister has suffered enough, Arthur answered silently.

They sat in quiet for a long moment, each of them deep in thought.

"Go and rest," Arthur said finally. "We have a long day ahead of us tomorrow. We need to reach the other end of the forest and the herds before the snow starts again."

Leaping Deer nodded and rose. His steps crunched across the snow as he strode towards his tent.

Arthur stood more slowly, and he and Warner struck off towards the tent they shared. The men were paired up for safety reasons, and it was easy for Arthur and Warner to share a tent when Warner was Arthur's official guardian.

When they were outside the firelight, Warner slid his hand into Arthur's. Arthur squeezed his in return, but he was unable to take his mind off the dreams surely awaiting him this night, or the coldness at his core no amount of furs and flames could warm.

His visions, while powerful, remained frustrating glimpses in time, often with no way for him to know when or how the events he foresaw would unfold. The strange abilities he and Tiana both possessed were beyond rational explanation. Since such sorcery was also forbidden within the city, he rarely had a chance to speak to anyone about it. None of the books in his father's expansive library addressed the odd abilities, and nowhere in his family history was there any record of deformities or special abilities. Whatever secrets his family kept were so tightly controlled, no trace remained.

Once, he found a sentence in the records kept by his forefathers, not pertaining to the family itself but detailing what happened during the first few decades after the Old World collapsed, when many strange events were recorded during the Age of Darkness, when the world existed in permanent stage of night for a century. Along with the waking of the Ghouls – human predators from a bygone age – during this period, the book had referenced a second awakening.

The hands of men shattered the world, but it was also the hands of men that coaxed magic from the land and began to repair all that had been broken.

Arthur had been puzzling over the sentence every day since the bounty hunter began interfering in his dreams. Were his abilities and Tiana's telekinesis considered *magic?* Or was this description figurative in nature? How would tracking game and seeing the future, or Tiana's diverse mix of abilities, heal the world?

There was no one to ask, and even if there were, no one would dare answer the son of the Hanover leader known to burn men and women at the stake for merely uttering the word *magic*. At a loss to explain his and his sister's deformities, Arthur was resigned to quietly finding alternate methods to protect his sister. If he did not find a way to stop the bounty hunter, or his father, or any others attempting to murder Tiana, by her birthday, all he cared about in the world was lost.

"Do you hear them?" Warner's whisper was terse.

Except for my sweet Warner, Arthur added with a glance at Warner. Their forbidden romance, which could earn them both being burnt at the stake, was as troubling as how Arthur was going to keep Tiana alive.

He lifted the flap from one of his ears. In the distance, on the side of the forest opposite the direction he had traveled from the city, wailing screams had begun to fill the night. No human or any other kind of animal made a sound so horrible.

"Ghouls," he murmured dismissively. "Our force is too large, and our fires too many, for them to attack." His eyes were trained to the north. "In the Free Lands, we would all be safe."

"If they exist," Warner said.

"They *must*."

"How will we ever know for certain?"

Arthur fell silent. Unless he went north, he would never know. Such a journey would never be approved by his father. Even if it were, he dared not leave his sister alone for the amount of time it would take to explore the far north. If the trials standing between the city and Free Lands existed, he was not likely to make it there alive. He estimated he had two months until his vision came true. His sister's immediate chances of survival were far more pressing than leaving her to find the Free Lands.

Except ... the Free Lands might hold the key to saving her.

There was no right answer.

"Let us sleep, assuming we can," he said and turned towards their tent, frustrated again by the problems for which he had no solutions.

"Rest. I am on the night watch this evening," Warner replied.

Arthur faced him. He started to reach for his friend and lover and then stopped, clearing his throat. Warner smiled, his blue eyes dancing with amusement and dark hair hidden beneath his hat. Cautious about being too open in their displays of affection, unless one of the ambitious Shield members dared to approach his father, Arthur also resented his inability to openly express how he felt and live the life he wanted.

I need to know if the Free Lands are real for me as well as for Tiana. This time, the thought was tinged with anger.

"Be well and safe," he said awkwardly.

"You, too, Arthur." Warner turned and walked away, towards the corral where the horses were kept on the prairie side of the encampment.

Arthur stepped into his tent, warmed by a fire at its center. The earth at its base had been cleared of snow and was covered in furs. The satchels and rolls containing his and Warner's possessions were neatly stacked in one corner.

Arthur stripped out of his weaponry and placed it beside the pallet making up his bed. He tossed his boots and outer coverings, except the scarf he kept with him at all times, and stretched out on the pallet.

Every night for the past few weeks, he had fought sleep, and every night, he had fallen into slumber despite his best efforts to remain awake. He dwelled on his discussion with Leaping Deer. Before learning the man chasing him in his dream really existed,

Arthur had often debated whether the dream was literal, or if he were being warned of general danger towards his sister.

His fear grew when he found Aveline, a woman from his dreams he had never met before. Yet he felt more confident, not less, after speaking to Leaping Deer. It was a relief to know the threat to Tiana had a face and identity. He would send a team of assassins after the bounty hunter before he reached Lost Vegas. If everyone knew about this native possessing dark spirits, then he would be easier to find.

"I'm coming for you, Black Leg," Arthur said firmly to the dream waiting for him. "If I fail to catch you by spring, I will take Tiana to the Free Lands. Either way, you will never be near enough to harm her."

Arthur's eyes drifted closed and his body relaxed.

MOONLIGHT REFLECTED OFF HIS HAIR, rendering it silver, while the brush of grass against his legs tickled. Arthur, in the body of his sister, ran hard through the prairieland, against the strong wind. He knew without looking over his shoulder that the skinwalker pursued, and he ran faster. He had tried many times to lift his eyes from the grasses before him to the horizon in the hope of determining where exactly he was. The city of Lost Vegas was surrounded by the prairie, which ended at the forests and then picked up on the other side of the woods. Was he running close to Lost Vegas? On the other side of the forest?

Or ... somewhere else completely? The plains stretched for at least a thousand miles, if not more. He could not imagine where his sister could have gone. She had no sense of direction, no knowledge about the geography of what lay beyond the city, aside from what he occasionally taught her of the world.

He was able to look behind him and at his feet and nowhere else, so he focused instead on his clothing. At first, he had assumed he wore the sleeping gown he always saw Tiana in. It was hard to focus in the dream, especially when he was trying to run away from a bounty hunter sent to kill him. He managed to tune in to his clothing and realized it was a pale blue dress, thicker than a sleeping gown but far simpler in design than any Tiana had worn for official events. Soft, leather moccasins were on her feet. Her hair was down, as it often was, and her soft blonde curls bounced with each step.

The dress was not the only difference he noticed this time; a bracelet wound around Tiana's wrist, consisting of colorful beads accentuating a central, flat stone. He squinted to make out the marking on the stone. Not words, but a picture etched in stone ...

From behind, someone grabbed his shoulder. He was yanked out of the dream.

Arthur lurched awake, his instincts blaring and his senses alert. The soothing crackle of the fire was the only sound in his tent. He trusted his otherworldly instincts, as unnatural as they were. At the moment, they warned him of danger. He lay still without being able to pinpoint what threat lurked in his tent.

"Do not move," Warner whispered from somewhere behind him. "Do not even blink."

Arthur stared at the ceiling, trusting his friend. Warner was silent in whatever he did. From his peripheral, Arthur spotted another of the trusted members of his inner circle, a man his age named Henri. Henri was creeping forward stealthily, his eyes pinned to something near Arthur's leg he was unable to see.

"One. Two. Three." Warner counted.

Three of Arthur's friends pounced when Warner uttered the last number. Arthur held his breath. Simultaneously, the three of them stabbed downwards with knives into the ground around Arthur's body: Warner near Arthur's head, Henri beside his left leg and Sayed beside his right arm. Arthur glimpsed the writhing of snake bodies in response to the strikes and remained in place. His friends lifted their targets one by one.

"Rattlers," Henri said, holding the snake run through by the blade of his knife.

Arthur sat up. Each of his grim friends had killed one of the snakes. He looked around, but his unusual instincts whispered that the danger was gone.

"Sayed saw Marshall Cruise leaving your tent," Warner said and flung the snake out the door of the tent.

Better Marshall than Black Leg. Arthur thought with wry amusement.

"Not completely unexpected," he said and climbed to his feet. "Matilda's family has long sought to usurp mine. I am only surprised he did not wait until we were farther from the city. He did not strike me as dumb before this night." As he spoke, his thoughts went to his sister. Did Marshall act alone or with the permission of his family? Was this the first step in a coup or an isolated incident? "Warner, Henri, Sayed," he said to his friends. "I owe you all a life debt." He smiled warmly at them.

"You would have done the same for any of us," Henri replied. "We can teach Marshall a lesson for you, if you wish it."

I want him dead. Arthur was quiet. With the dream of the skin-walker chasing him fresh, and his adrenaline lit by the danger, he knew better than to speak the words forefront in his thoughts. For all he knew, Marshall was the one who would hire – or had hired – the skinwalker to kill Tiana.

Murdering the brother of his stepmother without a trial and his father's permission would cause his father a political headache. Matilda and Marshall's father was the wealthiest man in Lost Vegas from an ambitious family; it was foolish to believe they had no support or allies among the elite.

A hunting accident, however, was completely explainable. Arthur's father would not object either way to the death of someone threatening his heir, but it was easier for others to accept a hunting accident than vengeance. It was expected only half Arthur's men would return, and he could invent a tale that made it sound like Marshall had died with honor rather than being poisoned or killed in a duel, as Arthur planned.

"I will handle it," he said quietly. "Henri, leave before dawn. Return to the city and warn my father to be wary."

Henri nodded. "I will leave immediately."

"Sayed, skin and cook the snakes. Make sure Marshall receives more than his fair share at breakfast," Arthur said with a smile. "Do not look so grim, my friends! I am alive and our hunt is just beginning! It promises to be an eventful few weeks."

Warner shook his head. "Have you no fear, Arthur?"

"None," Arthur replied. *At least, not when it comes to my own life.* His sister's was an entirely different matter.

He listened to his friends banter for a moment, his thoughts on the dream. With some satisfaction, he realized he had not seen Aveline in his dreams this night. When he sent bounty hunters after Black Leg, would the native, too, disappear when no longer a threat?

SEVEN

TIANA'S LIFE, Aveline learned, was filled with empty hours of soli-
tude interrupted by sleep, food and the occasional visit by an irritable
Matilda, who came for drugs and left poisoned tea that Aveline
promptly threw out.

The Hanover girl never objected to anything, including Matilda's
ongoing abuse. She wilted and stayed still, not moving until Matilda
was gone. Despite knowing she should never empathize with
someone she was supposed to murder one day, Aveline pitied the girl
trapped in her room and treated like an animal by the one woman
who should love her. She tried to tell herself it did not matter, that
none of this was her concern, without success.

As each day passed, Aveline grew more restless without the
ability to train or spar and angrier with Matilda's visits and Tiana's
submissive reactions. She had nothing to do but sit, stew and miss her
father.

Tiana read and sewed all day long, hobbies that left Aveline
almost crying from boredom. In all Aveline's fantasizing about
becoming an assassin, she had never once considered there were lulls
between action and danger or long periods of ... nothing. She had

grown up listening to her father's tales, to those of Karl and other assassins, with wonder and envy and never bothered to ask what happened when they were not on an adventure.

I can't bear this until spring! Aveline thought. Worse, the more she thought about Rocky being in the prisons of the Shield, the harder it was for her to justify lying around all day without actively seeking a way to free him.

A week after assuming her new duty, she lay on the floor, eyes on the ceiling. Tiana sewed so quietly, Aveline glanced frequently in her direction to ensure she was still present. The girl had not looked up once since meeting her. She embroidered silk with her back to Aveline, no matter where the lighting in the room was.

Without the daily dose of poison, Tiana's features had returned to a healthier shade of peach, and she smiled more often.

"Are you hungry?" Aveline asked, desperate for something to do.

"You have been stuffing me full of food the past few days. I've eaten thrice today already, and we have yet to eat dinner," Tiana pointed out.

"You're too skinny. You need to eat more."

"I am not hungry."

Aveline sighed. "How do you live like this?" she complained.

"How would I know what I am missing?"

"You wouldn't. But don't you ever wonder?" Aveline twisted her head toward Tiana, who sat on the bed.

Tiana's hands lowered, and her head lifted as she thought. "Will you laugh if I tell you the truth?" she asked hesitantly.

"Probably," Aveline replied. Over the period of a week, Tiana had stopped wilting whenever Aveline was too straightforward. The girl was not ready to face the world outside her room, but she was progressing each day towards discerning the difference between harmless sarcasm and malignant words spoken in earnest.

"I think about leaving the city all day long," Tiana replied.

"Why don't you go?" Aveline asked.

"Where would I go? How would I travel? Who would show me how to survive?"

"You have money. You could pay someone." Aveline grimaced. Tiana had a point. She would not survive two steps past the entrance of her room for long without help.

"My father has money. I have nothing."

"Your books would sell well."

"But I love them."

"Fine. Stay here your whole life."

"Aveline, do you not fear the unknown? The future?" Tiana asked.

"I don't really think that way. On the streets, you learn to live in the moment. It's acceptable to *hope* for there to be a future, but if you aren't paying attention to what's in front of you, you die," Aveline explained.

"I have nothing to do but think. Have you heard of the Free Lands?" Tiana asked her.

"Rumors," Aveline replied vaguely. "I heard traders mention them when I went to the markets."

"Then they exist."

"They might. It wouldn't matter if they did. I never want to leave the city."

"I do. I want to go to the Free Lands," Tiana said with rare conviction. "How many books would I give someone to take me there?"

"Burn me, Tiana. You can't just give someone a few books and tell them to take you somewhere."

"Why not?"

"You don't have any idea how the world outside your room works!" Aveline exclaimed. "What if the person steals your books and leaves you in the inner city to die? What if he leads you in the forest and does the same there? Or worse, sells you to the slavers or to a brothel?"

Tiana sighed. "I understand. I would not know who to trust. I could be sitting next to someone who wanted to kill me, and I would never know."

Aveline blinked, uncertain how to respond. It was the second time in as many days an innocent statement by Tiana had hit too close to the truth. Aveline sensed there was more depth to the Hanover girl than she initially assumed.

Uncomfortable with Tiana's too accurate guess, Aveline rose and paced. Her gaze settled on the boarded up window in Tiana's room. "I haven't seen the sun since I got here a week ago! Have you ever even been outside? You're whiter than a Ghoul."

Tiana giggled. "I go outside once a year."

Aveline shook her head. If she were Tiana, she would be consumed by madness. The isolated girl appeared too accustomed to being imprisoned by her own family to question it. That she had aspirations of going somewhere so far away from here surprised Aveline.

"This is ridiculous." Aveline went to the window. "The least we can do is open this damn thing so we have fresh air!" She dug her fingers into the area between wood and sill and yanked.

Tiana gasped. "No, Aveline. You must not!"

"Why not?" Aveline asked with a grunt.

"Matilda will be angry."

"Your stepmother is a bitch. It's in her nature to hate everything you do, so why not be happy doing it?"

Tiana said nothing.

The wood boards gave an inch. Aveline dropped her hands and stretched towards the table to grab one of her steel weapons. "Time to see how strong metal is." She shoved a pointed stake into the windowsill and pushed on the end, creating a lever. One of the nails popped out, and she went onto the next.

"She will know I did not do this," Tiana said.

"I don't care."

"I do. I do not wish her to harm you."

Aveline laughed. "If she sends me away, you will have no more strawberries. Is this what worries you?"

"You should not laugh at me." Tiana's voice held a note of sadness.

"Toughen up, Tiana," Aveline ordered. "Has your father forbidden you from taking down the boards like he has everything else?"

"No."

"Then you can bitch at me or help me."

Aveline neither knew nor cared what Tiana would decide to do. This was for her own sanity, to prevent her from going stir crazy. She needed the sunlight and to smell the city she grew up in.

After a hesitation, Tiana moved to the other side of the window and began tugging the board loose. Aveline loosened a few more of the nails and found most of them were rusted and rotted in place, as if the window had been covered for many years before Tiana assumed residency in the room.

"Pull," she said and gave her side another yank.

Tiana did so, and the board splintered, groaned and then gave. It snapped off fast enough to knock her down. Aveline almost fell with her but caught herself and kept the board from falling on the blonde girl.

"We did it!" Aveline exclaimed and put the heavy wood down, leaning it against the table. She peered out of the window, admiring the view overlooking the city and surrounding prairie with glimpses of the forest visible from the top of the largest structure in the city. The day was a typical gray, cloudy mid-winter day, but the moment the wintery air chilled her lungs, Aveline began to relax. She belonged outside, not trapped in the tiny room.

Tiana joined her, and Aveline heard her breathe in deeply several times.

"Beautiful," Tiana murmured. "Had I known this awaited me, I would have taken the boards down myself long ago."

"No you wouldn't have," Aveline replied, amused.

"I would have *thought* about it," Tiana said sheepishly.

"Don't you ever ..." Aveline glanced at her ward, and the question stopped in her throat.

In nearly every way, Tiana appeared normal. That was, until Aveline saw why Tiana kept her gaze downcast. She had no pupils. Or maybe, her eyes were made up solely of pupils. Aveline was not certain which was correct. Tiana's almond-shaped eyes contained inky black irises that filled the entire eyeball with only a fleck of white peeking out on either side and no differentiation between the pupil and iris. The unnatural condition was impossible to miss once Tiana looked up.

The blonde girl's smile faded when she realized Aveline was staring at her. She quickly averted her eyes to the ground again, whirled and ran to the closet. Tiana slammed the door closed, and Aveline heard the slide of the lock into place.

"Burn me," she muttered. Unprepared to witness Tiana's deformity, Aveline had reacted differently than she would have liked. It had taken a week for Tiana's fragile trust to emerge, and Aveline had destroyed it in seconds.

Aveline went to the closet. "Tiana? You can come out. I didn't mean to stare."

No answer. Aveline sank down with her back to the door, uncertain what to say. "It's not that bad," she said.

"It is so!"

"You aren't missing a leg or something. I understand why you don't leave your room, because your father would probably burn you at the stake but you're not ... ugly."

Tiana's soft sniffling reached her.

Aveline rolled her eyes. "Tiana, I don't care if your eyes are strange. My father massacred a thousand people in three days. I didn't judge him for it and I don't judge you for your eyes."

"You should," came the choked response. "When you understand everything, you will leave me or hate me or –"

"Why? Because your horrible family does?" Aveline snapped.

"No. Because ..." Tiana's mumbling was too choked by crying for Aveline to understand.

The ever-present charge in the air became almost stifling, until the hair on Aveline's arms stood up on end. Movement from her peripheral drew her focus away from Tiana. Aveline sprang to her feet before she was able to register who – rather, what – was moving.

Pillows were lifting into the air off the bed, followed by the coverings and then by the bed itself. The armoire was next to float, then the vanity and everything on top of it. Aveline's weapons floated into the air next.

Aveline blinked. She rubbed her eyes to ensure she was awake then reached out to one of the knives drifting towards her. She plucked it out of the air. It was solid, cool and heavy in her hand.

"Are you ... are you doing this?" Aveline asked.

"Y...yes."

So maybe Tiana had a few, extremely unusual traits working against her. Aveline absorbed the sight of the hovering inanimate objects in silence. She had never heard of anyone lifting objects without touching them, and she had no idea why Tiana's eyes were so strange. Granted, the daughter of the Devil, who carried the blood of a demon, was not normal either. Until this incident, however, Aveline had never considered more people than the members of her family had been touched by demon blood.

"Is this magic?" she asked.

Tiana did not answer. The furniture and belongings settled onto the ground.

Uncomfortable with the display, Aveline nudged the bed to confirm it was too heavy for one person to lift. How had the frail girl hiding in the closet managed to use her mind to do this?

Why did it feel hot in here?

"I'm going for ... food," she said loudly enough for Tiana to hear.

Aveline fled the room faster than she intended to, blaming it on the heat and electrical charge. In the week she had been with Tiana, she had become complacent, not in guarding her ward, but in asking questions to satisfy her insistent instincts. After the display, her insides were wired and her inner voice agitated.

The energy did not release her until she was at the elevator. Only then was Aveline able to coax her tense shoulders back into place. She shivered. Part of her was amazed by Tiana's gift, but it was the buzzing instinct of warning that bothered her. She never sensed danger from Tiana – but there was a threat in Tiana's magic this time, as if the floating furniture were a few harmless drops of rain foretelling the approach of a violent thunderstorm.

Aveline was in the basement before she had completely shaken off the unnerving sense of being caught in a spider's web of electrical currents. She sought out George and, unable to find him in either of the places she knew to look, she roamed the corridors in the hopes of crossing paths with him.

He was not around. She ventured into a part of the basement she had never visited before, as restless from a week trapped in the room as from the buzzing energy of Tiana's unusual skill. The lights flickered out, and she froze in the darkness. Within seconds, fire sprang to life in the sconces stationed beside the electric powered bulbs.

The corridor was dimmer, and she began walking again, glancing at the torches. She had forgotten how much friendlier firelight was. Electricity was amazing, but she missed the warmth of dancing flames lulling her to sleep each night.

Shouting emanated from ahead. The hallway sloped downward to make room for a ceiling thirty feet in the air and massive bays on either side of the hall that far exceeded the sizes of barracks, kitchens and anywhere else Aveline had visited.

Her step slowed, and she shifted to the balls of her feet as she neared the door from where the voices came. The wide, wooden door was cracked open, and she nudged it farther into the room, curious.

This bay extended several hundred feet from the door and was fifty feet wide with a thirty foot ceiling. Her gaze fell to the curled, metal devices thicker than her legs and twenty feet tall in the center of the bay, and she stared at them, uncertain what

exactly she was looking at. There were dozens of these structures extending all the way to the far wall, a forest of twisted
metal.

An older man with white hair and a handsome, young man her
age with dark hair and wearing a burgundy sash were arguing near
the front of the devices. Aveline pushed the door open.

"Hey," she called.

The two stopped and faced her, startled.

Too late, she realized she'd spoken aloud. Hoping they didn't
know who she was, or that she was supposed to be mute, she went
ahead. "What is this place?"

Both glanced down at her sash.

"Go. Fix it!" the older man ordered the younger and spun to face
the door. "This area is off limits or did you not read the sign above the
door?" he demanded of Aveline.

"I don't read," she retorted.

He froze mid-step, mouth agape, before he managed to speak.
"You must be the street dog assigned to the Hanover girl."

"That's me," Aveline confirmed, unfazed by the common deroga-
tory name.

The older man smiled suddenly. "Come! I have questions
for you!"

She moved farther into the room, unable to take her eyes off the
metal structures. "What are these?" she asked.

"This is where electricity comes from," he replied.

"Really?" She lifted her eyebrow quizzically. "Where is it?"

"Where is what?"

"Electricity."

He appeared taken aback. "Do you know what electricity is?" he
asked with a frown.

"Lights?" She shrugged.

His mouth fell open, closed and then opened again.

"Maybe you should fix it, and I can talk to her," the younger man
said, joining them. "Forgive my master. We rarely have visitors,

unless someone comes to scream at us for the lights being off. Did you come here to scream at us?"

"No," Aveline replied. "Why are the lights off?"

"If you do not know what electricity is, how can you possibly understand any answer we give you?" the older man lamented.

"What he means," the younger man said with a patient but pointed look at his master, "is that electricity is a complicated process with many challenges, such as consistently keeping the lights on. When the Old World collapsed, we salvaged as much technology as we could, but there have been problems since then preventing us from returning to the level we once were."

"I understood that," Aveline told the older man pointedly.

The younger man laughed. "My name is Jose and this is my master, Mohammed. He is the smartest man in the city."

"Possibly the known world," Mohammed added.

"Possibly the known world," Jose repeated with a smile that told Aveline he had long since grown accustomed to his master's oddities.

"I'm Aveline," she said.

"If you are not here to yell at us, why have you come to visit?" Jose asked.

Because I can't stop feeling like something is wrong here, and I don't know what else to do except keep busy. The answer was much more complicated than she felt like explaining. "I was wandering around and heard you shouting. Thought I'd see why," she replied.

"Jose, do you not know who this is?" Mohammed poked his slave. "Tiana Hanover's slave."

"We have heard about you," Jose said. "I thought you were seven feet tall with fists made of steel."

"No one has fists of steel, Jose," Mohammed chided him and spun, striding towards the towering metal trees.

"He does not always understand humor," Jose said quietly. His light brown gaze was on her, and Aveline peered up at him, uncertain when she had met anyone with kinder eyes or a brighter smile. "He is brilliant, though, and manages to keep the electricity on most of the time, unless one of the electromagnetic waves hit, which they do every forty eight hours or so."

Aveline frowned, concerned not only for Tiana but for herself. "I don't know what that means. Will these waves endanger us?"

"No. They are of no concern to anyone but us down here." Jose's grin was dazzling, and heat unfurled within her lower belly in response.

They gazed at one another too long.

"Shall I give you a tour?" Jose asked at last.

Aveline found herself nodding, mesmerized by the man in front of her in a way she did not recall experiencing before. Was it his straight teeth? The warm shade of his eyes? His husky, soft voice? He was tall with wide shoulders and lean, indicating he performed some kind of exercise, though his hands lacked the callouses one obtained when training with weapons.

"This is our control station area, where we can monitor the flow of electricity to every point in the building. Well, when it works, we can," Jose said, oblivious to her scrutiny. He motioned to a wall of tables inlaid with bulbous buttons and the darkened, glass panes that resembled windows above them.

At Aveline's doubtful look, he continued. "It is far more impressive when the electricity is working." The tips of his ears turned pink in embarrassment.

"Hmmm. What are these metal trees?" she asked, uninterested in the control station. She walked towards the towering spires.

"Metal trees?" Mohammed echoed from somewhere within the structures. "Is this what our world has come to?"

"We rarely have visitors interested in what we do," Jose said apologetically. "This is where electricity is generated. A river runs beneath the city, and we use it to power our internal grid."

Aveline did not understand at all what he meant. For the sake of not offending his master further with her ignorance, or alerting Jose to the idea she was not as smart as he seemed to think she was, she nodded.

Jose showed her a separate control station, their break room and residences, and a warehouse where more metal trees waited to replace any of those that became broken by the strange waves he mentioned. Some of his explanations became convoluted, and many were beyond either her desire to understand or her limited education. Assassins were not hired because they could read or write or figure out how to use a river to power light bulbs. They were successful because they read people and situations and understood how to survive. Even so, she was able to appreciate the mind it took for Jose to work in such a place.

" ... and that's it," Jose said, returning them to their starting point.

"You really are the smartest people in the city," she said, impressed.

"Possibly the world," Mohammed corrected her.

Aveline snorted. "Possibly the world," she repeated, eyes on Jose, who was grinning.

"You get used to him," he said quietly.

"Jose, did you ask her yet?" piped up Mohammed from within the forest of metal trees.

"When one has guests, one does not ask the kinds of questions you often try to," Jose scolded the older man gently.

An exasperated sigh was his response.

"What can the smartest man in the world possibly want to ask *me*?" Aveline countered.

"She has opened the door, Jose," Mohammed said.

"Now you may ask," Jose replied. "But be respectful, like we discussed."

Mohammed appeared from behind one of the metal trees, clutching a toolbox in his knobby hands. "My dear Aveline, I am grateful you chose to visit us this day." He glanced at Jose, who nodded in amused approval. "If I may ask, does Tiana exist?"

"Yes," Aveline replied, trying not to laugh at Mohammed's pained expression as he attempted to be polite.

"You have seen her?"

"Every day."

"May I ask what she is like?"

The level of his curiosity caught her off guard. Were they asking because they suspected Tiana had special abilities, or because no one had ever seen the mysterious Hanover girl outside of events where she was veiled from sight?

"She's very sweet, very honest. She embroiders all the time." Aveline picked up her sash and motioned to the flowers Tiana had sewn into it. At the center of the pops of color was an eagle like the one tattooed on Tiana's shoulder. "She likes to read."

"She is educated. This is wonderful." Mohammed nodded. "Her stepmother says she is of a sickly nature. What a beautiful, noble woman to care for her stepdaughter." He sighed wistfully.

Aveline bit back her retort. She disliked every aspect of Matilda but grudgingly admitted it was not wise to say so, no matter how much the woman deserved to be widely despised.

Jose was watching her.

Aware of how much time she had been away from her ward, she decided she had learned enough about electricity for the day. "I had better go," she said. "Thanks for showing me around."

"Wait! I have something for you to take her!" Mohammed cried. He darted into the room where he shared a bunk bed with Jose.

"I had heard the opposite about Matilda Hanover," Jose admitted for her ears only.

"Not my place to say," Aveline said with great control.

"Tiana is fortunate to have you." Jose smiled.

Aveline said nothing, suspecting he already knew enough to understand why she was quiet on the topic of Matilda.

"I rarely ever leave here. Someone has to look after Mohammed and his metal trees," Jose said with another winning smile. "If you ever want to come back or ... if you ever have electricity problems ..." He cleared his throat.

Aveline gazed at him, startled. His cheeks were pink, and he ducked his gaze. Uncertain how to respond, or even what was appropriate to say, she was silent. The daughter of the most feared assassin in the city had never been propositioned before or even considered it possible. She had been attracted to many men without imagining what happened if one of them were fascinating enough for her to pursue.

Jose was one of those men fascinating enough to pursue. Smart, kind and with pretty eyes that made her insides flutter whenever he looked at her. That he, too, noticed *her* unsettled her. She was accustomed to men viewing the Devil's daughter as off-limits.

Mohammed returned with a small pouch, dispelling the light tension between them.

"I made these when the twins were born," Mohammed said and tugged two necklaces out of the pouch.

"Twins?" Aveline echoed, grateful for the distraction from the rare uncertainty of her thoughts.

"Tiana had a twin. The twin was born with a deformity, so her father ordered the other child and his wife burnt at the stake," Jose explained quietly.

But if Tiana's twin was deformed ...Aveline was unable to process the thought fully. Had Tiana's father burnt the wrong daughter?

"Her father would burn a newborn as well as his wife?" Aveline asked, appalled. This truth was even worse than Tiana's factual declaration of her mother's fate.

"It is the law. He had no choice," Mohammed said.

"It is a harsh law," Jose said. "Why we do not send the deformed to the Free Lands, where they have a chance to live in peace, I do not know."

"It would be better than murdering children," Aveline agreed, thoughts on the young girls sentenced to the butcher. The outer city had its horrors, and the inner city did as well. Jose's solution was much more rational than burning or eating or enslaving children no one wanted.

"Many people believe Tiana is deformed, too, or perhaps something else is wrong with her," Mohammed said. His focus was on detangling the two thin silver chains holding pendants. "She is never seen in public."

"If that were the case, she would have been burned at birth with the others," Jose reasoned.

"Ah. Done." Mohammed held out the two necklaces to her. "She can decide what to do with the second."

Troubled by the latest revelation contributing to Tiana's tortured existence, Aveline accepted them. "These are timepieces." She calculated the resale value in the inner city and decided they were of little more value than Tiana's blue perfume bottle. The pure silver chains the pendant watches hung from would fetch enough bread for a week.

"They are powered by kinetic energy!" Mohammed declared.

She held them away from her warily.

"Kinetic energy is movement," Jose clarified. "It is nothing forbidden. The clocks use the energy of your everyday routine to tell time."

"Hmm." It certainly sounded like magic to her, but so did their explanation of electricity.

"They have one more quality you will appreciate." Mohammed reached out and placed them beside one another. The faces behind the moving hands began to glow. "When they are close to one another, they will light up."

"Is that more ... kinetic ... uh ..." Aveline started.

"Yes," Jose said.

"No," Mohammed replied simultaneously.

The two exchanged a look, and Aveline waited.

"Is that part magic?" she prodded.

"Magic is forbidden," Mohammed declared.

Jose said nothing.

Reading between the lines, Aveline pocketed the two necklaces. "Thanks." She looked at Jose, wanting to tell him she would return, if he earnestly wished it.

The older man was gazing at her expectantly.

"I will make sure she receives these," Aveline said finally. She turned away, disappointed she had not thought to tell Jose she wanted to visit again when she had the chance.

"Will you tell me how she likes it?" Mohammed asked anxiously.

"Yes. I can come back." Aveline gazed at Jose as she said the words.

"Today?" Mohammed asked.

"When her mistress allows it," Jose said gently.

The older man rolled his eyes and then turned away, stalking back towards the metal trees.

"Soon," Aveline said.

"I ... *we* would like that," Jose answered.

She turned away before he witnessed the heat in her cheeks and left, navigating the hallways until she reached the elevator. Mohammed's insight into the death of Tiana's sister was disturbing, but the exchange with Jose left Aveline energized in a positive way for once, if not hopeful about making a few friends while she was here. Spring was far away; she needed someone else to talk to from time to time and had enjoyed his company.

Her upbeat mood lasted until she reached Tiana's room and recalled what had driven her away. Aveline did not sense the elevated charge she had when she left. She had not determined what to say to convince Tiana to leave the closet and not be as concerned about what Aveline thought of her unique abilities.

Aveline debated going to the kitchens for strawberries before changing her mind. She was not one to avoid confrontation, though it was hard for her to temper her normally quick tongue and sarcasm when dealing with Tiana.

She unlocked the door and stepped inside. Her instincts warned her something was off before her senses had a chance to register what.

The closet door was open, and the bathroom door was halfway shut. The window filled the room with cold light. Tiana was nowhere to be seen.

"Tiana?" Aveline strode to the closet first. Its interior was dark.

The girl was not present. She turned – and her gaze went to the half-finished cup of tea on Tiana's vanity. "Burn me!"

Aveline went to the bathroom and pushed the door. Something heavy blocked it, and she pushed her head through the opening. Tiana was unconscious on the floor, her forearm bloodied and a knife in her hand.

"Tiana!" Aveline shimmied through the narrow opening and bent beside the blonde girl. She assessed there was not enough blood loss to threaten Tiana's life and leaned in closer until she could smell Tiana's lips.

The faint scent of poison was present.

Muttering curses, Aveline half-dragged, half-carried Tiana out of the bathroom and stretched her out on the floor. She yanked the assassin's kit Karl had given her from the bottom drawer of the armoire and dumped it out beside Tiana. Aveline searched it quickly. Good assassins carried multiple kinds of poisons. Great assassins knew to bring the antidotes, too, in case someone was targeting him or her.

Aveline found the oil she needed and snatched a cup, filled it with water and dropped in several drops of the antidote. She propped up Tiana's shoulders and poured the mixture into her mouth.

Tiana swallowed without waking.

Aveline shook her head. "You foolish, stupid girl." She lectured herself next for not thinking to tell Tiana the danger of accepting anything from Matilda ever again.

Replacing the contents and then tossing her bag into the armoire, Aveline lifted Tiana onto her bed. She hurled the teacup and saucer out the window before bandaging up Tiana's bloody forearm and then sitting down at the foot of Tiana's bed. It would take a few hours for the effects of the antidote to appear.

Aveline pulled the two watch pendants from her pocket as she waited. She played with them until they bored her then fingered the flowers Tiana had embroidered onto her sash. One pink, one yellow, one purple. They were small, pretty pops of color.

Checking Tiana again, Aveline stood in the center of the room, restless. Pink had returned to Tiana's cheeks, and she was breathing deeply in slumber. She would have to sleep off the effects of both poison and antidote.

Aveline cleared her bedding from the center of the room and eyed the space. Training there would be a challenge. She would have to be more in control of her limbs in order not to knock over anything or run into the wall or furniture. Sick of doing nothing, she tied her long hair back at the base of her neck and moved to the center of the room to perform one of the defensive martial art forms her father had taught her.

EIGHT

THE NEXT DAY, Tiana had recovered, though her coloring was paler than Aveline would have liked. She had tried to make up for leaving Tiana exposed with not one but two bowls of strawberries. Tiana was too kind to blame her, but Aveline hated knowing she had failed her ward in more than one way.

"You don't have to hide your eyes from me," Aveline said for the tenth time.

Tiana hesitated and clenched the sash she was embroidering. She was facing Aveline for once, which was progress, but she still refused to look at her impatient guardian.

"Don't worry about it," Aveline said, sensing Tiana was not ready for this step. "What are you sewing?"

Tiana picked up the silk to show her. "For Matilda."

"She poisons you and you embroider her a scarf?"

"Veil," Tiana whispered.

Aveline bit back the lecture at the tip of her tongue. "No. Just ... no," she said and stood from her spot on the floor. She snatched the veil from Tiana and went to the window. She threw it out, but a gust of wind blew the thin square of silk back in. Aveline balled it up and tossed it out again, only for the wind to push it back.

"Are you doing that?" Aveline demanded.

Tiana giggled. "I do not control the wind."

Aveline muttered curses and snatched the nails she had pulled from the window. She placed them into the center of the veil before balling it up once more and tossing it. This time, the veil plummeted towards the street.

"No more making pretty veils for someone who wants to murder you," Aveline said firmly and faced the room again, hands on hips. "If you can move things with your mind, why don't you throw her out the window next time she comes in?"

Tiana gasped. She touched her bandaged arm. Aveline had not asked why she cut herself. She had a friend who did the same and claimed it was a release of sorts and helped her feel better. Tiana had only cut herself once since Aveline had been in her life.

"I am deformed," Tiana said. "I shame my family by existing, and I am grateful they let me live."

Aveline stared at her. The words were soft and quiet – and factual, just as Tiana's unfeeling statement about her mother's death had been. The Hanover girl truly believed what she said. It was beyond Aveline's ability to understand either the conviction of such beliefs or that someone like Tiana held them.

"I want you to have this." Tiana twisted around and retrieved the pendant watch Mohammed had sent. She wore one and held out the second to Aveline.

"Me?" Aveline gazed at the outstretched hand holding the pendant. This time, she did not calculate how much she could sell the chain for. An emotion far less pleasant than anticipating where she would spend the money was in her belly. She had warned Tiana once about considering her as a friend and was beginning to question her own indifference to the girl. "Why?"

"Who else would I give it to?" Tiana reasoned. "You would object if I gave it to Matilda, would you not?"

"Vehemently."

"Then I wish you to take it."

Still Aveline hesitated. The two pendants were created for sisters, people with a bond stronger than that between a guardian and her ward or potential target. They lit up when close to one another and the light within them faded when the two pendants were apart. The symbolism was not lost on her, even if she were a lowly street dog with no formal education.

It's just a necklace, she told herself. *It means nothing.*

Aveline accepted it, unable to name the uneasy emotion in her blood. She pulled it over her head, and it settled on her chest next to the plain locket George had given her upon her arrival.

Tiana smiled.

"I heard someone else discuss the Free Lands," Aveline said and returned to her position sitting on the floor. She pulled out her new weapons to polish, again, needing the distraction and to remain active.

"What did they say?" Tiana asked eagerly.

"They seemed to think they exist."

Tiana sprang off the bed and went into the closet. Aveline watched her, confused. When the girl neither slammed the door closed nor returned, she stood and followed. The light in the closet was on, and Tiana was kneeling on one side, gazing at a tapestry embroidered with flowers covering half of it, as if it were a work in progress.

"You did all this?" Aveline asked when Tiana did not speak. The tapestry lining one wall of the closet was ten feet long and eight feet tall. "It must have taken you years."

"I started when I was young." Tiana pointed to one corner. "You can tell how poorly I embroidered."

Tiana's early attempts were more skilled than anything Aveline had seen in the inner city markets. She knelt next to her ward, gazing at the array of flowers, geometric designs and meandering whirls, vines and twirls in too many colors for her to name.

"This is us." Tiana rested her fingertip at the bottom, center, of the tapestry, directly in front of where they knelt. "And these are the Free Lands." She stood and touched an area six feet from the ground.

"Ummm ... what?" Aveline asked, brow furrowing.

"You must not tell anyone."

"I don't even know what I'm looking at."

"A map."

"But these are flowers and plants and ... I don't know what some of these are."

"Think of the blue as water, the brown as roads. These are trees," Tiana pointed to a ring of green, upside down triangles. "These are prairies." She tapped yellow lines. "I have spent almost eight years collecting information about the Free Lands, where they are, and how one might reach them."

Aveline studied the ornate map. "What are these?" She touched a flower.

"Villages, towns and cities. Purple for the friendly natives, pink for non friendly natives, and orange for the non-natives."

Aveline traced a finger from the largest of the flowers, the one Tiana claimed to be their city, and followed a slender brown vine upward, across yellow prairies, through green forests, past multiple flowers. She dropped her hand and looked up to where Tiana had placed her hand on another large flower. The Free Lands appeared close, until Aveline began to think about how far it was from Lost Vegas to the mountains a few days ride away. The mountains were designated as gray triangles in Tiana's artistic map and were at a point of about a third of the distance between Lost Vegas and the Free Lands.

"How do you possibly know the location of a place no one can confirm exists?" Aveline asked, baffled.

Tiana whirled and hurried out of the closet, returning seconds later with a book. She dropped to her knees beside Aveline. "Because of this." She opened the book and showed Aveline the writing scrawled across the pages.

"I can't read," Aveline said impatiently. "Does it tell you where the Free Lands are?"

"This book was written twenty years after the Old World ended," Tiana said. "It does not say where the Free Lands are, but it says where they are *not*. It describes the journey the survivors of the Old World took when they sought refuge, before coming to this city. I used the information in books and what I have learned over almost a decade to create this map."

As Aveline listened, she turned from skeptical to considering. The amount of time and level of obsessiveness it took to create such a map bordered on madness. But it was Tiana's glowing features, and her direct gaze – the first time she had chosen to look straight at Aveline with her deformed eyes – that alerted her to how serious Tiana was about leaving the city.

"Is it accurate?" Aveline asked, growing concerned.

"If they exist, yes. This is how to journey there."

"So you know the path to take but not if *there* exists."

Tiana nodded.

"You wouldn't go to these lengths if you don't already have a plan to leave the city."

Tiana looked away. She closed the book and hugged it to her chest.

Growing concerned, Aveline observed the distance Tiana would have to travel to reach the mythical place. It would take weeks, without the Ghouls, natives, mixed terrain and seasonal obstacles guaranteed to test even the most intrepid explorer.

"Tiana, you can't be serious about this." Aveline waved her hand towards the Free Lands. "Your own stepmother nearly killed you in your room. How do you think you'll survive outside of the city?"

"I will not survive if I remain here."

"You can't know that." Even as she spoke the words, Aveline knew how right Tiana was.

"I will die on my eighteenth birthday, if I do not leave the city first." The Hanover girl's voice was hushed.

"How do you know?" Aveline asked coolly, mentally reviewing everything she had said and done since arriving to ensure she had not tipped off Tiana somehow.

"I can do more than lift furniture with my mind," Tiana answered. "Sometimes, I dream of the future, and in these dreams, I see my death."

Aveline was silent.

"My father cannot afford to let me live past eighteen. I must leave the city before that day."

If Tiana knew Aveline was the one to kill her, she gave no indication, which worried Aveline even more. How many other people were there waiting in the shadows? People smarter and less obvious than Matilda? Perhaps those who hired Karl to kill Tiana?

Of all the questions Aveline had for Tiana, none of them seemed safe to ask without tipping off Tiana that the danger she dreamt of was real.

"What else can you do?" Aveline asked instead.

"I do not try to do any of these things," Tiana replied. "It is forbidden, and I try so very hard not to do anything, but I cannot always control what happens."

"You seem to control lifting furniture well."

"It happens when I am distracted or upset or crying. When I become aware of it, I can stop it, but that is all. I can do nothing about the dreams or about hearing the thoughts of those around me."

"You can read minds?" Aveline echoed and shifted uncomfortably.

"No. Single thoughts, and very rarely. Once a month, perhaps."

Burn me. Aveline was going to have to be more careful about where she allowed her mind to wander when she was around Tiana.

"Matilda screamed every time I looked at her for the first month and when my bed floated, she fainted," Tiana said. "Why do my abilities not shock you?"

Because I have a blood curse of my own. Aveline was not ready to share her secret, even if Tiana had chosen to disclose hers. "How do you have these ... abilities? They were inherited?"

Tiana nodded. "It is why my father burnt my mother," she whispered.

For once, Aveline wished she had thought to ask her father more about the devil's blood. Where the curse started, why it happened. It was not possible for her and Tiana to be related, which meant there were potentially many more people with a similar kind of inherited ability.

Aveline looked from Tiana to the map, uncertain what to think. Tiana deserved a chance to live outside her room but was not in any form prepared for what lay beyond her door. Aveline wrestled with herself, with her contradicting duties, and the growing sense that the issue of Tiana was much more complicated than she could guess. The question she had been avoiding for a few days – how someone locked in her room rated the level of dedicated attention Tiana received – returned. Aveline did not want to become more involved, to under-stand why so many people wanted Tiana dead, to empathize with her eventual target.

But two months was a long time to try to ignore her persistent instincts and what was before her eyes. Two months was a long time to fight the urge to help brighten Tiana's day or worse, help her find out more information about the one topic that made her face glow.

"Promise me you will not run away without telling me," Aveline said at last.

"You will help me?"

"I wouldn't go that far. I don't want to leave the city. But I'll make sure you aren't dead by the time you reach the main floor."

"Very well. I will not." Tiana sounded disappointed.

"Why would anyone want you dead?" Aveline asked with some frustration.

"My father cannot risk exposing my deformity, or it will cost our family our position and lives."

"And Matilda?"

Tiana shrugged. "Perhaps she knows my father wishes it?"

"Anyone else?"

"I do not know anyone else, aside from Arthur, who hired you to protect me."

"Who kills you? In these dreams?" Aveline ventured.

"Someone I have never seen before."

Aveline almost sighed and then sat back on her heels, agitated. Who else had been hired to assassinate Tiana? How deep did this conspiracy to murder the Hanover girl run? If Aveline failed in her secondary duty, she would never become an assassin. Who, then, was her competition?

"Tell me everything you've seen in your dreams about your death," she directed Tiana.

Tiana started to comply when they both heard her door swing open and smack the wall behind it, announcing Matilda's entrance.

"No. Tea." Aveline mouthed to Tiana.

The Hanover girl nodded, but Aveline doubted Tiana would disobey Matilda if she were ordered to drink poison. Tiana's backbone was severely lacking, and her sincere belief that she deserved to be mistreated was going to make Aveline's job protecting her even harder.

Tiana exited the closet first, eyes on the floor, as she assumed her normal position seated on the bed.

Aveline trailed her.

Matilda was at the drawer where she kept her drugs. She lifted one of the vials to the light of the window with a frown.

"Slave," she snapped, turning to Aveline.

Aveline ducked her head quickly. She neither smelled nor saw any cups of tea.

Matilda's eyes narrowed when she saw Tiana, the only sign she was surprised to find the girl perfectly well.

"You. I need my medications from the apothecary, and my useless personal slave cannot be found," Matilda said to Aveline. She held out a purple pouch. "This contains money and a list. I have counted the ounces in this purse. If you return with anything less than two ounces, I will have you burnt for theft. Do you understand?"

Aveline nodded.

"The apothecary is located at the border of the outer and inner city, on the east side of the fish market. Place this in your hair, and he will know to approach you." Matilda held out a bright purple feather.

Aveline accepted both purse and feather. The fish market was a landmark for those in both areas of the city because of its smell. The area Matilda described, however, was not reputable in the least, which supported Aveline's assumption the medications Matilda sought were illicit drugs banned in the outer city by her own husband.

Her plan to wait until Matilda was gone before vacating was quickly thwarted.

"Go. Now," Matilda ordered.

Aveline left reluctantly. She calculated the distance and time and realized she would have to run at least one way in order to return before dusk, when Tiana was likely to be in more danger. Although, she was always in danger with someone like Matilda in the adjacent room.

Unwilling to leave Tiana alone for too long, or at all with Matilda present, Aveline walked out of the room and down the hallway. She hid around a corner and waited several minutes, until she heard Tiana's door slam closed once more.

She peered down the hallway to confirm Matilda was returning to her chambers. Aveline pushed away from the wall and raced through the apartment towards the elevator.

Her first excursion outside in a week was far more invigorating than she expected. She ran with newfound appreciation for the ability to stretch her legs and the harsh winter wind. Even the over-whelming scent of the fish markets was unable to dampen her joy at being free of Tiana's stuffy room. As she hurried to find Matilda's drug dealer, Aveline began to form a backup plan. She always carried a knife or two with her, in case the apothecary needed encouragement to do as she asked.

The fish markets were at the center of the city's two major sides, patrolled by Shield members, and divided in half by a wide road. Aveline slowed when she crossed the bridge leading between the outer and inner cities. She continued to the east side of the fish market, ignoring the curious looks she received from those she passed. She picked up at least two hopeful pickpockets. Mindful of them, she expertly observed those she passed to pick up any threats or attempts to coordinate robbing her. The green sash had little meaning to the residents of the inner city, but the fact she was a privileged slave in clean clothing with nice boots would be noticed by the hawks of the streets.

Aveline tucked the feather behind her ear when she reached the eastern part of the fish markets and began to weave deliberately through the crowds. Five minutes passed, ten, twenty. Three pickpockets approached her, one around the age of eight and two much older, closer to her age. She rebuffed all of them and remained wary for the next attempt, because, in the inner city, there was always someone else waiting to pounce.

Impatient to be back by dusk, she shifted the feather so it was more visible and began to widen her route pacing back and forth along the eastern edge. Several native merchants displayed their handmade wares on blankets beside a building at the edge of the fish market. Her gaze lingered on the goods often before she decided to take a closer look.

Aveline paused with her back to the dwelling beside the natives' display. Baskets and leather and wooden goods were displayed by two elderly native women, each of whom possessed silver hair that reached their ankles and leathery, wrinkled features.

Catching sight of her, one of them nudged the other, and they both watched Aveline. Neither spoke, but their long looks caused her to lift her eyes from the goods to the women.

"Mixed," one of the natives said.

Aveline pursed her lips.

"Was your mother or father native?" the other asked.

"Mother," she said in a clipped tone.

"And you are a slave?"

She did not respond, not wanting to invite further questions from strangers about her position with the Hanover's.

"Do you know your tribe?"

"No," she said.

One of them clucked in disapproval, and Aveline crouched beside a handmade leather good she recognized. "Dream catcher?" she asked and picked up one of the five displayed.

"It is," one of the native women replied.

"Do they work? Will they stop ... nightmares?" She did not know what else to call Tiana's visions.

One of the women picked up a dream catcher and handed it to her. "This one will."

Aveline studied it. Black leather, beads, feathers and sinew webbing, all of which appeared to be high quality.

"Do you remember your mother's name?"

Aveline glanced up. "Walks with a Limp," she answered.

"Her tribe," the other pressed.

"I don't know," Aveline answered. "She was a slave brought to the city twenty years ago. My father fell in love with her and purchased her. She died giving birth to me. How much?" She motioned to the dream catcher.

"Quarter ounce," one of them answered.

"Quarter ounce?" Aveline replied. "That's two days worth of food!"

One of the women leaned forward and gripped the silk sash, rubbing the silk between her fingers. "Will you trade this?"

Aveline fingered the sash for a moment. Tiana had embroidered the flowers and eagle for her.

All the more reason to trade it, she thought, recalling her dual purpose in being with Tiana.

"Take it." Aveline lifted it over her head and handed it to one of the women. "Thanks." She rose and walked away, tucking the dream catcher into her pocket as she began to pace the edge of the fish market again.

Just when she began to think Matilda had been trying to expel her from Tiana's room for some nefarious reason, Aveline sensed someone approach. She turned and saw a slender, tall man making a line straight for her.

"Come with me," he said, breezing by her.

Aveline obeyed and followed him through the throngs of people at the market towards a quieter street lined with shanties that appeared to be propping each other up. He entered one that smelled so heavily of pungent herbs and chemicals, she almost gagged. She left the door open in an attempt to circulate the air while the apothecary went to his desk. Along both walls were various glasses containers, pots and other supplies. Drying herbs hung from every inch of the exposed ceiling rafters.

"What did she ask for this time?" the man asked and withdrew a box of empty glass vials from beneath his desk.

Aveline handed him the list and watched him read it.

"Tell your mistress arsenic is hard to come by," he complained.

Bitch, Aveline thought to herself. "What else does she want?"

"Her usual. Two ounces of Devil Powder and three of Old World Death," he replied.

"One to push her up, the other to bring her down," Aveline murmured. She opened the pouch again, this time observing the amount of money Matilda had given her. "She pays below price."

"In exchange for recommending me to her friends," the dealer replied. He leaned down and pulled a dark colored glass bottle from another box. He began to pour the pure, white powder inside into vials.

"Do you have Ghoul's Fancy?" Aveline asked.

The dealer stopped and looked up. "You aren't the slave she normally sends," he said.

"No, I'm not. Now, do you have Ghoul's Fancy?"

"I do," he confirmed. "For her or for you?"

"Mix it in with the Old World Death. Replace the arsenic with sugar."

When he did not move, Aveline withdrew one of the weapons she had brought. She met his gaze, her own cold, hard. "My father was the Devil. He trained me to use dozens of weapons and to kill in more ways than you have ounces of medicines in this shack."

Her words had the affect she wished. The dealer sat back, listening.

"You can do as I say, and survive, or you can disobey me, and I'll mix it myself after I slit your throat," she finished.

After a minute, he began to laugh. "The Devil's daughter? Here?" He shook his head. "If your mistress refuses to pay for what she –"

Before his sentence was complete, Aveline had plunged one dagger into his hand, pinning it to the table, and held a second to his throat.

The dealer gave a cry of pain. His eyes widened. "You ... you cannot threaten me! I have powerful clients who –"

"- who won't know what happened because you'll be too dead to tell them!" She twisted the knife in his hand.

He grimaced.

"Do as I say." Aveline lowered the knife from his throat without removing the one in his hand. She stepped back and waited warily.

His good hand trembling, the dealer sloppily filled vials halfway with one powder then half with another before shaking them. He sealed five vials with corks before withdrawing a sixth and filling it with sugar from the jar on his table.

"Good man," Aveline said. She released the knife. "That blade is steel. It's worth more than the medicines." Collecting the vials, she tossed him one of the ten ounces Matilda had given her for the medications then whirled and left.

Expecting him to raise the alarm with others of his ilk, Aveline left his shanty and broke into a hard run as she tore through the fish markets and back towards the structure where she now lived. Thrilled by the workout and brief escape, she could not help smiling when she reached the great pyramid. Before returning to Tiana's room, she ducked into a quiet hallway in the basement and opened the pouch. Claiming seven of the ounces, she hid them in a pocket before double checking the vial supposed to contain arsenic. It was indeed sugar; Tiana's teas would grow sweeter without killing her.

Pleased with herself, Aveline grabbed dinner from the kitchens and returned to the top floor and strode through the apartment, just as dusk began to darken the sky. She quickly deposited food on the table near the window in Tiana's room before going to Matilda's door and knocking on it.

A flustered slave answered. Her eyes and nose were puffy and red, and her cheek blazing crimson as well. By the wrinkled sash, someone had grabbed her, and by her limp, Aveline assessed the slave had been thrown down at an angle that hurt her.

Anger flared within her, but she forced herself to remain silent. Aveline handed the slave all six vials as well as the purse with two ounces remaining. The slave said nothing but claimed everything and closed the door.

Aveline stared at the ornate mahogany wood inches from her face, recalling the emotion she had experienced when the two girls at the brothel had been sentenced to the butcher.

Those in the city forced to suffer deserved better than to be controlled by people like the Hanover's and Matilda. It was the fault of the city leadership that the inner city was unable to feed its residents and children were eaten instead. It was also Tiana's father who allowed a woman like Matilda to abuse her slaves and Tiana, and who kept his own daughter living in poverty.

Aveline returned to Tiana's room, her upbeat mood ruined. Tiana was standing beside the table, holding her plate of food as she gazed out over the city. She had divided up the portion so each had half, and Aveline took her plate and sat on the ground.

"I cannot wait to see the sunset in spring!" Tiana said.

Aveline did not respond. She ate the venison, unable to taste meat for the first time without wondering how many innocent children she had inadvertently eaten.

"Did you go far?" Tiana asked her. "Did you see anything wonderful?"

"The city needs to be burnt to the ground. There's nothing wonderful about it, anywhere, at all," Aveline snapped.

Tiana turned away from the window. "Are you bleeding?"

Aveline glanced down. Some of the apothecary's blood had splattered her clothing.

"No," she answered.

"Where is your sash?" Tiana asked, dismayed. "Did someone take it from you?"

"No," Aveline replied. "I traded my sash for this." She shifted to pull the dream catcher out of her pocket and tossed it to Tiana. "It's supposed to help with your nightmares."

"It is beyond beautiful!"

Aveline rolled her eyes at her ward's too chipper exclamation.

"How does it work?"

"When bad dreams come, they get stuck in the web," Aveline explained. "My father taught me about these. My mother was a native, and my father did not want me to grow up without understanding who she was. I slept with one of these above my bed."

"You never speak of your family." Tiana sat down before her. "Are your parents alive?"

"No." Aveline bit off the word, hoping, for once, the Hanover girl took a hint and stopped talking. Tiana, of course, was oblivious to most social cues, since she rarely spoke to anyone.

"I am sorry to hear that," she said. "Was your mother beautiful like you?"

Aveline's eyebrows lifted. "Beautiful?"

Tiana nodded. Her gaze was on the ground. "Your hair is so long and shiny, and your bones do not protrude like mine. Your eyes are normal, the same color as the night. Your face is shaped like a flower."

"A flower?" Aveline's agitation softened. She felt her cheeks self-consciously. "My father said she was the most beautiful woman in the city."

"Then you do look like her."

"You are some sort of mad," Aveline said, unable to stop her smile. "I am not beautiful. You are."

"I am deformed." Tiana frowned.

"You're not deformed. If you had a mirror, you would know this."

"My father banned mirrors when I was four."

Aveline set her plate of food down and reached to the armoire drawer where she kept her few belongings. She pulled the assassin tool kit out and rummaged through it. Assassins used light reflecting off mirrors to coordinate attacks when more than one assassin had been hired for a job.

She retrieved the round mirror and pulled it free from its leather case. It was the size of her palm, large enough for Tiana to see her reflection.

Aveline handed it to Tiana, who took it slowly. Her gaze was instantly riveted to the reflection, and the Hanover girl stared, her breathing shallow and her body tensing.

"You see?" Aveline asked.

Tiana did not answer.

Aveline returned the satchel to its drawer, and her gaze fell to the envelope her father had entrusted to her, which she dared not open. Her fingertips grazed it, and she recalled too clearly how he had looked the last time she sat before him. Shaking her head to clear the vision, she sat back down to find Tiana had not moved an inch.

"Well?" Aveline prodded.

Tiana blinked. She was pale, and her eyes filled with tears. "It is so much worse than I thought." The words were choked, and she lowered the mirror. "No wonder everyone who lays eyes on me wishes me dead."

"What? No, Tiana, your eyes are –"

"I should have been burnt at the stake!" Tiana hopped to her feet and dashed to the closet.

Before Aveline could react, she heard the closet door lock and the sound of Tiana sobbing.

Aveline retrieved the mirror and dream catcher from the floor and released a long, controlled sigh. Dealing with Tiana gave her a headache, not because Tiana was mad, but because Aveline had to remind herself frequently to be gentle towards the skittish girl. If she were dealing with anyone else, she would drag her ward out of the closet and give her a stern lecture about her childish behavior and how her tantrums would hinder her survival in the world outside the city.

Replacing the mirror in her satchel, Aveline went to the door and sat down. She rested her head back against the wood and gazed at the ceiling. At a loss as to what to say, and doubting the weeping Tiana would listen, Aveline slid the dream catcher under the door. She listened for several minutes to hear if Tiana was calming down.

"Tiana, you will never be strong enough to leave the city if you cry about everything," Aveline said in frustration. "You have to toughen up, remember?"

Her words were met with heartfelt sobs.

Rolling her eyes, Aveline stood and went to the table to finish her dinner.

Tiana did not come out for food or when Aveline yelled through the door that she was going to bed. Aveline turned out the lights and stretched out on the floor. The light from the closet casted a golden glow around the edges of the door. By the time Aveline drifted to sleep, Tiana had stopped crying without leaving the closet.

I hope the dream catcher works, Aveline thought as she slid into slumber.

NINE

"A NIGHT HUNT?" Warner asked. "For what purpose?"

Arthur declined to answer aloud, aware his honorable friend would come to the dishonorable conclusion soon enough. He tied an axe to the saddle of his horse, whose breath rose in puffy clouds towards the dark sky. Arthur draped a blanket over the horse's rump to shield the gelding from the cold and then double-checked his own overcoat. Winter was jabbing his skin with an icy finger. It took a moment of searching before Arthur located the button he had missed. He promptly sealed the tiny opening.

"Arthur," Warner said with a sigh.

Hearing the realization in his voice, Arthur gripped his lover's forearm with his gloved hand. "Justice."

"You mean vengeance."

"I would not be my father's son, if I let a man like Marshall try to kill me without consequences."

"No. You would be a better man than your father." Warner pulled his arm away and stepped back, anger in his blue eyes.

Arthur debated trying to soothe his friend's feelings. Warner was a trained soldier from a good family, low enough in standing not to be a threat to the Hanover's. He did not always understand how much more difficult it was to retain a position at the top of the social hierarchy. Arthur admired his friend's unerring sense of honor and fairness, of right and wrong, because he himself was often lost in the political intrigue defining his position as the sole male heir to the Hanover legacy.

"We both know I am not my father, because I have your heart to guide my actions," Arthur said softly. "And that I must play the part of a true Hanover sometimes. If Marshall had not called me out, I would not have to respond."

Had Arthur any doubt about his plan, he would have shed it when he considered any danger he was in, his sister faced as well by becoming vulnerable should something happen to him at the hands of Marshall's family. His father would call the events of this night a lesson, and Marshall's family would understand it as a warning, no matter how it was covered up.

Any attempt on the life of the Hanover children had to be met with brutal retaliation. There could be no mixed messages, no mercy, if Arthur was to preserve his family name and assume his father's place one day. What happened then, he had not yet determined, except it would involve becoming the man Warner believed him to be.

"You are so much better than this," Warner retorted stubbornly.

"I do not expect you to understand why I must do this, Warner."

"But you *will* do this?"

"Yes."

Warner searched his features. "Then let me accompany you. I am your sworn guardian, the greatest warrior the Shield has produced in two generations, since my grandfather last held the distinction."

"No," Arthur said with rare firmness. "If anything goes wrong, I need you to protect my sister."

"Marshall is taking three men with him."

"And how many times have I defeated him during mock battles? You train with me. I am second only to you in skill. If you truly feared

I could not handle him, you would be on your horse, prepared to follow me to battle, not trying to convince me to stay. You know what this is." It would have been easy to order Warner to stay, but Arthur cared too much for how his lover felt, so he reiterated the truth both of them knew.

Warner stewed silently.

Arthur finished checking the gelding's girth and turned to face his unhappy friend. "If I do not return by dawn, you know what you are to do."

"Return to the city and your sister."

"Good."

"But I will search for you first."

"No, Warner." It was Arthur's turn to sigh. "You do not understand how vulnerable my sister can be. She knows nothing of the world outside our home. If anything should happen to me, it will only expedite the plans others may have for her demise. Without any heirs, my father's position will become unstable quickly."

"You ask me to rebel against my better judgment."

"If you care for me, you will do this."

Warner blew out a breath of air. "You know I do. You know I will always do as you ask as much as it displeases me."

"Thank you, Warner."

Warner walked away. Arthur did not pursue him. He trusted no one more than Warner to ensure Tiana was safe and to protect her secret, if discovered. As angry as Warner was, he would always do what was just and right.

Unlike me. Arthur had been raised to survive the political world his family inhabited where one's standing was as fragile as the ice on a pond on a warm spring day. One day, he might be able to escape with Warner somewhere like the Free Lands. But in the meantime, he had to play the role of his father's heir.

Mounting his horse, Arthur guided it towards the four men waiting for him at the edge of the clearing.

After leaving the city, the hunting party had stuck to the forest as they headed northeast, skirting unfriendly native villages and tracking their game as they rode. The herds of buffalo whose tracks they trailed were less than a day away. The first kill was always granted to the ranking member of the hunting party, accompanied by a select few, and usually occurred at dawn, before the official hunting began. Arthur's request for a night hunt held special meaning for the man he requested to accompany him, who had reluctantly accepted, with the understanding accompanying Arthur for the first kill was not the honor it was made out to be.

"Evening," Arthur said and halted his horse. He leaned forward onto its withers and looked over the three guards accompanying the man who tried to assassinate him in his own tent a week and a half before.

"Evening," Marshall replied. "Where is your lapdog protector?"

"Sleeping, I imagine," Arthur replied. "If the Hanover heir can ride in these forests without his guard, surely the Cruise heir can do the same, unless your family crest does not represent a lion's courage but the fact it sleeps all day."

Marshall stiffened at the quiet, nonchalant dare. "I do not wear the lion crest for myself but to remind others of the Cruise legacy and the glory no other family in Lost Vegas can claim."

Arthur refrained from rolling his eyes. Marshall's family boasted often of the meaning behind their lion crest. The courageous founder of Lost Vegas, Charles Cruise, had braved impossible-to-imagine odds to establish the first settlement after the Old World perished. The Cruise line ruled Lost Vegas for a mere fifty years, throughout the Age of Darkness, before Arthur's forefathers managed to wrench power away from the wealthy family and hold it for four and a half centuries.

"Go and rest," Marshall told his guards. "I will return by dawn."

The men obeyed without question.

Close in age to Arthur, Marshall possessed the striking features that ran in his family and the same sense of entitlement fueling his sister's mistreatment of Tiana. While competitive, Marshall had the disadvantage of a kind father, whereas Arthur was raised with the firsthand knowledge that ruthlessness was the true legacy of the Hanover's.

"Shall we?" Arthur motioned to the forest.

"After you."

Stifling a smile, Arthur nudged his horse forward and started into the forest. Marshall followed. Arthur led them away from the encampment, to the north. They passed their scouts and continued onward into the cold, quiet night, riding parallel to the prairie.

Judging by the smell of scat, upturned earth and fur, the buffalo herd was large. Arthur did not see any of its members on the rolling plains, but the scents were strong and the grass flattened where the herds had traveled. He ventured out of the forest, towards the wide swath of beaten down grass and darkened snow.

They rode for half an hour, following the wake the herds had left.

"To what do I owe the honor of accompanying you in place of your lapdog?" Marshall asked at last.

"We were educated by the same tutor. I am confident you can figure it out," Arthur replied.

Marshall said nothing.

The hair on the back of Arthur's neck stood on end suddenly.

He pulled his horse to a halt, uncertain what his senses were warning him of. He loosened the ties of his hat in order to hear without the fur and leather blocking his ears. The night was still and quiet, with the exception of snow crunching beneath the hooves of Marshall's horse.

"Very well. If this is where we are to duel, then let us be on with it," Marshall stated in a hard tone. He dismounted and yanked two weapons free from the horse, a double-headed axe and long knife.

Arthur glanced at him and then towards the forest. Grass rustled in the stiff, breathtaking wind, and the light gray clouds glowed overhead, illuminating his surroundings without the need for moon or stars. They stood at the bottom of a low, rolling hill, amidst other hills, in grasslands edged on one side by the forest and the other three sides by the sky.

What manner of threat was invisible? Not Ghouls or unfriendly natives, the only known dangers in the prairielands. Arthur dismounted and grabbed a lance and double-headed axe, unable to explain or shake off the cold slithering down his spine. It felt as if someone stood behind him, preparing to strike. When he turned, no one was present. He began to suspect this was an extension of his strange magic, yet it was neither a vision nor his ability to track game, the two unnatural skills he was aware of possessing.

He turned a full revolution, listening to his humming instincts as he did. The magic warning him was similar to the tracking magic he used to find game. It whispered faintly of where the threat was without defining what it was.

Someone, or something, was at the edge of the forest, waiting and watching.

Yet Arthur saw nothing.

Marshall sighed impatiently. "You invite me here for one purpose and stall our inevitable encounter?"

"I am glad your father has three more sons. He will not miss you, and neither will I," Arthur replied.

"It is not my death we should be discussing."

"What provoked your attack, Cruise?" he asked roughly. "The timing and place were beneath a man as intelligent as I thought you to be."

Marshall was quiet, lifting and lowering the axe in nervous agitation.

"Only one of us will live to speak of this night. I wish to know the truth," Arthur insisted. He focused on his opponent, but his instincts tugged his attention back towards the forest. "Speak, Marshall."

"Murdering you was not my intent in joining the hunt this year."

Arthur's eyebrows shot up. He chuckled. "Your family has resented mine for four centuries, and you did not intend to murder me by placing venomous snakes in my tent?"

"Of course I meant to *try* to murder you, but that was not my original intent behind joining the hunt."

"You speak in riddles."

"Not every heir within our circles wishes you dead and to take your place. Not every member of the outer city plots the demise of the Hanover's. I came this year so we might have a moment to speak. The snakes were to gain your attention and to test you."

"I have never heard anything more ridiculous!" Arthur exclaimed, genuinely surprised.

"There is talk you are not like your father. It is said you could lead the city in a way he would never consider." Marshall's explanation was spoken slowly, carefully.

"And this drove you to try to murder me? Because I am a different man, and whoever backs you disapproves of this fact?"

Marshall fell quiet. His weapons were lowered to the ground, his head tilted towards the sky.

The sense of being watched or ... stalked distracted Arthur once more. He made a show of swinging his axe, as if warming up, and faced the forest. The danger was still one moment, moving the next. It began to shift along the tree line he and Marshall had followed northward.

"It was not a real attempt on your life," Marshall spoke finally. "I was certain to be seen leaving your tent by your lapdog. The location of the attempt, less than a day's ride from the city, was planned in case you reacted as your father would and slayed my men. But you didn't react as your father would, which is why I have been hoping to speak to you in private. You are not like him."

"I am more patient than my father," Arthur said. He was unusually grateful for the discussion. A battle would find him too distracted by the strange danger to be effective.

"Some would say more honorable as well. He has alienated many with his corrupt system of justice and unilateral decisions to burn ..."

Arthur tuned out. Marshall was agitated to the point he was starting to yell.

The hidden danger passed them, headed south, towards the encampment. Whatever or whomever it was, it remained hidden in the forest. The farther away it went, the more the threat faded from Arthur's awareness, only to be replaced by inexplicable urgency lighting his blood on fire, as if his instincts understood the intentions of a threat he could not see. Arthur tilted his head, unable to make sense of what he felt.

He thought of Warner at the encampment and planted the butt of his lance in the ground, leaning against it with a frown. This danger could not possibly pose a threat to the contingent of well-armed, experienced Shield soldiers. Ghouls knew to avoid them, and an attack by unfriendly natives was not likely in this location or before the great hunt went underway. Historically, skirmishes with the natives came after the hunt, or in the heat of it, when the chaos was great enough to hide ambushes and attacks. The Shield members killed during the Winter Hunt almost always died during or after the initial attack on the herds. If not for the city's desperate need for food, Arthur would not be in the wilderness risking his life.

Further confusing him was the knowledge he had never experienced such a feeling when it came to the natives on any of the five hunts he had participated in.

The danger tripping his instincts was picked up by his unusual ability and therefore, could not be fully of this world. The only other time he experienced such a confounding jumble of emotions was ...

... the dream.

Arthur pulled his lance loose and strode back to his horse.

Marshall trailed off from his tirade before asking, "What are you doing?"

"Something is amiss. I must return to camp," Arthur replied. He secured his weapons, alarm shooting through him.

"At this very moment?"

Hearing Marshall's derisive tone, Arthur paused as he reached up to rest his hands on the saddle. "Stay if you like and await me. I will happily kill you upon my return."

"Did you listen to anything I said?"

Arthur had not paid attention to most of what Marshall said, though he heard enough.

"What you speak of is treason." Arthur swung up into the saddle. "You wished me dead then decided, because I did not kill you in return, I was somehow interested in hearing what you consider to be my father's offenses. If he has offended so many people, they can take the matter to his council of advisors."

"Your father burns anyone who speaks out against him!"

"Then I suggest you hold your tongue. Your opinion of my father carries no weight with me." Arthur turned his horse to the south and squeezed his calves. The gelding burst into a canter.

Adrenaline spiked within him, and his ears filled with the sound of his beating heart. Urgency turned to desperation, the same he experienced in the dream where he ran from the skinwalker. Arthur leaned forward and urged his horse to run. The danger was gone, too far ahead of him for him to sense. He raced along the tree line, waiting until he was parallel to the encampment before entering the forest, where he was forced to slow.

The pounding of hooves behind him as his would-be murderer chased him was no match for the blood slamming through his veins and the tiny voice inside screaming at him to hurry.

The first sign something was very wrong came when he reached the position of the scout stationed the farthest from camp. The gelding shied and stopped so suddenly, Arthur was flung forward in the saddle.

He murmured to the uneasy horse and patted its neck, searching the darkness for what had spooked him. Not caring who he tipped off, he pulled a portable torch created by one of his father's scientists and lit it quickly. The brilliant light blinded him. When his eyes adjusted, he was able to see what had startled his horse.

The scout positioned here had been impaled on a low tree branch. His blank eyes were open, and an expression of terror was frozen on his features. What appeared to be massive claw marks had pierced his winter clothing all the way to his bones, and his insides were exposed. The kill was fresh enough for blood to drip into a pool beneath him.

For a long moment, Arthur was stuck between reality and the vision in his dreams, between trying to understand if he had interpreted the dream incorrectly and whether this was the same creature – Black Leg – or something different. He had clearly seen Tiana's frame and the moon, as well as felt the warm-cool breeze of spring in his dream. This was not the right place or time for the skinwalker to appear, but his instincts, his sense of knowing, were the same as when he saw the creature in his dream.

"Burn me!" Marshall's exclamation snapped Arthur out of his confusion. "How big was the bear that did this?"

"It was not a bear," Arthur replied. He dug his heels into the horse's belly to keep it from shying and rode past the gruesome sight.

"What do you mean not a bear?" Marshall demanded. "A mountain lion the size of a gorilla?"

Arthur did not care to explain what it was, or how he knew, to anyone, least of all Marshall, who trailed him like a lost puppy. The path through the forest was winding, narrow and overhung with branches. On the way towards the plains, he had the time to maneuver around obstacles. With urgency fueling his actions, Arthur only grew frustrated when smacked by a snow-laden branch or forced to move around a small pond he had barely noticed two hours before.

His doubt a skinwalker – as scary as it was – was any match for a small army began to fizzle when he ran across the next line of scouts. This layer of defense contained five men – all brutally mauled and discarded without any of them appearing to have drawn a single weapon.

Arthur did not stop. Before he reached the final layer of defense, he glimpsed the campfires through the trees. He glanced at the bodies making up the third layer of security around the camp but hurried onward, his eyes trained to his destination. No sounds of fighting came, and no alarms were raised.

His heart skipped a beat then began to race even faster as he thought about Warner.

When Arthur broke through the forest into the meadow where the majority of his men were camped, he halted the horse and stared.

No one stirred. Mauled bodies littered the entire area while campfires continued to burn brightly. The horses were safe in the makeshift corrals at one end of the clearing, and the tents still stood where they had been erected.

Arthur dismounted, once more caught in a surreal state, this one brought on by shock. He walked through the dead, unable to comprehend how one skinwalker had done all this, and how a meadow of trained soldiers were unable to stop the creature. At least these men had been warned; many of them were clutching weapons in death. Blood soaked into the snow, frosting the meadow in red sludge that clung to Arthur's boots.

His eyes fell to the tent near the center of the encampment that he shared with Warner. Barely able to breathe through his tight chest, Arthur walked towards it, his stomach twisting in anticipation of what he would find.

"Ah, Sayed," he murmured when he drew nearer. A trusted friend from youth, Sayed lay near Arthur's tent, as if his friend had thought to come to his defense when the skinwalker attacked. "Ever the good soul." He had been slashed through and lay with his weapons in hand.

Arthur knelt and closed Sayed's eyes, thanking him quietly as he did so. He owed the dead man one life debt and might have owed him two, had he been present for the attack. Arthur could not repay him, but would visit his family upon his return and offer up whatever service or payment he could.

Dread and sorrow were heavy in his stomach. He rose and moved on, seeking the one face he was terrified of finding.

No body lay outside his tent. Unlike the other tents, which had not been touched, the skinwalker had slashed through both sides of

Arthur's tent. Arthur peered into it. Warner's weapons and overcoat were inside, though the man himself was not.

Arthur knelt by the footprints beside his tent, trying to remain calm enough to make out what happened. Judging by the size of the paw prints, the skinwalker had taken the form of a great cat potentially larger than a horse. Warner's boot prints were beside the skinwalker's; he had challenged the creature, as Arthur knew he would.

Blood was on the ground, though it was impossible for Arthur to guess whose it was. The paw prints turned into the bare footprints of a man staggering away for several steps before they transformed once more into those of a great cat.

Warner had somehow managed to stun the creature no other man could stop. Proud, concerned, and distressed by the idea he would find Warner's body nearby, Arthur trailed the paw prints towards the next tent, where the creature attacked other members of the Shield. He turned away and retreated to his tent and this time, followed Warner's boot tracks. They went in the direction of the corral before becoming jumbled among the prints of others.

What had happened next? Arthur closed his eyes and called upon his tracking skill to determine if Warner survived. He steadied his breathing, which had grown erratic, and focused on finding Warner.

Without a token to convey the direction his target had gone, his tracking magic presented him with an image instead. Warner had continued onward to the corral and then beyond, moving southwest. Arthur's ability could not tell him if Warner escaped on a horse, but it did tell him the skinwalker eventually left camp and headed southeast.

Warner was alive, or had been, when he left camp, and the skinwalker had not seemed interested in following him, or he would have taken a different course.

Arthur sighed, relieved. If any man could withstand a monster, it was Warner. Wiping his face, Arthur began walking again, searching for survivors among the dead. He circled the camp, checked the forest edging it, then returned to his horse.

From what he could see, only his tent was attacked, and no horses or wagons or supply trunks were disturbed. Why, then, had the creature sought out the army? And why had it spared Arthur and Marshall after stalking them to the plains? Did it seek someone or something here? It did not seem possible for there to have been time for the creature to determine if who or what he sought was present. He had entered camp on a rampage, slaughtered everyone within minutes and left no survivors. Was this carnage indiscriminate?

Marshall stood nearby, features pale and mouth agape, while Arthur wracked his thoughts for an explanation based on what little he knew of the mysterious skinwalker from his dream.

He surveyed the decimated camp once more before taking his horse's reins. The urgency had faded, though his emotions had not yet processed the savagery around him. He could not stop thinking about what came next, of Warner and Tiana in the hands of the skinwalker.

"What kind of animal did this?" Marshall whispered, stricken.

"The kind we dare not meet," Arthur replied. He mounted his horse, eyes facing the direction Warner had gone. "Mount up."

Marshall faced him, astonished. "We cannot leave the bodies without a proper burial. Some of these men were almost our equals."

"If we wish to survive, then we need to move fast and not stop until we reach the friendly villages near the city or the city itself."

Marshall stared at him.

"Ghouls, unfriendly natives and whatever did this stands between us and our destination. Do you really wish to alert any or all of them to our presence by remaining or burning a hundred bodies?" Arthur pressed. "We were both trained to lead. Think like a leader."

"You mean for me to think like a Hanover and leave our contemporaries to be eaten by animals and their belongings stolen by scavengers!"

"Very well. Then think like a Cruise. What is the name of the last man to survive the wilderness alone?"

Marshall flushed. "Charles Cruise."

Arthur waited for his rival to make a decision. Marshall was not stupid; once his emotional outburst passed, he would understand Arthur's logic. In any other situation, Arthur would not care to wait for Marshall to decide or bother waiting for him at all. However, in the five hundred year history of Lost Vegas, only one man had escaped the dangers outside the city, and his group had started with fifty refugees. The odds of surviving were better, if Arthur had at least one companion.

While his hands shook from suppressed emotion, he mentally forced himself to look to the future and his own life. His father would not have flinched at the sight of blood and death, let alone paused to wish his fallen friend farewell. Arthur was aware of this, just as he was aware there was no one to judge him, unlike every action he undertook in the city. Marshall was too preoccupied by the massacre, and any other witnesses to Arthur's failure to act in a manner similar to his father's were dead.

Aside from their lives being at risk, if he did not return to the city, his sister would be in danger from the same creature that destroyed his camp. He had already seen this in a vision.

Arthur also had a secondary motive for leaving quickly, one he dared not share. Warner was out there somewhere in the forest, alone, and missing the gear he needed to protect him against the elements. If they rode fast, they might encounter him before he froze or worse, ran into one of the dangers standing between them and the safety of the city.

Dazed, Marshall looked around the clearing, his gaze resting on the tent bearing the lion crest. He strode to it and crouched. Rooting through the pockets of a slain soldier, he pulled something from the body, studied it, and pocketed it.

Arthur leaned over and grabbed the reins of Marshall's horse. He nudged his gelding forward, after Marshall, pulling the second horse with him. If he looked too long at the dead, his sense of honor would compromise his plan. Marshall was right about the men deserving a proper pyre, but Arthur's focus was on preventing the loss of more life rather than grieving those who were gone.

Arthur kept his eyes trained on either Marshall or the corral to the southwest, tense and waiting for the sense of otherworldly danger to return.

"Come, Marshall. You cannot help the dead now. They are better off where they are, as spirits in the sky."

Marshall stood and then rubbed his face hard, as if unable to wipe away the sight before him. "We need to warn those friendly to us and the city. A beast this large must be stopped before it hurts more people."

Arthur neither cared about others being hurt nor objected to Marshall's reasoning. Traveling alone was a death sentence; if they were together, they stood a greater chance at making it home.

Marshall mounted his horse. Arthur wheeled his towards the southwest and Warner and carefully made his way across the meadow, not wishing to cause further harm to the bodies of those he had known.

Pausing at the corral, each of them harnessed two horses to take with them and then left the gate open, so the others could run free.

Arthur darkened the torch as he moved into the forest. From the direction of the buffalo herds, he heard the familiar shrieks of the Ghouls. They were far enough not to concern him for the moment. But what happened tomorrow night? Or the night after? And if the Ghouls found Warner first?

One day at a time, Arthur, he lectured himself. Above all, he had to maintain a clear head and judgment unimpeded by emotion, if he were to see the two people he loved most again.

TEN

TIANA DID NOT SPEAK to Aveline again until a full four and a half days after her meltdown. Time had never passed so sluggishly for Aveline or been filled with such a lack of activity, and she found herself eating constantly as a means of staying occupied.

If the Hanover girl had it in her to be spiteful or vengeful, Aveline would have chalked up her silence to passive aggressive attempt to punish her for the mirror incident. But Tiana was neither of those, and Aveline heard her cry too often during the days of silence to assign malice to her actions.

Tiana was devastated, and nothing Aveline said helped the distraught girl recover.

Aveline downed the last bite of a berry filled pastry that had become her favorite since she discovered them in the kitchens. She grimaced, about to remark aloud how boredom would drive her into obesity or insanity by spring, when Tiana spoke at last.

"I had a dream about you last night," she murmured.

Finally. Aveline looked down from the ceiling she had been staring at. Her back was to the wall beneath the window, which gave her the ability to see most of the room, except for the depths of the closet and bathroom. With her weapons cleaned, and her daily exercises finished, she had been trying to determine how to spend the unbearably long hours stretching between lunch and dinner.

"A dream or one of your visions?" Aveline asked warily. She dared not mention the mirror incident for fear of driving Tiana to tears or back into her closet. She was anxious to move on from the unexpectedly horrible attempt to help Tiana feel more confident about herself.

"Some dreams I know to be dreams, and some visions I am certain are of the future. But often, there is a vision or dream too disconnected from what I know of the world for me to determine which it is." Tiana shrugged. Her eyes were on the veil she was embroidering. She had not smiled since the mirror incident, either, and had barely eaten. "I saw you but did not understand the circumstances."

"What happened?"

"You were outside the city with two men I have never seen before. They were ... are or will be ... it can be confusing." Tiana sighed. "Friends. They are your friends."

"What were we doing?" Aveline asked, intrigued.

"You were agitated and worried. I think you were looking for me."

"You weren't there?"

"Your necklace was dark."

Aveline touched the timepiece dangling from her neck. Tiana's was bright, given their proximity.

"One of them was named Rocky," Tiana added. "You never spoke the other's name."

Aveline dropped the pendant, gazing at Tiana in uneasy surprise. Witnessing the furniture lifting off the floor at random times was less unnerving than Tiana's even stranger ability to glimpse the future.

Rocky's alive. At least, in this version of Tiana's vision. Aveline almost sighed at the revelation she did not end up causing her friend's death. Unwilling to discuss Rocky, who was trapped in prison, pending Tiana's murder, Aveline searched her mind for a series of events that would allow Rocky and Tiana both to live. When she came up with no such scenario, she focused again on Tiana. "What else?"

"There was not much to it."

"What about details? Was it light or dark? Were we dressed for winter or spring?"

Tiana paused in her sewing, pensive. "It was dark and cold but not winter. There was no snow on the ground but I could see your breath."

"Just three of us?"

"That I saw, yes."

Aveline tapped her fingers against her kneecap absently, thoughtful.

"I have seen this Rocky person before," Tiana said. "If you know him, then perhaps the other dreams are real, too."

"What other dreams?"

Tiana began embroidering once more. "I see him when he visits. He has come here daily for the past four days. Maybe he searches for you."

"It's not possible!" Aveline said with more emotion than she intended.

Tiana tensed.

With effort, Aveline quieted her voice. "How can you know this?"

"I know nothing with certainty. But if you know he exists, and I have never seen him before, then is it not possible he may be waiting for you where I see him?"

"It would be sheer madness, if so."

"How are you so certain he has not come?" Tiana asked, perplexed. "How can you doubt his presence here and yet believe my ability to see fragments of the future?"

For once, Tiana made absolute sense. Aveline snapped her mouth closed. Karl had told her Rocky was in prison, but what if her friend found a way to escape? What if Karl had negotiated his release early? Was it possible she worried about Rocky, when he was completely safe? She did not doubt, if he were released from prison, he would find her.

"Where is he?" Aveline asked, standing.

"In my dream, he waits by the southern entrance and stops every fourth slave who passes him. I cannot hear what he asks them, but each one of them shakes his or her head, and then moves on."

Before Tiana had finished speaking, Aveline was at the door. She left her ward secure in her room and raced through the Hanover's apartment, barely able to contain her excitement.

Ten minutes later, she reached the bottom floor of the great pyramid and hurried to the slave entrance she had never had a need to visit. When she reached it, she stopped just inside. The door was propped open, allowing the scents of the city and chill of winter to enter.

Rocky was not there. She waited and paced, venturing out into the cloudy, cold day briefly to observe the immediate area, in case Rocky had chosen to wait outside.

Disappointment sank into her. Rocky was nowhere in sight. Had Tiana's dream been wrong? If so, how could she know about him at all?

"Aveline."

She turned at the familiar voice. Jose, the assistant to the madman with the electric trees, stood nearby in his cloak, as if he were leaving for the city. His warm eyes and wide smile mesmerized her before she had a chance to blink.

"I meant to visit," she blurted out before she could stop herself. "But ... duties."

"I rarely leave. When you wish it, you are welcome to visit," he replied.

Why did his gentle response leave her cheeks warm? Aveline tore her gaze away from him, not liking how abruptly unaware of her surroundings she became when she saw him. With him standing before her, she could see, hear and smell only him. If an army of Shield soldiers approached, she would not notice them until after they had subdued her.

"Where are you going?" she asked.

"My master has had one of his coughing fits. I go to fetch herbal tea to help him," Jose replied.

"They have tea in the kitchens."

"He insists upon a tea a single merchant in the entire city sells," Jose said.

A smile slid free as Aveline recalled the eccentric man in the basement. Mohammed was better off with Jose than with her as an assistant. She would be nowhere near as patient with the madman as Jose appeared to be.

"You are waiting for someone?" he asked, glancing past her.

"No. Just needed some air," she lied.

An awkward silence fell between them, ripe with tension and self-consciousness she was unaccustomed to.

"I must go," Jose said and cleared his throat. "My apologies. Nothing would please me more than staying to talk, but if I do not return by dusk, my master will grow even madder with worry."

Aveline stepped out of his path, wanting to respond without knowing for certain what the right words were. She had seen where Jose worked and lived and yet, realizing he was about to walk away, she experienced the sudden urgency to speak, as if this were the last time they would ever meet.

"I would be ... happy to visit tomorrow, if that's ... happy to you." She mentally kicked herself. Of all the words to choose, why had *happy* – which she could not recall ever using – escaped her mouth twice?

You're a fool, Aveline! She yelled at herself.

"That is happy to me." Jose was grinning.

Mortified, Aveline nodded and spun, walking away quickly. Only when she had turned a corner did she release a deep sigh.

Assassins were dutiful, honorable and skilled – but never happy. What was it about Jose that left her stumbling verbally and fevered? For all she knew, he was an assassin, her competition, or some other sort of degenerate.

Lecturing herself about how dangerous it was to lower her guard around a stranger, however handsome he was, she descended to the basement to walk off the strange tension the run in with Jose caused.

The halls were quiet and cool. Afternoons were generally inactive until dinnertime, and few slaves passed her in the halls. It was as her senses returned to their normal state of awareness that she noticed the brush of cotton on cotton behind her. The faint sound would have been impossible to distinguish in a crowded market or elsewhere in the inner city. But here, in the near silent hall, it was unmistakable.

Someone was following her at a safe distance. The women she had bested on her first day as a slave were not likely to be ready to challenge her again any time soon, but it was always possible they had friends who witnessed the exchange who were.

Aveline navigated the underground maze easily and led whomever followed down a corridor lower and narrower than most, and away from the flow of normal foot traffic, in case she drew blood. The hallway ended in a t-intersection, and she went left, walked four steps and then halted. Pressing her back against the cool wall, she eased a knife free from the small of her back and waited.

Silence. Her stalker had stopped.

"Avi?"

She froze, not expecting the quiet voice.

"I know you're there."

Rocky could sense her as well as she could him. She lowered her knife and eased to the corner then peered around. He remained a safe distance way, pending her reaction.

"How ... where ... Rocky, what're you doing here?" Uncertain where to start, she put her weapon away and closed the distance between them, slinging her arms around her best friend. Her thoughts raced, a jumbled mix of astonishment that he was alive, incredulity Tiana had really envisioned him, and confusion over how either was possible.

Rocky hugged her. "Looking for you!" he said with his normal humor.

Relief washed over her. He was solid and strong in her arms, a reassurance he was indeed free and safe. Recalling the emotion she experienced when she heard he had been captured, she felt the anxious tension within her unravel without realizing it had been coiled in the pit of her stomach since hearing the news.

She released him and stepped back. Like any good assassin, Rocky was making an attempt to fit in. He wore the clothing of a slave, though the pants legs were too short on his tall frame and the sleeves of his shirt did not quite reach his wrists. He wore a sash, twisted in a way no real slave would wear it. Still, his attempt at dressing like a slave had granted him access to the pyramid.

"We have an agreement. We'll always find one another," he said firmly, though his eyes were warm. "When I heard you were *here*, I didn't believe it!"

"When did Karl get you out? Did he send you?" she asked.

"Karl?"

Movement came from down the hall as a slave passed through an intersection.

Avi glanced past Rocky before taking his arm and tugging him down the vacant hallway where she had been waiting to ambush her stalker. "Yes, Karl! He sent me here on my first mission," she explained as they rounded the corner.

"Karl." This time, coolness was in Rocky's tone.

She faced him, searching his features quizzically. "You say his name as if you have never heard of him before. I assume he got you out at some point the past two weeks? Or did he send someone else?"

"Out of where?"

"Of prison. Where you were sitting because the Shield caught you that night instead of me!" she exclaimed with a small laugh. "What is with you, Rocky?"

Rocky was frowning.

Aveline amusement faded. "What's wrong?"

"I wasn't in prison," Rocky replied. "After we got separated, I went to our rendezvous point, but you never showed."

She blinked, uncertain how to respond.

"It took me a week to find out where you were," he added.

"Why would Karl claim you were in prison?" she asked. "Did he at least tell you where to find me?"

"Avi, Karl left the Guild the day after your father was killed. He's working for the Trench," Rocky said, referring to the Guild's competition. "He told the Guild you were dead. They held a ceremony for you and your father."

She was silent, stunned.

"I never would've known you were alive, or here, if some irate apothecary hadn't shown up at Guild Main demanding payment for medicines he claimed had been stolen from him by the Devil's daughter. No one else listened to him, but what he said sounded too much like you for me to ignore."

Rocky's words were moving at the speed of sludge through her mind. If any other person stood before her, she would never believe any of what was said.

"You're saying Karl lied about what happened to me to you and lied about you to me," she stated.

"It seems that way."

"Why?"

Rocky shrugged. "Rumor has it he was paid off by someone. You say he hired you for a mission?"

She nodded.

"Against Guild rules?"

She nodded again.

"And that didn't bother you?"

"He said he'd get you out of prison if I did it, and he'd sponsor me to become a full assassin," she whispered. The reality of what Karl had done began to register. She had silently questioned why he was working outside of Guild practices but never suspected he was deceiving her about his intention to help her or flat out lying about Rocky being in trouble.

Dread sank into her stomach, along with hurt. "There must be an explanation. What reason would he have to lie to me?" she mused aloud.

"Maybe he heard the Guild wasn't going to appoint him the leader, as he hoped. You know people's motivations can be complex."

"Karl helped my father raise me. He's family! If this is true, then he betrayed everything my father stood for, everything I thought *he* stood for! He would never leave the Guild if my father lived!"

"Burn me, Avi. I don't know why it all happened, only that it did happen," Rocky replied. "I was never in the Shield prison or in any danger at all, and the entire Guild was stunned when he left."

Rocky's presence was too damning for her to deny Karl's actions had been undertaken with no good intentions towards her. But what was he doing? Why? If his promises to aid her were false, had he been truthful about hiring her because of her demon cursed blood? About wanting Tiana dead? He had known too much about who Aveline was hired to protect for it to be coincidence.

"Karl is a smart man. He knows your weaknesses," Rocky said. "He probably knew I'd try to find you, if he didn't lie about you being dead."

She warred with herself for a moment, wondering who she should trust: Rocky or Karl. When she met Rocky's gaze again, she knew the answer. Karl had been her father's advisor – but she knew little about him aside from how close they were and how well he treated her, until her father's death. In comparison, she understood the depths of Rocky's loyalty from years of experience.

She would never doubt Rocky.

"I'm glad you're well, Rocky," she managed.

"What reason would Karl have to send you here?" he asked, motioning to the pyramid above the basement.

She did not answer. Of all the emotions Aveline thought she would experience upon learning Karl might have betrayed her, sorrow was an unwelcome surprise. It ran deeper than fury. Even the devil in her blood was subdued. On the night she lost her father, she had lost Karl as well without knowing it.

The longer the quiet stretched, the more she thought about the assignment Karl had given her. She hated the relief trickling through her sorrow, as if some part of her – an instinct she had not wanted to acknowledge – had never wanted to hurt Tiana in the first place.

"Avi?" Rocky's soft voice drew her gaze to his face. "I know Karl was close to your family. We can find him together."

"No," she said and then shook her head. "I mean, yes, I want to find him, but Rocky ..." Uncomfortable with expressing emotion, she drifted off.

"It's Karl," he finished for her. "And you just lost your father. You don't want him dead, even if he has betrayed you."

She nodded, grateful Rocky understood without her explaining it. "I want to talk to him before we do anything else."

Rocky studied her. "It'll be dangerous to approach him."

"He's supposed to contact me in two days," she replied. "I'll request a meeting in person."

"Somewhere in the open where I can observe from the shadows."

"I won't go without you," she agreed. "I trained with him as well. It would take both of us, if it comes to that." *I hope this is a huge misunderstanding.* The longer she considered what Karl had done, though, the less she believed it possible he had done this for a reason other than to serve his own needs, whatever those were.

"It is good to see you, Avi. I feared you were dead for a week," Rocky said. "I never felt so alone."

Aveline forced herself out of her mind and smiled at her friend.

The pain of losing her father remained fresh, and she did not want to know how it would have felt to lose Rocky as well. Orphaned at an early age, he had been mentored by her father and loved by her as a brother from the day they met. His suffering, too, was of Karl's devising, and Aveline shifted further away from her denial of what Karl had done when she imagined her best friend feeling the pain she did.

"I'm alive, Rocky," she said. "We'll figure this out together. I want to talk to Karl, to hear the truth from his mouth. If justice is needed, we will burn him."

"So no Guild until after we meet with him."

"I think that's best. Don't tell them I'm alive. Maybe bringing in Karl will be enough to win over a new sponsor and make up for taking on an assignment prior to becoming a real assassin," she said.

"If Karl hired you under the guise of sponsoring you, the Guild's council won't hold you responsible."

"I was hired by someone else," she replied. "I took the position here before Karl assigned me a mission."

Rocky's eyebrows went up.

"I'd be in trouble either way," she said. "I can't explain this all now but I promise I will soon."

"You have more allies than you think you do. Come with me to the Guild after we confront Karl. We can explain everything."

"Let me make this right or ... as right as I can," she replied, thoughts on her father's spirit watching her from the sky. Her gut instinct about Karl's request had been right, and she ignored it. Her father would not be pleased with her for this or for accepting a position guarding Tiana before Aveline was an official assassin. "I broke two rules. I wouldn't feel right asking the Guild to sponsor me, knowing I've disappointed my father."

Would her father want her to leave Tiana and return to the Guild or stay and carry out her duty? Aveline had taken an oath to protect the girl, but she had done so before becoming an assassin. The thought of abandoning Tiana, even if she were coerced into accepting the assignment, did not sit well with Aveline. At the very least, she wanted to ensure Matilda was no longer a threat.

She recalled her father's lecture about fulfilling one's vows, no matter what the circumstances, and waffled with her decision before coming to a conclusion. She should not have accepted this assignment, but she did. She was therefore obligated by her promise to Arthur.

"Is this electricity magic?" Rocky asked, eyes on the bulb overhead.

Aveline snorted. "Yes. I cannot be gone long from my post. Do you have time to go somewhere with me quickly?"

He nodded.

Reeling from all she had learned, she could think of nothing but grabbing a snack. Aveline led him through the hallways to the kitchens, which were always occupied and bustling. As soon as one meal was over, the staff began clean up and preparing for the next. The constant activity meant no one noticed two additional slaves as they slipped in to snag some of the pastries cooling on a wooden table.

Aveline loaded up a sack with them and led Rocky out of the kitchens and back towards the southern entrance. When they reached the door, she handed him the bag.

"Will you come back tomorrow afternoon?" she asked.

"Without a doubt," he replied and accepted the treats. "You are safe here? You have weapons?"

"I do," she confirmed. "I'm safe and overfed." She patted her belly.

Rocky nodded in approval. "I'll see you tomorrow." He turned away and began walking.

"Rocky," she called.

He faced her again.

"Thank you," she said with emotion. "For coming to find me. For not giving up on me."

"It's just us now. We have to take care of each other," he replied. With another quick smile, he left.

She watched him, too preoccupied by all she had learned to know where to start. The idea Karl had turned against her, against the Guild, was nearly too wild for her to accept. A small part of her continued to deny it, while her instincts whispered everything Rocky said and believed to be true were supported by Karl's discussion with her.

Realizing she was standing near the door, staring dumbly outside, Aveline retreated to the elevator and returned to the Hanover's apartment. She did not want Tiana to suspect she was distressed – or discover anything if she read Aveline's mind. Aveline went in circles mentally, trying to understand Karl's betrayal so soon after her father's death.

Unable to sort through her tangled thoughts and feelings, she finally ceased pacing through the quiet apartment and went to Tiana's door.

It was cracked open.

Aveline's guard went up, and she paused to listen. The sound of someone beating on the closet door was muffled. Aveline pushed the door open silently.

What is this? She thought, startled by the sight before her.

Matilda was pounding her fists against the closet door hard enough that her hands were bloodied. Her eyes were wild and bloodshot, her nose red, and her hair mussed. She appeared possessed as she smashed the door over and over, impervious to pain.

Aveline closed the door to Tiana's room behind her, assessing the situation. Matilda had been quiet and absent the past few days, since Aveline returned from the apothecary. Ghoul's Fancy, the drug she had mixed in with Matilda's normal powders, was supposed to elevate moods to the point one did not know what was dream and what was reality any more. Aveline had hoped the euphoric high would prevent Matilda from hurting Tiana or trying to poison her again.

Matilda sagged against the closet door, breathing hard. A knife was on the vanity near her, and she picked it up after a brief rest and jammed the blade into the lock on the closet.

What had happened?

The sound of Tiana crying came from the closet, reassuring Aveline that the Hanover girl had used her brain for once instead of wilting when Matilda hurt her.

Aveline opened her mouth to speak before recalling Matilda thought her mute. So she opened the door and slammed it closed, as if she had just entered.

Matilda straightened and faced her, her blue eyes glazed. Her nose was running, and drool leaked from the corner of her mouth. She steadied herself against the wall with one arm outstretched.

She was high or drunk or otherwise not herself, but this was not the effect of Ghoul's Fancy. What had the apothecary mixed into the drugs, if not what Aveline requested? Anger slid through her. She added him to the list of those she planned on murdering when this assignment with Tiana was over. The apothecary would share the same fate as those running the brothel and butchering children for meat.

Possibly the same fate as Karl.

Aveline was not ready for this thought. She gritted her teeth in response to the pain of betrayal that slid through her and focused on Matilda, who was squinting at her to determine who she was.

"Slave," Matilda said finally. She pushed herself away from the closet. "Open this door."

Matilda was too far out of her mind to notice Aveline's shrug. Was she high enough to forget Aveline was mute?

"I do not have the key," Aveline ventured.

"What?" Matilda snapped. "Someone must have it!" She careened towards the vanity and began yanking out drawers and dumping them. When she did not find the key, she went to the wardrobe and did the same.

Aveline moved to the closet door and knocked softly. "Tiana? Are you hurt?"

The sniffling stopped. "N... no."

Matilda kicked clothing with a loud curse. "Where is the key?" she shrieked.

Aveline felt the door give behind her. Tiana peered out, her eyes and nose red from crying. Her face showed Matilda had landed a couple blows before the girl ran to hide in the closet.

"Stay here," Aveline said. "Hide if she tries to get you again."

"Come in here with me!" Tiana whispered urgently. "She is utterly mad. She will hurt you!"

"I can take care of myself," Aveline assured her and moved away.

Tiana protested, and Matilda whirled. She started forward, knife raised.

"Whoa!" Aveline said and moved to intercept her. "You're not right in the head, Matilda! Stop this now!" She pushed Matilda and gripped her wrist.

"Leave me be, slave!" Matilda hissed and shoved her. "If the freak's father will not burn her, then I will carve those ghoulish eyes out of her head!" Spittle sprayed Aveline as Matilda spoke.

Up close, Matilda was even less herself than Aveline initially thought. The woman's gaze was unfocused and her pupils dilated to the point her eyes were almost completely black. The blood vessels in her neck had begun to rupture, creating a network of purple webbing. The veins in her arms, neck and face were bulging.

"Let's be calm about this," Aveline said quietly, uncertain how to talk sense into Matilda, whose eyes were trained on Tiana. "You are ill, Matilda. If you don't seek out your physician, you will suffer more than you already are."

The hair on the back of Aveline's neck rose, but it was not from the crazed woman she was trying to subdue. The armoire was floating, along with all the belongings Matilda had dumped onto the floor. Tiana was too upset to control her strange ability.

Matilda looked at Aveline, away, then back. Her mouth fell open, and surprise registered across her features.

"You are not mute!" she exclaimed, squinting at Aveline. "George claimed you had no tongue!" Her arm dropped, and confusion replaced surprise. "Why does my head hurt so?" She clutched her temple with one hand.

"I don't know, but let me help you. We can go get help now," Aveline said and shifted closer.

"But you have no tongue. How can you speak?" Matilda asked.

"Matilda, please. You are not well," Tiana pleaded softly, drawing near.

Aveline waved her back.

"Those eyes." Matilda was staring at Tiana again. "You deformed, crippled, sick demon! I will cut them out and then your tongue, slave, before I burn you both!" She launched at Tiana.

Aveline blocked her again with her body and was driven back by the force of Matilda's charge. The woman raked nails down Aveline's face and plunged the knife towards her mouth. One leg buckled as it hit the vanity, and Aveline careened dangerously, struggling to avoid Matilda's knife and catch her balance. She knocked into Tiana, who had emerged from the closet. The Hanover girl was sent sprawling into the middle of the room.

Matilda wrenched her arm free and stumbled away, towards Tiana. Aveline hit the ground and launched back up, diving between stepmother and stepdaughter as Matilda's knife hand plunged downwards toward a helpless Tiana. Aveline calculated the angle of the blade as she moved. With luck, she would take a hit to the shoulder, maybe her upper back. It would anger her without disabling her, so she could disarm Matilda and throw the insane woman out.

What happened next was not an event Aveline would ever be able to describe to anyone else.

Tiana screamed, and the world rippled as an invisible shockwave tore through everyone and everything around them. Aveline's breath was knocked from her body, and one ear popped painfully then began to ring. She was flung across the room and slammed into the door. Lights exploded behind her eyelids, and she fell to the floor.

The ringing and sharp pain of her ear prevented her from sinking into unconsciousness. The back of her head pulsed from where it had hit the wooden door, and Aveline sought to pull herself out of the in-between state. Urgency was at the edge of her mind, agitated by the sensation of being caught in a cobweb of currents.

A new sound, that of someone banging on the door to Tiana's room, helped ground her.

Aveline's eyes fluttered open. Vertigo swept through her, caused by the damage to her ear. Her stomach roiled, and she clutched at the floor to try to steady herself. Sitting up, she touched the blood trickling from her hurt ear and struggled to make out what had happened through the sensation of the world spinning around her.

"This is the Shield! We order you to allow ..." The shout was accompanied by more banging on the door.

Tiana was hunched over in a pool of blood, clutching a knife, rocking and mumbling. Matilda's body sprawled out beside her, still.

Alarm and concern prevented Aveline from letting the vertigo drive her to the floor. She staggered up, tripped, and lurched to her feet once more. She dropped to her knees beside Tiana, unable to see clearly what the Hanover girl was doing until she was within arm's reach.

" ... bleed the evil out. I have to bleed the evil out. I ..." Tiana was saying over and over.

The sensation of twirling and spinning began to subside. Her senses were delayed but working, though her brain remained sluggish after the blow to her head. Aveline began to catch up with her surroundings and specifically, with the girl before her.

Rocking back and forth, Tiana's arms and legs were bloodied, her gown soaked with red. She was cutting herself as she mumbled and had shredded one forearm and both her thighs.

"Stop." Aveline snatched Tiana's wrist.

" ... have to bleed ..." Tiana pulled away.

Aveline snatched her arms and shook her. "Stop, Tiana!"

Tiana's ghoulish, black eyes were unfocused as she stared at Aveline. "Aveline," her voice trembled. "You live."

Aveline lifted her face as Tiana stretched out a bloody palm to her. "I do." Before she could ask what had happened, her gaze fell again to Matilda's body.

Aveline released Tiana with one hand and stood up on her knees, shuffling closer. She reached out to Tiana's stepmother and then froze, her hand halfway to the still body.

Where was Matilda's head?

Tiana was breathing hard and quick. She clutched Aveline's arm. "Forgive me," she whispered, panicked. "I feared she would hurt you … I lost control … please forgive me! I did not mean for this to happen!"

You did this? Aveline stared in disbelief. Matilda's head was nowhere to be seen. Too much blood formed puddles on the floor to stem from Tiana's self-afflicted wounds alone. The ringing in Aveline's ear became louder, along with the shouting from beyond the door. The sound of an axe splintering wood jarred her. She shook her head, grappling with her own weakened state.

"You have to hide!" Tiana told her urgently.

Aveline shifted back and sat before her.

"He will burn you!"

"Tiana –"

"Quickly! If they see you here, they will murder you!"

Aveline glanced down. Covered in the blood of the two most powerful women in the city, holding Tiana's knife, and seated beside Matilda's headless body, even dazed Aveline understood being discovered in such a state by the Shield did not bode well for her.

Tiana sagged.

Aveline caught her. "You're hurt."

"Bleed the evil out," Tiana said again, her voice growing weak, distant. "I thought I had killed you. Forgive me, Aveline."

"Stop it!" Aveline snapped, irritated. "It isn't possible for me to hide. I won't dive out the window, and you need me here to help you."

Tiana's eyes fluttered closed. "Behind the tapestry."

"What?"

"Go behind the tapestry."

The door began to buckle. Aveline lifted her head too fast, and the room began to spin again. What was wrong with her? Why did she feel as if she had been caught beneath the hooves of a stampede of horses?

"Please, Aveline. They will not hurt me. I am a Hanover. But you are my only friend. I cannot lose you." Tiana was fading. Blood loss and shock were too much for her, and her eyes closed as she fell unconscious.

Aveline hesitated, hating the thought of leaving Tiana in the middle of this disaster.

An axe made it through the door, which meant the Shield soldiers would soon follow.

Aveline debated but then stood. If she were thrown in prison now, she would never know who else threatened Tiana or be able to help. She had to make this right, which started with fulfilling her duty to the Hanover girl.

Besides, if the Shield discovered Tiana's eyes, someone would need to be able to rescue her, if her father decided to burn her.

Setting Tiana down gently on the floor, Aveline leapt to her feet and was hit by a wave of dizziness. She staggered to the closet and inside. Blinded by the spinning sensation, she stretched out her hands to catch herself against the wall. Her palm went through the wall. She tumbled helplessly forward, through the tapestry and into the dark, hollowed out space behind it.

Aveline landed in a heap and gripped her head. At the sounds of the Shield soldiers smashing through the door, she stilled her breathing and sat up, afraid they would find her. From the footsteps, she counted three of them.

Silence followed, and she inched close to the tapestry to hear.

"This is her," the voice was hushed.

At first confused, Aveline recalled that no one but her had ever seen Tiana. She silently cursed the soldiers for stopping to stare at the elusive Hanover daughter instead of rushing to help her.

As if hearing her thought, one of the Shield members stomped across the floor towards Tiana. Another began belting commands. The sound of sheets tearing was accompanied by a soft-spoken order to lift Tiana carefully.

Only when she was convinced the Shield members were acting to help Tiana did Aveline ease back from the tapestry. She shifted into a more comfortable position and stretched back with one arm, expecting to find a wall close behind her.

Her fingertips grazed nothing. The light from the closet, diluted by the tapestry, lit her immediate surroundings. She twisted to peer into the darkness and began to realize the hiding place was not completely dark. Ten feet away, a similar patch of faded light was present and another fifteen feet after that, a second. She could not gauge how far the tunnel went.

Aveline climbed to her feet slowly to prevent the vertigo from returning. She tested her body and frowned. The strange shockwave had hit her hard. She was fatigued, worn, her muscles shaky and skin crawling from Tiana's magic. Her left ear continued to ring faintly, and she could barely hear out of it.

Stretching her legs, Aveline began to walk towards the first patch of light down the darkened tunnel. She braced herself against one wall as she moved, afraid of collapsing and alerting the Shield soldiers to her presence.

She reached the lit area. Aveline started to lift the covering hiding the tunnel entrance from those on the other side before she noticed light piercing a peephole. She went to it and leaned against the wall, peering into the adjacent chamber.

She recognized the gilded chamber immediately as Matilda's. Her eyes fell to the still form of a slave in the middle of the floor. Blood darkened the carpet beneath the slave's head. One of the gold candlesticks Aveline had admired lay beside the woman's head, the heavy base bloodied. It was the same slave she had seen beaten by Matilda before.

I'm definitely going after the apothecary first, she vowed. The drug he had mixed in pushed Matilda over the edge, and now, two people were dead. Aveline had wanted the threat to Tiana to disappear – discreetly. There would be no hiding two murders in the Hanover household.

Her demon's blood stirred with her flash of anger. Another wave of dizziness swept through her. Aveline sagged and lowered herself to the ground. The world was growing dark and fuzzy around the edges, her muscles starting to give out.

Please forgive me ... you are my only friend. I cannot lose you. Tiana's desperate words rang in Aveline's mind louder than her damaged ear, along with the Hanover daughter's previous assertion her father meant to murder her soon.

Until that moment, Aveline had only known one other person who would kill to protect her, and that was Rocky. Tiana did not think herself worth saving, but she had taken a life in order to help someone she cared about.

"She's madder than I first thought," Aveline murmured.

What would happen to Tiana, once her father found out what had happened?

Aveline's last flicker of urgency died, replaced by the overwhelming need to sleep. Any sense of protectiveness she should have possessed about her ward crumbled beneath the oppression of looming unconsciousness.

Aveline rested her head on the cool floor and closed her eyes. As she slid into unconsciousness, she saw the map Tiana had created of the Free Lands in her mind's eye. Tiana would not live past two days outside the city or a few weeks in her room. Was it possible to protect the Hanover girl, or was she simply doomed?

Lost Vegas series
Aveline (Amazon, Amazon UK)

Tiana (Amazon, Amazon UK)
Arthur (Amazon, Amazon UK)
Black Wolf (Amazon, Amazon UK)

Love Lizzy's young adult titles?

Continue reading for an exclusive excerpt of "Broken Beauty" followed by an exclusive excerpt of "Halloween!"

TIANA

ELEVEN

FIVE HUNDRED YEARS AGO, the world fell asleep with a sigh and never awoke. The long night turned into the Age of Darkness, a hundred years where the sun was unable to penetrate the night, and was followed by the Age of Dusk, where the world was stuck in twilight for fifty more years. Human predators - from an age predating all recorded knowledge -arose from the darkness, awakened from their hibernation by the changes in the Earth. They were called the Ghouls. Strange deformities, some of a physical nature and others of a mental nature, took hold of many survivors.

Between the Ghouls and the shortage of food, no one knows for certain how anyone survived. Stories from the Age of Darkness are scarce. Either people were too busy surviving to write down what happened, or the records were destroyed by later generations. Some oral traditions remain and are either too morbid or too fantastical for anyone with sense to grant them any credence.

Whatever happened in the Darkness, some people survived. They found their ways to the remains of cities and huddled together with fire, learning to hunt in the dark. A man named Charles Cruise led a thousand people across the Great Plains to Lost Vegas. He was among the ten people who survived the journey. He and those with him re-established the city. They scoured the countryside for more stragglers and rescued them, until there were two thousand people living in the abandoned city.

Fifty years after he arrived, the first Hanover appeared in the city. His sudden arrival, too, is shrouded in myth and few details, except that, upon arriving, he was in control of the city within a year. The Hanover's seized power and never released it, forever displacing the elderly but highly respected Cruise founder of Lost Vegas.

Fifty years passed with no mention of what occurred anywhere in any records. No history is written until the skies turned from night to twilight to day, one hundred and five years after the end of the Old World. During the dark age, deserts had turned fertile, and bodies of water shifted. The tundras of the north spread south, while the forests of the northwest pushed into desolate expanses in the southwest. It is said the ocean was twenty miles closer to Lost Vegas than it used to be. The world changed in the Darkness. Those from the Old World would never recognize what happened after their era ended.

When twilight lifted, and daylight returned, the survivors were able to see what remained of the Old World: the crumbling structures and equipment, none of which the second and third generation survivors understood, and ... the dead. It is said ninety-nine out of every hundred people died during the dark age. Skeletons littering the cities and plains were commonplace and became a source of materials for weapons and homes. No one knew who the dead were anymore, so no one bothered to bury them.

The return of the twenty-four hour day brought stability and wealth to some, but also introduced new threats to the residents of Lost Vegas.

The First Peoples, the natives of the continent, arose with the dawn, more powerful than they had ever been, and bearing the resent-ment of a people oppressed for hundreds of years. They bore great hatred for the loss of their people, lands, and traditions at the hands of the Europeans who claimed the continent a thousand years ago. Tribal rivalries and traditional enemies were forgotten in the face of a common goal to drive out those who had stolen what was rightfully theirs. The Natives swept across the continent to reclaim their ancestral lands.

Three hundred and fifty years of wars ensued between those living in the settled communities similar to Lost Vegas and the Natives who roamed the wild, wide stretches of land between cities. Many isolated cities that once flourished – Phoenix, Reno, Austin and most of the cities of the Great Plains – perished during the Native Wars. It is said the cities along the Eastern Seaboard fared better, for many of them had been established on points of military advantage. They were also close enough to one another to help defend each other from attacks.

After three centuries of war, even those First Peoples who bore the deepest resentment towards the descendants of pale-faced European invaders either died or tired of death. Truces were called, and autonomous cities negotiated peace with the natives neighboring them.

With the common enemy and cause replaced by peace, the traditional rivalries among the tribal peoples returned. The coalition that nearly achieved dominance over the entire continent, for the first time since Europeans set foot in the Americas, splintered and cracked, until it was no longer a functional coalition. Natives fought one another for a short period and on occasion, still skirmish over disputed territory.

Our city is surrounded by a buffer area and the territories of three Native peoples: our allies, the Newe, to the west and north; the neutral Kutsipiuti who wish for peace, and whose lands are to the west, south, and north; and the Diné who have claimed an eternal blood war against the city and whose lands lie to the east and south.

The cities remain islands in the midst of forests, mountains, and plains. Each is self-ruling, with a feudal type system of governing that varies some from city to city. Little is known about those cities in the far east and south. The Free Lands are rumored to be to the north, from the direction Charles Cruise originally journeyed. No one, even the Natives, can confirm they exist.

Nothing is known about the state of the rest of the world.

THE ELECTRICITY FLICKERED OUT, as it did often, and was replaced instantly by the warmth of candles.

Tiana set her pen down beside the journal in which she wrote. She reread the brief history of the world – as she had come to understand it – with dissatisfaction. How was it possible to sum up five hundred years of history in *two* pages? How were there so many missing parts? Starting with why the world fell into Darkness in the first place. How her ancestor displaced the savior of Lost Vegas and seized control. Why the isolated city had survived the Native Wars when no other city for a thousand miles did. Where the records for most of the five hundred years were, because she couldn't believe there were so few.

Her questions were endless, and so was her headache. She had had it since the horrible day when she accidentally murdered her stepmother.

Candlelight danced on the desk beside her journal, and a happy fire blazed in the hearth. Both helped to dispel the gloom of late winter, when the sun set far too early. The door to her new apartment – which used to belong to Matilda – opened. Tiana tensed instinctively and ducked her gaze, going still.

"Your dinner," announced a familiar voice.

She sneaked a glance at the blind woman standing in the doorway to ensure she was alone. Tiana rose and crossed to her, accepting the tray and pausing to pat the guide dog accompanying the blind woman before turning away.

The fallout from the Matilda incident continued two weeks after it happened. Three slaves were ordered blinded by her father and reassigned to her. They were led through the pyramid and apartments by specially trained dogs whose leads were attached to the belts of the slaves. But several days blind did not give the women the chance to understand their new limitations, and Tiana had taken pity on the slaves several times a day. If she did not meet them at the door for her food, there was an almost absolute chance her tray ended up on the floor by accident.

The slave entered her chamber and took up a position near the door, four feet out from the wall she could not see. The awkward distance drew Tiana's glance more than once as she sat at the dining table where Matilda used to sit.

Her meager belongings fit on one nightstand, whereas it had taken a dozen slaves three days to strip Matilda's possessions out of the spacious apartment that now belonged to Tiana.

I hate this room, she thought and looked around at the garish wallpaper, heavy drapes, and bright bedding. She could almost feel Matilda's presence here when she was alone. While Tiana did enjoy some of the modern comforts long since absent from the closet where she was trapped her entire life, she would gladly trade the trappings for her old room back. At least there, she had felt safe in her own private space.

"What news is there?" she asked to distract herself from the unease present since she set foot in this room.

"Your father burns the last of the Cruises today. The riots among the outer city earlier this week are gone. He burnt those who protested his treatment of the family that founded Lost Vegas."

Tiana's appetite fled. Her father's solution to the Matilda crisis: burn the Cruises, under the guise Matilda had first enslaved and then used magic to try to kill his daughter. Word had spread too fast for him to contain. From the Shield members who discovered Tiana, to the slaves who were watching, to the physicians who helped save her life, all the residents of the outer city knew by dusk the same day.

Her father could not burn the hundreds of people who knew or heard about Tiana's living conditions, and the circumstances in which she was found. But he could force his council of advisors, who Arthur often referred to as political prisoners, to sanction the destruction of those who tried to murder a Hanover.

Tiana suspected a greater truth. This was vengeance, political and personal, and nothing more. Her father bore the Cruises a grudge long before Matilda's death. As always, the Hanover leader had managed to spin crisis to his advantage and come out on top. Her father's ruthless political sense of survival never failed to impress or scare her.

With a lineage honored more than her own, the Cruises were respected in both the inner and outer cities. Tiana was not surprised to hear of the protests, or of her father's decision of how to handle the Cruises. How many people had died, because Matilda had a bad day, Tiana reacted with her forbidden deformity, and the two of them forced her father's hand?

"What of my slave Aveline?" she whispered. "Is she alive?" She held her breath as she waited for a response.

"The Shield has her. Your father has not made his wishes public, but she has not been burned."

Tiana sighed, grateful yet confused as to why her father hadn't burned Aveline, unless he was too busy with the Cruises. He had never had a problem finding extra wood and fire with which to burn someone before, though. Did he sense what she did about Aveline? That the slave was special? Did he know his own heir had hired the teenage assassin? Her father respected Arthur more than anyone. Was this why he hesitated?

Not knowing Aveline's fate made Tiana ill.

"You may go," she whispered, distraught. "I do not wish to be disturbed again today."

The slave left, and Tiana listened for the door lock to click into place before she moved. Pushing herself back from her table, she gazed out the window to her left, which looked out over the city. Fresh snow carpeted the roads and roofs as far as she could see but did nothing to disrupt the normal flow of people through the streets. The city seemed unaware of her father's latest purge or perhaps, feared lifting their eyes from the ground long enough to acknowledge what was happening. No one who challenged her father lived.

Dusk, as well as the low clouds gathering for a snowstorm, prevented her from viewing the mountains she longed to see again.

Locked in her new prison, without her brother or the friend she'd come to adore, she couldn't help feeling ... trapped.

A light tap at her door was followed by the slide of the bolt. She braced herself, afraid of discovery, and exposed without her secret hiding place between the walls.

"Your slaves said you wished not to be disturbed, but I have news." George, her brother's most trusted slave, entered.

Tiana faced him without looking up. Twice he had come to see her before her incident with Matilda, and since then, he had visited several times. He would never look directly at her, but she sensed in him what she had in Aveline: someone she could trust. If her brother trusted both, then Tiana would as well.

"Forgive me for intruding. If you prefer I return later ..." he said when she didn't move.

Tiana turned to face him, her eyes on the ground as well. "No, please remain," she said quickly. "Have you news of my brother?"

"Your father sent search parties. No word has been received," the slave reported.

To make matters the worst possible, Arthur's message about the Cruises trying to attack him had reached the city two days before, further supporting their father's impetus to burn the Cruises. Adding to her father's fire: yesterday, a Native had come to the leader of the Lost Vegas and claimed to have found what was left of Arthur's base camp – with every last one of its occupants brutally slaughtered.

If there was one thing their father cared about, it was his heir. To lose Arthur now, in the midst of political unrest, would see the Hanover's toppled after ruling for four hundred and fifty years. Tiana had no memory of ever hearing of any Lost Vegas leader being a woman. The Hanover's had always produced heirs.

"Your father is being pressured to name an additional heir, if Arthur is not found soon," George reported.

Tiana's thoughts went down the list of cousins who lived on the floor below theirs in the great pyramid. "Who has he chosen?" she asked.

"It is believed he will name you, his natural daughter, along with the name of the Hanover cousin you are to wed on your eighteenth birthday."

Tiana said nothing, not wanting to dwell on a world without Arthur. Her father's shrewd political move was what she expected: enough to keep the family in power.

"You have become useful to him now," George added more quietly, as if afraid someone would overhear.

"At the expense of my brother," she replied.

"Your brother's sole concern lately has been finding a way to keep you alive past your eighteenth birthday. If your father betroths you to a cousin, he will ensure you are alive to wed, even when your brother returns. After Arthur's disappearance, your father would be foolish to believe anything other than you are needed to live to produce heirs."

"My father is many things, but he is not a fool," she agreed, while keeping her own opinion private. "I can think of nothing but my brother's safety." Tiana did not care about her own life or what happened in three weeks, when she turned eighteen, or what her father's true intentions were, because he never revealed them. To assume one knew, or to underestimate the head of the Hanover clan was a recipe for being burnt at the stake. Her father might keep her around for a while, but if Arthur feared for her life, she would not doubt their father's original plans – whatever they were – remained in play.

"You and Arthur share rare gifts. If anyone can survive, it is him,"

To speak of such deformities, even in private, was to tempt fate. Tiana did not respond to these words and asked instead, "Can you help Aveline?"

George released a sigh, and Tiana hid her smile. His reaction to the slave's name left her no doubt as to his feelings for her. "She is beyond my ability to help. Your father has his personal guards monitoring her," George replied. "For what it's worth, I do not believe he intends to burn her. If I hear more, I will inform you immediately." With a bow of his head, he turned and strode towards the door.

"Wait," Tiana called after him. She fiddled with the bracelet she wore once more, debating whether or not she should ask him of an additional favor.

George obeyed.

"Do you know what this symbol means?" she asked and held out her arm to display the bracelet.

He turned and approached but stopped six feet from her. His eyes stayed on the bracelet.

"It appears to be a Native rune," he said. "But I have too little experience in dealing with them."

"Can you find out?"

"Of course."

She lowered her arm.

"If I may ask, was this among Matilda's belongings?" he asked, puzzled.

Tiana almost smiled. They both knew Matilda would never own something as simple or inexpensive. "No," she replied. "But I will say no further."

George bowed his head again. "I will make inquiries. Quietly, I imagine?"

"Yes," she replied.

"Very well." George left her alone.

Tiana looked down at the bracelet. She had found it among Aveline's meager belongings, which were lumped in with Tiana's when the slaves moved her things from her old room to this one. Her guardian had possessed assassin tools, a medicine pouch – and the bracelet, sealed within an envelope. Tiana had opened it out of curiosity and then worn it to feel closer to the friend whose condition she knew nothing of. She hoped to be able to return it personally to Aveline one day.

The wooden cabochon framed in brass at the center of the bracelet was old enough for its surface to be scuffed and the brass to display a colorful patina. It was supported by a soft length of braided leather. It had felt too large at first, but had then shrunk to conform to Tiana's wrist. Carved into the wood was a symbol Tiana had never seen before, even in her history books about the Natives.

The symbol had to have meaning, and the bracelet personal value to Aveline, if the assassin had kept it and nothing else from her past life.

Restless to know more about Aveline and Arthur, Tiana was about to return to the window when a trickle of energy, resembling a draft of cold air, brushed her skin. She closed her eyes to better view the faint vision she knew was coming and prayed she saw Arthur alive.

A MAN, hiding in the brush. But not a man. This was ... a beast ...

Or ...

Present in the vision, she squinted to see better. Whether it was dusk, or the vision was dim, she could not tell. The skies were cloudy but not dark, and ... voices hummed in the air around her. She was not alone, wherever she was.

The man ... beast ... man ... shifted to his feet.

Puzzled, Tiana drew closer, struggling to see what hid in the brush beside a tent. The image fluctuated between man and large animal several more times, before she saw them at the same time. A man inside the animal. He was ... hiding inside the great bear. Or perhaps, he was representative of the great bear's spirit? She was unable to determine exactly what was before her.

The great bear towered twice her height, but the man ... he was as tall as her brother. She came up to his chin. Rather than peer into the eyes of the animal, Tiana concentrated on the man. His face was blank, aside from dead, empty eyes. His upper body bore tattoos, and his long, dark hair – much like Aveline's – gave away his Native birth. Sensing her, the man inside the beast lowered himself as if to pounce, and the creature bellowed loudly and swiped at her. She had experienced enough visions to know it could not harm her. Its claws passed through

her, and she stepped closer as the beast and man merged then sepa-
rated again.

"I see you," she said to the man, ignoring the beast.

Rather than run, the man started towards her. Sensing danger for
the first time in the vision, Tiana stepped back quickly. He reached for
her with one hand ...

THE IMAGE VANISHED, and she opened her eyes, alarmed. Never in any of her visions had anyone else been aware enough to try to touch her! It was as if he saw *her*, the real her, not the person in the vision, which was impossible!

Tiana shivered. The sensation of a chilly draft left her, and she returned to the window, unable to explain what she had seen, where she had been, or when except ...

"I was ... will be outside the city," she whispered, surprised. Facing a bear-man held no appeal to her, but sometime, in her own future, she was going to leave this forsaken city! Who was with her? Certainly Aveline, even if the slave claimed she had no desire to leave Lost Vegas. Tiana would go with no one else, except her brother, who – as their father's only male heir – was not about to give up his family name to escape with her. He was also currently missing, unless the vision meant he would return and take her out of the city.

Why, and more importantly, how, had she left? Her glimpses of the future occurred far less frequently than her brother's. They were nowhere near as detailed or long as his, but to date, all of them had come true.

Even the one about Matilda.

Tiana's excitement faded. Despite everything, she had never hated her former stepmother. Matilda deserved better, and the memory of what Tiana had done to her left her disgusted at herself.

Murder. She had *murdered* someone! Familiar distress crept through her, and tears filled her eyes. Although she could hear Aveline telling her she would never survive outside the city if she did not stop crying, Tiana was not able to stop whenever she thought of how right Matilda had always been about her.

What if Arthur were permanently lost outside the city, and Aveline was burnt at the stake? Who could Tiana trust? How would she ever see the Free Lands or escape her father or survive her eighteenth birthday?

She huddled up in the middle of her new bed and sobbed.

TWELVE

"I SEE YOU," the whisper was distinctly female and so soft, it could have been breathed by the air itself.

The Native bundled in furs, down, wool, and leathers spun, his skin pricking with the awareness of a hunter accustomed to prey that sometimes fought back. The wintery forest behind him was silent, blanketed by snow that seemed to have chased all the animals into hiding and rendered the trees lifeless.

Normally, when this voice spoke to him, he was asleep. What did it mean that this spirit sought him out when he was awake? And what exactly did it *see*? This lost spirit was not one of those whose lives he had taken, and it followed him too closely for him to believe the encounter was a coincidence. It had begun to speak to him several weeks before, when he entered the territory shared by the Sutai Cheyenne and Lakota.

He was invisible among men and beasts alike, a creature of neither world and of both. He did not fully exist, and he could never die. Neither night, nor light, nor anything touched by either, he was flesh and blood, and yet, he did not fully exist.

"You see nothing, spirit," he said gruffly to the trees whose branches were frosted with a foot of snow, "for I am nothing."

The errant spirit that often haunted his dreams did not respond.

The padding of his guide brought him back to his senses, and he faced the direction he was headed. A black wolf – with a belly swollen from the pups she would bear in a matter of days – waited for him, a stark contrast against the white world. Her golden eyes lingered on his face, as if she sensed what he felt.

It was dusk, but the coming of night did nothing to slow his progress.

"Go," he ordered her.

The wolf trotted forward, her belly swaying from side to side with her movement.

He sensed people long before he saw them. A faint scent or sound in the air, the shift of wind as it parted around manmade structures in its path. And of course, the faint sounds of heartbeats tapping the base of his skull, a warning he would momentarily be upon others, and soon be in pain.

The wolf paused at the edge of a small village at the last point possible before it became unsafe for her to proceed among those who would harm her.

He stopped beside her. Already, the tap in his mind had turned to a steady pattering. There were too many heartbeats to count in the village, which put its population over a hundred. If he did not need supplies, he would bypass this place and wait to stop until he found somewhere smaller.

His eyes examined the wounded leg of his guide quickly. The skin around her injury was infected, and he did not have the medicines needed to prevent a fever from afflicting her. Time was not on their side, and with the additional burden of the pups she carried, she was slow to heal. He dared not put her life, and the spirits of her pups, at risk by waiting too long to treat her.

The Native swirled his cloak off and draped it over a low tree branch, maneuvering it with practiced skill. He created a small tent out of its folds then knelt, impervious to the cold snow, to place a pelt made of rabbit fur and felt on the ground at the base of the tent.

He shifted back and motioned to the wolf, who obediently entered the makeshift cave he created for her. She paced in a circle several times before settling.

The Native rose and sprinkled the outside of the cloak with handfuls of snow. When the lines and structure of the tent were difficult to distinguish from the rest of the snowy tree trunk, he clapped snow from his hands and started towards the quiet village.

Each step increased the pulsing of heartbeats, and his fingers quivered as they brushed the hilts of his knives.

Like most villages close to a large city, this one consisted of traditional Native housing and what remained of the town that used to stand here during the Old World. Traditional housing was used for living quarters, while the surviving buildings from the Old World covered in withered vines served as community gathering places and storage facilities. Electricity glowed in one window, where many of the village's occupants appeared to be.

The tapping became a discordant thumping. Too many heartbeats were in the building for him to consider entering, so the Native kept his distance and quickened his pace as the heartbeats began to beat hard enough to cause pain.

He entered a narrow street lined with semi-permanent abodes, wincing. Stopping in the middle of the street, he sought to center himself and hopefully, take the edge off the pounding in his brain.

Someone spoke from the door to one tent, and he turned. A little boy the same age he had been when *they* came for him stood in boots, cheeks already rosy from the frigid night and uncertain gaze on him.

"English," the Native said gruffly. His tribe's language was not spoken on this side of the continent, or anywhere he had ever been.

"You are a guest?" replied the boy in halting English. "For the wedding vows?"

"Yes," the Native lied without hesitation. "I am hungry, and I need medicines."

The little boy appeared to be processing his words for a moment before he nodded. "Come," he said and stood aside, holding open the door.

The Native entered the warm interior brightly lit by a fire at its center and lamp with a pink bulb. The boy was alone, which did nothing to help the Native's pounding head, not with the proximity to the rest of the villagers.

He removed his cloak and scarf and sat beside the fire.

"Wait. I bring food," the boy said and then ducked out of the tent before the Native could reply.

He tossed the long braid of his hair over one shoulder. The tent was too quiet and warm. Without a distraction, the beating in his head took on a pitch that alerted him he was close to the edge. Each person's heartbeat held the power of a strike and he was being pummeled to his limit. A familiar sense came over him, that of sliding out of himself, away from the pain. He closed his eyes. His breathing became labored, his clothing tighter, the pounding deeper, as if each person's heartbeat slammed into his spirit.

"Soup," the boy said.

The Native opened his eyes and realized how far he'd fallen out of himself again. He straightened from his slump.

The little boy handed him a bowl of thick venison soup and a cloth napkin loaded with fry bread and bite-sized sweets from the celebration. The scents alone were enough to ease the beating of his brain.

The Native wolfed down the soup, ignoring the spoon the boy placed beside him and drinking it straight from the bowl.

The child squatted across from him, watching curiously.

The Native lowered the bowl and wiped his mouth with a sleeve before setting the empty dish aside. The stew slid through him, warming him from the inside out for the first time in weeks.

"You are hurt?" the boy asked and pointed to the Native's leg. "What is wrong?"

"No. I need medicines for a friend," the Native said. He slid his left leg, which was misshapen and clad in black leather, under the length of the long coat he wore. The child's question left him no doubt as to his innocence. An adult would know what his black leg meant.

"Medicines," the Native said.

The boy rose and went to one of the boxes stacked on one side of the tent.

The Native ate all the sweets and breads while he watched the child sort through several satchels and jars. After a moment, the boy frowned.

"More soup," the Native said and rose. He held out the bowl. "I will do this."

The boy nodded and took the bowl, happily skipping out of the tent and into the snowy night.

The Native went to the trunk and began filling his satchel with jars of poultice, clean bandages, and a bottle of penicillin.

The pounding in his head increased in intensity, as if a hundred guns were shooting through him, and he hunched his shoulders. The sense of sliding out of himself returned, along with the faint whisper of spirits emanating from his black leg, where the dark magic had trapped them. For a long moment, he stood, neither fighting the sensation nor surrendering, but gauging his chances either way.

Singing came from outside the tent. The party in the central compound had moved into the neighborhood where the people of the village lived, marking the end of the celebration.

His fists clenched, and the satchel fell to his hip. Sucking in deep breaths, the Native's fingers twitched closer to his weapons. His skin and clothing were growing too confined, and he snatched his cloak and scarf and draped them on.

"Two soup," the boy said, entering the tent, his high-pitched voice at odds with the deep pounding. He held out two bowls proudly.

The Native grabbed the bowls. The beating was becoming too much for him to withstand, and he left the tent. Stumbling, he careened into someone he could not see through his pain and dropped to his knees, splashing the soup. Pain lanced each thought and every breath. His body swelled, tearing the stitches of his clothing, and he dropped the bowls completely to grip his head.

The Native flung his head back and roared, a sound that was neither human nor animal but something in between.

The singing around him fell silent. As usual, when he shocked a crowd, there was a collective pause, as the hearts of each person skipped or slowed. And then they began again simultaneously, smashing him with a singular, jagged strike of unbearable agony.

Obsessed by the need for silence, the Native let the pain transform him. His clothing fell away in shreds, but the winter did not reach his skin through the thick layer of fur that raced across his body. This time, when he roared, the sound of a beast left his lungs.

The spirits whispered more loudly, competing with the jarring heartbeats. The Native lashed out to stop the maddening pounding. Blood splattered his fur and filled his mouth at the dizzying movement. The heartbeats were soon accompanied by screams, both of which lessened the more he freed the spirits possessing him to act.

He tore through the wedding procession and guests. With so many dead, the pounding eased without releasing him completely from the spell, and he smashed through tents to silence those lives, too, before chasing down the few who tried to run.

In the end, long after dark fell, the spell released him, and he collapsed in the middle of the now silent village, sucking in ragged breaths, human once again.

Silence ... it was all that brought him peace and relief. Not one heartbeat filled the space around him for a thousand feet, and he relaxed in the snow, too fevered from his activity to feel cold. He dozed, waiting for the final flickers of pain to subside. After some time passed, he roused himself and stood.

Now that the village was his to pillage, he took his time selecting the best and warmest clothing and raiding the medicinal supplies. The Native removed hunks of meat from the village's meat locker before stopping by the central building where the ceremony had begun to partake of the sweets and soup.

When his energy was restored, he left, hauling his treasures on a sled behind him.

"Wolf," he growled when he neared the makeshift tent where he had left his guide.

She did not appear. Assuming she was asleep, the Native dropped his plunder nearby and went to the opening of the tent.

"Wolf," he called again and dropped to one knee to peer into the tent.

His guide was gone.

Unable to believe his eyes, the Native stared at the empty space and then reached in to pick up the rabbit fur, as if his massive canine could fit beneath it. He sprang to his feet and searched the snow around the tent, his vision as sharp in the night as it was in the day. Snow had begun to fill in his footsteps, but shallow dents remained.

"Here."

The Native's head snapped in the direction of the little boy's voice. He went still, uncertain how a child had sneaked up on him.

No heartbeat pelted his brain.

Tilting his head, the Native gazed intently at the little boy from the village. The child smiled, and his cheeks remained rosy. The only difference between earlier and the form before him: the deep, black gash across the child's chest, from where the Native had ripped his lungs out with a single stroke.

"This is their trail," the boy said and pointed. There was no accent in the spirit's words, no hesitation, as there had been when he spoke broken English in the village.

The Native approached warily. He had never seen a spirit this clearly, only heard their whispers.

The shallow indentations of two people on foot were beside the boy. One pair of footsteps led them to the tent where the wolf rested, and a second pair led away.

The Native knelt to observe more closely. No paw prints were present, indicating the she-wolf was carried away. He could not imagine his guide going with anyone willingly. If anything, becoming a mother had made her even less tolerant than he was of other humans. She had been sent for *him* and allowed no one else near her.

He breathed in deeply without smelling fresh blood. His guide had a bandaged leg wound, and the trace of old blood was in the air.

They had not hurt her. At least, not here, or within a thousand yards of here.

He glanced towards the sky. The stars were hidden, but his internal sense of time told him he had been in the village for several hours, long enough for the snow to conceal all but the beginning of their path.

"How long ago did they leave?" he asked the spirit that lingered nearby.

"Two hours," the boy replied.

The Native's heart began to race, and familiar heat flushed through him as his body prepared to transform in response to his ricocheting emotions. He stood, peering into the forest in the direction the footsteps had gone.

Who had taken his guide?

Did they know what he would do to them, once he found them?

He calmed himself, aware he needed his human mind engaged.

"You should hurry," the spirit called. He had moved twenty feet away at the blink of an eye. The boy disappeared.

His plunder forgotten, the Native began to run in the direction the footsteps had gone. They ended abruptly, a quarter mile away, and were replaced by the unmistakable scent, deep hoof prints and cold scat of two horses. The men had mounted up and then set off towards the west.

The spirits were whispering again, insistent and mournful he had failed to protect the sacred guide granted him.

The harder the snow fell, the faster he went, fearful of losing all traces of those who stole his guide. In the distance, he heard the shrieks of the Ghouls. They could not sense him, but for the sake of saving time, he would have to avoid rather than confront them, if he wanted to follow the tracks of those he now hunted before the snow completely covered them.

THIRTEEN

"HAVE I told you how bad this idea is?" Marshall Cruise hissed. "Even for a Hanover?"

"Five times so far," Arthur Hanover replied. The heir to the ruling dynasty in Lost Vegas adjusted the bundled wolf in his lap with a grunt. The pregnant beast weighed over a hundred pounds and glared at him with golden eyes whenever he shifted her into a position she did not like.

At the moment, the fingers of one of his hands were trapped beneath her body and as numb as his nose and cheeks. Snow fell in silent sheets, too thick for them to ride faster than a walk.

"We saw what that monster did to our people, to the people of those two villages," Marshall continued.

"I know." Arthur glanced at the wolf. It was a rare day when he was not fully confident in his decisions, and today was one of those days. "We stick to the plan. If you do not like it, go back. I did not ask you to accompany me." Even as he said the words, he understood his chances of surviving alone were nonexistent.

"I came for the sakes of all our friends, not just Warner. He is probably dead by now, too," Marshall said quietly. "No one can survive this alone."

"We have!" Arthur snapped.

Marshall sank into sullen quietness.

All traces of Warner, Arthur's protector and lover, had long since vanished.

They had followed the tracks of his friend, until they intersected with the sometimes human, sometimes bear prints of the skinwalker that had indiscriminately slaughtered the entire party making up this year's Winter Hunt. Warner's footprints had been lost in the final snowstorm of late winter, and Arthur had followed the skinwalker in the hopes of being led to a nearby village where he would find his lover.

The skinwalker indeed led them to a village – and then slaughtered everyone in it.

No trace of Warner remained. Neither had they found his body, which gave Arthur hope that his friend had escaped the beast a second time. Warner would know to head to the city, but Arthur was at a crossroads. The very creature that had slaughtered Arthur's soldiers, and the village, also threatened Tiana.

The decision to pursue the threat was not an easy one, and Arthur made it knowing he may never see Warner again. It was easier to convince Marshall to follow the skinwalker. The Cruise heir believed this to be a mission of vengeance, and in a way, it was.

They trailed the skinwalker into four villages. Half of those the skinwalker entered were graveyards by the time he left. All but once, Arthur and Marshal had arrived to the village in time to witness the skinwalker departing, accompanied by the wolf, the only living creature that appeared immune to his carnage. The animal was of importance to him, and Arthur had hatched a plan to lure the skinwalker into a trap of their devising.

Justice was called for. But Arthur's secret hope was to prevent the vision replaying in his sleep every night, where this very skinwalker pursued his sister across the plains. If Marshall chose to claim this was revenge to the residents of the affluent Lost Vegas outer city, then he was welcome to. As long as they stuck together, Arthur did not care what the philosophical son of the wealthiest man in Lost Vegas believed.

"He could've made it back to the city by now," Marshall said.

"I hope so," Arthur murmured.

"I'm impressed by how much you care. It shows you to be a different kind of person than your father."

Not this again, Arthur thought. He rolled his eyes without admonishing his companion. He had exhausted his desire to counter Marshall's well thought out arguments about how terrible the Hanover dynasty was for the survival of Lost Vegas. So his father was a tad aggressive in sending people to the stakes, but the Hanover's were the reason the city survived the past four and a half centuries. When his father was gone, and Arthur was in charge, he could change things. It was only a matter of time.

Marshall's radical solution, overthrowing Arthur's father and the ruling council, sounded as rational to Arthur as his father burning everyone with deformities. He had stopped listening to Marshall's ramblings.

The wolf's head snapped up, and she planted her legs against the horse's body, wriggling.

Arthur stopped his horse and dropped the reins to try to grab the furry black animal, but she leapt free of the horse and landed in a puff of snow beside him.

"Burn me!" he muttered and flung himself off the horse to recapture the she-wolf.

"Arthur," Marshall's voice was quiet, urgent.

The wolf bounded a few steps away then lowered herself to the ground, preparing to pounce.

"Stay mounted, Marshall. She almost attacked you last time," Arthur said and circled his horse. The wolf appeared to accept his presence where she would not Marshall's.

"Arthur!"

Irritated, Arthur twisted to see Marshall in the darkness. Between the white snow, and white clouds, the night held an eerie glow. The only sound was that of horses snorting and the wolf's low, deep growl.

Marshall was pointing into the forest, his jaw slack, and a knife in one hand. Arthur looked towards him then back, realizing the wolf and his companion were both facing the same direction.

Shifting around the trunk of a tree, so he could see what they did, Arthur's breath caught in his throat.

Skin and hair whiter than snow, eyes and lips blacker than hell, sharpened fangs too large for their lips to cover, the ethereal monsters from nightmares floated more than walked, not twenty feet away from Arthur's position.

"Ghouls," he breathed.

Silent, except when hunting, the nocturnal predators were believed to have been awakened during the Age of Darkness, after falling into hibernation during the early days of mankind. Unlike most predators, which could survive off of multiple kinds of meat, the Ghouls hunted humans exclusively, rendering the insatiable creatures the largest threat after nightfall and the monster in nearly every ghost story Arthur had ever heard.

Arthur did not dare reach for his weapons, or even to breathe. By the silence behind him, from the direction of Marshall, the Cruise heir had paid attention to the briefings given to them about how to handle a Ghoul encounter. The only way to survive once the Ghouls spotted someone: flee.

But if the monsters were silent, they had not caught the scent of the human yet, in which case, it was highly advisable to become a statue until it was safe to flee without drawing the creatures' attentions.

Arthur remained as still as humanly possible. How had the creatures not noticed them? Their olfactory were known to be better than any animal's; how did they not smell Arthur, Marshall, or the horses?

They melted in and out of the blanket of snow that fell. Ghostlike in appearance, they nonetheless possessed physical bodies like any animal and could be killed. A grouping of them consisting of ten highly skilled warriors, whose weapons were unknown, for anyone who was close enough to determine such, died at their hands. In all the years the Ghouls had patrolled the night, Arthur could not recall one report about how the monsters slaughtered the humans they crossed.

Have mercy, he thought, as one of the creatures turned its head towards him. Halfway hidden behind the tree trunk, and halfway exposed, Arthur did not dare move. A chill worked its way through him, wrapped around his muscles, robbed him of breath, and held him paralyzed.

The wolf growled more loudly and paced out in front of him before lowering herself to the ground once again.

Arthur tried to warn her to quiet, but could not move or speak. His muscles did not respond to his commands any longer. He could move his eyes – and that was all.

I cannot die before I save Tiana. He strained against his body, a prisoner.

The wolf snapped at the creatures. Two more Ghouls glanced their way, and Arthur began to panic silently, certain he would die where he stood.

The creature staring in his direction turned away. Just as suddenly as the chill froze Arthur in place, it released him. He sucked in a breath, unable to help his body's impulsive response to the release.

The wolf straightened, her teeth still bared.

Two of the ghouls' gazes lingered on the beast, and Arthur glanced towards her, too, unable to explain how a dog could discourage predators like the Ghouls.

Similar to his own breathing, he heard Marshall panting. Arthur remained where he was until the last of the Ghouls disappeared into the snowstorm.

As if content the threat was gone, the wolf sat on her haunches, ears twitching between Arthur and the direction the creatures had gone.

Arthur sank to the ground beside the tree trunk, trembling.

"When it looked at me, I couldn't breathe." Marshall's voice was hoarse, scared.

"Me neither," Arthur said.

"We were vulnerable. Why did they not attack?"

Arthur's gaze settled on the she-wolf. The canine was standing beside his horse, as if to tell him it was time for them to leave. "The wolf," he said. "I don't understand it, but she scared them away."

Marshall was silent for a moment.

Recovering from the most terrifying moment of certain death, Arthur rose.

"Ghouls fear nothing," Marshal said. "Nothing ... normal, that is."

"Then the answer is plain." Arthur strode to his horse. "This wolf is not normal."

"Probably why the skinwalker travels with it. You do not think the wolf is one, too, do you?"

Arthur eyed the she-wolf, who was gazing at him with intelligence in her golden eyes, as if she understood them.

"She is far too small to be anything but a wolf," he answered. But he heard the doubt in his voice and hesitated to lift her onto the horse's back.

"The horse would know," Marshall said. "From what we have seen, horses do not like skinwalkers."

They don't like wolves, either, Arthur thought. Their horses had completely ignored the wolf since they captured it. Marshall was correct. This was not a normal wolf.

Anxious to be away from the place where they spotted the Ghouls, Arthur hefted the wolf onto the horse, supported her while she wriggled into a comfortable position, and then mounted.

"I take back everything I said about the wolf," Marshall whispered. "I am glad we grabbed her."

"Right now, so am I," Arthur agreed.

"I would fight a skinwalker over a Ghoul every day of the week."

"I am not that optimistic. I have seen you fight," Arthur said, unable to stop his smile. "Your chances against either are not promising. Maybe you can talk them to death, as you try to do me on a daily basis."

"Then you do the fighting," Marshall snapped. "I will be sure to tell your father this horrible plan was all your idea."

"I thought your plan to usurp him involves putting me in his place."

"Plans can be changed."

Arthur snorted. He positioned himself the best he could with his stolen treasure, and then signaled the horse to continue on its path. Leery of the direction the Ghouls had gone, he shifted their course. The wolf had somehow protected them once, but he was not about to take the chance she would do it again. After all, if she understood they were in danger, she probably knew she did not belong with him.

"How do you know we are going the right direction?" Marshall called from behind him.

Arthur held out his hand and visualized their destination. A whirl of snow circled his palm before piling up at the tip of his middle finger, confirming they were to continue going straight. "I paid attention when Running Deer taught us to navigate," he replied icily.

"So did I. And yet you always know where we are going, while I do not."

Arthur was silent.

Marshall knew nothing of the particular kind of deformity that ran in the Hanover family. If he did, he would be able to manipulate Arthur or their father, and Arthur was not about to give his political rival the chance to destroy his family's standing, no matter how much he agreed with a few of Marshall's views.

Lowering his hand, Arthur petted the wolf's thick fur absent-mindedly, unable to shake the strange sense the Ghouls were waiting for them around the next bend. What bothered him more: recalling a claim Matilda – Marshall's sister – had made about Tiana.

Tiana had the eyes of a Ghoul.

It did not seem possible, since their mother was a human, but neither did it seem possible for both Arthur and Marshall to be rendered immobilized by a single *look*. To the best of his knowledge, the Hanover's had rarely ventured outside the city, let alone survived a Ghoul attack or somehow managed to survive and breed with the creatures that survived off of human flesh.

Tiana's physical deformity was exactly that – a deformity. Her eyes resembled a Ghoul's, but that was the extent of the similarities. Birth defects were diverse. Because of one resemblance, it did not mean his sister was a Ghoul. If she were, then so was he, as they had the same parents!

His night had been too stressful for him to feel reassured by his logic. Arthur focused on their destination, the cave where they'd chosen to ambush the skinwalker, and shivered, unable to help it when he recalled how the Ghoul had looked straight through him.

"Thank you," he whispered to the wolf. "I do not know what you did, but I am grateful to be alive."

The animal was dozing. The snow was falling hard enough for her fur to be almost white.

Arthur pulled up his hood to shield his eyes, and his horse plodded on. The cave was close and contained natural coverage from rocks and trees that would limit the skinwalkers ability to identify the traps within before he was upon them.

The forest cleared ahead of him, though he was unable to identify the river until he was nearly upon it through the snowstorm. Arthur halted his horse at the embankment lined with a trail, leading down to the river, and he frowned.

The river had been a sheet of ice, covered by snow, when they came this way several hours before.

"A boulder must have come loose," Marshall said, drawing his horse to a halt beside Arthur.

A steeper embankment hedged the opposite side of the river, tall enough for a boulder to build the momentum needed to pierce the ice. Beneath the solid surface, the river still flowed. Gray water splashed out from the middle of the hole onto the ice. Frozen tendrils and streams gave the splashes the appearance of wax surrounding the base of a candle.

They both studied the scene quietly. Whatever had broken the ice had sunk into the hole it created when it hit the river. Arthur gauged how far out the ice had cracked in order to find a crossing point.

The sudden shriek of a Ghoul split the air from the direction they had come.

Arthur jerked and twisted to see behind him, expecting the creature to be close enough to paralyze and eat them.

"They're a quarter mile off at least," Marshall said, facing the way they had come. "But let's not wait to see if they picked up our scent."

"Agreed." Arthur urged his horse forward, parallel to the river for a short distance. When he felt certain the cracked ice had not traveled this far from the hole, he loosened the reins to allow his horse to pick its way down the embankment towards the river.

A second shriek drew his gaze hastily to the forest. "I never want to meet those things again!" he said.

"Nor I." Marshall was at his side. "I don't believe in magic wolves as much as I do luck."

"After what we saw, I believe in magic wolves," Arthur returned.

"You go first. Maybe your magic wolf will warn you if the river isn't safe."

Arthur focused on crossing the frozen river. He ventured forward at a slow walk, not wanting to risk the horse slipping on the slick surface buried beneath a foot of snow. The wolf stirred, as if she, too, were concerned about the shrieking Ghouls.

"Be still," he ordered her quietly. "We're halfway across." His eyes went to the gaping hole in the river some twenty yards away.

"Solid?" Marshall called.

"I'm still here, aren't I?"

The embankment ahead of them came into view, beyond the falling snow. Four yards from safety, a deep crack resonated from beneath the ice.

Arthur stopped the horse and looked down but was unable to make out whether or not he was in danger.

"Marshall," he said. "Are you on the ice?"

"I am."

"Go back."

Silence.

"Did you hear me?" Arthur asked.

Another Ghoulish shriek pierced the air, this time closer to the river.

"I'll take my chances with the ice," Marshall replied.

"Then cross at an angle! The ice here is damaged."

"I can't see you clearly. Are you across?"

"Not yet." Arthur's heart was beating hard.

"Dismount. Take some of the weight off."

Arthur had been debating that approach. Marshall voicing it aloud helped him decide. He swung his leg over the horse's back and dismounted with the softest landing possible. The ice held, and he reached up slowly to dislodge the wolf from the horse's back. One of his feet slipped, and he careened backwards with the she-wolf clutched in his arms. He landed on his back with a grunt, the animal squirming in his arms.

"Arthur?" Marshall called. His position had changed; his voice came from almost parallel to Arthur, several meters upstream.

No cracking came from beneath him despite the hard fall.

"Fell. I'm fine," Arthur said. He released the wolf, which leapt to its feet.

Several Ghouls were screaming in chorus and sounded as if they would reach the river soon.

"Hurry!" Marshall shouted above their racket.

He rolled and rose carefully and then reached out and slapped the horse on its rump. "Go, Tawny!" The horse jolted forward and trotted to safety, trailed by the sound of crackling ice.

"I'm across," Marshall reported.

"Grab my horse," Arthur directed him. "I'll be right there." He shifted away from the weakened ice before starting forward towards the shore.

Only when he set both feet on the frozen bank did he release the breath he was holding. Marshall was waiting, mounted and holding the reins to Arthur's horse.

"Let's get out of here," he yelled over the sound of Ghouls.

"Without her?" Marshall pointed.

Sudden silence made his shout ring out across the river.

Arthur turned, already suspecting what he would see. Concentrating on his own journey across the ice, he had assumed the wolf knew to follow him.

Her figure was a slash of black against a white world matched only by the large, piercing, unnaturally black eyes of the Ghouls. Ten figures lined up on the opposite side of the river.

Abrupt silence replaced their shrieks.

The she-wolf's low growl was the only sound not muted by falling snow. She had paced to the center of the river once more and was glaring at the creatures, teeth bared.

The monsters watched her, as if they were trying to decide whether or not to face off with the otherworldly wolf.

For the first time in his life, Arthur was able to see the Ghouls full on, in a way no one else had ever lived to tell of, without trees or fear clouding his judgment as they had during his first encounter. The creatures had human forms, though their features were decidedly not human, and their fingers twice the length of a normal man's. They were of a similar height, perhaps six feet tall, dressed in white furs over white robes, slightly hunched, and bearing no weapons he could see.

The cracking of ice pulled Arthur out of his fearful daze, and he tested his body to ensure he had not been frozen in place again.

While he was unable to see the ice beneath the snow, he saw the subtle shift of snow above the crack. The broken ice was slowly making its way towards the wolf at the center of the river.

"Let's get out of here while we can still move," Marshall whispered.

"We can't leave her." Arthur's eyes went to the she-wolf that stood alone in a silent battle with the Ghouls.

"This was a terrible plan. We can escape now and just go home!"

Anger warmed Arthur from the numb tips of his ears to the cold feet in his boots. He wanted to punch his companion in the throat. Or better yet – toss Marshall to the Ghouls. His friend made sense - their plan was probably going to fail at this point, if they were forced to keep running from the Ghouls that had their scent.

"I'm not leaving without her," he said firmly and shot Marshall a look.

"Don't be stupid!"

"She saved our lives once and now she risks her own to do it again," he said. "Go, you coward. I always said you Cruises were nothing but talk. None of you have contributed to our city in any way since your ancestor discovered the city five hundred years ago!"

Marshall appeared surprised rather than angry.

Not caring what the Cruise heir decided to do, Arthur snatched a length of rope from his saddlebag and tied one end quickly to the branch of a tree overhanging the river. He stripped off his cloak, weapons, and over garments to eliminate as much of his weight as possible. Gripping the other end, he took a deep breath and stepped onto the frozen river. He walked forward slowly, eyeing the shifting snow as the broken ice expanded several feet away.

The wolf's growls remained the only sound. Afraid to look at a Ghoul and lose his courage or worse, end up immobilized, Arthur stayed focused on steady breathing and on the she-wolf displaying more courage in this situation than Marshall Cruise would over the course of several lifetimes. The sound of a horse scaling the embankment did nothing but anger him more, and Arthur struggled to put his disappointment and fury at the Cruise family aside to focus.

The tug of the rope at his hand frustrated him more as he realized he did not have enough length to make it all the way to the center of the river.

The breaking ice was close to the she-wolf's back legs.

Arthur released the rope and continued.

"Hey there," he said when he was within a yard of the wolf. "If you can understand me ... the ice is breaking. You need to move."

The animal did not answer but continued to glare and growl at the Ghouls lining the river.

The shifting snow was at her feet.

"You have to move," Arthur said more urgently.

The wolf's growl ceased, and Arthur held his breath, praying the ice held.

One of the Ghouls wailed, and the wolf snapped in its direction.

Arthur sneaked a glance at the rope seven feet away.

Something smashed into the ice on the other side of the wolf.

Arthur glanced up, startled. One of the Ghouls had hefted a rock the size of the wolf and flung it into the ice.

"No, no, no," Arthur whispered.

Everything happened at once.

A Ghoul shrieked. This scream was different – not the normal hunting cry, but jarring enough for Arthur to sneak a look towards the line of creatures.

A massive bear had tackled one of the Ghouls, drawing the attention of all of them. The strange scream was one of pain. Blood spurted from the body and splattered the white world with crimson.

The ice groaned and cracked beneath the she-wolf.

Arthur dived for her just as the river's frozen surface crumbled beneath her feet. Frigid water splashed his face, and his fingers grazed her fur as she fell. Before he could adjust, he felt the ground give out from beneath him, and he plunged into the icy river below. The shock of cold was followed by a mouthful of water.

Arthur surfaced, sputtering water, and gave a strangled cry at the searing cold. His vision blurred by droplets, he saw only white and red on the embankment. More wailing filled his ears.

The she-wolf was beside him one second and then suddenly, gone, sucked under the ice by the river.

"No!" Arthur shouted. His hands already going numb, he tried to grab her, only for his wooden fingers to fumble. The river shoved him against unmoving ice. He sucked in a deep breath and ducked under.

Where is she? He demanded of the magic that allowed him to navigate without maps or the visibility of sun or stars.

The river pushed him. Something grazed his hand, and he snatched at it without reaching it.

Again! He ordered the magic.

The river pushed him again, and this time, he collided with a mass of wet fur. Unable to feel his fingers, Arthur wrapped one arm around the she-wolf and extended the other into the cold water. His lungs burned with their need for air, and the edges of his mind were frosting over from the cold.

River bank! He ordered his magic.

The river pushed him over and upward, towards the surface. Arthur stretched up – and his hand, then his head and shoulder, were met by solid ice. Panic began to form in his mind, and he pounded on the ice as hard as he could, until the warmth of blood brushed his face.

Leave me. The voice was so soft, he barely heard it above the frantic thoughts of survival circulating around his mind.

The she-wolf was limp. Was it possible she had spoken to him?

Unable to focus his much needed energy on anything other than breaking through the ice, Arthur continued to pound. Pain radiated through him, warming him, fueling his desire to make it through the ice.

But the ceiling standing between life and death did not budge.

Desperation crept through him, along with the shadows around his mind, closing in, suffocating him mentally as his lungs screamed for air.

Leave me. The voice was stronger, louder.

No! Arthur held the wolf against him more tightly, or so he hoped, since he was quickly becoming unaware of his body and unable to control it. His fist fell away from the ice, and he began to sink into darkness, and coldness, and the unforgiving depths of the river.

The water pushed him upwards again, keeping him afloat when he wanted to let go and die.

A sharp object slashed his shoulder, cutting him deep enough to draw him from the darkness. Arthur peered into the river again and saw the flash of ... something before it fell close to his head. In the far corners of his mind, he recognized the shape of an axe.

Up, he ordered his magic.

The water shoved him upward, towards the axe. He collapsed against the ice.

Up!

The water pushed harder, until it felt as if his insides were being crushed.

The axe fell again, and the ice shattered around him.

Arthur bobbed to the surface. The cold air felt warm after the frigid water, and he struggled to move a body too frozen to do so. He ducked under again, and this time, someone reached in and dragged him back up. His eyes closed. Though he heard the movement and sounds of the world, he could not process them well enough to make them out. One second he was in water. The next, he was being hauled onto the bank.

"Arthur!" This cry was familiar but far off, as if it came from across a vast canyon.

Arthur's eyes opened, and he blinked without being able to clear his vision.

"Breathe, Arthur!" the blurry form above him ordered amidst wailing too fantastical to be real.

Did I survive? He thought doubtfully.

Something slammed into his chest. Arthur choked and then began to cough. He was pushed onto his side, and he threw up water before he began to suck in huge breaths of air.

"Oh, burn me. Burn me ..." Marshall was muttering over and over, between pants.

Arthur coughed and breathed, and his senses began to return. He felt ... hot. And cold. And hot again. His body was heavy, his extremities immobilized. He lay still and slowly became aware of his situation. Unable to speak let alone raise his head, he searched for the wolf through his blurry gaze.

A blob of black was beside him, and the scent of wet fur was thick in his nostrils. Afraid the animal had not survived, Arthur made a gurgling sound as he attempted to speak.

The blob of black shifted towards him, and the she-wolf's pink tongue licked his forehead.

Ouch. Arthur tried to move away. Her tongue felt scorching and rough. It left a trickle of hot energy everywhere she licked him. The streak of heat began to spread through him, searing him from the inside out.

Arthur arched as the strange agony pierced him to the core, reawakening his body in a way nothing natural ever could. Seconds later, he lay, breathing heavy and blinking rapidly, aware of everything from the rocky, cold, sandy bank he lay on to the shrieks of pain from the Ghouls to the landing of snowflakes on his cheeks and forehead.

The too intense sensations lasted a few more seconds, before both the energy and intensity of his world faded to normal levels.

Gasping for air, alarmed by the wolf's strange ability, Arthur rolled onto his stomach. All his limbs were healed and had returned to working order, to include the fist he pounded into a pulp, and the icy shadows were gone from his mind. His clothing remained drenched and cold. He pushed himself into a sitting position and gazed at the two figures on the bank before him.

Marshall was soaked and pale and beside him, a broken axe at his side, along with coiled rope. He had draped his cloak around the shivering, panting she-wolf.

"You did not run," Arthur said, unable to hide his surprise. He had written Marshall off as the weak-willed, philosophical, spoiled son of a man content to spend his entire life fostering the reputation of his ancestors rather than making the city better, as Arthur's misguided father tried to.

"I did not want your father to burn me at the stake for leaving you," Marshall replied.

Was there more to the Cruise heir than Arthur ever allowed to be possible? Mettle, perhaps, a touch of courage, or even honor?

"I believe you now. She is magic," Marshall said with a glance at the wolf who now seemed content to sit beside him. When they had met, she refused to allow him within five feet of her, while Arthur had no problem approaching. "So are you, Arthur."

Arthur's features shuttered.

Sudden silence was as jarring as the screams of the Ghouls.

Grateful for the distraction, Arthur climbed unsteadily to his feet. "We need to warm her up." He held out a hand to Marshall, who accepted it. Pulling the Cruise heir to his feet, Arthur released him and then bent over to rub down the wolf with the cloak.

"Arthur," Marshall said.

"I know. She is tougher than both of us, but I just want to make sure her fur does not freeze."

"Arthur." This time, Marshall sighed in irritation.

Facing him, Arthur was about to ask what his companion wanted when the words died on his lips.

The skinwalker stood in the middle of the ice, his face and hands red with blood from killing the Ghouls. He was in human form again, a tall Native of indistinguishable age, with piercing brown eyes and the stillness of a predator about to pounce. The man held an otherworldly presence, as if he were not fully present, despite appearing solid.

Arthur eased to face him fully. There was no mistaking the man from his visions, the one who, one day in the near future, would chase Tiana across the plains and probably kill her.

He also became suddenly aware his plan was never going to work. He had no weapons to confront the skinwalker who had massacred ten Ghouls without a single wound to show for it.

"I think he wants his magic wolf back," Marshall whispered. "And I think we should give it to him."

Frustration unfurled within Arthur, along with acknowledgment he was not going to win this, if it became a battle.

"I think you're right," he said reluctantly. Twisting, he motioned to the wolf. She shook off the cloak before trotting forward. When she reached him, she looked up with her golden eyes and nudged him with her nose, then continued onward.

The she-wolf circled the skinwalker and sat on her haunches beside him.

He continued to glare at Arthur. Without speaking, he turned away and began to cross the frozen river.

"Wait." The word was out before Arthur knew exactly what he was going to say next. "Please." He started forward.

The Native stopped.

"Are you mad?" Marshall snapped quietly and snatched his arm. "This is a truce. Let us take it and leave with our lives!"

Arthur shook him off and ventured several steps closer, slowing his pace to ensure the skinwalker was not about to transform. He could think of no other way to help Tiana, and he doubted – no, he *hoped* – never to be this close to a skinwalker ever again. "Just ... wait." He glanced over his shoulder at an astonished Marshall and gauged the distance to be far enough for the Cruise heir not to hear him. "I have seen you in a vision."

The Native turned.

"I have a recurring vision that began months ago," Arthur rushed on.

The skinwalker lowered his head and glared at Arthur. "What are you?" he asked in a low growl.

"I do not know," Arthur replied honestly. "But I know our paths crossed for a reason, and I know I have seen you many, many times before they did. Will you listen to me?" Acutely aware of Marshall inching closer, Arthur tried to keep his voice as low as possible. He glanced at the she-wolf, who was watching him. "She spoke to me, did she not?"

After a pause, the Native nodded.

"My abilities are not of my understanding," Arthur continued. "But I know, without a doubt, what I saw of you will come true."

"What is this vision?"

Arthur was quiet, debating what to say, how much to reveal. When it came to his sister, his first instinct was to protect her, not reveal her danger to the very man who threatened it. But how else did he explain the circumstances he wished to prevent than by addressing them directly?

"You try to murder my sister," he said finally. "This happens this spring, in a location I do not recognize."

The Native's scrutiny intensified. "For what reason?"

"Reason?" Marshall echoed with an uncomfortable laugh. "We saw what you did to those two villages. Do you need a reason?"

"Shut up!" Arthur snapped to him before addressing the Native. "I do not know."

"What form am I in?" the skinwalker asked.

Arthur blinked, not expecting the question. He shifted his gaze towards the sky, recalling the visions. "In each one, it's different. But mostly, you are in my vision as you are now. On rare occasion, you are a bear, and at times, a wolf and other times ... a creature I do not recognize from this world."

"But mostly this form," the Native repeated.

Arthur nodded. He waited for an explanation.

None came.

"I wanted to find you and well, I planned to kill you to protect her," Arthur admitted. "I am aware the odds are not with me this day. I want to hire you for the sole purpose of not murdering or harming my sister. It is my understanding you are a mercenary. My family is very powerful and very wealthy. I can give you anything you request."

"It so happens this is my fee," the Native said with a glimmer in his gaze.

"*What* is your fee?" Marshall asked.

"Whatever he dictates," Arthur said. "Correct?"

The Native studied him. "How will I know her?"

Not expecting this question, Arthur hesitated again. His instincts warned him not to answer, while his heart was desperate to utilize this interaction to his advantage, since he was not likely to receive a second opportunity.

"Your mark," Marshall said, nudging him.

Arthur pulled off his shirt and twisted to reveal the eagle tattooed on his shoulder. It was the mark of every Hanover, given to them shortly after birth. "She bears this mark, in the identical place on her body. It is unique to us."

He replaced his shirt. When he faced the skinwalker, the Native was striding away. His wolf trotted ahead of him.

Arthur's mind was not on him but on the uncomfortable memory sliding through him. Before the skinwalker attacked his camp, he had been talking to their Native guide, Running Deer, and Warner about the visions. Running Deer claimed the skinwalker could be hired – and that his price was unknown, for no one who ever hired him spoke of what they paid, except to say it was not money.

"I assume if he leaves us alive, he agrees," Marshall said, puzzled.

They both watched the skinwalker disappear into the snowstorm and forest, but neither of them moved for some time. Arthur suspected he and Marshall were feeling the same thing: wariness, laced with fear, after the encounter with the monster that killed the inhabitants of two villages, their encampment, and ten Ghouls.

"You should've asked him why he killed everyone in our camp," Marshall said.

"After what we saw him do in the villages, I don't think he had any reason," Arthur replied.

"Except your tent was the only one destroyed."

Arthur did not know what to say to this statement, for he had been thinking along a similar line.

"No vengeance for us this day," Marshall muttered. "Will you insist we track him tomorrow, after what we saw him do to the Ghouls? Or will you display some common sense for once and agree to return home?"

The longer they lingered, the less sense Arthur made about all that had happened.

"Let us go home," he said quietly. "We will need half my father's Shield to take on this kind of opponent."

"Agreed." Marshall spun and strode towards the horses located at the top of the embankment. "Maybe when we stop next, you can tell me about your deformity and what we were really doing here, because it had nothing to do with Warner."

Arthur scowled and trailed. While Marshall's bravery and persistence in helping him was impressive, Arthur was not about to trust the secrets of his family to the heir of the only other family in Lost Vegas with a legitimate claim on the city.

Marshall stopped so fast, Arthur collided with him. Before he could speak, Marshall whispered, "We might have a new problem."

Arthur looked in the direction where his companion faced.

Natives armed with firearms – weapons outlawed in the city after the riots of twenty five years ago – and traditional bone or iron weapons lined the top of the embankment, so still, they could have been statues, if not for the puffs of air each exhaled.

How long they had been there was impossible for Arthur to guess, just as he had no way of knowing if they had seen the two of them interacting with the skinwalker boogeyman even the Natives feared.

"They are Kutsipiuti," Marshall added. "Neutral."

"Then I will simply inform them of who I am, and they will allow us safe passage," Arthur said confidently.

"The arrogance that runs in your family is astounding," Marshall snapped quietly. "We have no agreements with them. For all intents and purposes, we are trespassing. And that one," he pointed, "is Diné, our enemy. Your father may be able to bully people around, but you cannot. Not out here, when we are exposed, vulnerable, and alone."

"And I suppose only the great Cruise heir can negotiate with them?" Arthur retorted.

"My family has been forced to be diplomatic for generations, while yours unleashes a new generation of madness upon us all every few decades. The Cruises have survived ten generations of Hanover madness, have we not?"

Arthur grounded his teeth. It was not the appropriate place or time for them to fight about whose family was lesser in its dedication to the city's survival. "Then go negotiate. If you fail, we will try it my father's way," he managed to say.

Marshall nodded. His jaw was clenched, and he was paler than usual. He pulled off his weapons and made a show of laying them out in the snow. Lifting his arms, he then began following the trail up the steep bank towards the Natives.

None of their observers made a move to fire upon them, though no one moved forward to greet Marshall either.

Arthur shivered, aware of how exposed they were, with the treacherous river behind them and no horses to flee.

At least I found the skinwalker, he thought. With any luck, the Natives would have news of Warner.

FOURTEEN

THE DREAM ABOUT ARTHUR FADED. Upon waking fully, Tiana understood it was not a true dream, but one of her fleeting visions.

She sat up, clenching the blankets hard enough for her fingers to ache.

Arthur was alone. Cold. Imprisoned? She had the sense he was somewhere he did not wish to be but could not see deeper into his surroundings to identify his circumstances. Except ... she knew where he was. He had drawn a familiar symbol in the dirt at his feet. Did he know she would see him, or did he draw absently?

She released her grip on the bedding and swung her legs off the bed. The marble floor was cool beneath her feet, and she snatched her clothing to dress. After a lifetime of being sealed away from the world, she had made it clear to the slaves that no one was to close the window, no matter how cold its draftiness made her room.

Seconds after she finished dressing, Tiana jumped at the loud knock at the door. She took up her usual guarded position, behind the table, near the window, with her shoulders hunched and her eyes down. The chilly morning breeze leaked through the window to graze her bare forearms, and she shivered.

The door opened. "Forgive me for disturbing you so early," George began. He closed the door behind him, sealing off their discussion from the two blind slaves in the hallway.

Before Tiana could respond, he spoke again.

"Warner returned."

Tiana looked up. "Arthur?" she breathed.

"Warner was alone. But he gave us hope to believe your brother is alive before collapsing," George replied. "Their camp was attacked, and Warner was the only person to escape. He said Arthur and Marshall Cruise were away from camp for the ceremonial first hunt."

Tiana's heart was in her throat, her mind swimming with questions. The messenger Arthur sent back had warned his father about the Cruises planning to target his heirs. Why had he ridden off with Marshall, if he knew the danger? "And then?" she asked.

"That's all he knows," George responded.

Her hope was all but dashed. "Who attacked them?"

"Bears."

Her brow furrowed. "Bears?"

"A group of them."

"Bears don't travel in groups, and should they not be hibernating?" she asked, recalling what she had read about the animals in one of her books.

"From what I understand, because of his condition, what he said made no sense, and this was an interpretation of what he likely meant."

"What exactly did he say?"

"I'm uncertain. My information comes indirectly from those who encountered him. They said a group of bears," he replied. "And he asked if you were safe."

"That was kind of him." Warmth bloomed in her cheeks. She had always thought Warner was handsome, and Arthur boasted often of the fighting prowess of his closest friend. "Is he well?"

"His fingers and toes are frostbitten, and he had not eaten in some time. He was dehydrated and sickly, but your father's physician believes he will recover with rest."

"Good." Tiana did not say what she wanted to, that she wished she could see Warner and speak to him herself about what happened. The desire melted as soon as it formed. She had been confined since she was a child. Her surroundings were different, but her father's intent to keep her hidden had not changed.

How, then, did she help her brother? Her father would never let her leave, and he was not likely to grant her request to speak to him either. She saw him only during the official events the family attended.

"Your father has already sent soldiers to the Hunt site to find Arthur," George added.

They will not find him. "Thank you for letting me know."

George bowed his head. "If I learn more, I will inform you immediately."

Tiana waited for him to leave before she crossed to the spacious closet, where she had hung the partially completed project she began as a child: the map disguised as a lavishly embroidered tapestry. She studied it, reviewing what she had pieced together of the outside world over the years.

Arthur had explained to her the general location of where the Winter Hunt occurred, and she touched the spot on the map, wishing she could touch her brother. The territories of at least two Native tribes ran between the city and the popular hunting spot, which was on the border of one of the tribes – the Diné – that declared eternal war on the city and its inhabitants. The danger every year came from this tribe. Their lands bordered with a people that wanted nothing to do with war, the Kutsipiuti, and which valued peace over alliances with anyone. It was out of respect for this peaceful tribe, whose members often negotiated with the city and its enemies, that the war between two ruthless enemies had stopped years before.

Her finger slid across the uneven threads of the tapestry to rest on the symbol Arthur had drawn in the ground. He had somehow wandered several days eastward from the hunting fields, past two villages, past the blue threads of a river, and along the territory of the neutral Natives neighbored by the city's enemies.

He had drawn a waterfall in the dirt, a plot of land that traded hands often between the neutral Natives and the city's enemies.

With the final gust of winter blanketing the world in snow, and stuck with a Cruise, Arthur was not likely to survive long, if he were forced into the territory of their enemies or worse – captured by them. In any circumstance, her father's men would be too far away to help Arthur before he was killed or starved or died of exposure.

The sense of urgency in her breast was not new, but knowing what she did now, that her brother was exposed and alone, too far for those dispatched by her father to help him, she could not help hating herself more for being so helpless.

Aveline had told her many times that she would never survive a day in the city, let alone outside Lost Vegas.

Thinking of her friend, Tiana gripped the pendant dangling in the middle of her chest. It was identical to the one Aveline wore, and she touched it absent-mindedly whenever she thought of her guardian.

Tiana had spent the better part of her days in bed reviewing how to circumvent her own weaknesses. Her conclusion: she needed Aveline, or perhaps, now that he had returned, someone like Warner, to help her navigate the great world beyond the city to find Arthur.

Her greatest challenge, though, was not one she could puzzle through. How did she escape her room, which was always locked, without anyone noticing, long enough for her father not to catch her? And what would she do, if she did escape? How did she free her brother, if he were imprisoned?

If she could escape her room, would Arthur's longtime protector be well enough, and willing, to venture into the forest again to find her brother? Or had his near-death experience soured him on trying?

I cannot talk to him to ask, she realized.

Her whole life, she had fantasized about running away to the mythical Free Lands to the north, without experiencing the frustration unfurling in her breast.

What had changed, aside from her room? Had murdering Matilda, or meeting Aveline, altered her perception of remaining hidden away for the rest of her life? Was Arthur's danger so great only someone with nothing to offer could help him? She was useless here – she would be less than useless trying to help him.

With her birthday looming, and the visions of Arthur as well as those detailing her death the night of her eighteenth year fresh in her mind, she felt the urge to try, no matter how useless everyone thought she was.

Tiana dropped her hand from the tapestry with a deep sigh.

For the first time in her life, she was not able to accept her fate with her normal grace and resignation, not when her brother's life was on the line.

Tiana dragged a satchel out of a trunk at the foot of the map. She chewed her lip, torn between subsiding into the helpless girl she always felt she was and the woman who wanted her freedom. She pulled the contents of the satchel free and studied them. Based on what she knew of the world outside the city, she would need a change of clothing, basic medical materials, a second pair of boots, a map she had drawn, and the money she had found in Aveline's belongings.

It did not seem like enough, though, and she puzzled over what else she was missing. She dared not ask George or the slaves. After a moment, she shoved everything away, tears of desperation in her eyes.

Why did she bother planning to escape, when she knew she could never survive on her own? Was the world, and Arthur, better off without her in it at all? What purpose did her life hold, except to be an inconvenience to everyone around her?

Tiana wiped away tears and left the closet to rest, think, and plan.

DOZENS OF FLOORS BELOW, Aveline sat in a cell little larger

than Tiana's former room. She had been paraded through the prison that existed beneath the servants' floors of the great pyramid, and then deposited into a cell with no windows and a solitary light that flickered annoyingly, when it worked at all.

Two weeks after being caught by the Shield, she could not stop berating herself for behaving in a way no professional assassin ever would. The guards had followed a trail of blood to her location within the walls and arrested her, while she lay on the floor, floating between consciousness and the dark unknown, dwelling on her non-existent chances of taking Tiana to the Free Lands.

"Tiana would make a better assassin," she mumbled ruefully and rested her head back against the cool wall. She absently toyed with the pendant around her neck. It glowed, an indication Tiana was relatively close. As long as the two were not across the city from one another, a tiny light remained deep within the center. "I'll figure something out, Tiana. I don't think we'd ever make it to the Free Lands anyway."

The room was heated to a comfortable temperature, the bed unusually cozy, and her three meals a day heartier than what she had eaten on the streets but not quite to the quality reserved for Tiana and the other privileged members of the outer city.

Her prison was better than anywhere she had lived, even when her father was alive. They had slept under piles of furs during the winter to combat the dreadful drafts in his cabin. More than one winter, she had awakened to find her weapons frozen together.

Smiling, Aveline closed her eyes and recalled the simpler days with her father. The Devil of the inner city was feared by everyone – and loved her as the night did the moon.

Her warm memories slid away as she recalled her last night sitting beside his body. She had not had the chance to mourn him in private. Now that she did, she experienced only ... fury towards Karl, who betrayed them, and towards herself for not being more aware. Not sorrow or anything else she expected, but anger so intense, it left her sweating and her clothing too tight, while the Devil's blood within her demanded to be sated.

Her father had always warned her against releasing her anger. Aveline recalled his stern words and could not help wishing she could hear him say them aloud again, one last time. She would happily listen to him lecture her, if it meant he was still alive.

His loss consumed her anger, and she slumped, defeated by the battle within her. She was sweating again. For the past week, she had begun to sweat profusely for several hours a day and blamed the poor circulation of the air in her cell.

She stretched out her legs and rubbed her eyes before fanning her face. Between meals, she worked out in what ways she could in the confined space and took naps out of boredom. The only way she could tell how many days had passed was by counting how many times she was brought eggs for her breakfast.

She counted the marks she had etched into the wall.

Thirteen days. She had not spoken to anyone, and knew nothing of what had happened to Tiana. Screaming at the guards, begging them, throwing her food – nothing had made any difference, and she had sunk into general apathy around day five.

The window on the door – where guards pushed her food through to her – slid open. Aveline obediently rose and placed her breakfast tray on the table, so the soldier outside could reach it. She sat down on the bed and watched the window slide closed, prepared to spend another day in solitary confinement fighting her boredom.

To her surprise, the window opened again. She waited, wondering if they had brought her more food for some reason, only to hear the soldier outside her cell speak.

"Place your hands through the window."

Aveline remained where she sat, uncertain if she had heard him or if her mind had finally snapped after her days of silence.

The soldier repeated the order.

She rose and obeyed, sticking her hands through the window. Cool, metal cuffs encircled her wrists.

The soldier opened the door, and she pulled her hands back through. The metal cuffs were heavy and connected by a thick chain. Two heavily armed soldiers stood ready outside her door.

"Overkill for a little girl like me, don't you think?" she asked, trying to portray herself as not a threat. The second she spotted a viable exit, she was taking it. If the soldiers were caught unaware, her chances of escape were better.

Neither spoke, though one motioned for her to walk down the hallway.

Aveline did so, frowning when she saw the hall ended in a dead end, some three meters ahead, and only one door was located between her cell and the dead end. She paused in the doorway of the second room and peered in. It was three times larger than her cell and consisted of two chairs and four lights dangling from the ceiling.

"Enter and be seated," one of the soldiers ordered.

Anxious to leave her cell for good, Aveline welcomed the change from her normal routine and entered the room. She chose the chair facing the door and sat, gazing around. There was even less here to keep her attention than in her cell.

She jingled the iron chain between her hands and sank down into the chair until the base of her skull rested on the chair's back. Gazing at the light overhead, she waited to see how much less interesting her stay in the prison could get. Were they cleaning her cell, and that was why they placed her in this room? Was she to be interviewed? Executed?

Something! She thought, out of her mind with the need for fresh air and freedom.

She sat quietly for some time, until the chair became too hard to be comfortable. Shifting, Aveline sat up straight just as the door swung open. A tall man with reddish hair stepped through. Well-dressed in tailored clothing and custom boots, he smelled lightly of weapon oil, walked with a carriage stiff enough to look painful, and wore the trimmed goatee that was currently in fashion among the men of the outer city.

Within seconds of his entrance, she had no doubt as to his elevated status, even if she did not know exactly who he was. Warden? Wealthy patron?

"Your father was rumored to be the Devil," he began.

She blinked, not expecting him to know her exact identity, or to confront her about it in his first breath.

The man drew the second chair towards him and sat facing her, his posture straighter than the chair. At this distance, she became aware of an odd, familiar tingle in the air around him, almost too faint to notice, except that it made the hair on her arms lift enough for the movement to tickle.

"You were hired to protect Tiana Hanover, were you not?" he asked.

Aveline shifted. From her short time as Tiana's protector, she had discovered more duplicity about the circumstances of her job than she ever thought possible. She definitely knew better than to trust anyone in Tiana's inner circle, except maybe Arthur.

"Let me rephrase," the man said when she remained silent. "I know you were hired to protect her."

Aveline glared at him, not caring for the dismissive way he talked to her.

"And you no doubt discovered her ... deformity."

Aveline did not respond.

"I know you are not mute," the man said. "Just as I know you are the daughter of the Devil and why you are here."

Was it bait? He spoke too confidently for her to believe him to be lying about her circumstances. "How?" she asked. As far as she knew, only Tiana's brother – who had hired her – had any idea who her father was.

"It is my duty to know."

An awkward silence dropped between them. His charged air became powerful, and she shifted in her seat. She recognized the sensation from when she dealt with an agitated Tiana, who somehow managed to fill the air around her, and throughout the entire apartment belonging to the Hanover's, with the strange charge, whenever she was upset.

Tiana had claimed her brother was also deformed in this way, capable of seeing future events in the manner of a clairvoyant. The sheltered girl had claimed their mother possessed the deformity, which was why she was burned.

Instincts whispering, as they did often around Tiana, Aveline leaned forward, interested suddenly in the man before her.

"You're Tiana's father," she said.

"I am."

"How is that possible?" she pressed. "I thought her deformity originated in her birth mother."

The Hanover ruler's gaze cooled even further. "You are sharp. Like father, like daughter."

Aveline frowned, uncertain if he referred to her or to his own daughter. She dismissed the thought, doubting her father had ever met the man in front of her, who had issued a large bounty for the chief assassin's capture long ago. "What do you want?" she asked instead. "Me to admit I murdered your wife, so you can burn me?"

"Is that what happened?"

"Sure. Knocked her head clean off," Aveline said without hesitation. Tiana openly feared her father, a tyrant known for burning dozens every week. Aveline was not about to give him ammunition to murder his daughter.

"And..." he prodded.

"That's it."

"You did it to protect her?"

"Of course. That's why I was hired, right?"

Tiana's father gave nothing away. His features were calm and colder than the newly fallen snow. With a receding hairline and pale blue eyes, he radiated control, from the careful placement of his hands on one thigh to his rigid posture. Her father had possessed his own game face, his public persona, which was similar to this man's.

"We both know you didn't do this," Tiana's father said finally. "I know what my daughter is."

Aveline studied him. Once again, she sensed he was not trying to bait her. He had either figured out what Tiana did or confronted his daughter, who did not have the sense to lie.

"Is that why you locked her up in a cell worse than those in your prison?" she snapped. "Punishment for being different?"

"My relationship with my daughter is complicated."

"You don't have one!"

"She is alive, is she not?" he countered softly.

"You massacred her twin and mother. Tiana would have been better off burning as an infant than imprisoned her entire life," Aveline snapped. "If that wasn't enough, you let Matilda starve and drug her."

"In this, we agree. Had I not spared her, or entrusted her care to my deceased wife, I would not have my current problems," he agreed. "Tiana should have been burnt at the stake as a child, and I regret not following through with my instinct."

Aveline stared at him. He said the words with the same matter-of-fact tone with which Tiana spoke about her mother's barbaric death. Aveline's father would never have spoken about his late wife or daughter in this manner, and it was beyond Aveline's ability to understand how any man could. Her father was the Devil, but Tiana's father was the real monster.

"Here we are," he continued, unfazed. "My son hired you, but I did not think he believed her danger to be from Matilda, or he would have warned me before he left the city."

"Then you are both fools. It was obvious to me the day I met Tiana," Aveline replied. "Matilda was poisoning her slowly every day."

"I have dealt with the Cruises," he said. "What I am uncertain about is how to handle you."

"I'm surprised the solution isn't to burn me like everyone else."

The Hanover patriarch was quiet for a moment before he leaned forward, elbows on his knees. "Seventeen, almost eighteen years ago, a man from the streets did me a favor. Not because he cared for me or for what I wanted. In fact, he loathed everything I stand for. But he understood inaction to be ... dangerous. Not just to himself but to those he cared about."

She frowned. "What're you talking about?"

"Discovering you in the center of my household, and understanding who and what you are, as well learning my own son sought you out, I am left in a position where I cannot simply burn you," he continued, ignoring her question. "The Devil's blood you carry makes you valuable."

"I don't understand," Aveline said, listening carefully. "You're saying you knew my father?"

"We met but once, during the Devil's Massacre. You are familiar with the massacre?"

"Of course. Over the course of three days, my father unleashed his Devil blood and slaughtered a thousand people, by hand, on his own," she said, pride in her voice.

"This is what you were led to believe?" Tiana's father had arched an eyebrow.

"It's what happened. Why wouldn't I believe it?" she retorted.

"The Massacre occurred, and the Devil's blood was involved. But your father was not the Devil who slaughtered a thousand people," he replied. "Your mother was. Your father stopped her."

Had she not been so surprised, she would have laughed. "That's ridiculous! My father was the Devil. Everyone knows this!"

"Has there been another massacre since that one?"

"My mother died in childbirth. My father lost his mind and went on a rampage. If anything ever happened to me, he might react that way again, but nothing ever did."

"Hmm." Tiana's father was not impressed. "What if I told you there were several other massacres, in the villages and cities within two hundred miles of here, corresponding to the two hundred years in which your mother's life spanned, and leading up to the arrival of your mother in my city?"

Two hundred ... what is going on? Aveline was caught too off guard to process his question.

"Your mother could not control her deformity, but you appear to be able to, perhaps because you are a half-breed," he observed. "If your time in solitary did not cause you to react, then I believe your father's blood may be the key to stabilizing what you are. Unless ... have you reached your eighteenth birthday?"

Aveline's mouth opened, but no words would form, for she had no idea how to retort such a statement. She began to wonder if she had lost her mind in solitary confinement, and this entire discussion was a hallucination.

But would not her hallucination make sense to her, if it stemmed from her own mind?

"There is the idea your Devil's blood will not emerge until you are eighteen," Tiana's father said, un-fazed by her shocked silence. "When do you celebrate your birth?"

He waited this time. After a moment, she answered. "Next month."

"On the nineteenth, by chance?"

"Around there. I don't know the exact date."

"You and Tiana share more than your unusual deformities," he said. His gaze lit up – and Aveline had the distinct feeling it was not for a good reason. "How fortuitous."

She stood and pinched her arm to ensure she was awake and in her right mind. The air around them crackled with his charged energy, enough to make her edgier than before. When Tiana used her bizarre abilities, it was overtly evident. The air was filled with that same charge, but Aveline was unable to pinpoint what the Hanover patriarch did. Was he trying to alter her mind? Would she know if he were? What else could he be doing, if he were using his power without any sign of what he did?

Her cell was starting to look far more appealing than a conversation with a madman. "What do you want?" She bit off the words.

"Arthur found you for a reason. Not anyone – *you*. The bearer of the Devil's blood, despite the fact I never revealed you or your father's identities to him." Tiana's father paused, pensive. "There must be a reason for this, and I can think of only one. If he believes Tiana's danger to be so great, only you can save her, then I cannot interfere. At least, not until he is found and returned to the city, when I can question him about his visions."

Aveline hid her surprise. The Hanover leader knew his son was deformed and did not treat him as he did Tiana.

"It is in your benefit not to reveal her secret, just as it is to my advantage not to reveal yours. I would not wish my enemies to know what kind of guard dog I have, until you destroy them," he continued, oblivious to her flush of anger. "Your mother slaughtered everyone who came near her, except for you and your father. I believe you will share this discretion and ability to protect those you are charged with protecting."

"For the last time, my father bore the – "

"Believe what you will. As long as you know to protect my daughter with your deformity."

"And if I can't control my Devil blood on my eighteenth birthday?" she snapped.

He shrugged one shoulder elegantly. "I do not feel this is a problem." Tiana's father stood. "You will cause no further trouble, unless my daughter is in danger. In which case, you may transform into whatever form you must to save her."

What was he talking about? The Devil's blood rendered her father invincible. It did not change his form!

Tiana's father strode to the door.

Aveline remained where she was, reeling from the conversation. Of everything he had said, she could not get over the idea he somehow thought her mother was a two hundred year old monster!

"Wait!" she cried as he opened the door. She wracked her

thoughts to uncover the insistent instinct that was worrying her about Tiana. "Tell me why."

"Why ... what?" he replied.

"Why you spared Tiana as an infant and why you wish to protect her now," she replied.

He closed the door and faced her. "Hanover's never harm Hanover's," he replied.

Did the man who torched children, women, and the poor every week actually *love* his daughter? Aveline studied his face, but saw no affection whatsoever. Was this merely some sort of twisted sense of duty, since he seemed incapable of love?

"You had no trouble burning her twin," she pointed out.

"Think on that, and you will understand the answer," he said and then opened the door.

Before she could react, he had exited.

Aveline remained where she was, even though he left the door open. She was trying to understand what he was talking about, or how much of a madman he had to be in order to alter the events of her past and claim to want to protect Tiana in one breath then wish she had died as a child in the next. No logical explanation formed for his assertions about her family or even about his own daughter.

She concluded he had to be utterly insane – the unpredictable madman he was rumored to be on the streets.

She had never met someone she did not think she could figure out. What would her father say about the madman? How would he advise her to proceed?

Carefully. Her instincts were whispering again, this time in quiet warning. Tiana's father was the most powerful person in the city, and he was insane. That made him dangerous.

A soldier appeared in the doorway.

She shifted her stance, in case he tried to grab her.

"You are to report to your former duty station," he directed her. "All offenses have been officially pardoned, and you are to perform to the standards required of you."

Aveline promptly held out her arms, not about to miss the opportunity to be free. Of everywhere she could think of going, Tiana's room was at the bottom of the list, below her own prison cell. But she also wanted to check in on the Hanover girl before leaving the pyramid for air and to find Rocky, who was probably worried about her.

And ... something about the certainty with which Tiana's father spoke left her wanting to reaffirm what she knew of the Devil's Massacre. For a moment, she thought Tiana's father was going to insist the Devil had murdered his wife – Aveline's mother – to stop the massacre. The Hanover patriarch had stopped just short of such a statement, which struck Aveline as odd. If he were pushing his mad perspective of the past on her, why not finish the narrative he started? He had not hesitated to make any of his other ridiculous claims.

Why am I entertaining his version of events at all? She asked herself, perplexed. Her life had changed in every way since her father's death but this felt ... different. Was she under the influence of Tiana's father without knowing it? Were these thoughts hers, or planted by him?

The soldier freed her hands and removed the restraints, draping them over his arm as he replaced the keys at his waist. He stepped aside and motioned for her to walk ahead of him.

The second soldier led her through the underground prison and to a stairwell. He escorted her through the servants' area and then to the main floor before leaving her at the service elevator.

Already, Aveline could breathe more easily and had even sneaked a peek through one of the open doors to see the mud churned snow and grey morning. She was antsy with the need to feel free again and experience the bite of winter after her solitary confinement. Eager to ensure Tiana was alive and safe, Aveline rode the elevator to the very top of the pyramid and exited past the guards standing on duty in front of the Hanover's apartments. She barely glanced towards the finery and opulence that had once engaged her attention, only slowing when she reached the cul de sac at the end of the hallway where the personal rooms of the Hanover's were located.

The door to Tiana's room had been removed.

Aveline frowned and stepped into the small space. The furniture was gone, the window boarded up once more, and the closet with its secret entrance into the walls sealed up by concrete. The tiny room had been scrubbed of blood and dust alike.

"She was given Matilda's room," George said from behind her.

"Hi, George."

"I wish I could say this is a pleasure."

"Good to see you, too." Aveline faced him with a grimace.

He held out a familiar set of clothing in slave grays, with a green sash. She glanced down at the clothes she had been wearing. If she smelled, she was used to it, though she looked forward to bathing soon.

"Thanks," she said and accepted the clothes. "Anything I need to know about?"

George folded his hands in front of him. "No."

"All right." Already at her limit with the passive aggressive slave, Aveline turned towards Tiana's door. It was locked. From her peripheral, she saw George hold out the key.

Not much has changed, she thought, irritated to know Tiana was still locked away like a prisoner.

Then again, the Hanover girl was probably safe locked in her room, where her madman of a father was not reminded of how he should have let her die so long ago.

Aveline drew a deep breath, hoping her friend was well, and uncertain what to tell her about the conversation with her father. Anxious to check on Rocky, Aveline debated returning later before she decided to see Tiana first.

Please don't cry, she begged Tiana silently and drew a deep breath. She had no idea what kind of a mess Tiana would be after what happened the last time they were together. Was the Hanover girl even able to leave her bed?

FIFTEEN

AVELINE UNLOCKED the door and opened it. She stepped inside the doorway, gaze settling on a woman in slave clothing standing near the middle of Tiana's room.

The window was open, and Aveline felt her body relax of its own accord as she breathed in the smells of the city and winter. Tension slid out of her, and she sucked in a deep breath. She closed her eyes, pretending she was outside.

"Pursy, you are dismissed," George called into the room.

Aveline opened her eyes and stepped out of the doorway. The woman at its center turned towards George's voice, took a step, and then tripped over the rug. Aveline started forward when she noticed the woman's eyelids had been sewn shut. Startled, she stayed where she was as the blinded woman shuffled to the door before leaving.

"What –" Aveline started.

Before she could say another word, Tiana had flung her arms around her with such force, Aveline barely caught her balance in time to prevent them both from tumbling to the ground.

"I knew you had to be alive!" Tiana's high-pitched squeal made Aveline flinch.

Pleased to see the girl, Aveline was nonetheless not accustomed to open affection. She pried Tiana off her and pushed her back, holding her at a distance with her hands planted on the blonde girl's shoulders. "You don't hug assassins," she said firmly. "Okay?"

Tiana nodded eagerly, smiling widely. Her deformity –pupil-less black eyes that swallowed the whites of her eyes – caught Aveline off guard again, but she managed to hide her revulsion this time.

"Where were you?" Tiana asked. "Did my father hurt you? Did you hear about the Cruises?"

"Were you crying?" Aveline countered, studying Tiana's sun-starved features.

Tiana sighed. "I know." She continued to smile. "But everything's going to be okay now. I have it all figured out."

Burn me. What could that possibly mean? Aveline did not feel prepared to ask.

"Are you hungry?" Tiana asked. "I eat real food now, all day long." She spun and hurried across the cavernous bedroom to a bowl of fruit on a table near the bed. "Look! All this is mine!"

Aveline watched her. She was also unable to look upon Tiana the first time without recalling when they had last been together. Tiana was limping, and her arms remained bandaged, the results of her self-inflicted wounds, when she tried to kill herself after murdering Matilda with magic.

But it was the subtle changes in Tiana that Aveline noticed more. Tiana wore real clothing, not the sleeping gown she used to live in all day long. She had not hesitated to look Aveline in the eye. Her cheeks were flushed pink. While her frame was no heavier than before, she walked with a spring in her step and held her head up.

"Look. Bananas!" Tiana exclaimed and hurried back with the bowl of fruit. She held it out to Aveline.

Aveline took an apple absently then caught Tiana's wrist. Fresh blood marred the bandage on her arm.

Tiana pulled her hand back self-consciously and ducked her gaze.

"You're still cutting," Aveline observed.

Tiana offered no explanation. She returned to the table and replaced the fruit. She held her arm against her chest. "You look well. My father did not hurt you, did he?"

Aveline shook her head. She did not know what to say to Tiana about the bizarre meeting with the Hanover patriarch. "He said he would do nothing about me until your brother returns."

Tiana's smile faded. "If he returns."

"What has happened?"

Tiana drew a deep breath and then told her everything: the burning of the Cruises, the blinding of her servants and the news about her brother that brought tears to Tiana's eyes.

Insane doesn't do Tiana's father justice, Aveline thought after she had heard it all. She had not expected the Hanover leader to respond as fast or decisively as to massacre the entire Cruise family. Even street dogs like Aveline understood the significance of eradicating the descendants of the city's much-revered founders.

"I missed a lot," she said in the pause that followed Tiana's story. "Are you being treated better?"

"If Arthur does not return, my father will likely marry me off to someone to produce an heir, so the city stays under the family's control," Tiana said with a frown.

"Like a broodmare?"

Tiana nodded.

"You plan on agreeing to this?" Aveline asked.

"What choice do I have?"

None, with a father like hers, Aveline knew.

"I am happy you are here," Tiana said with a small smile. "Do you think we should rescue my brother?"

Aveline had forgotten how blunt the sheltered girl could be on occasion. After meeting Tiana's father, she no longer wondered where it came from.

"Absolutely not," she said without hesitation. "I'm certain your father sent out people to find your brother."

"He did. Over twenty of them, and he is dispatching a second party to hunt for the meat we need." Tiana grew serious. "Arthur's protector made it back to the city. He can go with us to find Arthur. It will only take two days to reach Arthur, and then maybe we can negotiate his release in a day or two and return two days later."

"Didn't you say your father already sent Shield soldiers to find him?" Aveline asked, brow furrowing.

"Yes, but they will not find him," Tiana replied. "That is why we must go."

"Let's take a step back," Aveline said. She had also forgotten how difficult it was to deal with Tiana sometimes, for the Hanover girl had no common sense whatsoever. "How do you know they won't find your brother?"

"I saw him in one of my dreams. He is not where they are looking for him," Tiana answered.

"You did not think to tell your father this, before he sent the Shield to find him?"

"I did not know until this morning," Tiana replied. "Now that you are back, we can go."

"Absolutely not," Aveline said firmly. "It's not safe for you, especially not in the middle of the snowstorms we've been having."

"But who will rescue Arthur?" Tiana pressed, the high-pitched note in her voice revealing she was likely to cry soon. Her lower lip trembled.

"Don't start," Aveline warned. "You'd be of no use to him. You'd be dead in a day."

"Warner is the greatest warrior in the city. He will escort us," Tiana insisted. "Besides, I will be dead soon, if I do not act. I have told you my dream. Maybe this is why – because Arthur does not make it back."

"We don't know that!"

"You know he would never let anyone hurt me. If I die in my visions, then this must be why." Tiana's unguarded expression was a combination of sorrow and hope.

"I've never left the city, Tiana!" Aveline exclaimed. "In the city, I can keep you alive. One we leave, I might be able to hunt, but I don't know how to navigate terrain like a Native would, and I can't speak the languages of any of the Natives, even if I'm a half-breed."

"Warner can, and we can ask your friend Rocky to –"

Aveline stared at her. Tiana had never been insistent in their time together, and she had never discussed anything at all with this much enthusiasm or emotion. The sad little girl who huddled away in her room had transformed, and Aveline was at a loss to explain how or why. Was this the effect of Matilda being gone? Without someone to crush her spirit, was Tiana blooming?

Is this a good thing? Aveline could not help but think. If Tiana gushed about marrying a wealthy man, Aveline would be annoyed but understanding. But Tiana's dreams were of a dangerous nature, of escaping the city, and she had put enough thought into it to include Rocky and draw a map, which she held up for Aveline to see.

"Is this about your brother or the Free Lands?" Aveline asked.

Tiana flushed.

"You don't plan on coming back, after we find him."

The Hanover girl fell quiet.

Of every nightmare in existence, Aveline could think of none worse than taking Tiana outside the walls. Not because Aveline did not wish to help her friend, but because she believed doing so would be the fastest way to see Tiana hurt, probably dead, within a day.

With no sense of the world outside the pyramid in which she lived, Tiana's eyes glowed with excitement, and Aveline could not help but feel ill prepared to deal with the girl she was charged with protecting.

"Tiana, this is my home. I'm a seventh generation assassin. I want to take my father's place one day. Why would I want to leave?" Aveline asked, frustrated already. Whether it was the time alone with her thoughts, or the lack of control over her changing world, Aveline felt ready to explode. She was sweating again, too, adding too her irritation.

"We can come back," Tiana said reluctantly. "Will you think about it?"

I'd rather burn, Aveline answered silently. "Let's just ... slow down. I'll talk to George and have him tell your father that Arthur isn't where they think he is. The simplest, and safest, solution is to let them handle it, and for you to stay right here," she reasoned aloud. She could think of nothing worse than hiking across the wilderness while Tiana cried about ... everything.

Tiana's features fell into sorrow, and she folded in upon herself, the way she had when Matilda used to scream at her.

Aveline groaned. "Don't look at me like that!" she exclaimed. "I'll think about it, okay? We will find some kind of ... I don't know. Middle ground." Even as she said the words, she had no idea how that was even possible in this situation.

But Tiana smiled, and Aveline was reminded of how she had always tried to balance Tiana's delicate feelings with the harsh reality of their world. Maybe sneaking Tiana out for a day trip into the city would be enough to satisfy her curiosity.

"I haven't been outside in two weeks," Aveline said. "I need some air and to check on my friend Rocky. He's probably worried about me. We can figure out what to do about Arthur when I get back."

"Very well," Tiana replied.

What is she thinking? Without another word, Aveline tossed her clothing on the table near the hearth, turned, and left.

Aveline strode through the Hanover's luxurious apartment and rode down the servant's elevator. She had stepped outside, into the brisk winter morning, before she registered where exactly she was.

Aveline sucked in winter air that stung her lungs and shook out her newfound tension after the talk with Tiana.

Could nothing stay constant in her life long enough for her to find her footing?

She stood in place, observing the daily activities of the city dwellers, before striking off in the direction of the inner city to search for Rocky in one of the many hiding places where he was known to stay.

Her mind went from Tiana's mad request to Karl, and her step quickened. She had seen his face in her dreams every night while trapped in prison. What was worse: she experienced the same sense of loss when she thought of him as when she thought of her father, albeit lesser in intensity. How was it possible for her to mourn Karl, the man who betrayed her father and lied to her?

Hours alone to think had resulted in her acceptance that there could be no misunderstanding, no explanation, for what Karl had done. What remained now was finding out *why* and just how far Karl's betrayal ran. She was resolved to hearing the truth directly from him, and fulfilling the oath she took to protect Tiana, before she appealed to the Guild for inclusion as an assassin.

Guild. Arthur.

Aveline cursed under her breath, suddenly recalling the reason why she, too, should have been concerned about whether or not Arthur made it back alive. He had paid off her father's debts in exchange for protecting Tiana – and he had promised to become her benefactor, and buy her a sponsor, so she could join the Guild as a full-fledged assassin.

Without his influence, she would need to secure a new benefactor, or at least, curry favor with sympathizers who would not begrudge her for breaking the Guild's rules. Without a benefactor, her chances of becoming an official assassin were slim. She was likely to remain an apprentice until she had backing.

Arthur was not the only option, but he was the easiest option for her to find favor with the Guild and follow in her father's footsteps.

The Hanover's were quickly becoming the source of a massive headache. Determined to focus on her task at hand, she pushed all of them from her mind.

Aveline glanced at the cloudy sky, uncertain if her father were watching but hoping he might not be, until she had righted her breaking of his sacred rules. She shivered in the cold wintery day.

More snow was beginning to fall, and she had been too anxious to leave to be concerned with finding a cloak or heavy coat.

Had Rocky learned more about Karl and his abandonment of the Guild while she was missing?

Avoiding Guild Main – the headquarters of the assassins – was necessary, since her existence was not widely known, and she did not want wagging tongues to spread word to Karl.

When she reached the familiar footpaths and roads of the inner city, Aveline broke into a run to keep warm. Snow had been cleared or beaten down on the main walkways while four-foot tall piles sat on corners and blocked alleys. Several times, she was forced to take different routes than normal to avoid ice or snow piles.

She checked three of Rocky's normal spots without finding him before stealing a coat from an unaware passerby. Aveline took up a position in an alley near one of the major suppliers of weapons to watch for Rocky. There was always a chance he was on a mission, but she suspected he would not accept one if she were missing. Assassins visited this merchant regularly to purchase new wares or trade worn ones or, in the case of Rocky, to test and handle a bone sword he could not yet afford to buy.

Several hours passed while she waited. Aveline remained at the mouth of the alley until her toes were numbed from the cold snow beneath her feet, and she was shivering. Only when she did not feel as if she could stand another second in that spot did she leave. Rocky had not been by all day, which left several more options as to where he could be within the inner city. None of them were appealing, though, not when she had not thought to bring weapons and dreaded running into anyone who might know her.

Impatient to find Rocky and upset with herself for being unprepared to face any problems she ran into, Aveline pushed away from the building she leaned against and left the weapons' merchant area of the market. Rather than head back to the outer city and Tiana, she found herself on another familiar path, this one towards her home. She pulled up the hood of her coat far enough so no one could see her features as she passed the impoverished residents of the inner city.

Passing a butcher's, she missed a step, recalling the source of the fresh meat hanging from hooks in the window. Aveline shuddered and suppressed a flicker of Devil's fire within her.

One day, she would be ready to take on the brothels that sold young children to butchers to feed the inner city. One day, she would return to her birthright: the Guild. Both of those events would have to wait until after she had found Rocky and confronted Karl and learned the truth about Karl's betrayal.

Aveline reached her father's cabin and stopped across the street.

Her home had been burnt to the ground. She studied the ashes, distraught by the destruction, and feeling unusually vulnerable. Her whole life had passed in the cabin. She had always imagined she would live there until she was old and white haired, caring for her elderly father, while they both reminisced about their exciting careers as assassins.

She could never go home again. The sense of being adrift, and overwhelmed, returned. She had no idea what to do, or where to live, when her mission protecting Tiana was finished. Arthur had promised to buy her a sponsor in the Guild, but if he died outside the city, he could not help her at all.

Had he known how tightly her fate would be tied to his own and Tiana's?

Why did the Hanover siblings suddenly seem like they could become permanent fixtures in her life, when she wanted them to be a mission that helped her become who her father wanted her to be?

"What are we waiting for?" Rocky's low voice melted from the air behind her.

Aveline released a sigh, grateful her friend was alive and well. "You. I've been stalking you all day."

"I've been waiting for you where you work."

She turned and saw him in the same ill-fitted slave's clothing he had worn the last time they met. A smile escaped. Rocky was a welcome splash of darkness against the heavily falling snow.

"Where were you?" he asked.

She gave a bitter laugh. "Long story. Did Karl burn my home down?"

"Looters, I believe," Rocky replied. "Karl's deep in hiding. Some of the Guild members think he's outside the city somewhere."

"Where? Why?" she demanded.

Rocky smiled. "He angered a lot of people, and many of them happen to be assassins."

It made sense, though she had yet to learn the full story behind his break from the Guild, aside from his anger at being shunned as its next leader. There had to be more, and a reason for his betrayal.

"Come on," Rocky said. "I have a new place near here. We can talk." His boots crunched in the snow as he walked away.

Aveline lingered, eyes falling again on her destroyed home. Her life had changed in ways she never would have guessed that night. Some part of her understood there was no going back, but she began to wonder how far off her intended path she had already drifted, and whether or not she would ever find her way back.

SIXTEEN

THE SECOND VISION of Arthur came with twilight, when the world outside Tiana's window was swallowed by a combination of snow flurries and darkness.

A draft colder than that emanating from the window brushed her. Tiana reached out blindly to steady herself as the image of Arthur appeared in her mind.

COLD ... alone ... bleeding ... Arthur sat in a metal cage, left out to starve. His head rested against the frame of his cage while blood dripped from various wounds into the slushy pink snow beneath his body.

"OH, ARTHUR!" she whispered. Her breath caught. The vision began to fade, and she started to open her eyes, when *he* appeared again. The man inside a beast.

The images morphed from night and cold into a cool spring morning. This time, she was able to make out her surroundings more than she had the first time she witnessed the man-beast hiding in the brush. She had returned to that moment in the future.

Tiana turned and made out the shapes of those she knew: Warner, Aveline, Rocky and two others. They were standing outside a tent, the only manmade structure within sight, speaking to a Native whose profile bore a scar down the side of his face.

In a flash, the scene changed again. One second, the beast was crouching in the brush, watching her friends. The next, he was a blur of fur and blood. The world righted itself, and she stared in shock at what remained.

Not one beast but two were fighting in the center of the small campsite. Rocky, Warner, and one of the strangers lay in pieces on the ground, while a smaller beast had materialized out of nowhere to challenge the first one.

The larger creature slammed the smaller one into the ground hard enough to daze it and then took a step back. The beast threw his head back and roared before he began to shrink and transform from a bear-like creature into a man once more. The man was watching the smaller beast stagger to its feet. Suddenly, as if sensing Tiana, as he had before, he spun to face her.

His features and body were blurry, and she was unable to make out the markings on his body, aside from their colors. Black, yellow, orange.

The man started towards her.

Tiana's eyes snapped open. She trembled with fear and sorrow for those who had died. Unlike most visions, this one had seemed real.

She stared out the window. The visions had seemed brief – mere seconds – but twilight had turned into full night. She had never experienced a double vision such as this one. Nothing about the two scenes appeared connected, except that they both occurred outside of Lost Vegas. Why was Arthur not among those facing the beast? Or had he been in the tent? Where had the second beast come from?

Her heart was pounding with urgency, her hands trembling.

Tiana went to the window, not realizing how hot she was until the cold night touched her warm cheeks. She leaned closer to the window, inviting the wind, while staring into the snowy night to see as far as she could.

Outside the city was dangerous.

Outside the city was Arthur.

How far in the future was her vision of Arthur dying in a cage? A dusting of snow covered the metal cage. Was he there now, or would he be there soon? The second occurred in spring, which put it far enough away she would know to warn those involved about the skin-walker lurking in the brush. She was outside the city, witnessing the event. Which meant, she had to leave at some point.

Why not now? Before I die on my birthday?

The vision of Arthur was in her mind. She dwelled on what she knew of the distances and timing separating the Winter Hunt and Arthur's location and concluded it was not possible for her father's men to reach him in time, especially when they did not know where to look for him.

Distraught, she paced and wrung her hands, helpless to assist her brother. She glanced from the locked and guarded door to the window.

"Wait for Aveline," she whispered to the insistent urgency clamoring for her to act before it was too late. Aveline had agreed to think about saving Arthur but had appeared reluctant. How long would it take Tiana to convince her friend to accompany her? How long did Arthur have to live?

Warner crossed her thoughts again. He was located on the medical floor of the pyramid. If she could leave her room, she did not doubt she could find him.

Her distress leaked into her surroundings. The bed, chairs, wardrobes, trunks, and tables all floated in the air, while smaller items such as her brush and hairpins swirled in an invisible storm.

Tiana gasped, realizing her magic was free, and quickly ordered everything to return to its place. She looked around, expecting Matilda to scream at her for the display, but nothing happened.

"You have to stop this, Tiana," she lectured herself. She wrapped a hand around her wrist, where she had last cut herself. Matilda had made her bleed herself whenever her magic acted up.

But Matilda was dead. When Tiana cut herself, she did so to relieve her anxiety and worry, not to try to rid her body of magic or as punishment.

Magic.

If she could lift random items around her room, could she unlock a door from within? For seven years, Matilda had forbidden her from using the magic and punished her when she did. Before the period of time when Matilda was in her life, Tiana used to amuse herself in her tiny little room by playing with her forbidden gift.

Had she forgotten all she once knew?

She crossed to the door and pressed her ear to it. No sound came from the space outside. It was too early for her father to retire, and her slaves disappeared until morning after her evening meal. On occasion, a Shield member would walk through on his rounds. For the moment, all was silent outside her room.

Tiana drew a deep breath and closed her eyes, focusing on the lock. She knew nothing of the mechanism inside the door, but she understood the bolts that slid into place when someone twisted the key. She focused her errant magic on moving the bolt.

For a long, torturous moment, nothing happened. She released the breath she held and rested her hand on the door to help focus her energy. She tried again.

The locks slid out of the doorframe with a chorus of clicks.

Convinced someone was sure to notice, Tiana backed away from the door and waited.

No one charged through the door to beat her or yell at her. She ventured forward and rested her hand on the cool doorknob then twisted it. It gave, and the door opened.

She stood in the open doorway, gazing down the long hallway leading to her freedom. The apartment was quiet and warmly lit.

Why have I never tried this before? She thought, and answered her question as fast. *Because I never had a compelling reason to leave.*

Arthur had never been in danger before.

Frozen in her doorway, afraid to move, Tiana argued with herself quietly about whether or not she should continue and if so, how. She closed the door and walked away from it. Her agitated magic threw everything into the air, and even her hair billowed and floated around her.

She warmed her hands by the fire then crossed to the window to cool her body before returning. Her gaze fell to the clothing Aveline had set on the table near the hearth, and her inner turmoil silenced.

Tiana touched the slave's clothing then picked up the tunic and shook it out. The light, gray clothing was meant for indoor wear, but she had the special cloak her brother had made for her, which would surely keep her warm anywhere.

With a flash of excitement, she limped to her wardrobe and flung it open. Her fingertips skimmed the formal clothing and cloaks, until she found the one she sought. Tiana pulled the thick cloak lined with furs captured by her brother from the wardrobe. Her heart raced, and she studied the slaves clothing and elegant cloak.

I can do this, she thought with recklessness she had never experienced in her life.

She changed quickly into Aveline's clothing then grabbed her satchel from the closet. She positioned it over her head and across her chest before swinging on the warm cloak. Tiana went to closet wardrobe when a flash of color caught her eye. She pulled her favorite veil out of the wardrobe, a brilliant pink length of silk she had embroidered with forest animals, and stuffed it in her satchel.

Approaching the door, she paused once more, afraid of what lie beyond her protected chamber, afraid someone might already know. She wanted to cry but knew Aveline would not approve.

Tiana pulled the hood of her cloak up over her head to hide her eyes in the depths of its shadows. She went to the door and opened it.

No Shield members – or worse, her father – waited for her outside. No one was there to stop her. Her will to leave began to chip away as she reviewed how daunting her challenge really was.

I have to save Arthur, she reminded herself. Tiana stepped outside of her room, into the hall, and pulled the door closed behind her. She braced herself for discovery, but no one confronted her.

She hurried through the apartment, hunched and fearful, and reached the servants' elevator without anyone noticing her. The two Shield members glanced at her then away when they saw her slave's clothing.

Tiana held her breath as she waited for the elevator car and clenched her hands together to keep them still. At long last, the elevator door slid open. She hurried into its depths and selected the floor for the medical bays catering to the privileged elite residing in the pyramid.

She reached the fourth floor and hurried off the elevator. The medical wing was lightly staffed, and she recognized the hallways and bays where she had been taken after the Matilda incident. Warner was likely staying in a room close to the one she had woken up in. Tiana rushed past the three medical staff members gathered in the waiting area. Her heart was beating so loudly, she was certain it was about to give out. Tiana skirted two more nurses in slave uniforms before reaching the hallway where those requiring close observation were kept.

She went door to door until she found Warner and then ducked inside his room and closed the door behind her.

Shaking from head to toe, she leaned heavily against the door and fought to catch her breath. A trickle of terror mixed with exhilaration as the thought she had not only left her room, but done so without permission, disguised as a slave.

"Who are you?" Warner's voice was thick and his words slow.

Tiana straightened. She had not thought this part through all the way. Warner had never seen her, even though she knew him from spying on the household. Arthur's bodyguard lay in a narrow bed. He was tall enough for his feet to dangle over the end, and his muscular frame was visible beneath the thin hospital clothing he wore. His hands were bandaged as well as his head and one bicep.

But his dark eyes were clear and sharp and trained on her.

Tiana was stuck between the inherent shyness stemming from never speaking to anyone in her life and urgency to help her brother.

"Are you ... Tiana?" Warner's gaze narrowed, and he pushed himself into a seated position.

She nodded, startled he knew her.

Surprise flickered across his features, along with confusion. "Is this another hallucination brought on by medicines?"

She shook her head. "I am really here."

"I had begun to think you did not exist," he said.

Tiana had no idea how to respond.

"Are you safe? Have the Cruises tried to hurt you?" he asked.

"No. My father burned them all," she said without revealing the danger she had faced from Matilda.

"Good. The bastards should all burn."

Another awkward silence fell.

"Arthur," she managed to say her brother's name without crying.

"He is still in danger," Warner said, frowning. "I understand your father sent every Shield member he could spare. I only hope they move fast enough to help him."

"They will not," she blurted out. Grateful for the opening, she drew near his bed, eyes on the ground and voice low. "He is in great danger, Warner. My father's men are not heading in the right direction. He will be dead before they find him."

Warner was silent. She dared not lift her head when she was close enough for him to see her eyes if he did. "You share his ... deformity," Warner said quietly. "The visions?"

Surprised her brother had revealed such a potentially damning secret to anyone outside the family, she could only nod.

"You have seen his danger?" Warner sat up. His tone took on an urgent note.

"I have," she answered. "I know where he is."

"Tell me where!" Warner sprang out of bed. His large form crossed the room to a trunk, and he yanked it open before pulling out the clothing of a Shield member.

"I will show you."

"You cannot go outside the city! If the Natives do not impede me, the Ghouls will hunt me as they did when I returned!"

Ghouls are real? She almost asked. Arthur had insisted they were fairytales told to scare children.

Warner yanked off his hospital shirt to reveal the thick muscles of his back.

Tiana's jaw fell open, and she turned away quickly before fanning herself.

"Where is he?" Warner asked as he dressed.

"I will only tell you when we are outside the city," she replied.

"Your brother would not approve of you leaving the city. I cannot in good conscience disobey him."

What he said made sense. But for the first time in her life, she had a plan, and she was not going to let Warner dissuade her. "After we find him, I am going to the Free Lands," she whispered.

The rustling behind her stopped. "Free Lands. Does your deformity tell you they exist?" he asked cautiously.

"My deformity tells me nothing of the sort. But it has revealed, if I am here on my eighteenth birthday, I will die. I must leave, but first, I must find Arthur."

The sound of his movement began again. "If you wish."

"You will take me?" she asked.

"I swore an oath to your brother to protect you. If there is danger beyond the Cruises within the city, then you are safer with me, are you not?"

"Yes," the word came out as a sigh, and her cheeks flushed hot.

"You understand you will anger your father doing this?"

"I do," she said. "As will you."

"I would risk anything for your brother, even being burnt at the stake."

So would I. Tiana's thoughts went to Aveline. She wished her friend agreed to accompany her but also knew the assassin in training had never cared to set foot outside the city. It was not fair to ask her to leave her home, even though Tiana wanted her friend by her side.

"Let us go, before I change my mind about you coming with me," Warner said. He whipped open the door and strode out.

Tiana scrambled after him, barely able to believe this was really happening.

No one stood in the muscular Shield member's way as he walked to a slave stairwell and trotted down. Tiana trailed him. While she was unfamiliar with most of the place she called home, Warner knew exactly which path would take them around any Shield members on duty and around the gathering areas for the privileged elite. Twenty minutes later, they emerged into the snowy night.

Tiana stopped and looked up. It was the first time in her life when she had been outside during the night, and without her father's permission. She was allowed to leave her room four times a year for special events requiring the entire family to attend. Those events, however, usually lasted a few minutes.

But tonight ... she was free!

The hood slipped back. Snow fell straight down upon her exposed face, stinging her cheeks with tiny, cold kisses, and stuck in her hair. She suppressed the urge to cry. Too many emotions were soaring through her for her to decide which she felt the strongest.

"I think I know this answer, but can you ride a horse?" Warner asked.

In her awe of the night, she had forgotten his presence. Tiana started to glance his way before realizing the hood had fallen down to her shoulders, leaving her deformed eyes visible.

She snapped her eyelids closed and clawed the hood back up over her head.

"Arthur told me," Warner said, a gentle note in his tone. "He does not hide his deformity from me. You do not need to, either."

Where had her brother ever found such a man? She did not know how anyone could look up on her eyes and not be repulsed.

"I cannot ride," she whispered. "I have never been around animals at all. Or trees."

"Neither of us can ride a tree," he said with a soft chuckle. "You are small enough for us to ride together. Come."

Her emotions surged and tumbled as she hurried after him. Every sound, from the crunch of snow beneath her boots to the swishing of her cloak, and every new sight, such as the paddocks where several horses in blankets were turned out and the streetlamps whose torches struggled to shine through snow, filled her with a giddy combination of delight and fear.

"Wait here," Warner told her and then walked into the stables.

The scent of hay and horses reminded her of how her brother smelled when he returned from a ride or a hunt. Homesickness for the only person she had ever truly loved caused her exhilaration to wilt. How did she find pleasure in the world, when she did not know if anyone could save her brother?

Warner emerged leading a saddled bay horse. Before he reached her, the horse stopped and lifted its head. The beautiful creature was taller than Tiana expected, with legs longer than hers and a small, chiseled head. She started to smile.

Warner murmured something she could not hear to calm it before starting forward again.

The horse neighed loudly in complaint. This time, it yanked its reins free from Warner.

"Sorry. He is usually friendly," Warner called over his shoulder. "Step closer. Maybe he needs to smell you first."

Tiana complied and walked forward, eager to see if the horse's coat was as soft and fuzzy as it appeared.

The animal's ears flattened against its head, and the whites swallowed half its eyes. It reared with a sound of panic rather than objection. The animal pulled its reins free of Warner then spun and bolted into the stables.

Tiana stopped, uncertain what to do.

"That was unexpected," Warner said, hands on hips. "Horses have many reasons for behaving the way they do. If he's lame, perhaps ..." He drifted off without sounding convinced. "Wait here. I'll find us another horse."

Tiana shivered and wrapped the cloak around her more securely.

Movement from the corner of her eye caught her attention, and she smiled at the two horses standing at the paddock rail, a good ten feet away. She approached them, admiring their large eyes and winter coats. The nostrils of one horse widened as it caught her scent. Its ears went back, and it brayed loudly. The horse beside it backed away from the railing and trotted to the opposite side of the paddock.

The first horse followed, kicking out with its back legs in her direction.

Tiana stayed where she was, disappointed. From what she had seen of horses, they seemed friendly. Did they sense she had no experience with them?

Warner returned leading a smaller horse. He drew near her, only for this horse, too, to plant its hooves in the slushy snow and refuse to move.

Tiana approached, and the animal reared with a neigh.

She stopped.

Warner tried to calm the horse down to no avail and finally led it back into the stables.

When he appeared a third time, he carried saddlebags over one shoulder. "They do not like you, so we will not be riding."

"Oh," she said. "Is it common for them not to like someone?"

"I have never seen it happen before," he replied as he walked past her.

At a loss as to why horses liked Arthur and not her, Tiana suspected her deformity was responsible without understanding how. Was it her appearance the horses did not like or her magic?

"Which direction are we going?" Warner called.

She shook her head to clear it. For whatever reason, horses disliked her. But they could still find her brother on foot.

"The Little Beard tribe's borders," she reported.

Warner muttered a curse beneath his breath. He swung one arm and made a show of balling up his bandaged fist and releasing it. "I have time to think this through," he said. "Come on. We have a long walk ahead of us, and we will need to hide from anyone your father sends after us. Luckily, your brother has a friend or two we can call upon."

Tiana trailed him, too excited to take note of the city as they passed through the northern edge towards the road leading out of the only place she had ever known.

SEVENTEEN

AFTER A RELAXING AFTERNOON and evening talking to Rocky, Aveline entered the great pyramid where the privileged members of Lost Vegas lived. She passed through the common areas on the ground floor, skirting a fete in full swing despite it being midnight, and arrived at the slave elevator. A few minutes later, she was walking through the quiet apartment belonging to the Hanover's towards Tiana's room.

A portrait of Arthur on the wall of the long hallway leading from the family areas to the individual rooms caught her attention, and she paused to observe it. It appeared recent; he was the same age as when she had met him at the brothel, where he rescued her from her fate.

She had spoken to Rocky at length about her options with regards to entering the Guild. He had agreed she needed a sponsor, which he – as an assassin and full member – was more than willing to do. However, neither of them possessed the type of benefactor she needed to back her pledge. The Guild thrived off of donations from benefactors. Rocky had been fortunate and found his a year ago by accident, when he saved a privileged member of the outer city from being trampled by a runaway cart. At twenty, Rocky was the youngest full-fledged assassin in the Guild, and he owed it to the man who gave a generous donation out of gratitude.

Aveline's plan had always been for her father to sponsor her. With the backing of the Guild's leader, she had not needed any other kind of benefactor.

Arthur's offer to act as her benefactor was currently her only real hope of entering the Guild anytime soon. Any doubt she had about his ability to donate a substantial sum of money, large enough for the Guild to overlook her breaking of two of their rules, had perished when she saw the luxurious apartment where he and Tiana lived.

Arthur was not the only option, but he was the easiest. Rocky had argued that she would find another potential benefactor, if she remained in the Hanover's service long enough to meet more of the wealthy members of the Outer City.

What she had not dared to reveal, however, was the one reason why she may not stay there long at all: Tiana's insane father. He knew what she was. She was in favor – for now. But based on how quickly he had burned every Cruise in existence, she understood too well how fickle his favor was. Unlike Arthur, who had followed through on his promises to her thus far, the Hanover patriarch would discard her once he had no use for her.

All of her internal arguing, and the discussion with Rocky, led her right back where she started.

Arthur would get her where she wanted to be.

Arthur's life was in danger outside the city.

Did her concern for him stem solely because of her desire to make her father proud? Or ... was it also because of Tiana, and the hope and fear she had witnessed in the Hanover girl's features when she discussed Arthur?

Aveline moved away from the portrait. After her stay in solitary, the conversation with Tiana's father, and seeing her home burnt to the ground, she decided only a good night of sleep was going to help her think straight.

She walked to Tiana's door and slid the key into the lock.

The door cracked open at the light pressure.

At once on edge, Aveline pushed it open all the way. A fire was burning in the hearth, and the rest of the room was dark.

"Tiana?" she called, once again irritated with herself for not thinking to grab a weapon or two at some point during her day.

No response.

Aveline went to the bed, where she expected to find Tiana this time of night. It was vacant. She strode to the closet, where Tiana used to hide when she was upset. It, too, was empty.

"Tiana?" Aveline called again, growing alarmed.

A pile of clothing lay near the table by the hearth, and the wardrobe was partially open. A chill went through Aveline, and she crossed to the desk. The map Tiana had drawn and placed there earlier was gone.

"Burn me!" Aveline muttered. She bolted to the closet, hoping the large map Tiana had been embroidering was located in the same place it had been in her former room. Flipping on the light, Aveline spotted the tapestry first, and the soft leather roll containing her weapons second.

Her weapons sat on a trunk, and Tiana had placed half a dozen needles around one of the many flowers located on the tapestry. Aware of her hidden system for disguising villages and terrain, Aveline studied the map.

The needles surrounded a village that was half red, half orange, indicating it was either on the border of the territory of an unfriendly tribe of Natives, or contested land. Aveline had never had a reason to ask exactly which one this particular flower was on the tapestry filled with flowers. She placed a finger on Lost Vegas – represented by the largest of the flowers – and then on the village Tiana had emphasized.

"Past the plains and into the forest, then onward to the plains beyond," Aveline said. Tiana's map was missing one key piece of information: a legend describing distances. Aveline suspected Tiana did not know distances, or the mountains would not seem so close to the city, as they did on the homemade map. She stood still, concentrating hard, until certain she had memorized everything the map had to offer about the location of where Tiana was headed.

With any luck, if she moved fast enough, she could find Tiana before the Hanover patriarch realized she was gone. Aveline did not want to know what he would do when he discovered his newly pardoned *guard dog* had allowed his daughter to escape outside the city. Whatever he decided, it would quash any chance Aveline had to enter the Guild, or even remain in the city, assuming she escaped his madness with her life.

Aveline tugged the necklace from her shirt that was given to her by Mohammed, the scientist in the basement who cared for the great trees that generated electricity. The stone was dark, indicating Tiana was not located in the apartment.

How long had she been gone?

She snatched her weapons off the trunk and raced out of Tiana's room, down the elevator, and back into the dark, snowy streets. Aveline sucked in cold air that burned her lungs. She started to run in the direction of the inner city and then stopped. Her hand went to the necklace around her neck.

Mohammed had a deformity, one he had been unwilling to admit to when she asked him about it. It allowed him to create the necklaces he had made for Tiana and Tiana's dead twin. When Aveline and Tiana were close, the necklaces came alive and grew bright. When they were apart, they were dark. Although, in prison, the light had been faint, not gone entirely, as it was now.

What kind of magic did Mohammed possess, and was it possible for him to make the necklace stronger? Or at least tell her how far away Tiana was, if the light at the pendant's center went out?

Tiana had not had too much of a head start, only a few hours. After a split second of debate, Aveline returned to the pyramid and raced to the nearest stairwell leading beneath it, to the part of the pyramid reserved for slaves and the day-to-day duties needed to keep the privileged elite living comfortably.

She hurried through the maze of hallways until she reached the section she sought. Slowing, Aveline's hair lifted at the power of the electricity radiating off the massive metal trees behind the doors ahead of her. She entered the large bay without knocking. The living quarters for the scientist and his slave were off to the side, and she strode through the area designated as a control center to the door leading into the private quarters.

Their door was locked. She pounded on it and waited. Unable to stand still without fidgeting, she shrugged her shoulders, paced, counted to five and then pounded on the door harder.

It opened, and the small scientist peered up at her. "Is the power off?" he asked.

"I need to talk to you about this." She held up the pendant.

"Aveline?" The handsome young man who appeared behind Mohammed stood close to Rocky's height and possessed dark hair, currently ruffled, and handsome features that made her temporarily forget her purpose.

"Hi, Jose," she breathed.

"Are you well?" he asked quickly.

"What is wrong with the power?" Mohammed asked and pushed past her. Dressed in a nightgown, he hurried to the consoles where Jose had told her they could control the electricity.

"Nothing," she said, blinking out of the trance she went into whenever she crossed paths with Jose.

"I came to see you and heard you were in prison," Jose said.

Her cheeks grew warm. "Long story," she mumbled. "But I'm back at my duty position now." Embarrassed Jose knew her personal business, she spun and went to Mohammed. "I need to know more about this pendant."

The elderly man blinked rapidly as he looked from the necklace to her face. "This is Tiana Hanover's?" he asked.

"Yes. The necklaces you gave me to give to her. She gave me one," Aveline rushed on. "How far away does she have to be for the light to be completely out?"

He appeared pensive.

"How far?" Jose repeated. "You mean ... she's not here?"

Aveline was torn about what to tell them. She needed answers, but she was not about to endanger their lives by revealing information for which Tiana's father might burn someone.

"She would have to be outside the city," Mohammed replied.

It was not outside the range of possibilities for Tiana to be so far, but that left Aveline with a second problem. Tiana would not know how to leave the city in the first place, or learn how to navigate it on her own in a few hours. She had to have help, which meant, someone who was going to help her stay ahead of Aveline, if she did not react fast.

"I have to go," she said and started away. "I have to find her."

"That is all?" Mohammed called after her.

"Wait!" Jose said and caught up to her. "Tiana Hanover cannot leave the city. Her father forbids both his heirs from leaving simultaneously. Which means ... did someone take her?"

Aveline ignored him with effort.

"Aveline, do you need help?" he asked quietly. "Is that why you came?"

Aveline stopped in her tracks. Help. As if an assassin, who worked in isolation, ever truly needed anyone else! She bristled, about to correct his assumption, when Mohammed spoke.

"Do you want me to make it stronger?"

"What?" she asked, facing him. "You can do that?"

"No."

Jose shook his head at his mentor. "He means yes. He can do that. It's forbidden for him to reveal his deformity, but he can make it stronger."

"Yes," Mohammed agreed. "Is she in danger?"

"Not if I reach her first," Aveline replied.

"I can make it stronger." He held out his hand and approached her.

Aveline whipped the necklace off and handed it to him. "Can you make it track her?" she asked.

He wrapped his hand around the pendant and closed his eyes. Light flared around his hand.

"I doubt it," Jose answered for him. "His gift is energy. Electricity. There are some very detailed principals I will not bore you with, but the pendants contain particles that recognize each other, which is why they light up. It is a form of electricity."

Aveline did not have time to comprehend what exactly that meant.

The light faded from Mohammed's hand, and he uncurled his fingers to reveal the pendant again. She plucked it out of his palm, uncertain she wanted to touch live electricity. The metal was warm but appeared otherwise normal.

"When you are within five miles of her, it will light up," Mohammed said. "But this is as strong as I can make it."

"Better than nothing," she said and pulled it on over her head. "You both must swear not to speak of this to anyone!"

"We all have secrets," Mohammed said. "If I may ask, where do you go?"

"It doesn't concern you."

"Maybe we can help," Jose said.

She hesitated.

"Fetch the battery-operated torches," Mohammed directed him. "She will need them."

Jose returned to their private quarters.

"I'm going east," Aveline replied.

Mohammed's eyes lit up. "Aaaaaahhhh. Perfect!" He strode towards the door of his quarters. "Jose! Pack the batteries and conductors! You have a delivery to make!"

"Wait, what?" Aveline asked. "He can't come with me!"

"You will need a guide. To the east are the enemies of the city," Mohammed said. "Jose is the only city dweller who can walk into their villages and not be harmed. If you take him, they will grant you safe passage."

Aveline's second refusal died on her lips. "How?" she asked instead.

"We share a common concern." Mohammed held up a square box.

Aveline frowned.

"Electricity!" he said with a sigh. "Jose takes them to the Diné monthly, and we are several days overdue with this month's delivery."

Her mind was racing. She knew exactly where Tiana was headed. If the Hanover girl had help, there was always a chance Aveline would not catch up to her in time, before she reached her destination.

"I don't care about the boxes," she said. "You're telling me Jose can get us into the Diné camp?"

"He can. And he knows the fastest way there, too."

"I have food," Jose said and held up a meal bar. "I can be ready in thirty minutes."

As much as Aveline wanted to believe she would find the Hanover girl by dawn and return her to the city, she had a feeling the situation was not going to work out the way she wanted it to. Jose's addition to her party, and his knowledge of the fastest route to the camp where Tiana believed Arthur was being held, would be of use.

"I will be back for you in thirty minutes," she said reluctantly.

He smiled, and heat flared within her.

She turned away before he could see her blush. Aveline left the bay housing the electrical center and glanced down at the pendant. At its center was a very faint light. Tiana was within five miles of the city.

She bolted and sprinted through the basements and up the stairs to the ground floor then out of the pyramid completely. She ran at full speed out of the Outer City and past the smelly fish market into the Inner City. She dared not enter the village of an enemy alone, even if Jose's guaranteed them safe passage. She could think of only one person she trusted to take on a village of Natives and ran straight to Rocky's.

Her Devil's blood was rising, stoked by her anger and worry. She could think of nothing worse than Tiana alone, freezing, and vulnerable somewhere outside the city.

EIGHTEEN

TIANA HAD NEVER SEEN a sunrise unobstructed by buildings or the boards that used to block the window in her former room. She stood on a flat boulder squatting near the edge of the forest and watched the sun crest the horizon. The snowstorm had cleared late last night, though the morning felt colder than the night had. The remaining clouds hovered near the horizon, reflecting pastel pinks, yellows, and blues as the sun hefted itself into the sky.

The winter air numbed the tip of her nose and her ears, but nothing penetrated the cloak her brother had gifted her. Beneath it, she was as warm as her cheeks were not.

Of everything that surprised her most about the world outside the city, it was the relative silence she found most striking. She had grown up with the sounds of the city outside her window without ever realizing just how noisy the city was. Here, on the snow-coated plains, with no one else in sight, she experienced a sense of peace she had never known before. The sun rose in revered silence, as if the rest of the world stood still to watch alongside her.

Tiana squinted, and tears stung her eyes. She lifted a hand to shield them from the brilliant, pale yellow sun but dared not miss any part of her first sunrise. With a smile stretching her stiff, cold cheeks, she could think of nothing more magical than this moment.

"We need to continue," Warner said from below her. "Are you rested enough to travel?"

"Yes!" she replied cheerfully.

"Come on down."

Tiana crouched and made her way down the boulder. She pulled her hood over her head instinctively, despite knowing Warner had already seen her deformity. Exhilarated by the first night outside her room, which was spent trudging through snow, Tiana had not slept at all during the two hours Warner allocated for them to rest. Her mind was on her surroundings, on the sky, the forest, Arthur, the snow ... there was too much to see for her to sleep!

"Here. I will have to hunt in the forest tonight, but this will keep us going today." Warner handed her food wrapped in a soft cloth.

She accepted it and glanced up at him then back. "Are you well?" she asked. "You look pale."

"I've not yet recovered," he admitted. "Exposure has peculiar effects on one's body. It makes you less capable of handling the extremes a second time." Dressed in the dark scarlet of the Guild and wearing a cloak, he appeared sickly with dark rings under his eyes.

Tiana unfastened her cloak and twirled it off with a shiver. "You can wear mine. Yours is not as thick," she offered.

Warner straightened, and his jaw clenched. "I am here to protect you, not the other way around."

"But if you are too cold to do so, does it not make sense to take my cloak?"

He gazed at her for a long moment before turning away and beginning to walk. "We need to move more quickly. Once we're in the forest –"

"The *forest!*" she squealed. With clumsiness born of excitement, Tiana managed to pull her cloak on without dropping her food as she ran through the knee-high snow after him.

Warner sighed.

Tiana passed him, eyes on the trees marking their destination. She tucked her food away so she had full movement of her body. She slowed only when the snow of the shallow valleys making up the rolling plains grew too deep.

By midmorning, the weather had begun to change from frigid to unusually warm, and snow began to melt around them and turn to sludge. The closer they came to the forest, the faster she moved, until she was running ahead of Warner, intent on seeing her first tree up close.

She reached the tree line and stopped, breathless. Craning her neck back, she followed the brown trunk of the tree as it stretched towards the sky. Pine needles dripped with melting snow and ice, and the scent of wet earth and pine swept over her with the breeze.

"They're so much larger than I thought!" she said softly in delight when Warner joined her.

He gave her another long look before starting forward into the trees.

"Should we not be going that direction?" She pointed towards the west.

"We will. We need someone to help us negotiate with any unfriendly tribe members we encounter. This close to spring, there's a lot of feuding over food, since everyone is pretty much out."

Tiana trailed him, more interested in the towering trees and patterns the melting snow made on the ground than in his explanation. Lost in her wonderment of the real world, she did not notice Warner had stopped until she collided with him. She blinked out of her fascination with the forest and stepped back. Peering around Warner, she gasped and ducked back quickly to tug her hood up over her head.

On the path ahead of him were three Natives, one of whom was carrying a firearm, the likes of which were forbidden in the city.

"It's safe," Warner told her over his shoulder. "They are allies. Wait here." He moved forward.

She peeked out at the forest from beneath the protection of her hood. Warner spoke slowly in the Native tongue, his hands held away from his body to show he was not a threat.

A branch snapped from behind her, and she turned. Two more Natives melted from the forest. Tiana crowded Warner, both excited and uncertain at her first encounter with the peoples who inhabited the great expanses between cities.

A short exchange ensued between Warner and one of the Natives before he lowered his arms and turned to her.

"We are going to one of their outposts," he explained. "The tracker we want will meet us there."

As he spoke, one of the Natives darted into the forest, towards the east.

"I have told them the truth of who I am. My family name is too little known to draw attention, but everyone for a thousand miles knows of the Hanover's. I have told them you are Tiana Burrows, my —"

"Wife?" she asked hopefully.

"Burn me, no!" he said, startled. "My sister."

Deep within her hood, Tiana's face grew hotter than the midday sun. "Oh. Of course."

Warner shook his head. "You do not need to hide your eyes outside the city. Your father burnt anyone who was different, but out here, there are many deformed people."

She pulled her hood farther forward anyway. "I do not wish to be seen as different," she objected.

"They already know one of us is, and since you're hiding, it's likely you."

"What? Why do you say that?"

Warner pointed to an area behind her.

She turned, not understanding, and started to face him, when she looked up. Her magic, responding to her excitement, was lifting the branches of the trees around her. Those nearest her pointed straight into the air, while those farthest from her influence had lifted a meter or so. It was not just the trees but the snow as well. Rather than drip downward, the canopy of snow that had gathered above them melted to the side, with rivulets of water traversing empty space until it met a tree trunk and ran down to the ground.

Unaware of what it had been doing, Tiana reined in her magic. The snow hovering over their heads dropped to the ground, and the tree branches floated back down into place.

None of the Natives appeared horrified by the unusual phenomenon, as those in the city would. They barely glanced at the shifting trees.

If Matilda were here ...

Tiana shivered despite the warm day. Thinking of Matilda made her wounds and scars alike ache.

"They may have a medicine man as well at the outpost," Warner said with a grimace.

She studied his features again. "You are not well, are you?"

"Well enough," he said shortly. "Let us not keep our hosts waiting." He began walking, following the Natives ahead of them.

Tiana trailed. This time, she made an effort to remain conscious of when her magic began to act out, so she could suppress it. No matter what Warner said, she did not think it prudent to display her deformities, when her father was likely trying to find her by now.

The Natives led them down another narrow path through the forest and stopped when they reached a small wooden cabin. Warner walked into it without hesitation. Tiana stepped up to the doorway and stopped.

The wooden interior reminded her too much of the room where she had spent seventeen years of her life.

"May I wait outside?" she asked, recoiling from the cozy, warm space.

"If you do not wander off," Warner said. He sat heavily on a bench running along one wall of the cabin. An elderly woman rose from her place cooking over a fire and sat beside him. To Tiana's surprise, the cabin had an electric lamp in the far corner to brighten the interior.

Warner's weary sigh disrupted her curiosity about the electricity available only in the great pyramid in the city.

Tiana almost asked him again what was so painful. The strongest man she knew was struggling, and yet, his stride was sure without any sign of a limp, and his gaze remained sharp, unlike the glazed look Matilda had worn when she was ill.

Speaking to him would require Tiana to enter the cabin, when she intended to enjoy her first day of freedom. She moved out of the way of another of the Natives and sat on the porch. Two horses were loose in a small paddock to the side, and wires providing electricity were strung up in the nearby trees. Once, long ago, Tiana had toured the lower levels of the great pyramid with Matilda and seen the room where an older man with wild hair made electricity. The outer city relied on an underground river, and she could not help but wonder what the Natives used.

The midday had grown too warm for her cloak, though a chilly breeze prevented her from doing more than unfastening the top button. Melting snow dripped into puddles or formed a muddy slush. Trees creaked in the breeze, and the forest was otherwise quiet.

Two Natives joined Warner, and she heard them speaking through the open doorway. The other Natives who escorted them this far had melted into the forest, leaving her alone on the porch to admire the world around her.

One of the horses whinnied, and Tiana became curious of the elegant animals once more. Would the Natives' horses react differently to her? She pushed herself off the porch and walked around the side of the cabin, slowing when she neared the paddock.

The horses shifted to the far side of the paddock and began pacing, their ears flipping forward and back, and their nostrils wide. While she knew little about horses, she understood their agitated behavior to be born of discomfort, if not fear. Disappointed once more, Tiana gave the paddock a wide berth and went toward a dirt road much wider than the trails they had taken through the forest. She recalled the map she had created out of years of eavesdropping and collecting tidbits of information from her brother and books. The road probably led to a village, though she was finding it harder than she expected to understand with certainty where she stood relative to the map.

She started to turn away when movement caught her attention. Tiana squinted into the forest, trying to make out what she saw. Brush shifted, and a sapling waved, as if someone or something had bumped it.

She glanced around then pushed her hood back and started forward, towards the movement. One of her few books had been on forest animals, and she was excited to see which one hid in the trees and brush around the cabin.

Entering the forest again, she made her way through sludge and bramble in the direction where she had seen the brush move. When she arrived to the spot, she saw no animals at all. Gazing around, she spotted more movement and started forward again.

For ten minutes, she followed the tantalizing clues left by an unknown animal deeper into the forest. At long last, she reached a clearing filled with small piles of snow and large puddles.

A low growl reached her ears, and she sought the source without finding it at first. The swishing of a tail came from her peripheral, and she spun, awed by the great cat crouching no more than five meters from her. With a coat as golden as the sun and eyes a shade darker, the great cat resembled the illustration in her book so perfectly, it could have been the very animal the author drew!

"You are beautiful," she whispered. "I believe you are called a cougar, are you not?"

The cougar growled again and glared at her. She studied it, admiring its thick coat and the smooth musculature beneath it. Its paws were larger than her hand, and wide, fuzzy ears pointed in her direction.

"I am a visitor in your beautiful forest," she told it. "I mean no harm." She smiled, knowing it could not possibly understand. Never in all her dreams had she believed she would ever be here, in the forest, confronting an animal she had read about in books. "This is the best day of my life!" she said, tears in her eyes.

After a long moment, the cougar rose from its crouch. Its lips uncurled, and it stood, relaxed.

Swallowing hard to keep from crying, Tiana took a cautious step forward, towards the animal. From what she read, cougars were not friendly. But she had also read that wild animals often did not view humans as dangerous, especially those who had a symbiotic relationship with the Natives who shared their territories. She wanted to see if it ran from her, as the horses wanted to, or if it would allow her to approach it.

The cougar showed no sign of fleeing. Neither did it crouch threateningly again or bare its teeth at her. Encouraged, Tiana crept closer and closer, until she was within arm's reach.

The cougar eyed her and then sat on its haunches, panting.

She stretched out a hand cautiously. The animal remained. When Tiana's fingertips met the thick, downy fur of its head, she grinned. She ran her fingers over its wide head to an ear and then to its neck. Shifting to its side, she buried both hands into the fur ringing its neck.

The cougar made a strange sound she took to be non-threatening. It rubbed up against her insistently. She scratched its neck.

How was it that horses ran from her but a cougar did not? Tiana stood with the great cat in the quiet clearing, scratching its neck and occasionally stroking its head, listening to the forest around her.

The cougar stood abruptly and tensed, staring into the forest. She followed its gaze and saw the Native half hidden behind a tree. A flare of panic lit within her, and she yanked up her hood, hoping he had not been there long enough to notice her deformity. The cougar shook itself out and slinked away, headed the opposite direction of the Native. It loped into the forest and vanished among the shadows.

Tiana stood, hunched and tense, and waiting for the Native to react as Matilda did, whenever she looked too long at her late stepmother with her deformed eyes.

"Are you ... hurt?" the Native asked in halting English.

She peeked towards him. He had ventured from the forest and stopped two meters from her.

"No," she replied.

"You ... know this ... cat?"

"No."

He was silent long enough for her to glance towards him again. The Native with dark hair and eyes was studying her. He appeared around her brother's age and wore layers of wool and fur.

A whistle came from the forest. The Native turned and placed two fingers to his lips, blowing a sharp response. He motioned for her to follow and led her back to the woods, towards the direction she had come.

Thankful he had said nothing about her eyes, Tiana followed him back to the cabin, where Warner was pacing.

Relief crossed his features as he spotted her. "Did I not tell you not to wander off?" he demanded.

"I am fine," she reassured him. "How do you feel?" Already, there was color in his features again.

He glanced towards three Natives, who spoke in hushed tones. One of them was the young man who found her in the clearing. "Better. The Natives have turned penicillin into tea. She gave me enough for a week." He lifted a canteen that he had strapped across his chest. "I see you met our tracker. His cousin was a friend of Arthur's and our guide for the Winter Hunt. He was with us in the encampment when ..." He drifted off, and a shadow crossed his features.

"When *what?*" she asked. She had been too absorbed in her quest, and surroundings, to ask him what happened.

"I cannot discuss it," he said in a clipped tone.

"Because my father forbids it?"

"Because it makes no sense, even to me, and I was there."

She opened her mouth to prod him into describing what had attacked her brother's camp, when the Native tracker spoke.

"No horses?" he asked quizzically, addressing Warner.

Warner shook his head. He responded in the Native's tongue, and the tracker glanced towards her. He nodded and pointed towards the road leading further west.

"We start there," he said.

"But we need to go east, do we not?" Tiana asked.

"Village ... death." The tracker stopped and spoke to Warner in his tongue.

"He says a village was wiped out, and they think the danger remains in the woods," Warner translated. He had tensed and was frowning.

She tilted her head, sensing he was not telling her everything the tracker said. Was it another tribe or an animal that wiped out the village?

"Trust me. We don't want to run into whatever it is," Warner said. "Are you well? Hungry?"

"I am well, thank you. We must find Arthur soon."

"I know that," Warner said impatiently. He motioned to the tracker, who began walking to the road leading the opposite direction Tiana wished to go. Trusting those around her, she nonetheless followed without objection.

The tracker stayed ahead of them about ten meters. Tiana made every effort possible to be normal and not to let the beautiful forest distract her and cause her magic to act out. The day grew even warmer, until it resembled spring rather than late winter, and the men with her shed their outer garments. She kept her cloak in place and the hood up, in case the Native looked back and saw her eyes or they met other travelers walking the road.

By evening, all signs of the recent snow had vanished beneath the heat wave, leaving a soggy forest. Their guide led them off the road at twilight and onto a muddy path through the forest, this time headed west.

They ate on their feet and continued walking after dark fell. Tiana's heels were blistered and her body beginning to ache from exertion and lack of rest, but she was too anxious to find her brother to consider slowing down or complaining. The moonless sky and shadowy forest conspired to prevent her from seeing more than a yard or two ahead of her, and the temperature dropped until her breath was visible once more.

She trailed the tracker and occasionally glanced over her shoulder towards Warner to ensure he was still present. Unable to make out his features, she hoped he was well enough to continue as long as they had to walk this night. Her focus turned from the forest to placing her feet the best she could. Mud clung to her boots and caused her to slide off the trail more than once.

A couple of hours after leaving the road, a high-pitched shriek rang out from nearby.

Tiana froze. The sound was followed by a wail, this one farther away. Soon, a chorus of eerie screams sounded.

Warner uttered curses she had only heard Aveline use before.

"This is why horses," the tracker said sternly.

"Horses are not an option!" Warner snapped in a whisper. "Are they close?"

The shrieks came from all around them, and Tiana struggled to match the frightening sounds with descriptions from her animal book. What kind of animal made such a horrifying sound? Not bears, or wolves, or cougars. Were these nocturnal birds of some kind?

Very large birds, she thought and flinched as another shriek sounded.

"Too close," the tracker answered. "This way. Run." He spun and darted forward.

"Warner, what –" Tiana asked, perplexed.

"Not now!" Warner snatched her hand and followed the Native.

Their guide plunged off the path into brush. Tiana allowed Warner to pull her along without making much sense of the darkness around her. Branches smacked into her face, and brush tangled with her cloak. More than once, she was brought to a standstill when she tripped over a fallen log or low branch. Warner hauled her back to her feet with sheer strength and carried her until she had her footing again.

She stole looks back when she could manage to but saw and heard no animal pursuing them. The strange cries remained at a steady distance from them. Whatever the men feared, it was not gaining on them.

The tracker led them to another trail, and the forest stopped impeding their escape. Tiana was soon breathless from the pace that showed no sign of slowing. Her hood fell away as she ran. Once or twice, she glimpsed flashes of white from her peripheral but when she tried to look directly at whatever it was, nothing was present.

They raced through the forest, across a wooden bridge straddling a half-frozen narrow creek, and back into the forest. She lost all sense of direction in the mad dash away from an invisible pursuer.

At long last, when she felt as if her lungs were going to explode in her chest, and her thighs were on fire, she careened into Warner, who stopped too suddenly for her to avoid him. He was panting, as was the Native, who stood near the mouth of a gaping cave.

The shrieks had kept pace with them and were circling closer.

"Go," the tracker breathed and gesticulated towards the cave. "Empty."

Warner led her into the darkness, and the Native followed.

"Warner, what –" she tried again.

"Hush!" he snapped. "Go as far back as you can." He released her hand and gave her a push towards the back of the cave. "No matter what, stay out of sight!"

Tiana tripped over a rock and steadied herself against the rough stone wall. The cave was tall enough for her to stand up straight, without her head reaching the ceiling, and too low for the men to do the same. She navigated the uneven floor and boulders of all sizes scattered along the floor. Focused on her task, she went as fast as possible, understanding the men's urgency without knowing what it was they feared.

She fell hard on her knees and hands. Tiana sat back with a

grimace. She wiped her hands on her cloak and peered around her into the darkness. The silence struck her as odd, and she twisted to face the mouth of the cave.

"Warner?" she whispered. She heard no sounds and sensed no movement indicating the others had followed her.

No answer.

Another shriek ricocheted off the walls of the cave, becoming creepier and higher pitched as it bounced around her. She covered her ears until the sound faded.

"Warner?" she called again, lowering her hands.

Her heart racing, Tiana climbed to her feet and turned around, heading back towards the front of the cave. Flashes of white filled the mouth of the cave, and she frowned. What were these creatures? Nothing in her book on forest animals remotely resembled what she glimpsed.

"Warner!"

No response.

Tiana neared the front of the cave, immersed in identifying what manner of animals had them surrounded. A flurry of movement, white fur and hair ...

Someone grabbed her around her arm and yanked her from the center of the cave to its edge. Pain fluttered through her as he gripped her forearm in the last place she had cut herself. She gasped, and a hand crossed her mouth.

Ghouls. She heard his thought in her mind.

They're real. Part of her had always known this to be true, based on how many different people had spoken of them, despite her brother's attempt to convince her the human predators were wives tales.

The tracker released her, and she shifted to face the mouth of the cave. Leaning around him and the wall jutting out from the side of the cave, she tried once again to make out what a Ghoul really was.

A sudden chorus of wailing left her covering her ears again, and she shifted back. Movement came directly across from them, from an alcove. Warner was staring out at the Ghouls, gripping his knives.

Just as suddenly as the wailing began, it stopped. She held her breath and lifted her hands from her ears without lowering them completely, in case the Ghouls started again. Silence came from the front of the cave. For a solid five minutes, no one moved, and Tiana barely dared to breathe, in case her breaths broke the quiet.

Finally, the tracker shifted past her, blocking her view, and motioned to Warner.

"No move," he whispered to her.

The two of them moved stealthily to the center of the cave. Neither spoke. Instead, they communicated through a quick set of hand signals. The two waited another few minutes. The tracker drew a firearm and knife, while Warner slid a sword free of its place at his back. The two were tense.

Tiana twisted her hands together beneath her cloak. She watched as they moved at last and approached the front of the cave with silent steps. They paused at the entrance of the cave before exiting. She started to relax, happy the threat was gone.

A flash of white moved with inhuman speed across the front of the cave. Deafening screams drove her to her knees and resounded off the walls. Pain shot through one ear, and it began to ring as loudly as the shrieking. She gasped and squeezed her hands over her ears. Dizziness fluttered through her, enough so, she struggled to stay balanced on her knees. A shout came from outside the cave, this one very human, along with what sounded like a small explosion.

Tiana hunkered down where she was. The silence outside of the cave was lost on her, until she recovered from the pain and ringing of her ears. Dazed, Tiana climbed to her feet, one hand over her hurting ear, and the other bracing her against the wall. She made her way to the mouth of the cave, concerned for Warner, and not about to remain in the cave if the creatures screamed again.

She stared at the tall creatures possessing a kind of ethereal elegance she did not know existed. They were more human than beast, with similar body structures, though their features left her no doubt as to how *in*human they also were. From skin white as snow, to eyes blacker than the sky, and fangs like the cougar's ... the Ghouls defied any idea she had ever formed of what one would look like. In her mind's eye, she had always believed them to resemble the great white bears of the north rather than a person.

A groan came from her right. Two of them knelt over the still form Warner, their faces and hands splashed with brilliant red blood, while three others crowded over them. The tracker's rigid, unmoving body was to her left.

Fear and horror shot through her, and she recalled the night Matilda had tried to murder Aveline. Adrenaline and energy coursed through her as she saw another friend in danger.

"Warner," the choked word left her mouth before she could stop it.

Two creatures slid between her and him, and she looked up, oblivious to the hot tears on her cheeks. Suddenly, she understood why Matilda had insisted Tiana's mother was a Ghoul. Their eyes were like hers – inky blackness that swallowed the whites of their eyes. They were peering into her soul, and she was viewing the emptiness of eternity in theirs.

The ringing in one ear became a buzzing. It filled her skull and trickled down into her body, where it met the uncontrolled magic responding to her emotions.

The unmistakable sound of teeth tearing into flesh nauseated her.

As when she hurt Aveline, and murdered Matilda, Tiana's reality took on a surreal state, as if she were not fully present, and definitely not in control. What was solid became transparent, blurred, and smeared, like an artist sweeping a brush across his canvas and somehow reversing dark and light.

"Stop!" She heard herself scream without feeling the words leave her mouth. A pulse of air, or energy, rippled out from her and swept outward. It knocked the Ghouls off their feet, and caused the trees nearest them to bend away. Trunks snapped, trees groaned, and the Ghouls fled.

Tiana sucked in a deep breath. Dark and light returned to their original places, and the world righted itself. She became aware of the cold night air seeping into the space between buttons of her cloak, and the tears that had dried and left her cheeks stiff. The ringing of her ear was back, along with a trickle of warmth running from her ear down the side of her neck.

"Warner!" she exclaimed and dashed forward. She dropped to her knees beside him and started to touch them then stopped. "Oh ... oh god ... Warner ..." Chunks of his arm and shoulder had been bitten away, and half his scalp was gone. Blood covered everything.

The tracker knelt on Warner's other side, his dark gaze assessing whereas Tiana's was too panicked to know where to look.

"Can you help him?" she managed. Tears flooded her eyes, and she wiped her nose on her cloak.

He nodded once before pulling off his satchel.

In the distance, she heard the screams of Ghouls. Tiana looked towards the sounds. The cries were moving away from them this time.

"His ..." the tracker said and then pointed.

She looked away from the forest to the satchel he indicated. It had been tossed into brush nearby. Tiana stood and retrieved it before crouching down beside the tracker.

Warner was not conscious, and his breathing was shallow and quick.

The tracker shifted away to start a fire before returning to bandage what he could of Warner's wounds. He used the medical supplies from both his satchel and Warner's. Tiana watched, helpless to do anything other than stay out of the way.

The tracker placed the blades of two knives in the fire then returned and rolled Warner carefully onto his back. He cut off the bloodied shirt and paused.

Tiana shifted forward to see what had his attention. The wounds in Warner's abdomen were not Ghoul made, for they were half-healed.

And unnaturally black.

"What is that?" she whispered.

"Marked," the tracker said. He studied the wounds without touching them.

"What does that mean?"

"Attacked. Not human. Not Ghoul. Not animal. This ..." the tracker paused, seeking the right words. "Beast. Marked him."

"Why?"

"Not kill first time. Will kill second."

"What kind of animal could do this? Ghoul?" she asked.

"Not Ghoul." He sat back. "Old animal with many forms."

"Many forms." She shivered. The vision of the man-beast replayed in her mind's eye. "Bear, wolf, human?"

"Yes. We call skinwalker."

She shivered.

Why had Warner not told her he encountered such a creature or that it hurt him? If she had known he would be in danger leaving the city, she would not have asked him to accompany her.

"The skinwalker will return to kill him?" she whispered.

"Yes."

Was this why the skinwalker had attacked them all in her vision? Had he come for Warner?

She huddled in her cloak. The Native worked quickly to stop Warner's bleeding, binding every wound except those on his abdomen. For those two punctures, he sealed them together using the superheated knives.

Warner did not move at all during the tracker's ministrations. After half an hour, the tracker sat back and released a deep breath.

"Must take to village," he said and wiped his face. "Will not live long."

Fear slithered through her, cold and deep. Tiana was not about to argue with him, but she could not help starting to panic at the idea she would not find Arthur in time.

"Healer in village," the tracker continued. "We take him. I take you east."

She swallowed hard and nodded. "Will he live if we get him to the village?" she ventured.

"Maybe."

It was not a no.

The tracker looked at her for the first time.

She started to reach for her hood, but he gripped her wrist. His eyes went from her to Aveline's bracelet to her face again.

"What are you?" he asked.

More tears spilled from her eyes. She pulled her hand from his grip and tugged her hood up with fumbling fingers. Tiana hid her face and hunched, waiting for him to turn into another Matilda.

Instead, he maneuvered a new shirt over Warner's head and began to clean up the area around them. He put out the fire next and then bent and hefted Warner over his shoulders. The tracker stood, paused to balance his load, and then began to walk.

Tiana scrambled to her feet and followed.

The clouds had cleared, and starlight reflected off what remained of the re-frozen snow to help light their path.

I will save you, Arthur, she promised silently. *No cage will trap you, and no skinwalker will harm you.*

NINETEEN

A FULL DAY and night's journey away from the incident at the cave, the skinwalker moved through the forest with the ease of one who had become part of the darkness after many years of exposure. Ahead of him, his guide trotted with grace and agility, untouched by the branches, mud, and bramble in her path.

A breeze stirred those pine needles and brush that had not frozen with the return of the cold this night. The wind ruffled the fur lining his cloak, and the feathers in his hair – and then moved *through* him, piercing his cloak, his skin, his spirit, and before sweeping outward to rattle the frozen branches ahead of him.

He stopped. A second later, when the breeze ruffled the she-wolf's fur, she halted, too. As one, they turned and faced the direction from which the unusual wind had come.

Stop! The new spirit spoke again. When she had whispered the words, *I see you,* he had felt unease, for he did not understand what she meant, or why she sounded satisfied, for it could not possibly bode well for him. In all his time alive, he had never met anyone capable of seeing him when he chose not to be hidden.

But this time, the spirit was distressed, and he sensed the words were not spoken to him. If she did not wish to talk to him, why did he hear her? Was this wind her, too? If he followed it, would he find the elusive spirit that danced in and out of his mind, outside his control?

"This way," said a small voice.

He glanced back towards the direction they had been headed. The spirit of the little boy he had gutted at the last village stood in his path.

"When I listened to you last, you led me into a nest of Ghouls," the skinwalker said gruffly.

The child smiled, his large eyes innocent. "You can trust me."

It had been a very long time since the skinwalker had been haunted by a *vengeful* spirit. He was accompanied by the spirits of those lives he had taken, but they were generally quiet and rarely ever confronted him.

The skinwalker revered all spirits, even those that sought to lead him into danger. If anything, he was amused by the form the vengeful spirit had taken.

"Be careful, child," he whispered quietly. "If you are lost here, or I leave you, no one will find you but the Ghouls."

The little boy's smile faded and seconds later, so did he. The greatest fear of a spirit was to be cut off from friends and family to spend eternity seeking others or a place they once knew. At least if they stayed with him, they were never alone.

The skinwalker faced the direction they had come. He spent a moment in thought, shifting only when his guide nudged his hand with her muzzle. He scratched her head absently.

"We have business awaiting us," he said finally.

The she-wolf did not object, and the skinwalker began walking once more. He left the trail to navigate the woods, alerted to danger by the vengeful spirit who wished him dead. His destination, a semi-permanent outpost belonging to the Diné, who migrated with the seasons and food supply, was less than a mile ahead.

He reached it ten minutes later, without incident.

Five heartbeats assaulted his mind, and he braced himself to stay among the painful racket for the night. His guide accompanied him towards the outpost. After the incident with the red-haired man, he dared not leave his wolf alone in the forest. Because of her condition, she was far less alert and agile than usual.

He came upon one of the scouts, a boy not yet out of puberty, and startled him. The skinwalker waited for him to regain his composure. He had never traveled this far west before in his life, so he did not expect a youth this young to know of him. The Diné were waiting for a messenger from one of his employers, and he was content to let them believe what they wished about him.

"We were expecting you earlier," the scout said and lowered his weapon.

The skinwalker owed no one any explanation and remained silent despite the expectant pause from the young man across from him. The scout glanced towards the great black wolf and lingered. She bared her teeth to growl at him, as she did every other human, until the red-haired man.

"Come with me," the scout said and turned to guide them towards the other heartbeats. "You are lucky the Ghouls did not smell you. You should not travel alone."

The skinwalker snorted at the boy's stern tone.

The windows of the wooden cabin glowed with warm light, and the scent of roasting meat made the skinwalker and she-wolf both quicken their paces in anticipation of a hearty dinner. The scout led him into the cabin and motioned for them to sit near the hearth.

"My brother will return shortly," he said. "He is negotiating on behalf of our father, who is too ill to leave his home."

The skinwalker said nothing. He did not wait to be served but prepared a plate of food for himself and one filled with meat for the she-wolf, whose tail wagged when he set the meat in front of her.

"She is beautiful," the scout said, focus on the wolf again.

The skinwalker nodded once and stuffed more food in his mouth.

"What is she called?"

He shrugged. She had never revealed her name to him, and he had never asked.

When the skinwalker and his guide were finished, they sat back from their plates. The skinwalker ran his hands over the wolf's body, checking for any new injuries or tangles in her coat. He worked out several small pieces of brush, changed the bandages on her injured leg, and then removed his cloak to relax. His guide stretched out beside him, trusting him to protect her while she dozed, which she did more often in her advanced stages of pregnancy. Her stomach bulged from her position on her side, and the skinwalker rested a hand on her belly to feel for any tiny kicks or movements from the pups within.

The scout was quiet. The skinwalker watched him from his peripheral, noting that the young man had been staring at his black leg in puzzlement for a solid five minutes. If he knew what it was, or anything about the legend, he would not be seated calmly in the same forest as the skinwalker.

As it was, the skinwalker was enjoying his relative obscurity among the western tribes. Obscurity was a trait he had not valued or missed, until he was free to enter any village or city without being chased out or attacked. In the East, everyone knew of him, and no one welcomed him, with the exception of the desperate or criminal, who needed his skills.

A second man bearing a scar down the right side of his face entered with features resembling those of the scout, though where the scout was barely out of puberty, this man had left his adolescence behind five years or more.

"You are Black Wolf?" he asked.

The skinwalker nodded and stood. He had been called by many names in his time and settled on this as his favorite, out of reverence to his guide.

The chief's eldest son extended a hand, and they shook briefly. He was a strong man with a direct gaze and the air of someone accustomed to being listened to when he spoke.

"I am Diving Eagle," he said. "My father's honor was greatly affected by his inability to meet with you himself. His heart is generous but weak, and he took the loss of everyone inhabiting one of our villages hard. You are fortunate not to have crossed paths with the beast that did it. No one was left alive."

"I travel with a guardian," the skinwalker replied.

"We have not seen her like in many generations here," Diving Eagle said.

"She is the last of her kind, but not for long," the skinwalker replied. "Your father's representative is acceptable."

"Thank you. Have you eaten?" Diving Eagle motioned to the food.

The skinwalker nodded.

"Good. Then let us discuss the prisoner."

The two of them sat, and the she-wolf settled beside the skinwalker again. He had been paid to secure the prisoner by any means necessary. The option to negotiate was available, but not required, by his employer, who had wanted to give him as many tools as his objective required. The skinwalker's plan was to eat, rest, and then murder anyone standing between him and the prisoner. He sat with no expectation of being interested in anything the proud man across from him had to say.

"First, we have moved the trespasser to a different location, known only to my father and me, for his protection," Diving Eagle began.

"Where?" The skinwalker asked.

"With respect, cousin, I know who you are working for, and I do not trust him to deal fairly with us. For this reason, the trade will be on our terms, not his," Diving Eagle said with equal parts firmness and quietness.

Smart, the skinwalker thought. Though, if this man's directness and aura were any indication, he should not have been surprised by the attention to detail and shrewdness with which he operated. Was this man the brains, or was his father?

"I will need to verify the prisoner is who I seek," the skinwalker said, testing his opponent.

"You must trust me that he is. We will deliver him in a time and place we determine directly to your employer. If this is not acceptable, I have three more men coming to visit me with regards to this particular prisoner's fate. My father has authorized me to conduct negotiations on his behalf, with the understanding I will only accept the deal that benefits our people the best."

He is the brains. The skinwalker had not operated on someone else's terms in a very long time. Privately, he understood this scenario occurred because he failed to snatch the man he sought in the forest several weeks ago among a large hunting party sent by the city to find meat. His ruthless, determined employer had sent him word of where to go next, and who he should speak to. Had he not failed, he would not be in this position. It was entirely his responsibility to do what it required this time to secure his target, even if that meant negotiating with words and not weapons.

The chief's son was sharp, which he expected from those he normally dealt with, but operating on behalf of his people, which was unusual in the skinwalker's line of mercenary work. Those who hired him tended to be men of little honor. His current employer was among them.

On the surface, Diving Eagle did not seem to lack honor. Still, the skinwalker sensed more to Diving Eagle's careful words. He spoke the truth, of which the skinwalker was certain, but managed to hide something about this situation as well.

The unusual circumstances of this deal were unlike anything the skinwalker had dealt with in quite a while. So much so, he was curious enough to want to see where this all led, and why such efforts were necessary to secure one man.

His guide did not warn him against this arrangement. She was dozing. If she deemed this man unworthy, or the arrangement poor, she would object.

"Very well," he agreed. "As long as I am paid."

"Thank you," Diving Eagle ducked his head once in a display of polite deference that was not required, given his important position, but which elevated him one step more in the skinwalker's opinion. "The precautions are necessary, given the identity of our prisoner."

"His identity is not my concern," the skinwalker said. "Ensuring my employer's offer is accepted is."

Diving Eagle studied him. "This particular man's identity would increase what you were paid to do here by tenfold at least. There is not a chief or city leader for a thousand miles who would not give everything he owned to capture this man. Another great war will start once it is known who has him."

The skinwalker rarely cared about the alleged importance of anyone. At the end of the day, no one he crossed failed to pay what he demanded of them.

"Arthur Hanover," the scout said from his position seated near the door.

"I am not familiar with his name," the skinwalker replied.

"His family has controlled the city of Lost Vegas for five centuries," Diving Eagle replied.

"Lost Vegas," the skinwalker repeated. "The legendary city no army has taken?"

"That very one. His father rules the city, and his only heir is our prisoner."

The skinwalker leaned back, impressed. "It was said fifty thousand warriors tried to take the city and broke against it like water a dam."

"If it were a hundred thousand, the results would be the same," the scout said gravely. "Everything you have heard is true."

"Are their walls so high?"

"There are no walls," the scout said. "There was for two centuries, but then they came down."

"Then how did the city survive the wars among our kind?" the skinwalker asked.

"Every warrior who tried, died."

The skinwalker lifted an eyebrow skeptically. This sounded like a child's tale, not reality.

"The truth is, no one knows. The last tribe that tried to take the city did so a hundred years ago, with fifty thousand warriors, and no one survived. No one alive knows exactly what happened that day. It is believed among those peoples around the city that a Hanover must always be in charge, or the city will fall," Diving Eagle said. "Why that is, no one knows, except it has always been this way."

I remember hearing about this when it happened, the skinwalker thought. He had been around twelve at the time and believed the numbers to be an exaggeration. It was clear there was some truth to the stories that spread two thousand miles.

"Those were our people," the scout said quietly. "It is why our blood war exists."

"Four hundred of our people survived," Diving Eagle added. "We were once the largest tribe on the continent and were reduced to beggars who barely survived the winter. My father has spent seventy years as our chief, rebuilding our tribe."

"You somehow retained your lands?" the skinwalker asked.

"The Hanover's have never been interested in taking our lands, only in preventing us from taking the city. We were forced to trade over half our lands for food and shelter and the pity of our neighbors." Diving Eagle's jaw clenched when he finished speaking, and the muscles of his cheek jumped in agitation reflected in the sudden fire in his gaze.

"How can one city withstand an army this size?" the skinwalker puzzled, searching his memory for any mention of the events. However, he had been too young and uninterested in the goings on of a place so far away to take note of this war.

"Everything you have heard of Lost Vegas is true," his younger brother explained. "The city is ... sacred. Built upon or with magic and ruled by a madman who burns his own people every week, and who is feared even by the peoples who want his seed wiped from the earth." He grew quiet then glanced quickly at his brother. "It is said the dead fight for the Hanover's."

"Quiet, brother," Diving Eagle said with a disapproving look. "Do not mix fantasy with reality. The city has never been taken. This much is true, but there are more practical reasons for why Arthur Hanover is the greatest prize on the continent," Diving Eagle said. "The Hanover's control all trade between here and the ocean. Many men would like to take his father's place, or at least, to seize what the Hanover's have guarded and controlled for five centuries. Wealth is the motivation, not some fantasy about the dead."

His brother rolled his eyes, as if this were not the first time he had heard this lecture.

"How did you come to capture the heir?" the skinwalker asked, intrigued by their tales of the mythical city and its ruler. He was attuned to magic in a way most men were not, and he sensed either the siblings spoke around the possibility that the Hanover's possessed some sort of magic, or did not know it existed.

"By accident," Diving Eagle replied. "He crossed into our territory with another man. We captured him at the river dividing our lands from those of our neighbors. When we realized who he was, we demanded our neighbors turn him over to be tried for war crimes against our people."

"At a river?" The skinwalker shifted forward in interest.

"Yes."

"Does this man have red hair?"

"He does," the scout said.

The skinwalker reached into one of his pockets and pulled out the crude drawing he had made of the marking the man who kidnapped his wolf had shown him as a means of identifying his sister. The skinwalker had not been hired to kill a woman in some time, but the man at the river had claimed the gift of clairvoyance. The skinwalker thought it prudent to recall the tattoo, for the man had offered to pay him anything – which was a price the skinwalker never turned down. It was also wise to listen to someone with precognition, a lesson he learned as a child.

"Does he bear this marking?" he asked and held out the drawing of the eagle.

"Yes. It is the Hanover crest," Diving Eagle said with a glance.

The skinwalker wanted to laugh bitterly. He had been tracking this very man and spoken to him without knowing who he was. In fact, the Hanover heir had done everything humanly possible to draw the skinwalker's attention by kidnapping his guide.

How had he missed so many signs? Or ... had his target's clairvoyance kept him a step ahead of the skinwalker, until now? Was this also how his family maintained control of the city, by foreseeing threats and acting to stop them?

The skinwalker dwelt on this then dismissed it. The city was none of his concern. Only Arthur Hanover was. His guide had allowed herself to be kidnapped by the stranger and never allowed any other human near her, aside from her companion. Had she been trying to tell him the man he sought was right before him, or was there something more to the Hanover heir?

He had not thought to ask her this, either, instead respecting her decisions and instinct.

"I understand now why so many people wish to possess this boy," the skinwalker said and tucked his drawing away. "He is powerful."

"His father is. The son appears ... different," Diving Eagle said.

"The son is powerful as well," the skinwalker said.

"We may underestimate him," Diving Eagle allowed politely.

The skinwalker snorted. It was rare when someone tried to treat him with the respect this man did. "My employer offers any amount of silver and gold and copper wires. Or anything else that can be bought with an endless amount of silver and gold. Whatever you desire of him, he will guarantee you. Any offer made by another, he will double it."

The siblings exchanged a look. Diving Eagle was too careful to read, but excitement and happiness flared across his brother's features.

"Does your employer understand what happens, if we turn the prisoner over to him? The potential war that could break out?" Diving Eagle asked.

"My employer's intentions and concerns are his alone," the skinwalker replied. "He has offered to pay any cost. I believe he does not care about a war."

"I would have to agree," Diving Eagle said softly. "We are not as eager for war. Our conditions will include preserving the life of the Hanover heir."

"What my employer does to him once he has paid for him is not your concern," the skinwalker said. "How is your blood war with the Hanover's to be settled, if you do not wish them dead?"

"In a hundred years, we will be in a position to challenge them," Diving Eagle replied. He released a slow breath, as if he had not agreed with his father's decision to spare the Hanover heir. "We will not attack, until we are guaranteed victory. We are a patient people."

"And a poor one. Hence the reason you need my employer's wealth. To reclaim your lands and honor," the skinwalker said, understanding.

"Our honor is not in question. Our position to influence others is," Diving Eagle said firmly. "We will win by building a coalition greater than any created to date. And yes, this requires wealth we no longer possess."

"Understood." The skinwalker hid the smile that wanted to creep across his face. Diving Eagle bore a hundred year old grudge as if it were his own. The skinwalker understood vengeance, but not vengeance for the sake of pride or for someone else's lost battle. He understood only true revenge: the kind that came after watching his family being cut down by a man like a Hanover.

"We are neighbors to the great city this man's father rules, and he will seek us out first, once he hears of all that has transpired. He cannot die. This is my father's decision," Diving Eagle said with effort. "If you cannot agree to this condition, on behalf of your employer, we cannot hand over the prisoner."

The skinwalker was quiet. He could lie and promise falsely, which was the easier route, second only to slaughtering everyone and taking the Hanover heir. Or ...

"I can guarantee his life," he began slowly. "But you will have to agree to pay my price."

"Your price?" Diving Eagle studied him once again. "I do not believe you understand how this negotiation works."

"I cannot guarantee my employer's actions, but I can mine. He will pay you what you ask for the prisoner, and you may hire me to ensure the Hanover heir's life, once my employer has him."

Diving Eagle folded his arms across his chest, unimpressed. "Would your price happen to be the same amount we receive from your employer?"

"The price is insignificant. I will not ask you to sacrifice your vengeance," the skinwalker replied. "I ask that I deliver the Hanover to my employer instead of you."

Diving Eagle frowned, and his younger brother appeared confused. "Why would you ask this?" the chief's son questioned.

"My reasons are my own. He will be safe with me, and I will protect him, should my employer decide to take his life." It was the skinwalker's turn to be firm. "I have survived every danger or threat for two thousand miles. If so many people wish to possess this Arthur Hanover, you will need my protection to deliver him alive."

There was a pause. The skinwalker could almost see Diving Eagle's shrewd mind working. If their tribe were in as poor of shape as the skinwalker suspected, Diving Eagle would understand the inherent danger in moving a prisoner through territories not his own.

"I must discuss this with my father," Diving Eagle said. "There is risk involved in allowing you to leave here with him. If you do not arrive to your destination, we will be held responsible."

"I can handle any danger I cross."

"Not the beast in the woods," the younger boy said in a hushed tone.

"Even the beast in the woods," the skinwalker said, fully aware he was the greatest threat in existence.

"Why would we trust you to deliver him in the first place?" Diving Eagle asked. "You are a stranger, working on behalf of someone else."

The skinwalker debated how to respond before he opened his satchel and pulled out a leather wrapped trinket the size of his hand. "Show this to your father. Allow no one else to see it." He said and held it out. "I will respect his decision."

Diving Eagle accepted the small item slowly. "I will consult with my father," he said. "You are welcome to visit our village and show him this yourself."

"We will remain here," the skinwalker said.

Diving Eagle stood. "I will return in the morning. If you need food or supplies, my brother will assist you." The chief's son left.

His brother ducked into one of two rooms off the main common area and returned with blankets and pillows. He set them down beside the skinwalker. "I must return to my duty. I am not far, if you need anything," he said.

The skinwalker nodded.

The boy left, and the skinwalker shook out a blanket to drape over his dozing wolf. He stripped out of his warm second layer of clothing and boots and wrapped himself in a blanket, content to sleep inside for the first time in months.

The crackling of the fire was joined by the wolf's deep breathing, and the beat of only two hearts. The chief's son had taken his escort with him, leaving his brother and another scout, both of whom were far enough away for their heartbeats to tap but not pound the skinwalker's brain.

He relaxed, full and content, and gazed at the ceiling overhead.

"Arthur Hanover evaded me once and then tracked us from the site of the hunt party," he whispered to the wolf. "Our paths are meant to cross, for more than this one reason, or he would not have taken you."

She breathed out a sigh. She had not just allowed the Hanover heir to kidnap her, but she liked him, too.

"You made the right decision," the vengeful spirit said with a giggle.

The skinwalker turned his head to view the child.

"Sleep well," the boy said before disappearing.

For a long moment, the skinwalker mentally ran through everything he knew about his current situation twice. While it was true he could not predict all the dangers he might face on this leg of his journey, he did know he was the scariest creature he would run across, and he could handle any kind of threat.

Was the vengeful spirit toying with him?

I will slay any danger I face, spirit. The skinwalker closed his eyes and slid into sleep.

TWENTY

TIANA and the tracker walked until dawn without stopping. The tracker kept to narrow trails and avoided the two dirt roads they crossed, opting to remain in the forest. With all sense of her direction gone, Tiana could not fight her rising worry. She had not slept to see if the vision changed, and no premonitions seized her during daylight.

The confrontation with the Ghouls, and lack of sleep, were beginning to dull her senses. The ringing had quieted in her injured right ear without leaving entirely, and she had wiped the blood from her neck. Her hearing was not what it should have been, adding to her growing disconnect with her surroundings.

Just when she felt ready to drop into sleep forever, they reached a small settlement among the trees consisting of concrete buildings and log houses. She tugged up her hood once more.

Bonfires burned periodically throughout the active village. They passed a group of women skinning and chopping meat to place into a concrete bunker lit by electricity, and men forming wood logs to be used for new buildings. The scent of food came from one direction, while, at the village's center, a massive pine tree had been wrapped in tiny lights and glowed.

She gazed up at it as they passed, admiring the symbols carved into the trunk.

The tracker continued walking. A couple of people called out to him, and he waved in response. He stopped finally in front of a medium-sized log house and entered.

Tiana followed him into a small clinic consisting of half a dozen beds, a hearth at each end, and vials, boxes and jars of medicine stacked on every level surface. Drying herbs hung from the ceiling rafters. A laboratory was off to the side of one hearth.

The tracker rested Warner on a bed and motioned for her to sit on the one beside it. Tiana did so, grateful for the chance to rest. She studied Warner's pale features and willed him to live through this.

The tracker returned with a middle-aged Native carrying several items, to include a stethoscope and a battery-powered torch. He examined Warner and spoke to the tracker.

"Your brother cannot be moved," the doctor said in perfect English. He lowered the stethoscope.

"Will he survive?" she asked.

"I cannot say. His condition is critical."

She said nothing, afraid to break down in tears.

"Laughing Tree says you are hurt?" he turned to her.

"I am well," she whispered.

"Ear," the tracker said.

She hesitated and closed her eyes, then removed her hood and twisted so her right ear faced the doctor.

"Punctured ear drum," he said before touching her. He gripped her earlobe and peered into her ear. "It will heal. Might be painful for a few days, but your hearing will return. I will give you medicines to prevent an infection." The doctor released her.

She pulled her hood into place before opening her eyes. "Thank you," she murmured.

"You are fortunate. People do not usually survive the Ghouls," he added and rose.

She said nothing. As with the Matilda incident, Tiana had no explanation as to what happened or how. That it was connected to her left her sick to her stomach, when she considered how strong her deformity could be and how little control she exerted over what happened to those around her when it was unleashed. Did her father know? Was her deformity connected to the dream of her death on her eighteenth birthday?

"Rest," Laughing Tree, the tracker, told her. "We leave night."

She glanced around, feeling exposed in the large bay and afraid someone was going to see her eyes.

"Safe," he added.

"Yes, you are safe here," the physician seconded. He approached, clothing in hand. "If you would like clean clothes?"

She glanced down, unaware of how muddy her own clothes had gotten. She accepted the offering.

"You may change here. No one will disturb you today."

She nodded and clutched the clothing to her chest. The two of them walked towards the exit and left, talking quietly. She waited until the door closed and then stripped out of her muddy clothing, changing quickly into the soft cotton clothes. She wrapped her cloak around her once more protectively and pulled up her hood.

She sat on the bed beside Warner, hesitating to sleep when he was so hurt.

"You will survive, Warner. You have to," she whispered. "You can come with me to the Free Lands. And Arthur, too, after we find him."

Tiana stretched back on the bed with a deep sigh. Expecting to stay awake out of discomfort from her unfamiliar surroundings, she closed her eyes – and dropped into deep sleep.

TIANA AWOKE to the crackling of a fire and the calming scents of herbs. She sat up, alarmed, not recognizing her surroundings at first.

Warner's body was on the bed beside hers, his chest moving up and down steadily, and she relaxed. Aside from the fires, the patient bay was kept dark, while bright light outlined the closed doors of the lab and other rooms off the main bay.

She swung her legs off the bed. Someone had placed a bowl of stew and bread on the nightstand between her bed and Warner's. Before the scent of the hearty food reached her, she had the warm bowl in her hand. Her stomach roared with hunger. She ate fast and with no concern for etiquette, since she had never been permitted to eat in public before.

"For ear."

At the tracker's voice, she looked up and instinctively reached for her hood with the hand holding her roll. He held out a piece of gauze. She glanced from it to his face before lowering her hand to take it. Tiana stuffed the soft gauze into her ear and continued eating, hunched over her food. Only when she had soaked up the very last drops of stew with her bread did she take a deep breath and straighten.

Suddenly aware the tracker had not left, she wiped her mouth on her cloak and then pulled her hood up.

"Horses," he said. "Ready?"

She nodded and stood. Her ear was achy. He handed her a satchel and a canteen similar to the one carrying penicillin tea that Warner had worn. The tracker walked towards the exit, but she lingered over Warner, worried.

Tiana leaned forward and touched his warm forehead. "I'll be back," she promised him. "With Arthur. Then we'll all go ..." She stopped. She had purposely not considered how her father would react to her breaking all of his rules and leaving.

The door opened, and the cool night air touched her cheeks. Tiana shrugged off the thoughts of her father and left Warner, following the Native.

As soon as the cold night air brushed her face, she smiled. A thrill ran through her, and she looked around at the dark village, barely daring to believe she had spent not one, but three days outside the city!

She had done it. She had thrown off her father's heavy-handed control and escaped. She felt sad for Warner, but not even his condition could change her mind about leaving. Nothing would ever make her regret having her freedom at last.

The lights in the houses, and circling the tree, flared to life. She had been too tired to pay much attention to the village when they arrived. Fully refreshed, she gazed at the strings of lights in the trees and wrapped around trunks with awe. The village appeared magical with the faint pricks of light, some of which glowed from beneath a thin layer of fresh snow.

"I would never leave here!" she exclaimed.

The tracker did not respond.

She turned and saw he was far ahead of her, waiting at a corral with two horses. She hurried after him and slowed when one of the horses began to show signs of panicking. The second horse, however, twitched donkey-sized ears but did not try to pull away or flee.

The Native nodded, as if he expected this, and motioned to a youth lingering near the entrance of the stables. The boy took the nervous horse away while leaving the calm one. The Native motioned her forward.

She approached uncertainly, not wanting to scare the beast. Its ears twitched faster as she approached, and it pawed the ground with its front hooves.

"Mule," the tracker told her. "Not scare easy."

Tiana reached out to touch the soft hair of the mule's face. It blew out a snort into her hand, and she smiled. It was the first domesticated animal she had ever officially met. His eyes were large, his ears larger, and his coloring brindle.

"He is beautiful," she murmured.

The tracker appeared pleased. "Faster on horse," he said. He stood to the horse's left side and motioned for her to join him. As if knowing she had no experience with horses, he picked up the stirrup and motioned to his foot, then showed her the reins, the saddle and saddlebags. She nodded, excited for her first horseback riding experience.

When he was done, he dropped a wooden box beside the mule. She stepped onto it, and he helped her mount before handing her the reins.

"Wait," he directed her.

Tiana nodded. She fumbled with the reins and settled into the saddle. The mule's warm body eliminated some of the night's chill. His hair was soft and his mane wiry. She admired the animal and added this first-time experience to her list of adventures she intended to share with Arthur and Aveline, when she saw them again.

The tracker left the stables atop a second mule and joined her. Stretching forward, he claimed her horse's reins.

"Hold." He said and motioned to the horse's mane.

She gripped its mane and smiled, ready to find and rescue her brother.

He led her out of the village at a quick walk. When they reached the nearest road, their speed picked up, from a jarring trot to a smooth, fast canter. Tiana clung to the horse's mane and squeezed the animal with her legs, until she had found her balance. The movement had a natural rhythm her body soon adopted. Her hood fell away, and the cold night swept through her hair.

The exhilarating pace soon left her intoxicated. The moody, partially cloudy sky above, mysterious forest, and invigorating wind only added to the happiness bubbling up within her. She grinned, feeling free of her oppressive father at last.

Her guide alternated between cantering and walking and remained on the same road, which twisted and turned through the forest. They passed no other travelers during the night. Only when dawn began to brighten the forest, and the sun rose, was she able to figure out what direction they went.

The sun rose at their back, though the air remained cold this day.

The tracker glanced back, and she met his gaze, relaxed and smiling. He shook his head and faced forward again.

Tiana took a drink from the penicillin water before sipping regular water and eating small bites from the meat and cheese given to her by the tracker the night before.

She was about to ask the tracker how far away Arthur was, when he halted his horse in the middle of the road and tilted his head, listening.

Her horse stopped automatically, and she gazed around at the forest. Even without her damaged hearing, she doubted she was going to pick up what he did, for he knew the forest in a way she could not. When he did not move, and nothing appeared in their path, she whispered, "What is it?"

His response was in his language. He tensed and released the reins of her mule, indicating for her to remain where she was. The tracker advanced on horseback.

Tiana lifted her hood over her head and waited for the danger he sensed to appear. When the tracker was a good twenty feet ahead of her, he stopped again.

Five figures on horseback melted from the forest and rode towards him at a slow walk. The tracker spoke to them at length, until Tiana's mule began to doze, and she grew concerned.

She twisted as the sound of hooves on gravel came from behind her. Four more Natives on horseback were within fifteen feet. They had halted, but their horses were already starting to show signs of anxiousness. They danced in place and tossed their heads. None of the men behind her spoke. They were all armed.

Gripping the mule's mane harder, she faced forward again.

The tracker returned to her, grim.

"You go ... them," he said and pointed.

"Oh. They will take me to Arth ... our destination?" she asked.

He grimaced. "We cross their lands. They take you there. Your brother pay and you come back." He spoke the words slowly and with effort.

She glanced at the men ahead of them with renewed interest. "Are they kidnapping me?" she asked.

"Stealing," he confirmed. "Me one. They many." He motioned to them. "I come back with brother."

"Very well," she said.

"I tell them ... eagle." He reached back to his shoulder and tapped it.

She cringed. "You were watching me change clothes?" she asked.

"No. Brother tell me. Eagle is safe."

How would the Natives know anything about the tattoo each Hanover bore? And why had Warner felt the need to explain its existence to anyone?

"If trouble, you do ... Ghouls," the tracker added quietly, gravely. "Okay?"

She nodded half-heartedly, confused about what was happening. Even if she dared call upon her magic to help, she could not control it. That this man and Warner had survived, when Matilda did not, was beyond her ability to explain.

"Is Arthur ... our destination close?" she asked.

"Yes. They have man you seek," he replied.

She almost sighed, relieved for the sliver of luck in circumstances she was doubting were fortunate.

But at least she was free of the city. Nothing that happened to her here would ever convince her otherwise.

"They will not hurt you. I tell them you special," he added and pointed to her eyes.

Tiana flushed, hating others knew of her deformity. "Thank you," she said. "Be safe."

The Native was frowning, as if he genuinely had not expected this complication. With a brisk nod, he rode past her and towards the four men behind her on the road. They parted to allow him to pass. He urged his horse into a trot then a lope and disappeared around a bend.

Tiana faced the five riders. None of them tried to ride near her.

Had the tracker warned them what would happen if they did? Why did horses despise her so much?

One of them motioned for her to follow, and the five ahead of her turned their horses and began to walk down the road.

Uncertain how to make her mule go, she remained where she was, stranded on the beast. She considered sliding off the mule but did not know how she would climb back without help. She stretched forward to try to reach the reins the tracker had left dangling but was unable to grab them.

"Can you ride?" one of the Natives behind her asked finally.

"No," she replied.

He muttered something to his companions, and one of them chuckled. The Native urged his horse towards her and made it three steps before the animal reared and whinnied. It lashed out with its forelegs in Tiana's direction then landed and bucked.

"I cannot be around horses," she called to him.

He slid off his horse and strode towards her, frowning fiercely. Snatching her reins, he draped them over the mule's neck. The Native effortlessly pulled himself up behind her and nudged the horse forward.

Tiana shifted to give him as much room as possible. With her cloak bunched between them, she was uncomfortable for the first time since being hoisted into the saddle.

They neared the five riders ahead but slowed when the horses grew agitated. The Native behind her mumbled under his breath and guided the mule towards the forest rather than the riders. He shouted a few words towards the others. One of them nodded, and he entered the woods via a well-trodden path wide enough for two horses.

Uncertain what to expect from her first kidnapping, she began to grow concerned. These Natives had her brother, but how would she find him, if she were a prisoner? Once she did, how would they escape? Would she be able to find her mule again? And if they could not escape on their own, how long would it take for Warner to recover enough to rescue her as well as Arthur?

A village appeared not far into the forest. It was much smaller than the tracker's and consisted of rawhide tents and makeshift corrals rather than permanent cabins and paddocks. No women or children were in view either, only men bearing firearms and traditional weapons.

The warrior behind her pulled the mule to a halt in front of one of the tents and slid off the animal's back. He motioned for her to do the same and draped the reins over a pole to the side of the entrance.

Tiana managed to climb off the mule without falling. The moment her feet touched the ground, she groaned. On horseback, she had not noticed the muscles used to keep her in the saddle. On the ground, her inner thighs trembled and her hamstrings burned from being used in a way to which she was not accustomed. She wobbled rather than walked to follow the Native waiting for her at the entrance to the tent.

He swept aside the flap covering the entrance and motioned her into the large space beyond. A fire burned at the center of the tent, its smoke funneling up through the hole at the center. Furs and rugs covered the ground. The man at the fire rose upon seeing her. Several years older than Arthur, he was lean, like the other warriors who confronted her on the road, and tense, as if the well-armed warrior suspected her of planning to attack him. His dark gaze was steely, and a scar ran down the side of one cheek.

He spoke a flurry of words at her escort, who answered just as fast. She heard her name mixed in among their tongue without knowing what was said. The frown and lingering glance of the man at the fire warned her he was displeased about something the other had said. He asked a question, and her escort answered with a shrug.

"You call yourself Tiana Burrows?" the Native before her asked.

She nodded.

He lifted his chin in a wordless order to her escort, who left.

"You bear a mark, as all the wealthy in Lost Vegas do?" he asked.

Hearing the edge in his voice, she hesitated.

"Show me."

Could he know what her marking stood for?

If her father did not care who she was, why would the Natives?

Tiana ducked her head then removed her hood and cloak. She loosened the shirt she wore and turned her back to him, sliding it down over one shoulder.

"You're a Hanover," the Native said, voice growing even harder.

She straightened her clothing and took a deep breath. "I came to find my brother."

"He is here," the Native confirmed.

Her heart leapt, and she silently thanked the tracker for bringing her the right direction. She bent to retrieve her cloak.

The Native snatched her wrist, and she froze. He tossed her cloak out of reach. His scent was that of forest and bonfire, and his solid frame larger than Arthur's. His body heat radiated through the clothing he wore. His grip was tight enough to start to hurt, but she was accustomed to pain after seven years with Matilda and did not flinch or complain.

The Native was quiet, brooding. She felt the intensity of his gaze, as if he wished to murder her with his eyes.

"You believe your enemies are beneath you?" he snapped. He snatched her jaw with his free hand and twisted her face towards him.

Tiana closed her eyes to shield him from her deformity.

He muttered in his tongue then spoke to her. "I look forward to peeling the skin from your body and killing you slowly," he said with a great deal of control. He shook her hard enough to knock her off balance. She caught herself against his hard frame, ignoring the fingers digging into the wrist that had not yet healed.

"What of my father? Will you send me back to him?" she whispered. She did not resist the angry Native, aware of how it would only infuriate him further.

"You will never see him again!"

"S... so, if I stay, you will murder me, and I will not be returned home?"

"You will never see your city again!"

She breathed as deeply as possible, given the awkward angle of her neck. "Very well. I agree."

He was silent.

"Did you offer my brother these same terms?" she ventured. She doubted Arthur would agree to stay. He had always held his father's good favor and a future as a leader in the city.

"Are you toying with me, or are you a fool?" he snapped.

"He does not intend to let me live past my next birthday. I would rather die free than under his control."

A low, gruff laugh emanated from the shadows in the back of the tent. A few hoarse words came next.

The Native holding her gritted his teeth loudly enough for her to hear, offered a terse response, and then released her.

"You are not foolish or toying with him, are you?" the second man asked.

Tiana peered through her eyelashes at the elderly man with a blanket draped around his shoulders walking slowing towards them. He leaned heavily on a cane. His leathery features were folded in wrinkles, though his brown eyes remained sharp. Uncertain how to answer the question, she said nothing.

"My father is the chief of our people. When he speaks, every man and woman beneath the sky answers," the Native beside her growled. He gripped her arm and shook her again.

"N...no," she replied. "I am being honest. Perhaps I seem different because I am deformed."

"The Hanover's burn the deformed," the elderly man said.

"Yes," she said. "My father does."

"What does he do to the daughter he did not burn?"

She did not wish to speak, but when the first man reached for her again, she shifted to display her arms and then turned her back to them and lifted her shirt over her head to display the various scars left over from her interactions with Matilda.

"Fitting treatment for a Hanover," the younger Native said and spat on the ground beside her.

"She is every bit his victim, son," his father chided.

"She is a Hanover, father."

Tiana lowered her shirt. The younger Native snatched her arm and peered at the bracelet she wore.

"Where did you find this?" the older man asked, limping closer. "It is not yours."

"It belongs to my guardian," she replied.

"What is it, father?" his son asked.

"Something I have not seen in a very long time," was the careful response. "If this belongs to your guardian, then we will act with caution." This was directed at his son, who nodded.

In the quiet that followed, Tiana risked a look at the elderly man, who was studying her hard. He shifted forward and placed a knobby finger beneath her chin to lift it. Tiana cringed but did not fight him, not wanting to disrupt his delicate balance or anger his son even further.

"It is true," he said in his low, gruff voice. "The Hanover's carry a deformity in their blood."

"My mother did. My father does not," she replied.

"You believe this?"

Tiana's cheeks grew warm, not because she cared to defend her father's honor, but because she truly did not know him well enough to say.

"It has long been rumored the Hanover's pass down special gifts to each generation," the elderly man said. He released her chin. "It is why your family maintains control of the city."

"My father spoke nothing to me of this," she replied. "I was not permitted to leave my room."

The younger Native shook his head and paced away. "Every Hanover should be locked away and beaten!"

Tiana gazed at his father, who lifted an eyebrow when she failed to react to the other man's anger.

"Son, return this to the man who sent it. I have given you my decision," he said and held out an item hidden inside a leather cloth.

The younger man took it slowly with a glance at Tiana. "I can send in several warriors to watch her, if you fear danger from her guardian."

"I fear nothing, son. We will be well alone," was the calm response.

"Father, she's a *Hanover*. Our blood enemy. She cannot be trusted."

"Do as I say."

His son did not object again but glared at Tiana before striding out of the tent.

She sighed when he was gone. He carried the air of someone accustomed to action, as opposed to his father's wiser approach of assessing what was before him before he acted.

"Please sit," the elderly man said and limped towards the fire.

She trailed him. "You do not wish to imprison me with my brother?" she asked. "I am a Hanover. I lied about my identity."

"If you would choose a slow death over returning to your father, you are no enemy of mine," he replied. "You bear the signs of his abuse too well to be insincere."

She flushed, embarrassed to be so easily read by strangers. "Is my brother well?" she asked.

"He is being treated as an enemy."

"He despises my father as well."

"Perhaps. But is your father's heir, which makes his guilt undeniable."

She sat and wrapped her arms around her knees. "Will you take him a blanket and tend his wounds?"

The elderly man titled his head. "How ... clairvoyance?"

"Among other abilities," she admitted. "His vision of the future is much better than mine, but I saw him freezing to death and bleeding. It's why I left the city. To find him."

"And rescue him?"

"Yes. I also hope to convince him to go north with me, to the Free Lands."

The elderly man was quiet, and she looked from the dancing fire to him. A flicker of warmth was in his otherwise hard gaze. "I will order my son to take him a blanket and tend his wounds."

"Thank you," she said and started to smile. "May I see him?"

He chuckled. "If I agree, you will stay with him in conditions befitting my blood enemy."

"I can survive anything," she replied quickly. "I've been poisoned, stabbed, attacked by Ghouls, and starved."

"Ghouls," he repeated, one side of his mouth pulling up. "You have no fear of death or torture?"

She shook her head. "I will happily die beside my brother, if that is our fate."

The older man was quiet long enough that Tiana's cheeks grew hot once more.

"My guardian thinks I'm crazy," she said, eyes on the bracelet.

"You are not mad or daft, though you may appear to be both," he replied. "Do you know what that marking stands for?"

"No."

"Where is your guardian?"

"I want to think in the city, but she may have followed me," Tiana said. "She's supposed to protect me, and I left her behind."

"This mark belongs to a tribe believed to be extinct," he explained. "They were from the northern reaches, where the snow never melts. It was said they moved south after the Old World ended and were scattered across the eastern side of the continent. The members of this tribe should not exist, and she is the second whose path I have crossed lately."

Tiana listened, fascinated by the account. "She has no idea about her past or any living family members," she said.

"She does not know what she is?"

"No. She is special, is she not?"

"If this is hers, passed to her by her family and not bought at a market, then yes," he stated. "Your father does not favor our people. He would not approve of a Native protector, if he did not know her capabilities."

"I do not know what he knows," she replied and dropped her gaze to the fire once more. "But if he knew she is my friend, he would send her away. He wishes to punish me for what I am."

Another long pause stretched between them before the elderly man spoke again. "I will grant your wish to see your brother, but not tonight. Tonight, you will enjoy my hospitality, out of respect for your honesty."

The idea of dying beside Arthur terrified her. But she also believed that, if anyone could figure out a way out of this mess, he would. She would rather suffer with him than survive alone. She just needed a few minutes with him, to alert him to her presence and ensure he was alive. He had to have a plan of some sort.

The older man rose and hobbled to the entrance. He left, and she released her breath. While his voice had remained soft, he had been evaluating her. She recognized the intensity behind his look from the few times she had dealt with her father. Both men had been trying to decide her fate, and she suspected both came to the same ultimate conclusion: Tiana Hanover had to die.

She swallowed hard. Part of her hoped Aveline had followed her, for her fighting skills might be needed to escape, while another part of her was leery of the attention the bracelet drew. What did the older man know about Aveline's past and her special ability? Tiana sensed the magic without seeing what it did. The last thing she wanted to do was drag her friend into a situation no one would survive.

After several minutes, a woman with a tray of food entered and set it down beside her. Wordlessly, she left the small feast consisting of quail, squash, and bread. Tiana began to eat and was joined soon after by the elderly man.

He returned to his seat across the fire from her. She glanced at him once then hunched over her food to eat quickly, in case he decided to send her to prison early.

"Your brother will be tended to," he told her, watching.

Her mouth was too full of food to respond. She nodded her thanks. When she finished what she suspected was supposed to be her last meal, she sat back and examined her surroundings.

"What wrong has my family committed against yours?" she asked.

"Fifty thousand and four wrongs," he replied.

Her brow furrowed.

"In the final wars between the city and its neighbors," he explained. "Your ancestor massacred all but a few of the members of my tribe."

No atrocity committed by her family would surprise her, even this one. "I understand why you hate us," she murmured. "And why you wish Arthur and me dead."

"It is not personal."

"I know. I just ask that I am allowed to die beside him."

"As much as this would please my people, my son in particular, another fate has been chosen for your brother," he replied. "Someone has made me an offer I cannot refuse, one that will rebuild all we have lost. Your brother has been traded in exchange for the means for us to seek our justice."

Her breath caught.

"Your value lies in the mark on your shoulder. No one knows you are here, little Hanover. My people would be pleased to see you take your brother's place."

Tiana squeezed her hands together.

The elderly chief studied her briefly once more. "You will face trial among my people for crimes committed against us by your ancestors. I believe, even if your father is ashamed of you, you are of great political value, more so once your brother is gone. I may have a use for you beyond the satisfaction your death would bring my people."

She waited, sensing he was not yet certain how best to use her against her father.

"You will have a day with your brother to say your farewells," he said finally. "I will consult several other tribal elders before I make my decision about your fate."

"I do not fault you at all," she said earnestly. "Thank you for granting your enemy this small favor."

"You do not plead, do not apologize," he said, smiling faintly. "Is your brother as brave as you are?"

Brave? She had never in her life been called anything close to this! "He is braver," she replied, puzzled. "Much braver. He hired my guardian, without my father's permission, and she saved my life once already."

"For the sake of your spirits, I am pleased to know the Hanover madness was not passed to either of you," he said. "Perhaps you will find the peace in the world beyond this one that you have not found here."

He is kinder than my father. A lump formed in her throat. How was he able to read her, when people like her father and Matilda had known her for years and never understood her pain the way he did?

"Thank you," she managed.

"Rest. You may take my son's bed this night." He motioned to a pallet on one side of the tent, in the shadows, covered in blankets.

Tiana rose and crossed to the bed. She sank down onto the soft mattress and pulled off her boots before climbing under the blankets. The bed smelled of his son, and she snuggled in the fur and wool, soon dropping into sleep despite knowing her fate would be decided tomorrow.

Rather than restful slumber, Tiana was assaulted by the familiar vision of the skinwalker lying in wait to attack her. The scene played over and over in her mind, each time a little different than before. More details formed with each iteration, and she made out the faces of the chief's son, Diving Eagle, Rocky, Aveline, Marshall Cruise, two other Natives, and ... Arthur, who had never been present in this particular vision before.

Each time, the skinwalker morphed into a beast and massacred everyone, or killed most of them before the smaller skinwalker appeared to challenge him.

Every recurrence, someone she cared about died in her arms. Sometimes it was Aveline and other times it was Arthur. The scenery never changed. Neither did the time of day, the position of the tent, the brush, the distance she stood from the others. The people were often different.

Stuck in a lucid nightmare, she was unable to break away from the repeating vision, and likewise helpless to stop the skinwalker from slaughtering her friends.

No vision had ever done this before. No vision had ever been this vibrant, where she could feel the cool brush of a spring breeze, smell wet earth, and feel the warmth of Arthur's blood when he collapsed in her arms.

Tiana ended each dream sobbing and shaken. As the night progressed, she managed to rein in her emotion long enough to think. In the seconds between iterations, she tried to make sense of what she saw and more importantly, why it continued to replay in her dreams.

What am I missing? Why am I seeing this? Why does it change?

She wracked her half-sleeping mind for insight and recalled how Arthur once explained that the visions changed when the circumstances leading up to them changed. If true, then was she seeing potential versions of the future? Had the future not yet been determined fully?

Before she could process more thoughts along this line, the vision began again.

Tiana spent the night trapped in sleep, reliving the events of a potential future she had been experiencing for several weeks over and over.

She awoke crying and distressed by the idea of Arthur dying in her arms.

TWENTY-ONE

"WHAT'S THAT SOUND?" Aveline asked and pushed herself up from the hard ground. She had been deep asleep when a loud thumping jarred her out of slumber.

"What sound?" Rocky sat nearby sharpening a knife, his eyes trained on their surroundings.

"That ... pounding." Aveline frowned. "Hmm. I don't hear it. Guess it was in my dreams." She settled back onto the ground and gazed at the sky. With no fire, she was warm beneath a thick blanket, though the cold winter night brushed the exposed skin of her face.

Rocky shivered beneath his cloak, while Jose snored quietly nearby, oblivious to everything.

Restless, Aveline sat up and huddled in the blanket. "It's too quiet out here," she muttered and shuffled over to Rocky.

"I kind of like it," he replied. "No one hunting for us."

"Except the Natives who murder everyone who leaves the city."

"Jose says that will protect us." Rocky pointed to the three items the electrician had lain out on a boulder near their camp in a shallow valley between two hills. The tool and two metal objects meant nothing to Aveline, but Jose had insisted the Natives expecting him would understand what he carried and leave them alone.

"I have to find Karl," she said for the tenth time that day. She was constantly at war with herself about whether or not she should have left the city at all. Tiana was hers to protect, yes, but was vengeance not a priority as well?

"We will," Rocky said, unfazed by her persistence. "At this point, you know the city is locked down."

With both his children gone, Tiana's father was likely burning people left and right for details about where either of them were. Every time Aveline thought about him, she frowned. "We can't go back without her," she surmised.

"I'm wondering if we can go back at all," Rocky pointed out. "You will be hunted like your father was."

"Like father, like daughter," she murmured. Tiana's father had made an identical statement, one that left her perplexed as to his meaning even after she had mentally reviewed the conversation several times. "Hey, Rock, did you ever hear any weird stories about the Devil's Massacre?"

"Weird?" He glanced towards her. "You mean, aside from the fact your father slaughtered a thousand people in three days' time with his bare hands?"

"Have you heard any variations on the story?"

"Of course not. I heard the tale directly from him."

It has to be magic. How else had Tiana's father managed to introduce such doubt into Aveline's mind?

"Why?" Rocky asked.

"No reason." Uncomfortably warm beneath the blanket, she tossed it off. For a split second, she thought she heard the strange pounding again, coming from the direction of Jose. She held her breath to listen, and it was gone.

"How are we going to find your friend once we're in the village?" Rocky asked.

"Luck," Aveline replied in a growl. "We're going to have to break away and wander around until we find her. This might help." She lifted her pendant. "It'll glow brighter when I'm closer to her. Asking about her would draw too much suspicion, and Mohammed says these people are enemies of the Hanover's."

"Who isn't?" Rocky said with a smile. "Maybe we can use that to our advantage. You're no fan of the Hanover's either."

"Their father, no," she agreed. "Tiana is different. I think Arthur is, too, though I haven't spent enough time around him to know for sure. He did pay off my father's debts as promised."

"You have a good sense of people. If you think he can be trusted, then I believe you," Rocky replied.

"I'm not sure yet. I do think he will do anything he can to protect Tiana. We can use that to keep him in line."

"I hope they feed us," Rocky said after a pause. "I can't eat any more of Jose's bars."

Aveline snorted. Jose had brought enough food with him, but it was in the form of dense meal bars, each of which required a full canteen of water to choke down. They worked in that everyone was energized throughout the day, but the taste and texture had grown stale after their first full day of travel.

"I wonder if your father ever thought we'd leave the city," Rocky mused.

"I doubt it. He always told me I needed to stay where I was."

"We had to try it once, right?"

Aveline shrugged. "I keep thinking of everything I should have asked him before he died. About the Devil's blood curse. The Guild. About my mother. Other questions I didn't know I needed to ask. Karl. What he knew of the outer city." She sighed.

"He may not have known a lot of those answers, or he would've refused to tell you," Rocky said. "No one, not even you, were allowed to mention your mother if he didn't bring her up first."

"I don't think he ever got over losing her," she said. "You remember the shrine he built in our cabin?"

"I do. The last shirt she wore, a few feathers, a candle, and a braid of her hair."

"I should've taken some part of her with me, but all I could think about was him," Aveline said, recalling the night her father died. "He was my world. It wasn't like I remembered her anyway. I think I cared about her, only because he did."

"I remember her. Glimpses mainly. I was super young when she died," Rocky said. "But I do remember her giving me candy. She was really pretty."

"Shut up, Rock," she said and rolled her eyes. "I was being serious."

"So am I."

"You *can't* remember her! You would've been ... what, two?"

"I was four. My mother had just abandoned me, and your father brought me to your home. You were big enough to crawl," he insisted. "I remember everything for about a two week stretch."

"Rocky, please! My mother died during childbirth!"

"What? No. Unless your father brought home some other Native to raise us, she was alive for a few months after they took me in, and then she was gone."

Aveline stared at him, seeking some indication he was jesting. It was not like him to joke about something this serious. His features were relaxed as he focused on his knives, without the telltale hint of humor always present when he told a joke.

"You really think you remember her?" she asked at last.

"I know I do."

What was she missing? How did Rocky recall a memory that should not have existed? Why did Tiana's father also insist Aveline's mother had lived through the childbirth her father claimed had killed her? What reason would her father have to lie about anything to her, let alone when her mother died? It could not have been more than a few months difference between Aveline's birth and Rocky's arrival to the family.

"I'm going to sleep," she said and rose. She returned to the small nest on the ground she had created earlier and rested on her back to stare at the clear, dark sky. Anger prevented her from feeling the chill of winter. "You swear you remember her, Rocky?"

"Yeah," he said. "I remember her carrying you in one arm and me in another when we went ... somewhere. Market, maybe."

This makes no sense. Aveline rolled onto her side, placing her back to him. Rocky could be wrong, but he would not lie to her. If her father had smudged the date her mother died by a few months, why did it matter?

She breathed in and out deeply and closed her eyes, determined to rest. She needed to be at her best for the meeting Jose would have with the Natives' scientist the next day. She and Rocky were supposed to be his assistants, brought along to help carry more of the metal tools and parts their bags were loaded down with. She had no idea what to expect of her first ever meeting with Natives and was hoping no one asked why he did not simply bring another horse to carry the supplies.

Her mind skimmed through her worry over Tiana, passed her confusion about the different accounts of when her mother died, and rested on the heritage her mother had left behind. She had been raised to respect her mother's Native religion and to be proud of her heritage, but she did not know the basics about her mother's people: the name of her tribe, where they were from, or even why her mother chose to stay in the city, once her father bought her as a slave and freed her. Was it because of love? Did she not want to visit her family again?

Did she even have any family elsewhere? Did Aveline have aunts, uncles, cousins, or grandparents searching for her somewhere? If she did, and they were outside the city, did it matter? Aveline had no desire to remain outside the city and possessed little curiosity about her mother's people. The passing thought about asking her father who her mother's tribe was left without leaving a flicker of regret.

She had never known her mother and idolized her father, who

raised her to follow him into the criminal underworld of Lost Vegas. She had never desired anything else, not even now, on her first journey outside the city.

She began to drift into slumber. A faint thumping sounded at the edge of her mind. At first, its steady rhythm lulled her deeper into sleep. But soon, it grew louder and shifted from the recesses of her thoughts to the center, where it began to pound against her brain. A second rhythm joined it.

Aveline awoke fully, and the sounds faded once more. She closed her eyes and slid back into sleep, and the pounding returned. Her body flushed with fever, and she tossed and turned, trapped between sleep and consciousness.

"Avi," Rocky called.

She snapped awake. Disoriented, Aveline looked around her. She was about to lecture him for waking her up in the middle of the night, when she realized dawn lined the eastern sky. This time, the strange pattering in her head remained after she woke. The longer she listened for some sort of pattern in the sounds, she soon realized there were three separate rhythms, each with its own individual pattern.

"You all right?"

She twisted towards Rocky's voice. He and Jose appeared awake and were readying their horses. Embarrassed to be the one holding them up, especially in front of Jose, she rose. Her head felt woolly, and she was still sweating.

"Fine," she mumbled.

Rocky peered at her. "You ill?"

"Slept terrible," she replied. "I think there was a rock in the middle of my back all night long."

He nodded without appearing convinced.

"I'm not used to horses," Jose said. He was holding his reins and gazing at his horse with a grimace. "Anyone else sore?"

"Yes!" Aveline and Rocky chorused.

The incessant, erratic tapping baffled her. She surveyed their surroundings but was unable to identify the cause of the strange sound reverberating around her skull. Then again, she did not fully expect to see a source outside her head, for it sounded as if it came from *inside* her mind.

How is that possible? She shook her head.

"Meal bar?" Jose asked sheepishly and approached, holding out one of the bemoaned foodstuffs to each of them.

"I need real food," Rocky said acidly and snatched his.

"Thanks," Aveline said with a smile. Jose held her gaze a tad too long, long enough for both of them to flush, before he turned away.

If Rocky noticed the glances they sneaked at one another, he said nothing. Jose's attention, however brief the exchange, caused Aveline's body to flush warmer and cleared her mind.

"It's warm today," she complained and tugged off her cloak. She rolled up her sleeves as well and un-tucked her shirt. She pulled on her boots with reluctance, feeling as if she would explode if she could not remove more items of clothing instead of adding to her discomfort.

She finished tying the second boot and paused.

The ground was frozen beneath a thin layer of snow and the air chilly enough for her breath to rise in white puffs towards the sky. Yet the back of her neck was damp with sweat, and beads of moisture tickled the sensitive skin of her chest and back.

She straightened and rested the back of her hand against her forehead. Her skin was warmer than usual. She was uninjured, and she was not experiencing the same symptoms of illness she expected from flu or cold season in the city. She was hot and of course, the thumping had not stopped. Otherwise, she felt fine. Was the world beyond the city's limits making her sick?

I hate nature, she thought.

"Avi!" Rocky called again.

She shook out her arms and legs then stretched. She had gone to bed feeling sore from two days of horseback riding and awoken with burning thighs, aching core, and some other sort of illness she hoped subsided once she was back in the city.

Aveline mounted and ate her breakfast bar.

The three of them began at a slow walk through the hilly terrain making up the short distance remaining between them and the forests east of the city.

A quarter of a mile from their camp, one of the pattering sensations in her mind fell away, though the two original sources remained. It was not until another mile from camp that she heard the third rhythm return.

Her instincts tickled her senses, and she studied the hills to her right. If she had not known better, she would have guessed the tapping came from that direction. As she listened, the new rhythm slowed and became steady, much like a ...

Heartbeat?

That's insane, she thought. The closer she listened to the sounds, the more they resembled three distinct heartbeats. As a chorus, it was chaotic, adding to her misery. For several hours, she dwelt on the sounds. The third rhythm came and went often yet remained in the same general direction, either flanking them to the right of their path or ahead and to the right. She monitored the movement without understanding what or who was tracking them or even if that was what the tapping indicated.

A mile or two away from the forest, Rocky and Jose began to talk, disrupting her focus.

"So these guys know we're coming?" Rocky was asking Jose.

"They do. They should have spotted us the first night," Jose asked.

"Then they're okay with us being here, or we'd be dead."

"Not necessarily."

Aveline nudged her horse closer to the two men ahead of her. "What do you mean?"

"They tend to attack on their territory. If they're not happy I brought an escort, we'll know by noon, when we enter the forest," Jose explained. "But don't worry. I've never had problems with them over anything. Once they take an oath, they keep it, so long as we do, and they've guaranteed my safety."

"I hope that extends to us." Rocky reached for one of his weapons and positioned it closer to his dominant hand. Aveline did the same and eyed the forest.

"Does anyone know you trade with the city's enemies?" she asked.

"Not really," Jose said and cleared his throat. "No one asks. But the Diné have the most advanced electrical infrastructure of anyone within five hundred miles. It makes sense to trade with them, when we need materials to maintain the city's grid. In exchange, we, uh ..." he cleared his throat. "We kind of provide their electricity, too."

Aveline laughed. "This had to be Mohammed's idea!" she exclaimed, tickled by the idea of the Hanover's unwittingly providing direct support to their sworn enemies. It did not seem possible for a man like Tiana's father not to notice. If he were running the city, and obsessed with burning people, he probably did not have time to ask too many questions, she reasoned.

"It was," Jose confirmed. "We have better metal-smithing capabilities in the city. When the Diné need specific parts, we can make them. But we need the material, which is not cheap or readily available within the confines of our city. The Diné are master tradesmen and they have natural resources unlike anything the city could possibly dream of having. The relationship just kind of works."

"Sounds mad to me," Rocky said. "Especially since the inner city has no electricity at all."

"The Hanover's have never made the inner city a priority," Jose admitted. "But I don't know that you want them to. Edwin Hanover's attention brings only death and ashes."

"What an ass," Aveline murmured. "How can one man control an entire city anyway?"

"He's dangerous."

"But so are a lot of men. And yet only this man's family rules over everything. One man controlling people I can understand. My father was amazing," she said. "But a dynasty? How does it survive?"

"They're all mad," Rocky assessed.

I have to agree there, Aveline thought. As the only person among them who had met all three of the Hanover's, she was in a unique position to evaluate the family. They were different than anyone she had ever met, and each of them possessed some sort of forbidden magic as well. Was this magic somehow behind their power?

There was more depth to the Hanover's than she had been exposed to, and it was beyond Aveline's ability to comprehend what that could be. Neither Tiana nor Arthur appeared to have the temperament to burn hundreds of people. How could Tiana's random abilities, and her brother's foresight, help either of them hold on to power over an entire city?

Tired, frustrated, and growing irritated with the pattering in her mind, Aveline drank a full canteen of water to help cool her down.

"Are these your people?" Jose asked.

She lifted an eyebrow, and his cheeks bloomed with red.

"I meant ... do you know your Native birthright?" he clarified.

"I don't," she replied. "My mother was a Native, but I'm not sure from what tribe or even where her people lived."

"Maybe they can help you find out. If you want to know."

She shrugged one shoulder. He was trying to be helpful, and she cared too much for his opinion to tell him she did not want to learn more about her mother's people.

"Avi's going to be the head of the assassin guild like her father," Rocky said proudly.

"Hopefully," she added. "As long as we can find Tiana and Arthur."

"Do you have a plan for dealing with the Natives?" Jose asked.

She and Rocky exchanged an amused look. "We're going to steal our friends back," she said.

"Hmm. Do you have a backup plan?" Jose asked.

"Have a little faith, Jose!" she said with a smile. "Rocky and I are good at what we do."

Jose smiled in return without responding.

In truth, Aveline was not entirely certain what they would do, if their initial plan failed. Trained in stealth and all manners of violence, she trusted her skills and Rocky's to see them through this. And ... Tiana had a trick or two up her sleeve as well. If the Hanover girl set her mind and magic to escaping, Aveline doubted anyone would stand in her way.

A new pattering entered her thoughts. Four heartbeats. Two strong, emanating from her traveling companions, and two distant.

She glanced in the direction from which the new source of thumping originated and rubbed the back of her head. Why did it feel like the pounding was *inside* her skull, pummeling her brain? How was that possible?

She pulled her hair into a low ponytail and fanned her face, hotter now atop the horse and beneath the midday sun.

"There we go," Jose said. "That's the chief's second son, Red Moon."

"The kid?" Rocky asked.

Aveline shifted her focus once again from the sounds inside her head to the events outside. A boy around the age of thirteen or fourteen was loping towards them on a bay horse.

"He's my favorite," Jose said. "Always friendly and curious." He waved.

The boy waved in return.

"Just don't mention the Hanover's," Jose advised quietly. He drew his horse to a halt. "Hold out your arms to show you aren't reaching for weapons."

Rocky and Aveline followed his lead as the boy approached.

"Is that a gun?" Rocky asked.

"It is. The firearms edicts don't extend to our enemies," Jose answered. "Our allies do not carry them within a few miles of the city, but the Diné do as they please."

Aveline and Rocky both stared at his weapons as the Native youth approached, fascinated by the firearm they had heard of but never seen.

"I wonder if they'll let us shoot them," Rocky said, excitement in his tone. "I'm glad I came!"

"You can have that little toy," Aveline said with a smile. "They have shotguns, too?"

"They have a full arsenal. They claim to be the best armed for two thousand miles," Jose replied.

"Then how do they not take the city?" Rocky mused. "Swords and knives are nothing compared to firearms."

At Jose's hesitation, both assassins turned to him. "It's a long story," he said at last. "You can ask him. Red Moon loves to tell the story of why they hate the Hanover's and city dwellers in general. I'm not sure how much of it to believe, though."

"They can't think we're too much of a threat if they only sent him," Rocky said.

"Unless you count the two guys tracking us," Aveline replied.

Jose and Rocky both looked at her.

Unable to explain how she knew, and not certain she was correct, she focused on the youth approaching them. At about a hundred yards out, she heard the tapping of his heart join the rest of the rhythms in her mind.

Something must be wrong with me. Aveline was starting to feel unsettled by the strange developments inside her.

"Hello, Jose!" the boy called seconds later.

"Hi, Red Moon," Jose replied and lowered his hands. "How's life this month?"

"Life is crazy." The boy's eyes sparkled with mischief. "Who is this?" He looked from Jose to Rocky and Aveline.

"Friends who wanted to get out of the city."

"Ah. So the madman does not burn them. We have noticed the fires. Many more than usual." The boy gestured towards the city.

"Yeah. It's not a good place to be. This is Rocky and Aveline," Jose said. "This is Red Moon."

"You brought a lot of parts," Red Moon said, eyes on their bulging saddlebags. "My brother's day cannot possibly get any better now!" He spun his horse to face the forest and placed two fingers to his lips for a sharp whistle.

Two forms appeared from behind the hill in the exact location Aveline had identified. These warriors were well armed and seasoned, unlike the youth.

"Did you bring bars?" Red Moon asked Jose.

"Of course," Jose said and glanced back at Aveline. "Some people actually like my meal bars." He reached into his saddlebag, pulled out three bars tied with a ribbon, and tossed them to the boy.

"You can have all of mine, too, Red Moon," Rocky said with a snort.

"Excellent! Come!" The energetic boy urged his horse forward and trotted towards the forest, while the two seasoned warriors fell into step behind them.

"His brother pretty much runs things," Jose explained as they rode. "Their father has a bad heart and cannot handle too much stress. Diving Eagle manages the day to day."

"Is he as happy as this kid?" Rocky asked with a half-smile.

"Oh, no," Jose replied quickly. "Humor passed Diving Eagle over all together. If we see him this trip, try not to talk too much or get in his way. He tolerates us for the sake of the agreement his father made, and the supplies, but that's about it."

They fell into quiet, trailing the carefree youth ahead of them.

The sun was overhead when they entered the forest, and Aveline privately thanked every spirit in existence for the shade. The day had grown little warmer – but the sun agitated her fevered body to the point the lighter clothing and undergarments she wore were wet with sweat. The coolness of the trees was a welcome relief.

She finished off another canteen and tucked it away. Her mouth was dry, and the four heartbeats seemed to become louder when no one spoke.

Make that ... Six. No, Seven. Eight? Aveline fanned herself and flung her body off the horse with little grace. The horse's heat was only aggravating her fever, to the point she felt like either hyperventilating or fainting. She had no intention of passing out atop a horse and breaking her neck on the way down.

The boy led them towards a small cabin. Though she saw no one else in sight, she sensed the others' heartbeats through the pounding in her skull. Aveline walked, sweating and flinching from pain. The outside world was starting to fade away from her senses. Its competition, the thumping in her head, was too strong, too distracting. She felt herself slide into autopilot as she walked numbly behind the others.

Rather than stop at the outpost, the boy continued onward, into the forest. He and Jose rode side by side, talking easily, while Rocky observed their surroundings.

Half of the heartbeats fell away as they left the cabin, and Aveline breathed a sigh. Four was tolerable. Eight? She had begun to feel sick.

"You sure you're okay?" Rocky had twisted around in his saddle to face her.

"Yeah," she lied.

"You don't look it."

"Rocky, I'm fine. Just ... not a forest girl, I guess."

He frowned. "He says they have a healer, if any of us want muscle balm for the horseback riding. Maybe you should consider visiting their healer."

"I'm fine."

"I hear we get real food tonight. Maybe that'll help, too," Rocky said. "The kid is crazy about those bars."

Aveline made a face. "How?" she demanded and glanced past him. "I didn't want to hurt Jose's feelings, but they're terrible!"

Rocky grinned. "First time I've heard you say something like that."

"That they're terrible?"

"That you didn't want to hurt someone's feelings. Something you want to tell me?"

"Shut up, Rocky."

He laughed and faced forward.

In the quiet that followed, she considered asking him something. Anything. For a few seconds, he had distracted her from her physical discomfort.

Aveline focused on walking and not trying to understand why she suddenly felt like a stranger to her own body. The sense of sliding out of herself, of her mind floating, caused her to shake her head in hopes the sensation brought her back to herself. It worked – for a few seconds. And then she began sliding again.

"Rocky."

Was she speaking aloud or in her head? He did not turn, and she could not tell. Aveline opened her mouth and prepared to concentrate all her energy on speaking.

She felt them then. Five ... ten ... dozens of heartbeats, assaulting her all at once.

She staggered and caught herself against the horse. Pushing away, she shook her head and sought her balance.

The furnace raging in her blood was hotter than the fires Tiana's father used to murder the residents of his city. She was burning up ... falling out of herself ... being crushed beneath the pounding ...

"Avi."

Just like that, her world righted itself.

"I really think you should see the healer."

She blinked out of her mind and looked up to meet Rocky's gaze. The heartbeats had faded. Somehow, she had managed to follow the others into the center of a small village consisting of tents designed to be assembled or disassembled quickly.

"I'm ..." *fine*. By the look on Rocky's face, he was not making a suggestion. "Maybe I should."

"This isn't a normal fever." He stretched forward to lift a strand of her hair. It was soaked through with sweat. "You look like you went swimming."

"Maybe I'm allergic to the world outside the city," she joked. "Where's Jose?" She started to move around Rocky, who – along with his horse – were blocking her path.

"Healer first," Rocky said firmly and pushed her to face the other direction. "You need to be well to handle this."

"Handle what?"

"Tiana."

"She's here?" Aveline whirled. "Did Red Moon say where?"

"He didn't have to."

"What –"

"You're not well, Avi. Let's get you looked at. Then you can deal with this."

"Deal with *what*?"

He gripped her arm to turn her away once more.

Aveline tore free and maneuvered around her horse to stand in the center of the village. She stopped, uttering curses beneath her breath.

Tiana and Arthur were in the middle of the village at the base of a large tree. Arthur was in a cage, along with another man Aveline did not recognize, and both appearing worse for wear. The cage was chained to a tree. Tiana sat beside it, neither bound nor caged that Aveline could see. All three showed signs of abuse: Tiana's cheek, eye, and lips were swollen from fresh blows, while Arthur and the man with him were pale, bloodied, and wearing blood soaked clothing. Their wounds had been bound, but their clothing was filthy, as if they had been prisoners for some time.

Tiana was right, Aveline realized. Arthur was in bad shape. Their father would never have found him in time to save his life.

"Stop staring. You're drawing attention," Rocky said and pushed

Aveline aside. "We don't want them knowing –" He trailed off at the approach of two Natives, one of whom bore a scar down one side of his face.

"They are our enemies," the scarred man said in a hard voice. "At least we did not burn them as you city dwellers do to your own kind."

"Does that girl look like she could even *lift* a weapon?" Aveline snapped back. Fury pushed her fever even higher, and the pounding against her skull grew sharper, painful. She started to fall outside herself then wrenched herself back to the present, not about to let down Tiana.

"Why are you concerned with the fate of a stranger?" The scarred man glared down at her.

Aveline heard the warning, both from his tone and from her instincts. It was unwise to cause their hosts to pay more attention to them than they already did, especially since her plan relied on discretion. Unusually close to losing it, she struggled to explain away her behavior to the tense man in front of her. Her brain was being battered too hard for her to think straight.

Rocky rested a hand on her arm. "Pardon my friend," he said quietly. "She is ill. Fevered."

The scarred man did not move or speak for a long moment as he studied her. "Go to the healer. You will leave my village by dusk," he ordered.

Aveline had never wanted to hit anyone as much as she did him in that moment. He had no concern for Tiana at all, no compassion for the two men who barely looked alive. With effort, she suppressed the retort at the tip of her tongue and let Rocky pull her away.

"Thank you," he called. When they were several steps away, he hissed for her ears only, "That's the brother we weren't supposed to talk to, and you just pissed him off!"

Aveline groaned, partially from discomfort and partially because she realized what she had done. Their goal of spending the night, and slipping away with the prisoners before dawn, had been dashed, because she failed to hold her tongue.

"Dammit!" she muttered. "I didn't mean ... burn me! What is wrong with me?" She pressed the heels of her hands to her ears, but it made no difference in the intensity of the pounding.

Rocky pulled her hands away. "I have an idea." He glanced past her, towards the direction of Tiana. "Pass out."

"What?"

"No one will think twice of us if you're too sick to move tonight. Pretend you're about to die or something."

Funny. That's how I feel, she answered him silently. Without waiting for more encouragement, Aveline allowed her body to sag. The sense of falling out of herself returned, and she did not fight it. Suddenly, she was no longer *pretending* to faint. She slumped and then pitched forward, barely aware of Rocky catching her. His shout was garbled before it vanished into the dark recesses of her mind.

She slid into the place between consciousness and sleep. The pounding would not release her completely to slumber, but neither was she aware of her surroundings. Instead, she floated in and out of herself.

Tiana. This thought was accompanied by a burst of energy that almost allowed her to awaken, but it was soon swallowed by the hammering of heartbeats against her skull.

I never should've left the city.

TWENTY-TWO

TIANA SAW Aveline faint and straightened, eyes trained on her friend. Happiness bubbled forth within her and was quickly followed by concern. Something was wrong with Aveline. It was more than her sickly appearance; she was radiating energy strong enough for Tiana's skin to prick.

Arthur shifted in the cage beside her. "What ... is that?" he mumbled and opened the one eye not swollen shut.

"Arthur!"

When the Native guard glanced her direction, she lowered her voice to a whisper.

"I have been waiting since dawn for you to awaken!" Tiana told him. "I do not know how you are alive. There is so much blood."

"Me neither." He grunted and shifted within the cage. "Where is ..." His eyes settled on Marshall Cruise, who was slumped and unconscious in his own cage beside him. "At least you are ... wait. What are you doing here, Tiana?" He asked, swiveling his head to face her.

She smiled. "Rescuing you."

Arthur stared at her and then groaned. He rested his head against the cage behind him. "You should never have left, Tiana." He sounded far too tired to anger. "The world outside the city is not for you."

"I found you, did I not?" she countered.

"For all of a day, and then we both die out here. If the Natives do not murder us, the Ghouls will."

She frowned. "I saw a Ghoul. You said they were not real."

"If I told you they were, you would have wanted to see one!" he replied. "Burn me, Tiana! Why are you out here?" His anger was audible this time. "Why did you purposely place yourself in danger?"

She was quiet. What did she tell him? That she hoped to rescue him and then convince him to go to the Free Lands with her? At the moment, none of the plans she had intended to carry out were feasible.

"Where is your guardian?" he asked, calming. "If she brought you out here, I will burn her myself!"

"I left without her."

"This is worse!"

"Warner brought me but fell ill and remained with our allies while I went on ahead. They are supposed to return and ..." She stopped. It was too late to negotiate. Her brother would be gone with the dusk, and there was a chance she would be trialed and murdered by dawn. The memory of Warner's unusual wounds left her no doubt as to whether or not he was capable of traveling anytime soon.

"Warner," Arthur repeated. "He brought you here?"

She hesitated and then explained the circumstances of her journey. Arthur's haggard features grew dark and the lines of his face deep. When she fell silent, he did not speak.

Sensing her brother's anger, Tiana shifted and leaned against the cage to prevent her words from being overheard. "Father burned Marshall Cruise's family," she whispered. "All of them."

"All of them?" Arthur asked skeptically.

"Yes." She hastily explained the incident with Matilda.

Arthur did not appear surprised to hear of her magic. He listened in silence until she had finished. "Father finally found the ammunition he needed to justify burning the Cruises. If they threatened one of us, fine. But both of us?" He started to shake his head then grimaced and went still. "It does him no good to burn the entire city down to protect us when we will die out here! How did I not ..." He gave a sound that was part groan, part growl. "I deserve whatever these Natives do to me for not acting sooner." His gaze was on Marshall Cruise.

"You may have a chance yet. The tribe traded you to someone who wants you alive," she said.

"Nothing good can come of that, either."

"All you have to do is escape, and you can return and take father's place, so he does not hurt anyone else."

"That easy?" He snorted.

At a loss as to what to say to cheer her brother up, Tiana reached into the cage and took his hand. "We are together, are we not? Beneath a tree. Did you ever believe this possible?"

"Never," he said and sighed loudly. Anger left his features. "I wish the world were as simple as you try to make it."

"Can you not devise a way to escape?"

He was quiet, thoughtful for a moment. "Your magic. Will it listen to you, or does it act randomly?"

"Randomly," she replied. "Though it consistently works when someone I care about is threatened."

"It responds to your emotions?"

She nodded.

"We may be able to use that," he said.

"I cannot control it, Arthur."

"No need to control it out here among our enemies."

I cannot guarantee your safety, if I use it, she added silently, thoughts on Matilda. She had managed to murder her stepmother without seriously injuring Aveline. How that happened, and how she had driven off the Ghouls without killing anyone, was beyond her ability to understand.

The siblings fell quiet as several Natives approached. Tiana withdrew her hand from Arthur's and hunched, preparing for more blows. She had been placed beside her brother an hour after dawn, and several women from the resupply train visiting the warriors' outpost had taken out their anger with her family on her. She did not fault them, and no one hit quite like Matilda, who had been deliberate in her desire to cause the maximum amount of pain. When every one of the women had thrown a punch or kick, they had left her.

The group of five warriors paused four yards away and began speaking amongst themselves, in their language. The man who hated her family most of all – Diving Eagle – was at the center, glaring at her and her brother.

"He is the one we need to avoid," her brother whispered. "Those who captured us were allied to neither our enemies nor us. When he found out, he slaughtered five of them to capture Marshall and me. I would be dead, if his father had not ordered me not to be."

"Did he tell you why?" she asked, recalling the conversation she had with the elderly chief.

"Unfortunately, our family has too many enemies for us to bother tracking why they hate us," Arthur said dryly. Some of his familiar humor was back in his tone.

"Why is that, Arthur?" she asked, genuinely confused. "Why does our family resort to such measures?"

He hesitated before answering. "To protect our secret."

"What secret?"

"Father told me once that the Hanover's must remain in power, or the city would fall. I thought it was pride or arrogance. My unique deformities came into existence soon after. He told me these deformities are what give our family the right to rule, and which protect those around us."

"He lied about our mother," she said, dismayed.

"He did. Whether or not she was deformed, it did not matter. *He* was. Every leader of Lost Vegas has possessed certain gifts that allowed him to retain power and control."

"But he burned our mother and my twin."

"He burned a witness to your deformity and the child they thought was you," Arthur explained. "Our mother was not the only one who died that day. The attending physician and two nurses did as well."

Tiana twisted her hands together. Had she been too afraid to suspect her father was deformed or to ask him for details about her mother's death? For too long, she had simply accepted what her father, Matilda, and brother told her to be true. It was not until Aveline that she began to feel comfortable thinking for herself.

"Father has deformities," she said.

"He does."

"And he murdered a baby to protect me."

"He did."

"Then why does he punish me for what I am?"

Hearing the sad note in her voice, Arthur stretched to touch her then stopped with a groan. "He is also mad, Tiana. I have not wanted to acknowledge how mad, but I feel I cannot deny it much longer. Rather, I feel I will not be *allowed* to deny it much longer." He glanced towards the unconscious Cruise heir. "Our father cannot continue to massacre our people in the manner he has for the past twenty years. The Cruise's were rivals, but they had good people among them. Marshall is one."

Tiana followed his gaze. "What will we tell him?"

"Nothing," Arthur said firmly. "Not yet anyway. We will need his help to escape. He will not aid us, if he knows our father wiped out his family."

Tiana did not say what she thought, that their father was a blight to Lost Vegas and Arthur would be the kind of compassionate leader the city desperately needed. For all she knew, they would die this very day. "Aveline is here. She followed me."

"Good. Because I do not think I can walk, and I do not believe Marshall can either."

Tiana's gaze swept over his legs. One was twisted at an odd angle. "I can help you," she said. "I am stronger than you give me credit for."

"I hope so, or we will not make it out of here."

She swallowed hard. She was nothing like her father and nowhere near as brave as her brother. Was she strong enough to carry him? To fight off anyone who tried to stop them? To do what had to be done? She had never tested her limits, and she had rarely ever done something new without crying.

"You are not tied," Arthur said suddenly.

"No. The chief has been very kind to me. He knows I would not leave your side and did not feel the need to bind me."

"One blessing. We could use a hundred more." Arthur gave a rough chuckle. "Aveline will save you. I hired her for that purpose."

"She will always try," Tiana agreed.

"She is more than she seems. Soon, she will show everyone just how fearsome she really is."

"Maybe. I believe she may be ill." Tiana toyed with the necklace she wore identical to Aveline's. The light within the pendant was bright.

"She is not ill," Arthur said.

"You have had a vision of her? Of us escaping?"

"The nature of my recent visions, since entering the custody of the Diné, has been different than usual. Stronger. I have seen farther than I thought possible, and I have witnessed the materialization of secrets in those around me I did not know existed," Arthur said mysteriously.

"All night long, I was plagued by one vision. I am not like you in this, but I felt like I was there," she said in a hushed tone. "And when I woke, it lingered. The magic or ..." She shuddered, still able to feel the odd energy from the vision, the sense of being grazed by a cool breeze that did not exist.

"I feel it, too," Arthur said. "Someone here is very powerful and is enhancing our abilities."

The group of Natives fell silent, and Tiana glanced towards them. They were watching her brother. Fire burned in the gazes of all of them. One by one, each member turned away and left the tree.

"They really hate us," she murmured. "How does one come to loathe someone else with such passion?"

"Sometimes I believe our family deserves no less."

"But you ... *we* are different, Arthur. How do *we* deserve such hatred?"

"Such is the nature of a blood war. Reason has no place in hatred."

"You are not frightened?" she asked.

"Of course I am. After hearing what Father did to the Cruise's ..." His focus was on Marshall Cruise. "He saved my life, Tiana, more than once. How do I tell him his entire family has been wiped off the Earth by *our* father, our blood? How do I look at him knowing he represents every wrong our family has ever committed?"

"You tell him you are not the same as our father, and you show him who you are," she replied. "You show everyone. The Natives, the city, everyone. When they see in you what I have always known to be true, they will not wish you dead."

"You are always optimistic." Arthur forced a smile. "I admit, I never thought you would make it this far. I am proud of you, Tiana, and extremely disappointed at the same time."

"I want to be brave like you."

"Sister, you are far braver," he said with a hoarse laugh. "I left the city with weapons and an army, and you left with one man and hope. Here we are, in the same place, and you are better off by far!"

"You are laughing at me!" she said, face warm.

"On the contrary, I am sorry to have underestimated you our whole lives. If I thought you had this much mettle, I would have trained you to fight."

Stunned by the compliment, Tiana smiled, even though it hurt her bruised cheek. Resting her head back against the tree trunk behind her, she peered up at the pine needles.

"Have you ever seen anything so beautiful?" she breathed.

Arthur started to speak and then began to cough.

Tiana shifted closer to the cage, wishing she could remove it, so she could hug her brother. Blood sprinkled his lips and splashed across the hand he used to cover his mouth. She recalled too clearly how warm his blood had been when it soaked her clothing and coated her hands in the vision, and how empty his eyes had appeared once the life had drained out of it.

I cannot lose him. Ever.

"Arthur?" she asked in a trembling voice. "Are you well?"

He finished the coughing fit and sagged against the metal cage. "I will be."

"Have you had a vision of surviving?"

"No. But there is too much left for me to do in this world for me to die now," he replied. "I want to right the wrongs committed by our family. I have always felt a little adrift in Father's shadow. My fate will be different."

"I have never cared for your lofty ambitions, Arthur," she said softly. "I care that you survive."

He smiled faintly. "I will. I must."

A shadow fell over her, and she glanced up then away just as fast.

Diving Eagle knelt beside her. Tiana tensed and shifted away, expecting him to take out his anger when his father was not looking.

"For your wounds." He held out a cloth and jar of balm. "You will not be touched until after your trial."

She accepted the offering without speaking.

"You call us savages," Arthur muttered. "Look what you do to a defenseless girl."

"A Hanover is never free of guilt," Diving Eagle replied in a hard voice. "But we are not savages like your family. No one should have hurt your sister."

"And Arthur?" she asked hopefully.

"I am fair game, sister," Arthur answered before the Native could. "I bear the full brunt, since I am the Hanover heir."

"Exactly," Diving Eagle seconded.

Tiana was quiet.

The Native rose and strode a short distance away, where he replaced the current guard monitoring them.

"That was unusually kind for him," Arthur said. "His father likely had a hand in it."

Tiana dabbed the ointment on her lip, cheek, and around her eye. After initial stinging, the medicine numbed her pain. She passed it through the cage to Arthur.

"I need more than that," he said ruefully but accepted both.

She started to relax, when the brush of cool energy caused her to shiver. Arthur stopped in his ministrations of a wound in his arm and looked up.

"What is it?" she asked. The tickle agitated her, and she could not identify its source.

"I am not sure." He was gazing in the direction Aveline had been carried after she collapsed.

A blur of black crossed her vision as a large wolf trotted into camp, tongue hanging out of her mouth and stomach swollen.

Arthur murmured a curse.

Mesmerized by the first canine she had ever seen, Tiana shifted forward when she realized the animal was headed straight for them. Arthur, too, moved to the front of his cage.

The wolf stopped when she reached him and licked his hands. Her tail wagged. Tiana admired her thick, black fur and the grace with which even small movements were made.

"This is my sister," Arthur said to the wolf and motioned to Tiana.

Golden eyes turned to Tiana. Unlike the horses that fled from her, this animal's intelligent gaze seemed to peer right through her. It approached, nose extended curiously.

"Hold out your hand with the palm up, so she can smell you," Arthur directed her.

Tiana did so. The wolf nosed her and then licked her before walking closer and sniffing at the wounds and ointment on Tiana's face. She buried her hands into the animal's coat. A downy layer of fur lined its body, while a thicker, coarser layer of hair grew atop it. The wolf was not as soft as the cougar had been, though her coat was shiny and smooth.

"Tickles," Tiana said as the wolf licked her swollen eye. "I wonder how many babies she has?"

Six. The soft voice came from within her head. Tiana lowered her hands and gazed at the creature.

"Six," Arthur said aloud. "Can you hear her?"

"Yes. Is that normal?" she asked in surprise.

"No. *We* are not normal," he said with a hoarse laugh. "And neither is she."

"She's deformed?"

"Magical."

The wolf licked her face several more times, until Tiana giggled from the new sensation. The animal went to Arthur's cage, touched his hand again, then paused in front of Marshall and lowered her head to study the unconscious man.

"He is relatively well," Arthur said to her. "Resting."

As if satisfied, she trotted away.

"How wonderful," Tiana said. "I have seen such wonders on my journey outside the city!" She shivered, despite the warmth of the early spring day. "Arthur, what is this?" She waved at the agitated energy filling the air around her.

"I do not know." His eyes were on the wolf loping across the village. "Be prepared to run."

"Why?"

"Just in case."

Two people ducked out of the tent where Aveline had been taken. Tiana recognized Rocky, who was frowning. The Native with him darted to Diving Eagle. The two spoke briefly before the Native returned to the tent. Not long after, two Natives emerged, carrying Aveline between them on a stretcher.

"Oh, no," Tiana murmured, eyes on her friend.

"Agreed." Arthur's gaze was not on Aveline but someone else. He struggled to change positions in the cage. "Can you feel it?"

Tiana cocked her head. Aveline was awake on her stretcher and trying to get up. Tiana was not surprised that the proud assassin-in-training refused to be carried, even if she appeared ill. She struggled enough that the two holding the stretcher had to set her down on the ground.

Tiana smiled. "I do not notice anything –"

It hit her then, the sense of being back in the vision, of watching Arthur die, of being stuck in a recurring nightmare she was unable to escape. Emotions swelled within her, and she looked around wildly.

This was not the right place, not the time, or the circumstances drilled into her mind by the vision. Shaking her head to clear her thoughts, she reassured herself of where she was by grabbing Arthur's cage.

I am here now. The vision is elsewhere, at a later time, she told herself. Then why was she unable to release the emotion, the anger, sorrow, and horror, from the vision? Why did she feel as if what she feared most was about to occur? Her pulse raced, and adrenaline lit her blood on fire.

"Tiana?" Arthur asked.

"Yes," she whispered. "I feel it. What is it?" Already, light and darkness were sliding into one another as her deformity reacted to her emotions and the pull of energy radiating from the direction of Aveline. Tiana stood and breathed deeply to calm herself. Her magic was unpredictable when it was in this stage, and she feared hurting anyone around her.

What had the power to affect her? To enhance her brother's visions and influence her emotions and magic?

"Not a what. Who," Arthur said in a terse voice. "Someone very dangerous. Tiana, you need to ..." His voice faded, replaced by the sound of her own heartbeat.

Tiana saw *him* clearly for the first time. The skinwalker from her vision. Walking with the chief of the Diné, he was a tall Native of indistinguishable age. His features were lean and chiseled, his dark hair braided, and the air around him oddly ... still. His eyes were dead, and the exposed skin of the back of his hands, face, and neck bore tattoos matching the colors she had witnessed in the nightmare.

He passed Aveline, who had frozen on her feet and was staring, glassy-eyed, into the distance.

Light and dark began to mix in Tiana's vision. Everything changed – except for him. She saw all his forms at once: the man, bear, wolf, and otherworldly creature.

"Tiana!" Arthur cried.

She was moving without realizing what she did. Whether the skinwalker's magic fed hers, or her emotions did, she did not know. Tiana saw no one but the skinwalker, while the vision of what he would do at some point in the future replayed in her mind. The rest of the world smeared until the colors all ran together and faded away, no longer of interest to her.

The skinwalker looked at her, and she stopped, already knowing what he was capable of. He faced her fully.

"We meet at last, spirit." Was his voice aloud or in her head? She could no longer tell.

"You will not hurt my friends," she replied. A blast of air accompanied her words, and he was shoved backwards, into the trunk of a tree.

The skinwalker tried to wriggle free, but she kept him pinned without understanding how, except for the fact she wished it to be so. Tiana began to lose the sense of herself and her surroundings, to slide into the state she had been in when she murdered Matilda. With effort, she remained in her mind and walked towards the immobilized skinwalker.

His body remained human, while his shadow began to morph,

and suddenly, he was free of her, with his bear form towering over him. He charged her.

She stayed where she was. Her magic flattened the forest behind him without touching him, and Tiana lifted her hand to try to channel it better directly at him. At once, he was smashed onto his back.

The wolf form reared up behind him next, and he slid free of her magic. This time, he made it within inches of her before she shoved him away again.

"Tiana!" Aveline's voice was unusually loud, as if Tiana stood over her friend.

"You do not wish to kill me!" the skinwalker said.

"Shut up!" Tiana cried at him. "I know what you are! You will not murder my family, my friends!"

He released his animal forms, which lingered in the space around him, and faced her as a man once more. The skinwalker paced, growling deep within his chest and glaring at her, the epitome of a trapped predator waiting for her guard to drop so he could pounce.

"Tiana." Aveline sounded ... hoarse. Scared. Hurt.

"Release me! I will help her!" the skinwalker snarled. Tiana shoved him against a tree again to keep him still and began to crush him with her mind.

She spared a glance around to find her friend and made out Aveline's crumpled form among the reversed colors of her surroundings. Aveline was convulsing, not seven feet away.

"She is one of mine," the skinwalker growled.

"You are a monster!" Tiana returned. "She is my friend!"

"The bracelet you wear belongs to her."

Tiana blinked, not expecting these words. The skinwalker was writhing, pinned and dying, beneath her power. "How do you know this?" she demanded. No one, other than the elderly Diné chief, had known what the symbol was.

"It is the ... mark of my people. My kind." With effort, the skinwalker pulled something from his pocket and allowed it to drop to his feet. The leather wrapping fell away, revealing a medallion like the one Tiana had found among Aveline's belongings. "You can feel her energy."

Tiana looked at the medallion, identical to Aveline's, down to the wear and tear.

"Release me, and I will help her live," the skinwalker ordered.

Tiana hesitated. If he died today, he would not murder everyone she cared about at a later time.

Aveline might not make it that long.

"If I lie, kill me!" the skinwalker added. His face was beginning to cave in and yet, he showed no fear, no pain, only defiance. "She is not a full blood. She cannot survive her first transformation alone."

Was he lying? Tiana had no way of knowing. But he did possess the same medallion Aveline did, and the chief had mentioned running across two skinwalkers of late.

Aveline's body abruptly went still. Concern replaced fear, and Tiana dropped her arm. The world righted itself instantly, and the skinwalker landed in a heap at the base of the tree. He coughed and staggered to his feet.

Tiana dropped to her knees beside Aveline. The assassin-in-training radiated heat and energy. Her clothing was soaked with sweat, and she was paler than a Ghoul.

"Aveline!" she called urgently.

The skinwalker pushed her aside and took her place at Aveline's side. "Take her head in your hands," he directed.

Tiana studied him briefly before obeying. Her hands trembled from exertion, and she gently rested her fingers and palms against Aveline's head. Fire flew through her at the touch.

The skinwalker drew a knife from his belt and slashed his palm.

"What manner of spirit are you?" the skinwalker asked gruffly without looking at her. He reached forward for Aveline's hand and gripped her wrist.

"I am not a spirit," Tiana whispered, concerned for her friend. She flinched as he sliced open Aveline's hand. "What are you doing?"

"Full bloods can transform at will. Most half-breeds die during the first transformation. My blood will stabilize hers."

Aveline was muttering in her sleep.

As Tiana watched, color returned to Aveline's cheeks. The energy zipping through her abated, along with the heat.

"Release her," he growled.

Tiana did so. "She will be well?"

"For now. The same cannot be said for either of us."

She glanced at his face and then past him.

The entire village had ringed them. The forest on one side was gone as far as she could see. She sought a familiar face in the crowd, praying she had not hurt the chief who had been walking beside the skinwalker when she attacked him. Diving Eagle and his father stood side by side, and she was unable to tell which of them was grimmer.

"You have haunted me long enough, spirit," the skinwalker said. He was bandaging his hand and stood, knife in hand.

Tiana gazed up at him, recalling the vivid vision too well.

He snatched her throat.

Her magic exploded.

The skinwalker went sailing through the air, over treetops, and fell, disappearing into the woods a half a mile away.

She shook her head, and the colors of the world returned to normal.

Silence surrounded her. Aveline was breathing deeply, her body no longer curled, and her cheeks pink with health.

Tiana hugged herself, not wanting to cry when everyone was watching her. The tears came anyway.

"He is gone, little Hanover, and we will tend your guardian," he said in his low, gruff voice.

She faced the chief, who had approached and stood by Aveline's sleeping body, flanked by his son. The elderly man leaned heavily on his cane and was unarmed. His gaze remained direct, and he made no move closer to her.

"I am so sorry," she said. "I saw him and ..." Hot tears spilled down her cheeks.

"I believe you now, Father," Diving Eagle said. "The Hanover children are dangerous."

"Unlike their father, they use their gifts to protect rather than harm," the chief said. "Perhaps we should talk, little Hanover."

Tiana swallowed hard with a nod. Had Arthur witnessed what she did? Was he ashamed of her, as their father would be?

She lifted her eyes towards the tree where her brother was imprisoned, looked away and then back.

Rising onto her tiptoes, she stared at the cage.

It was empty.

"Where ... where are they?" she asked with a gasp.

Diving Eagle strode past his father and stopped beside her, following her gaze. After a split second, he bellowed orders to the warriors nearest the tree. They scrambled to obey and began searching the area.

Tiana stared at the cage. It was still locked. In the time she faced off with the skinwalker, Arthur, Marshall, and their shackles had vanished. Her magic had been directed against the skinwalker on the opposite side of the village. She had never controlled it this well before, and never used it purposely in this manner at all. She did not understand her limits any more now than she had before. Was it possible her deformity lashed out randomly at others? Were Arthur and Marshall sent flying as well? Or had she done worse to them? Was she so obsessed with stopping the skinwalker that she lost her brother?

Tiana began to shake, and tears blinded her.

Two warriors lifted Aveline onto the stretcher behind her, but Tiana was unable to take her eyes off the tree.

"Come, little Hanover," the chief instructed her.

What have I done? Tiana thought.

Lost Vegas Series
Aveline
Tiana
Arthur
Black Wolf

ALSO BY LIZZY FORD

Young Adult Fiction

Non-Series Title

The Door (teen sci-fi)

Between (paranormal) (2019)

Esme (teen paranormal)

Halloween

Thanksgiving

Christmas

Lost Vegas Series – young adult post-apocalyptic

Aveline

Tiana

Arthur

Black Wolf

Lost Vegas Series Omnibus

Spell Realm Series – young adult romantic fantasy

Water Spell

Dragon Spell (2019)

Moon Spell (2019)

Sword Spell (2020)

Omega Series – teen dystopia with Greek Gods

Omega

Theta

Alpha (2019)

Omega Beginnings Miniseries – individual episodes

Alessandra

Mismatch

Phoibe

Lantos

Theodosia

Niko

Cleon

Herakles

Omega Beginnings Miniseries Omnibus

Theta Beginnings Miniseries

Silent Queen

Mercenary

Shadow Titan

People's Champion

Theta Beginnings Miniseries Omnibus

Anshan Saga – new adult science fiction romance

Kiera's Moon

Kiera's Sun

Witchlings – young adult paranormal

Dark Summer

Autumn Storm

Winter Fire

Spring Rain

Broken Beauty Novellas – new adult dramatic fiction

Broken Beauty

Broken World

Broken Chains

Foretold Trilogy – young adult fantasy

Elle's Journey

Shadow Rising (2019)

Journey West (2019)

Voodoo Nights - young adult paranormal

Cursed

Erotic Romance

Non-Series Titles

Star Kissed (erotic sci-fi)

A Night Worth Dying For (short story, contemporary erotic thriller)

Trial Series – erotic paranormal romance

Trial by Moon

Trial by Thrall

Trial by Blood

Trial by Heart

Trial Series Omnibus

Heart of Fire – sexy dragon shifter

Charred Heart

Charred Tears

Charred Hope

Incubatti Duet – Buffy meets 50 Shades

Zoey Rogue

Zoey Avenger

Writing as SE Reign, erotica writer

101 Nights Box Set (featuring all seven serials)

Adult Sweet Romance

(no graphic sex scenes)

Non-Series Titles – 2014 - 2018

White Tree Sound

Black Moon Draw (fantasy romance)

Highlander Enchanted (historical romance)

Last Resort (2019)

History Interrupted – Time Travel Romantic Adventures

West

East

North

South (2019)

Super Villainess Chronicles – twisted superhero romance

It's Not Easy Being Evil

It's Not Easy Being Good

Starwalkers Serials (with Julia Crane) – new adult science fiction serial

Severed

Trapped

Exiled

Revealed

Escaped

Ascended

Starwalkers – Omnibus

Sons of War – contemporary military romance

Semper Mine

Soldier Mine

SEAL Mine

Rhyn Trilogy – new adult paranormal with demons

Katie's Hellion

Unnamed Series

Unnatural (TBD)

Short Stories

Santa's Ninja Elves: Natasha

Santa's Ninja Elves: Hunter

Snow Whisperers (retired)

Non-Series Titles – 2011 - 2013

A Demon's Desire (paranormal romance)

The Warlord's Secret (fantasy romance)

Maddy's Oasis (contemporary romance)

Rebel Heart (sci-fi romance)

ABOUT THE AUTHOR

I breathe stories. I dream them. If it were possible, I'd eat them, too. (I'm pretty sure they'd taste like cotton candy.) I can't escape them - they're everywhere! Which is why I write! I was born to bring the crazy worlds and people in my mind to life, and I love sharing them with as many people as I can.

I'm also the bestselling, award winning, internationally acclaimed author of over sixty titles and counting. I write speculative fiction in multiple subgenres of romance and fantasy, contemporary fiction, books for both teens and adults, and just about anything else I feel like writing. If I can imagine it, I can write it!

I live in the desert of southern Arizona with a pack of spoiled dogs.

Connect with Lizzy

Website: LizzyFord.com
Facebook: www.Facebook.com/LizzyFordBooks
Twitter @LizzyFord2010
Instagram: @LizzyFordAuthor

www.ingramcontent.com/pod-product-compliance
Lightning Source LLC
Chambersburg PA
CBHW022247020726
47496CB00004B/1101